"Engaging and mysterious, fast-paced and entertaining, *Red Jacarandas* reminds us that L.A.'s five hundred square miles still comprise America's most exotic territory."
—Ken Kalfus, author of *Thirst, Equilateral,* and *2 a.m. in Little America*

OTHER BOOKS BY JEFF POLMAN

1924 and You Are There!
Ball Nuts
Mystery Ball '58
Twinbill
The Invasion of Normandie

RED JACARANDAS

Two Screenplays

AFTERSHOCK
LOVED ONES

and a Novel

ONE EYE OPEN

JEFF POLMAN

Grassy Gutter Press • Culver City, CA

Front cover illustration by Greg Jezewski

Author photo by Carmen Patti
Book design by the author

Library of Congress Control Number:
2021920235

ISBN: 978-0-578-95771-5

◂ Introduction ▸

I spent much of my childhood in Western Massachusetts, happily being terrified at the Bing Theater. I'm talking double features of low-budget horror movies every Saturday afternoon—when they made those just for kids—and the place was packed and empty popcorn boxes flew through the dark air and you were lucky to hear one line of dialogue. But the scares from Roger Corman and William Castle and others were real and exciting, and likely led to me and my high school pals forming a Horror Movie Club years later.

I've been living in Los Angeles for forty years now, immersing myself in the city's unique brand of buried horror. L.A.'s sordid past—apart from its endlessly recycled Hollywood lore—has been paved over and forgotten whenever possible. Reading *Eternity Street*, John Mack Faragher's excellent and thorough account of frontier Los Angeles, it's uncanny how much murder and madness was baked into the region's dry soil long before the great Jewish storytellers arrived from New York to craft our golden monuments of make-believe that have been front and center ever since.

After a short but worthwhile career in weekly New England journalism, I arrived here in 1982 with yes, the dazzlingly original notion to write and sell movie screenplays. I hammered out twenty of them, sold two low-budget thrillers that were both produced and altered beyond recognition in the process, but also wrote a few others that still intrigued me enough to shake off their cobwebs and polish them for the first time in years. *Aftershock* and *Loved Ones* (p. 341) bookend a more recently completed novel *One Eye Open* (p. 129), and all grapple with the sun-kissed spectres of Los Angeles, the merciless demons of celebrity and insecurity that are ingrained here and infect our culture on a wider scale.

Red Jacarandas is the product of over a year of house-bound contemplation, and especially to fans of modern horror, I hope you find it deliciously unsettling.

—*J.P., Culver City, CA*

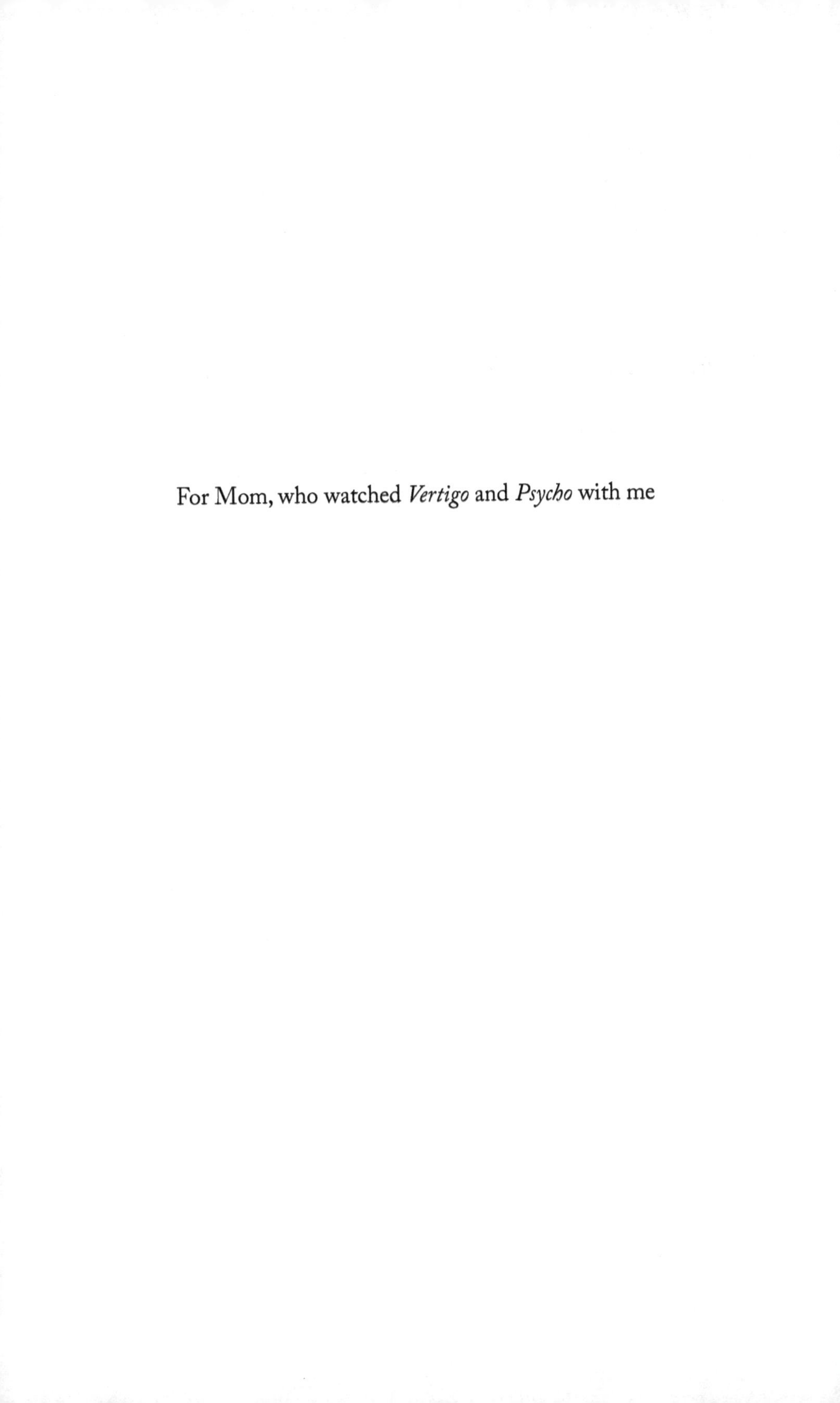

For Mom, who watched *Vertigo* and *Psycho* with me

"It's that time of year, when L.A. turns into a violet utopia with vivid clouds of blossoms lining the streets. The Jacarandas are the cherry blossoms of Los Angeles, with a sight and smell that is completely entrancing and have become one of the city's most recognizable trees....But then, there's the mess."

—Secret Los Angeles

AFTERSHOCK

Screenplay by
Jeff Polman

Registered WGAW

EXT. LOS FELIZ - AFTERNOON

Looking north up Vermont Avenue: a congested,
gentrified street lined with coffee shops,
trendy eateries, thrift stores, and the usual
sprinkled HOMELESS. In the distance we can
barely make out the Hollywood sign on Mt. Lee
through thick, late summer haze.

A ten-year-old Saab coupe is parked at a meter
across the street from NIGHTLIGHT BOOKS, where
a small group of PATRONS have gathered on the
sidewalk out front to socialize before slipping
inside.

Behind the Saab's steering wheel, SUZANNA
BRISTOL watches them with visible unease.
Late-40s and wearing a black satin blouse, her
auburn hair tied behind her pale, attractive
face with a yellow scrunchie, there's a fragile
air about her, an embedded anxiety in her eyes.

                    SUZANNA
          They're invisible, Suzanna...

She glances around first, then opens the glove
compartment, takes out a small silver flask and
downs a few sips of whatever's inside. Puts the
flask back in the glove compartment, then pops
an Altoid mint in her mouth and checks her face
in the rear view mirror.

                    SUZANNA
          Invisible...

Opens the car door.

INT. NIGHTLIGHT BOOKS - LATE AFTERNOON

Suzanna stands at a podium in front of a sign
reading MEET DR. SUZANNA BRISTOL, AUTHOR OF
"FINDING THE NEW YOU".

PULL BACK on a modest CROWD of about three
dozen attendees filling the aisles and a small
seating area.

                         SUZANNA
                    (reading from her open book)
               ...and yet there's no need to
               shine up your hardwood floors,
               or continuing the metaphor,
               to over-wash your cloth
               napkins. The New You is the
               person who deserves honesty.
               Who deserves compassion. Who
               deserves respect. Who deserves
               happiness...When everything
               in life seems to conspire to
               beat you down, the New You is
               the courage you find to pull
               yourself up.
                    (smiles and closes the book)

POLITE APPLAUSE. She nods gratefully.

INT. NIGHTLIGHT BOOKS - FIFTEEN MINUTES LATER

Suzanna sits at a back table beside a stack of
her books, pen in hand and sipping from a glass
of ice water. She signs one of the books for a
middle-aged EARTHY WOMAN wearing about a dozen
bracelets.

                         WOMAN
               I've only seen him once, but
               it was unforgettable. His eyes
               radiated.

                         SUZANNA
               Really. What did you say his
               name was?

                         WOMAN
               I didn't. They call him The
               Beacon. It takes three days to
               reach his compound by llama
               but it's worth it.

Suzanna smiles, a bit forced. Finishes signing
and hands her the book.

                         SUZANNA
               Thank you. I'll keep that in
               mind.

A DISTINGUISHED GUY in his 50s wearing a tweed
sport jacket gives her a book to sign.

                    GUY
          I heard you on that radio
          show in San Luis Obispo. Very
          engaging.

                    SUZANNA
          Thank you. Who should I,
          um...

                    GUY
          Dale Moody. That's with a Y.

She starts to sign the book. He studies her
hands, then her face.

                    MOODY
          I'm in behavioral metrics.
          Hit up most of the psych book
          events on the coast, and
          happened to be in town. Are
          you working on a follow-up?

The crowd squeezes closer to the table. Suzanna
gulps down some of her water and spills a
little on her blouse.

                    MOODY
          Doctor?

                    SUZANNA
          What? Oh—yes. I've been
          working on the outline, when
          I can get to it.

                    MOODY
          Great. Same subject?

                    SUZANNA
          Y'know...I really can't
          discuss that.

                    MOODY
          Of course. Understood.

He hands her a business card for something
called CONTROL CONCEPTS.

                    MOODY
          My center can always use a
          fresh mind. Stop by sometime.

He smiles at her, takes his signed book and
walks away. Suzanna waits till he's gone, then
discreetly lowers the business card beneath the
table and crumples it up.

EXT. VERMONT AVENUE - EVENING

Book publicist DENISE RAYNER escorts Suzanna
back to her car. Denise is smartly-dressed,
anorexic, an obvious go-getter.

                    DENISE
          I counted 38 at one point.
          Seen better, seen worse.

                    SUZANNA
          And a third of them needy or
          weird. Or needy and weird—

                    DENISE
          Come on. They bought your
          book. Isn't that why we do
          these?

                    SUZANNA
          Honestly? I don't know...

                    DENISE
          How could you not know?

They reach the Saab. Suzanna unlocks her
passenger door and leans against it.

                    SUZANNA
          I'm probably not supposed to
          tell you this, Denise...But
          one of my wealthiest clients
          is also suicidal.

                    DENISE
          You're right. You probably
          shouldn't—

                    SUZANNA
          Because when she was seven
          her mother bound and gagged
          her and locked her in a
          storage closet for 16 hours.
          Now how can my book, or 50
          minutes of my attention per
          week, ever erase that?

                    DENISE
          It's not your job to erase
          things, Suzanna. Just be
          there to listen, and to...I
          don't know, give them some
          guidance and hope?

                    SUZANNA
          Right. And if I'm lucky maybe
          they'll hear me.
               (Denise frowns at her)
          I'm sorry. I've just been a
          little tired lately.

                    DENISE
          Stressed is more like it.
          Maybe you should get more
          sleep. Or take me up on one
          of my unmarried male friends
          already.

Suzanna visibly tightens. Opens the car door.

                    SUZANNA
          You mean another emotionally
          unavailable one?

                    DENISE
          Oh, come on. Not all of them
          were. At least let me buy you
          a drink.

                    SUZANNA
          Thanks, but no...I think I
          just need some alone time
          tonight.

She gives Denise a quick hug and gets in her
car.

                    DENISE
              (under her breath)
          Says the alone time
          factory...

EXT. 101 FREEWAY - NIGHT

Suzanna's Saab cruises by the HOLLYWOOD BOWL
exit and over the Cahauenga Pass into the even
hazier murk of the San Fernando Valley.

INT. MEDITERRANEAN DREAM - NIGHT

A Greek-style fast food place. Suzanna waits
for her take-out order at a crowded counter,
checking emails on her phone.

An OLDER MAN in an ill-fitting canvas jacket
with wild grey hair sits at a nearby table with
his food. Suzanna makes minimal eye contact
with him, re-focuses on her screen.

The man's right hand suddenly begins to twitch.
A hunk of his gyro meat falls into his lap and
he switches the fork to his other hand.

His right leg shakes. Then his entire arm. He's
having some kind of fit. Suzanna gazes at him,
petrified. A BUSBOY, other PATRONS run over, try
and grab him as he tumbles out of the booth.
Lay him on the floor. Someone dials 9-1-1.

Suzanna's order is placed on the counter in
front of her. She pockets her phone, grabs the
bag and hurries out of the place.

EXT. THREE PALMS VILLAGE - NIGHT

A high-end condo complex in Reseda, surrounded
by tall, swaying palms and a gaudy fountain
out front. Suzanna drives her Saab through
an automatic gate and down into a dark,
underground garage.

INT. SUZANNA'S CONDO - NIGHT

She enters with a small stack of mail. Slides
out a <u>Psychology Today</u>, neatly places it on
a living room coffee table with a dozen other
magazines, each with only the title showing.

INT. CONDO - MINUTES LATER

Suzanna sits at a desktop computer with her
large Greek salad and glass of white wine.
Makes adjustments to a client spread sheet on
the screen. There are at least fifteen names.

                    SUZANNA
          Tuesdays suit you better,
          Robert...Trust me.

INT. BEDROOM - NIGHT

She exits the bathroom in a plain beige
nightgown, buttoned to the neck. Walks to a
small aquarium on her dresser and feeds a
couple of GOLDFISH inside.

Climbs onto her four-poster bed, sets up an
iPad on her lap and starts watching SEASON 3,
EP. 6 of a foreign crime show called NORDIC
MIDNIGHT.

                                        CUT TO:

INT. BEDROOM - DEAD OF NIGHT

The light is still on but Suzanna is fast
asleep, the crime show still going on her iPad.

Something wakes her, and she sits up. What was
that? The clock on her night table reads 3:41.
The curtain on her partly open bedroom window
is deathly still. As are the goldfish in her
aquarium. A couple of DOGS BARK somewhere in
the complex.

She climbs out of bed, walks over to check on
the fish——

And a VIOLENT EARTHQUAKE shakes the room.
Suzanna SCREAMS, falls down. The aquarium tips
over and SMASHES on the carpet. Panicked, she

scoots through the water, around the broken
glass and straight under the bed. DISHES SMASH
down the hall. CAR ALARMS go off everywhere. Her
goldfish flop around helplessly on the carpet in
front of her. The RUMBLING and shaking won't
stop. She covers her ears and <u>blacks out</u>...

INT. BEDROOM - MINUTES LATER

Comes to. The shaking has stopped, and she
can hear RESIDENTS shouting in the halls. She
slowly crawls out from under the bed and gets
to her feet. A LITTLE TREMOR rattles the place
and she grabs hold of one of her bed posts
until it stops. Runs down the hall.

INT. FRONT ROOM

Evades the broken dishes, the spilled books
everywhere. Grabs a jacket and her purse off a
chair and hurries out the front door.

EXT. COURTYARD - NIGHT

Practically EVERYONE in the complex has
gathered in the ground floor courtyard, and
are making their way through the main gate.
Bathrobes, pajamas, one GUY in his underwear.

Fire trucks with flashing red lights are out in
front. A FIREMAN blocks a door leading to the
underground garage and Suzanna approaches him.

                    SUZANNA
          Are the cars okay down there?
          I have to get to my car!

                    FIREMAN
          Your car is the least of our
          problems, ma'm.

Suzanna whirls around, sees that parts of the
second and third floors at the far end have
collapsed and RESCUE WORKERS are all over them
with high-powered flashlights.

                    MALE RESIDENT
                 (to the gathering)
          They've opened a shelter down
          the road at Reseda High! My
          van's on the street and I can
          take six or seven!
                    (to Suzanna)
          Need a ride?

                    SUZANNA
          Yes! Thank you!!

INT. RESEDA HIGH GYMNASIUM - NIGHT

Suzanna enters with some others, is handed a
blanket, pillow, and sleeping mat.

QUAKE SURVIVORS take up nearly every inch of
floor space. Both sets of high bleachers have
been folded up, loom over the gymnasium like
fortress walls. A young VOLUNTEER walks over.

                    VOLUNTEER
          This way, people.

Suzanna hesitatingly follows her. The volunteer
points to an open spot on the floor between two
families. Suzanna doesn't move, still somewhat
in shock. The volunteer takes her sleeping mat
and rolls it out for her.

Suzanna slumps onto the mat. Nervously eyes
one of the folded-up bleacher sections, a
yard or two away. A LATINO MOM beside her
slaps together the last of five peanut butter
sandwiches for her KIDS. Sees Suzanna staring
and silently offers her one. Suzanna half-
smiles, takes it.

                    SUZANNA
          I couldn't get my car out.
          Otherwise I'd be somewhere
          else.

The mom can't relate. Has already started
another sandwich.

INT. GYMNASIUM - AN HOUR LATER

Suzanna has managed to pass out again, but
another LOW RUMBLE wakes her.

                    SURVIVOR ACROSS FLOOR
                         (O.S.)
          Aftershock!

Basketball hoops at each end of the gym GROAN
and sway. A few people SCREAM. The bleacher
section closest to Suzanna CREAKS, starts to
roll back open. People grab their belongings,
scurry out of the way.

Suzanna stares at the moving bleachers.
paralyzed. Waits until they're a foot away from
her, then leaps up and races to the middle of
the floor. When the bleachers finally stop moving
she collapses. Throws the blanket over herself
and shivers—more out of fear than any cold.

EXT. THREE PALMS VILLAGE - MORNING

PULL BACK ON

Rescue vehicles everywhere, but two trucks have
also pulled every undamaged car out of the
underground garage and left them on a grassy
median in front of the building.

Suzanna arrives with some of the other
residents. Is thrilled to see her Saab one of
the survivors.

A handful of RESIDENTS have begun re-entering
the complex to fetch belongings.

                    PASSING WOMAN
          Hey there! Glad you're okay!
          Going in for your stuff?

                    SUZANNA
          Uhh...In a bit maybe.

She reaches in her bag, quickly fishes out her
car keys.

EXT. SIDE STREET - MINUTES LATER

Suzanna pulls onto a shady residential street a
mile or so away, and parks.

INT. SAAB - MORNING

Still wearing her jacket over her nightgown,
Suzanna talks on her cell phone.

                    SUZANNA
          Hi Dolores....Well, I beat
          you to it. Yes, let's
          reschedule next week and see
          what happens...And I'm glad
          you're okay...

A FEW MINUTES LATER

                    SUZANNA
          Right, right. Yes, same time
          next week. And I'm so sorry
          about your cat. I'm sure
          he'll turn up.

A FEW MINUTES LATER

                    SUZANNA
             (after a message BEEP)
          Hi Wayne, it's Suzanna.
          Pretty disruptive, right?
          Anyway, I'd like to
          reschedule your session to
          sometime next week, so get in
          touch when you can. Thanks.

She hangs up and the phone immediately RINGS.

                    SUZANNA
          Hello?

                    DENISE
                    (V.O.)
          Holy shit! Are you okay??

                    SUZANNA
          Yeah. Fine...Just a little
          shaken up.

                    DENISE
                    (V.O.)
          You should've seen us! Fred
          had me and the kids in a
          doorway hanging onto us, and
          it was like being on a surf
          board in a tidal wave with
          the thing going on forever!
          You were in a doorway too, I
          take it.

                    SUZANNA
          Um...yeah. Listen, I have to
          finish re-scheduling all my
          appointments. How about--

                    DENISE
          I'll check in later!

Denise hangs up. Suzanna pauses, then drops the
phone in her lap. Takes a DEEP BREATH. Checks
her haggard appearance in the mirror.

                    SUZANNA
          Coffee please...

EXT. COFFEE BEAN DRIVE-THRU LINE - MORNING

Suzanna's Saab waits with about a dozen other
cars, snaking out the driveway, into the street
and around the corner.

INT. SAAB

Suzanna is back on her cell, tweaking a phone
version of her client spread sheet while she
waits. The driver behind her BEEPS and she
looks up, realizes she's let two other cars
move ahead of her.

                    SUZANNA
          Crap...Sorry!

INT. SAAB - TEN MINUTES LATER

Suzanna drives with her large coffee, but the
street traffic in the valley is excruciatingly
slow. She has her car RADIO on.

                    LOCAL ANNOUNCER
                       (V.O.)
              ...USGS is calling it a 6.8,
              with its epicenter in the
              Reseda Hills.

She comes up on an entrance to the 405 Freeway
south and swerves up the ramp.

EXT. 405 - DAY

Less clogged than usual, Suzanna's Saab breezes
over the Sepulveda Pass to the West Side.

EXT. DOUGLAS PARK, SANTA MONICA - DAY

She stops next to a serene, tree-filled public
oasis and gets out with her coffee. Takes a
footpath into the park.

As expected, there are no people around except
for a DOGWALKER or two. The peace and quiet
is a godsend, and Suzanna takes it in as she
strolls along.

Then she turns a sharp corner around a wide
tree trunk and abruptly slows down.

Sees that she's stepped onto a Japanese-style,
wood-slat bridge rising over a koi pond.

She's suddenly unable to move. A very small
TREMOR shakes the earth, and the wood slats
under her shoes grind together with an
unsettling CREAKING sound.

Suzanna grabs hold of the bridge rail with her
free hand. Spills some hot latte on her other
one and the whole cup slips free, drops into
the koi pond.

She shuts her eyes, keeps them closed long

after the tremor has subsided. Finally opens
them again. Peers down at the brown coffee
fouling the fish water, then turns and walks
quickly off the bridge and back out of the park.

A DOGWALKER passes her.

                    SUZANNA
          Did you feel that tremor?

                    DOGWALKER
          Uhh...Nope.

Suzanna just keeps walking.

INT. SAAB - DAY

She drives west on Montana Avenue, agitated and
slightly delirious. STORE OWNERS are out on the
sidewalks, sweeping up broken glass from their
broken windows.

EXT. 7TH STREET - DAY

Suzanna's car crosses San Vicente Boulevard and
drops down the steep, curving hill into Santa
Monica Canyon.

INT. SAAB

The road winds down through lush vegetation,
past elegant homes tucked behind trees and
gates and walls and vines.

There's also a lot less visible quake damage
here. Suzanna slows down to marvel at the
canyon around her. It's like another world.

EXT. CANYON ROAD - DAY

The Saab cruises past a row of funky beach
shops, all of them closed. Comes up on an old,
tree-shrouded watering hole called THE SORRY
MAN TAVERN. It's front door is open. Suzanna
pulls into the nearly empty lot.

INT. TAVERN - DAY

A cozy, wood-panelled room. Old vinyl booths

with graffiti carved into many of their mahagony
tables. A bluefin tuna is mounted over the bar.
Coconut shells in each open window RATTLE in the
ocean breeze. Except for an OLD DRUNK SNORING
beside his half-empty beer glass at the bar, the
place is empty.

Suzanna approaches the bar, keeping a few feet
away from the drunk. Is about to knock on the
counter but hesitates. Loudly CLEARS HER THROAT
instead.

A door to a back room swings open and a chubby,
grey-bearded BARTENDER appears, toting a carton
of liquor. Flashes a smile when he sees her.

                    BARTENDER
          Howdy. What can I get you?

                    SUZANNA
          I don't know. Too early in
          the day for a glass of good
          Zinfandel?

                    BARTENDER
          What's too early?...

He pulls down a wine glass. Suzanna glances
around.

                    SUZANNA
          So no damage here, huh?

                    BARTENDER
          Find out for sure when the
          inspector comes. Far as I
          know only lost one case of
          Glenlivet. Now that's a
          tragedy.

                    SUZANNA
          You should see Montana Avenue.

                    BARTENDER
          I did. Damn thing hopped around
          town like a goofy grasshopper.
          Got a bunch of friends who
          didn't even lose a salt shaker.

He slides over her wine on a napkin. She takes
a stool at the bar and enjoys the breeze on her
face. The sound of the coconut shells. Takes
a large sip of wine, then sees her sleepless
reflection and wrinkled sweats in the mirror
behind the bar and looks back down at her glass.

Gets a sudden eerie feeling. As if someone is
watching her. She pivots on her stool.

A YOUNG MAN sits in a shadowy corner booth,
without a drink in front of him. His eyes are
fixed on hers. He wears tight jeans with the cuffs
rolled up, and a rumpled white denim shirt. His
longish brown hair is swept back off his tanned
forehead with some kind of gel. He's killer
handsome, but there's a deep, alluring sadness
about him.

Suzanna takes in his stare for a good three
seconds, then quickly turns back around. Has a
much larger sip of wine.

                    SUZANNA
               (under her breath)
          Keep dreaming, Suzanna...

The bartender ducks into the back room again.
Suzanna is sweating a bit. Slowly peers back up
at the bar mirror.

Doesn't see the young man behind her. She turns
around.

The booth in the corner is empty. Suzanna scans
the room, mystified. Notices the open door to the
parking lot just a few feet away from the booth.

A flyer tacked to the wall behind the booth
flutters off in a sudden wind gust and lands on
the table. Suzanna stands with her wine glass
and walks over to the booth to glance out at the
empty parking lot and hang the flyer back up. It
reads:

                  -FOR RENT-
          QUIET CANYON GUEST HOUSE
                849 EL MESA
          CONTACT BURTON REALTY

She's curious. Tacks the flyer back on the wall,
then snaps a phone picture of it.

EXT. EL MESA ROAD - DAY

Suzanna's Saab cruises up an even narrower,
twistier canyon road, flanked on both sides by
ancient Chinese elms. The leafy canopy is so
thick that only thin slivers of sunlight stab
through it.

INT. SAAB

Suzanna slows to a crawl, peering out at any
house numbers she can make out. The road ahead
ends in a cul-de-sac, and a padlocked iron
gate. 849 was painted on the wall beside it,
decades ago, a couple of the numbers barely
readable now.

                    SUSANNA
          Jesus...

She kills the engine and climbs out.

EXT. DRIVEWAY - DAY

It's unbelievably quiet here. A rodent or
bird SCURRIES into a nearby bush. Above the
property's high adobe wall, Suzanna can make
out the tiled orange roof of a large old
Spanish house, but not much of it. Through the
gate, the driveway curves up to the left and
disappears.

Suzanna quickly takes out her phone, goes to
the web site for BURTON REALTY. Types 849 El
Mesa into the search window. A message comes
up:

          PROPERTY PHOTOS UNAVAILABLE
          CONTACT REALTY OFFICE

                    SUZANNA
          Great...

She climbs back in her car. Gets a thought and
reaches behind the front seat for a gym bag she

remembered was there. There's a pair of extra
sweats inside.

EXT. DOWNTOWN SANTA MONICA - DAY

Wearing the cleaner sweats under her jacket
now, Suzanna enters an office building that's
considered a "high-rise" here, maybe 20 floors.

INT. BURTON REALTY RECEPTION - MINUTES LATER

A large, somewhat tacky but damage-free office
with old brown carpeting, badly painted
landscapes on the wall. A prim elderly
SECRETARY with her grey hair up in a bun lowers
her bifocals and smiles at Suzanna.

                    SECRETARY
          Mr. Burton is on a call but
          he'll be right with you.

Suzanna nods, takes a seat on a couch. A window
right beside her looks out on the beach and
Santa Monica Bay.

A door behind the reception desk opens and
MONTY BURTON appears with a five-star smile.

                    MONTY
          Hi. I'm Monty.

She gets up, walks over and he gives her a
quick handshake. In his mid-60s and fit, with
oval tortoise eyeglasses and a thinning,
layered haircut. He wears pressed white tennis
shorts and a dark blue polo shirt.

                    SUZANNA
          Suzanna Bristol. Hi.

He ushers her through his door.

INT. MONTY'S OFFICE - DAY

The window view in here is bigger, and somewhat
dizzying. Suzanna looks away from it and grabs
the nearest chair in front of his desk.

                    MONTY
Sorry for my casual look but
as I can see...
        (motions to her sweats)
It seems to be in style
today. Any damage at your
place?

                    SUZANNA
Enough. So I saw your flyer,
and saw the guest property on
El Mesa from the gate—

                    MONTY
A flyer?

                    SUZANNA
Yeah. On the wall at the
Sorry Man Tavern?

                    MONTY
Oh! That must've been from
the last time I rented it...
        (checks something
          on his computer)
I was just about to advertise
again, so...I guess it
doesn't matter. What do you
do, Suzanna?

                    SUZANNA
Well, I have a therapy
practice and write self-help
books. Out in the valley.

                    MONTY
How ambitious!

                    SUZANNA
But I'm a little sick of
the heat and congestion out
there. Your guest house
sounds kind of perfect right
now.

                    MONTY
Oh, it certainly is. The last
tenant left me in the lurch,
and I'm pretty eager to find a
new one. You live alone?

                    SUZANNA
Yes. I mean, I had a couple
of goldfish, but they didn't
survive.

                    MONTY
Condolences.
          (back on his computer)
Well, it's a pretty old guest
house, built in 1925, along
with the main house, which is
undergoing repair along with
the pool...

                    SUZANNA
Oh! There's a pool?

                    MONTY
Like I said. Being repaired.
But the guest house is a good
size with its own bathroom
and internet and it's awful
sweet for just a thousand a
month.

                    SUZANNA
Really. You have any photos?

                    MONTY
No, unfortunately.
               (grins)
Just the keys.

                    SUZANNA
Well, I kind of like to know
what I might be renting.

                    MONTY
Sure. Then I guess I'll have
to tell you.

He sets his computer mouse aside and leans
forward on the desk.

                    MONTY
          First of all, it's cooler
          there because you're closer
          to the water. Some days you
          get fog, but most of the time
          it burns off by the afternoon.
          And you can sit on one of the
          deck lounge chairs with a
          good book, or get some sun.
          Or enjoy a plum from the tree
          beside you. Or slide the
          chair under a hundred-year-
          old oak tree that spreads
          over the house. It's a
          wonderful place to read, or
          to write, or to just be.

                    SUZANNA
          Hmm...You're making this
          a lot easier for me, Mr.
          Burton.

                    MONTY
          Friends call me Monty. You
          can too.

                    SUZANNA
          Okay. Monty...

                                        CUT TO:

INT. OFFICE BUILDING ELEVATOR - DAY

And Suzanna riding the elevator back down,
staring at the two old keys in her hand.

                    SUZANNA
          Am I really doing this?...

Suddenly the elevator lights flicker. The lift
jolts to a stop and the entire thing CREAKS
and sways. Another aftershock. Suzanna buries
herself in the corner, shuts her eyes and waits
for it to stop. The elevator makes a METALLIC
POP sound, then resumes descending.

EXT. FRONT OF BUILDING - DAY

She practically stumbles out onto the sidewalk.
A handful of PEDESTRIANS pass, but none seem as
shaken as her.

                    SUZANNA
                (to one of them)
            Did you feel that??

One man shrugs, doesn't stop. Suzanna hurries
to her car, climbs in. Sits behind the wheel
and DEEP BREATHES a number of times until she's
recovered enough to start the ENGINE.

INT. SUZANNA'S CONDO - DAY

Suzanna picks up her dead goldfish with a paper
towel, dumps them in a trash can without
looking. Looks around at the absolute mess she
had feared. Unsure where to even begin.

EXT. CONDO BALCONY - MINUTES LATER

Suzanna on her phone, pacing. Three stories
below, a few RESIDENTS move back and forth
across the courtyard, carrying belongings.

                    SUZANNA
            So how's Des Moines, Deb?

                      DEB
            (V.O., nice but guarded)
            Oh, crazy busy as usual. Bob
            got another raise, meaning
            he's home even less. Teddy
            has an ear infection so he's
            out of school right now and
            bouncing off the walls—

                    SUZANNA
            Feel like some company? I
            don't know...Flat, solid
            ground suddenly sounds
            appealing.

                    DEB
                   (V.O.)
        Oh Suze. It's not really the
        best time.

                  SUZANNA
        Not the best time. Even for
        your sister?...I get it.
        Teddy's ear infection is
        obviously more important than
        my condo building caving in.

                    DEB
        (V.O. after an exasperated SIGH)
        Please don't do this.

                  SUZANNA
        Do what?

                    DEB
                   (V.O.)
        Make me feel guilty. We've
        been watching the news, you
        know, and they said the
        damage is contained, and
        there's plenty of shelters.
        Heck, at least you don't have
        to deal with tornadoes there.

                  SUZANNA
        Forget it, Deb. Just forget I
        called.

She hangs up. Is tempted to hurl the phone
over the railing, but stops herself. Goes back
inside.

EXT. EL MESA ROAD - DAY

Suzanna parks her stuffed Saab on the cul-de-sac.
Gets out with a packed carton and roller bag and
approaches the locked gate.

Takes out the keys and inserts the one that fits
into the padlock. It won't turn. She tries it
again. No luck. She CURSES, rubs the key on her
pants leg a few times, then tries it a third

time. Sets down the carton and roller bag. By
holding the padlock with her other hand she's
finally able to work the thing open. Swings the
GROANING old gate forward and heads inside.

The driveway curves up to the left, where a
canopy of wisteria needs to be ducked under.
She stops and takes in the property.

The vine-covered Spanish house rises on the
left, tucked behind a row of elms and spider-
webbed vines. There are black bars in front of
many of its windows, and a turret adorns the
top.

She passes a large, empty pool that looks more
neglected than it does needing repair. Weeds
grow up through cracks at the bottom, and only
half of the diving board is left. The sight of
the pool makes Suzanna a little uneasy, and she
keeps moving.

The spreading oak tree Monty mentioned bathes
practically everything else in shadow, and
that includes the charming Spanish-style guest
house, which is nearly as big as Suzanna's
condo. It's certainly more homey. Bougainvillea
flowers spread up its adobe walls and onto its
tiled roof. A flagstone deck wraps around the
front and side, two dusty lounge chairs and a
flowering plum tree visible.

A noticeable glow fills Suzanna's face.

                    SUZANNA
          Wonderful...

INT. GUEST HOUSE

She unlocks the place with the other key and
steps inside. A decent-sized living room area
with an old leather couch, mini-kitchen, and
a bathroom in the rear. The walls sport a few
framed photographs of early 20th century Santa
Monica.

She sets her roller bag and carton down, nods
in approval.

Then hears the slow grind of a TRUCK ENGINE
coming up the road.

                    SUZANNA
          Oh!

She races back out.

EXT. DRIVEWAY

Jogs down to the road, where a large pick-up
from SALGADO MOVERS has pulled up to the gate.

                    SUZANNA
          Hey! You might want to back
          that in!

Through the gate's bars, she can make out the
DRIVER and his PARTNER sitting in the front
seat. The partner is looking up the driveway
with trepidation. Shakes his head, mumbles
something in SPANISH to the driver. Adds a few
wild hand gestures and the driver backs out.
Turns the truck around in the street and we can
see Suzanna's four-poster bed roped up in back.

Suzanna swings open the gate, is about to
motion them back through it, but instead the
truck SLAMS into FIRST GEAR and just drives
away.

                    SUZANNA
          You have to be kidding me...
          HEY!

                                        CUT TO:

INT. GUEST HOUSE - MINUTES LATER

Pacing again, on her phone. The business card
for Salgado Movers in her hand.

                    SUZANNA
          I don't know! You tell me!
          They pulled into the driveway
          and friggin' changed their
          minds or something. Can't you
          contact Manny? I think that's
          who I talked to...

She idly walks to a large closet and slides
open its door. Stuffed under some extra blankets
is a rolled-up futon mattress.

                    SUZANNA
          Wait. Hang on a second...

She drags the thing out and unrolls it. It's a
fairly decent size, and in good shape.

                    SUZANNA
          You know what? Forget it.
          Tell them to just bring the
          bed over to E-Z Storage,
          on Ventura Boulevard near
          Coldwater. I'll call and tell
          them it's coming.

EXT. GUEST HOUSE - LATE AFTERNOON

Denise helps Suzanna carry two more cartons and
a couple of grocery bags in. Like Suzanna was,
Denise is blown away by the property's beauty.

                    DENISE
          Pinch me. And where's Gloria
          Swanson?

                    SUZANNA
          I know. Lots of old money
          around here, I imagine. And
          the realtor says the canyon
          plays tricks with sound.
               (loses her balance for a
                moment on the flagstones)
          Whoa. You must have felt <u>that</u>
          one!

                    DENISE
          Nope. I think this quake
          really rattled your bones,
          lady. Weren't you around for
          the Northridge one in '94?

                    SUZANNA
          No, we were living in Italy
          that winter. And Pasadena
          definitely didn't get the
          damage the west side did.

INT. GUEST HOUSE

They put the grocery bags on the counter.
Denise looks around, impressed. Eyes the plum
tree out on the deck.

                    DENISE
          Plum tree could use some
          love, though.

                    SUZANNA
          Really?

She gives it a glance. The white blossoms are
definitely a bit withered now.

                    SUZANNA
          That's weird. It looked
          pretty healthy yesterday.

Denise strolls around, checks out the framed
Santa Monica photos.

                    DENISE
          Huh. This one looks like the
          main house. Bet they had some
          roaring 20s parties back
          then.

                    SUZANNA
          No doubt...

She takes out a pack of new kitchen sponges.
Denise walks over, opens a cabinet for her
beneath the sink.

                    DENISE
          Hey. This yours?

Pulls out a dark green backpack and holds it
up. Suzanna looks at a name tag on top.

                    SUZANNA
          Not unless my name is
          Yolanda.

She zips it open. Slides out a couple of
college-level textbooks, a loose leaf binder,
and a handful of seed packets for various
vegetables.

                    SUZANNA
          Must be the last tenant's.
          She split without giving
          notice, apparently.

                    DENISE
          Bummer. Didn't even have a
          chance to garden.

INT. GUEST HOUSE - AN HOUR LATER

Denise has left, and Suzanna struggles with a
wi-fi router under the desk, which could be the
first one ever built. It BEEPS and CRACKLES when
she switches it on, sounds like an old dial-up
modem that's being strangled.

Her laptop still says NOT CONNECTED. She looks
back down at the router, follows its wires out
onto the deck.

EXT. DECK

Sees that a bougenvillea vine has been clawing
at one of the router wires that leads to a
phone line. She pries it free, hears a familiar
BOOTING UP sound and turns to go back inside--

And SOMETHING DARK shifts in the pool out of
the corner of her eye.

She spins around. Reluctantly peers into the
pool's empty abyss.

Whatever she thought she saw isn't there. An
oak leaf flutters down from the tree and she
shakes her head, goes back in.

INT. GUEST HOUSE - EVENING

Suzanna wears a headset plugged into her cell
phone while mixing a salad. The backpack with
YOLANDA P.'s name, address, and phone number
is a few feet away on the counter.

                    SUZANNA
          Yeah hi. Is this Yolanda?

                    YOLANDA
                (V.O., muffled)
          Si...

                    SUZANNA
          Good. Well, I found your backpack
          in this Santa Monica Canyon
          guest house I just rented.
                (hears no response)
          Hello?

                    YOLANDA
                (V.O., even quieter)
          I don't have a backpack...

                    SUZANNA
          O-kay...But this one right here
          has your name and phone number
          on it, so I figured you were
          renting this place before me and
          left it, or—

                    YOLANDA
                (V.O.)
          I wasn't there. Goodbye...

CLICK. Suzanna frowns in puzzlement.

                    SUZANNA
          If you say so...

She takes off her headset, then reaches over,
plucks the six or seven seed packets out of the
backpack and tosses them on the counter.

INT. GUEST HOUSE - NIGHT

Suzanna sits on the made-up futon, messing with a

BOOK OUTLINE on her laptop. She YAWNS.

A breeze outside RUSTLES the branches on the
oak and plum trees. Along with them comes faint
LAUGHTER, TINKLING GLASSES, and a SPLASH or
two. Some kind of nearby party.

Suzanna looks up from her laptop screen.
Listening to the sounds.

                    SUZANNA
          Oh please...On a Monday
          night?

At least a dozen people are TALKING and
LAUGHING now, but it's impossible to make out
any of the words.

She gets off the futon, opens the door to the
deck and pokes her head outside.

It's a clear night, under a half moon. She
scans the pool area, including an old vertical
shed on the far side. The oak leaves continue
to RUSTLE in the breeze. The party sounds are a
bit louder here, but are obviously coming from
somewhere else in the canyon.

                    SUZANNA
          Sound tricks for sure...

Turns and goes back in. Gives the futon an odd
look. The sheets and blanket are reversed on
the bed—and now face in the opposite direction.

                    SUZANNA
          Good one, Suzanna...

She quickly re-arranges them and slips into bed.

INT. GUEST HOUSE - MINUTES LATER

She's closed her laptop, turned off the light.
Can still hear the FAINT PARTY SOUNDS so grabs
her phone. Thumbs to a sleeping app called
TRANQUIL, chooses COUNTRY MEADOW, pops in some
earbuds and starts to fall asleep to the sound
of DISTANT WHIPPOORWILLS AND FROGS.

EXT. CANYON - DEAD OF NIGHT

The party sounds are gone, and have been
replaced by more natural ones. Dew DRIPS off
a palm frond. A MOCKINGBIRD goes through its
chirpy repertoire. A SQUIRREL darts into some
brush. The BARKING of a canyon dog echoes
through the trees.

INT. GUEST HOUSE

Suzanna's sleep app has gone quiet. A faint,
steady CREAKING sound from outside can now be
heard. Her eyes open, and she sits up. Looks at
her phone and sees it's out of juice. Yanks out
the earbuds.

The CREAKING is just loud enough to be
annoying. Gazing out the window, she can see
that the breeze has died, meaning it's not
coming from the oak branches.

There's also a dull yellow light coming from
somewhere. Hitting the wall above her bed.

She stands and walks to the window above the
sink.

The yellow light is coming from the turret atop
the main house.

                    SUZANNA
          Nice.

She finds her robe and slippers and puts them
on. Walks outside.

EXT. GUEST HOUSE

Much of the pool area is bathed in yellow
light. The weird CREAKING is louder outside,
but like the pool party sounds seems to be
coming from somewhere else.

She quickly makes her way around the pool,
trying to not look into it. Finds what appears
to be a little footpath, overgrown with
vegetation. Carefully makes her way down it to

the main house, peering up once or twice at the
yellow turret window.

Steps between two thick bushes and nearly
smacks into a high barbed wire fence! She
GASPS, hops back and looks in both directions.
The fence wraps around the entire house.

                    SUZANNA
          Sheesh...That's one hell of a
          "repair" going on, Monty.

She backtracks up to the guest house. Reaches
the pool area, now suddenly bathed in nothing
but moonlight. She spins and looks up at the
turret.

The yellow light is off.

Something in the pool SHIFTS out of the corner
of her eye again. She decides not to even look
this time. Hurries back into the guest house.

INT. GUEST HOUSE - MINUTES LATER

Pours herself a glass of sherry and takes it to
bed.

INT. SAAB - MORNING

Suzanna drives on a San Fernando Valley street
in her conservative work dress. Doesn't seem
fully awake yet.

Rolls up to a crosswalk, where a dozen or so
SCHOOL KIDS are being escorted across the road
by a TEACHER.

Suzanna stares at them, suddenly nervous. The
kids are eight or nine years old, all wearing
packs. She drops her eyes a second, reaches for
her phone to find her emails. Or anything.

Dares to peek back up.

The last BOY in the group has slowed down, and
is staring at her, odd concern on his face.

Suzanna trembles. The teacher takes the boy's
arm, moves him along and Suzanna resumes normal
breathing. Keeps driving.

INT. SUZANNA'S OFFICE - MORNING

Dimly lit, minimal decor, and no windows. You
get the sense she doesn't spend a lot of time
here.

ANNIE and PATRICE, a lesbian couple in their
30s, sit on the far ends of her soft couch.
Trying not to look at each other.

                    ANNIE
          That isn't what I said.

                    PATRICE
          I'm not deaf. I heard you.
                  (imitating Amy)
          "I left the closet years ago,
          Patrice. You're still afraid
          of the doorknob."

                    ANNIE
          Well, aren't you? Don't blame
          me if you can't admit it.

                    PATRICE
          And stop being such a bitch.

                    ANNIE
          Your parents are intrusive
          and annoying, Patrice. They
          need their Elizabethan family
          values ripped out of their
          skulls.

                    PATRICE
          Whatever. Getting rid of
          our second bedroom will not
          do that. They'll just be
          confused.

The women lapse into thick silence. Suzanna
has been sitting across from them in a chair,
making notes on a legal pad. She leans forward.

                    SUZANNA
          What I'm hearing...is that
          coming out is a very personal
          decision for Patrice—as it
          should be. Now Annie, if you
          truly care about Patrice
          and want her to grow, that
          decision should flower on its
          own. She has the right to her
          space, or if we extend the
          metaphor a bit, to her water
          and sun.

Patrice blubbers a little, breaks into a SOB.
Annie hesitates, then slides over on the couch
and hugs her. Suzanna eyes a clock on the far
wall.

                    SUZANNA
          I'm encouraged by this,
          guys...Why don't we start
          here next week?

She jots down a few more notes. The women
stand.

                    ANNIE
          Sometimes we think you're a
          cold bitch, Dr. Bristol.

                    PATRICE
               (wiping her eyes)
          But sometimes...like right
          now...I think you can help
          the most hopeless person on
          earth.

Suzanna isn't sure how to respond. Gets up from
her chair and both women move to embrace her.
Suzanna recoils.

                    PATRICE
          Bet you're real good at fixing
          things in your relationships.

                    SUZANNA
          Well...Not the best track
          record, I'm afraid. See you
          next week?

They nod and walk to the door, clutching hands.
Suzanna gathers herself.

INT. SUZANNA'S OFFICE - AFTERNOON

WAYNE leans forward on the same couch. Bouncing
his leg and mashing a piece of gum. He's in
his 40s, a balding, unattractive child-man in
a short-sleeve yellow shirt with sweat pools
under his arms.

                    WAYNE
          I don't know...I see guys do
          it all the time. It probably
          isn't that hard. Especially
          after a beer or two...Did I
          tell you about the pub I went
          to in Hollywood? It was after
          work, after I did my FedEx
          drop, and this girl with red
          hair was definitely checking
          me out.

Suzanna slumps tiredly in the chair. Very few
notes on her legal pad.

                    SUZANNA
          So what did you say to her?

                    WATNE
              (rocks and sweats
               a little more)
          I said...I said "You're
          real pretty. Wanna go see a
          movie?"

                    SUZANNA
          Okay. And how did she
          respond?

                    WAYNE
          How do you think?

Suzanna just looks at him, rapidly losing
patience. He slowly leans back, but keeps his
knee bouncing.

                    WAYNE
          I guess I didn't really say
          that. But I <u>wished</u> I did,
          definitely. I'll probably go
          back there next week, after
          my FedEx drop. Get to know
          her if she's there—

                    SUZANNA
          Wayne?

He goes quiet. Suzanna SIGHS deeply, leans
forward.

                    SUZANNA
          You will not meet a woman
          this way. You will find love
          when you find it in yourself.
          When you go to a bar or coffee
          shop to spend time with your
          thoughts. Or feelings. Or
          even a book. You will find
          it if you ever move out of
          your mother's house because
          your mere independence will
          create the self-confidence
          you've been lacking. And
          self-confidence can be an
          aphrodisiac.

                    WAYNE
          Yeah, but I can't really
          leave my mother.

                    SUZANNA
          I see. Afraid our time's up,
          Wayne. See you next week.

She jots down a few cursory notes. Wayne gets
up. Is about to say something else but stops
himself and walks out.

Suzanna takes a deep breath and goes to her
desk. Starts entering the session notes on her

computer. Feels a sudden chill in her arms and
pulls on a sweater that was draped on her desk
chair.

A light CHIME goes off. Suzanna frowns, clicks
over to her appointment schedule on the
desktop.

WAYNE B. was her last scheduled client at
4 p.m. She gets up, walks curiously to the
waiting room door.

EXT. SUZANNA'S WAITING ROOM

A very small room, with the only window in her
unit looking out on Moorpark Avenue.

And no one is waiting there.

Puzzled, she opens the door to the hallway.

No one is in the hallway either.

She thinks for a beat, uneasy, then slowly goes
back inside.

INT. GUEST HOUSE - EVENING

Suzanna finishes planting the seeds from
Yolanda's backpack in some small pots for her
kitchen windowsill.

EXT. GUEST HOUSE DECK - AN HOUR LATER

Suzanna sits on one of the lounge chairs with
her laptop, headset on, participating in a
podcast interview with MARTIN, an academic-
looking host on ZOOM.

                    SUZANNA
          Absolutely, Martin. The
          pandemic has seen a massive
          growth in not only personal
          therapy, but for families as
          well. Everyone is staying at
          home and being on top of each
          other, so to speak.

A cool ocean breeze kicks in. Suzanna brings
her knees up on the chair for added warmth.

                    MARTIN
                 (on screen)
          Of course...Um, before we
          wrap up, Dr. Bristol, I've
          been meaning to ask why you
          chose to be a therapist. Did
          it first come to you when
          you were in college, or high
          school, or middle——

                    SUZANNA
          College, yes. As I think
          I prefaced in my book, I
          attended Stanford, which has
          one of the best Psychology
          programs—

                    MALE VOICE
          Suzanna...

The voice was barely audible, mixed with the
breeze, but defnitely mournful.

                    SUZANNA
          One of the best programs...

Her ears perk up. She glances around.

                    MARTIN
          I'm sorry?

                    SUZANNA
          Er, one of the best programs
          for that in the country.

                    MALE VOICE
                 (a tad louder)
          Suzanna...

                    SUZANNA
          Did you hear that?

                    MARTIN
          Er—hear what?

                    SUZANNA
          Never mind. It's getting late
          here and I'm a bit tired.

                    MARTIN
          No problem. It's been great
          talking with you, Suzanna.
          Dr. Bristol's book is
          entitled "Finding the New
          You" and is available on
          Amazon and at all worthy
          bookstores.

A SCRATCHING SOUND comes from the empty pool.
Suzanna practically leaps out of the chair.

                    SUZANNA
          Thanks Martin! Have to go
          now!

She exits the interview. Stands, holding the
closed laptop in front of her like a shield.
Slowly inches up to the edge of the pool.

Whatever dark thing she thought she saw earlier
down there is shaped like a young, crouching
boy.

She shuts her eyes. Opens them again. The shape
is moving. Suzanna grimaces in horror and the
thing SCRATCHES furiously on the pool wall.
Then comes more into view and Suzanna nearly
faints with relief.

It's a SQUIRREL.

                    SUZANNA
          God almighty...

She sets her laptop back on the lounge chair.
Looks around for a way to help the animal.

Quickly goes over to the tall pool shed on the
other side of the area.

Like the front gate, the shed is padlocked. And
she has no key. Suzanna backs up, looks around
the side. Spots something on the ground behind
the shed.

A long, pool-cleaning pole with a net on its
end. She slides the thing out and takes it
around the pool.

Gets down on her knees, then her belly. Extends
the net end of the pole down far enough so the
squirrel can reach it. The critter doesn't move
right away, innately suspicious.

                    SUZANNA
          Come on, buddy. Don't be
          afraid.

The thing doesn't move. Suzanna GROANS and
retreats a little to give it "space". After a
few seconds the squirrel digs its claws into the
net, hauls itself up. Suzanna quickly lifts the
pole and gives the animal a gentle toss out of
the pool. Swipes her hands together in triumph.

                    SUZANNA
          Now squirrels I can help...

INT. GUEST HOUSE - DEAD OF NIGHT

A drenching spring RAINSTORM beats on her tiled
roof. Suzanna tosses and turns on the futon.

                    MALE VOICE
          (faint, mixed with the rain)
          Suzanna...

She sits up with a start. Did she really just
hear that again?

But now there are more sounds. The same TINKLING
GLASSES, LAUGHTER, and SPLASHING she heard the
night before.

                    SUZANNA
          In the frickin' rain?

She gets out of bed, goes to the window. Nothing
going on out there but raindrops, and now
there's a new sound: LITTLE KIDS TALKING IN
SPANISH.

She goes to her night table. Fumbles for her
cell phone and finds a RECORDING APP.

As a dull yellow light suddenly hits the wall
in front of her. She spins—

The turret light on the abandoned main house is
back on.

She takes one step toward the window, looks to
her left and SHRIEKS—

The YOUNG MAN who was watching her at the Sorry
Man Tavern stands in the corner. Completely
naked and dripping wet.

                    YOUNG MAN
          Suzanna...

                    SUZANNA
          GET OUT OF HERE!!

He doesn't move. She gets on her phone, dials
9-1-1. Grabs a long kitchen knife with her free
hand.

                    SUZANNA
          DID YOU HEAR ME??

He leaves the corner. She SHRIEKS again, raises
the knife and HE WALKS RIGHT THROUGH HER and
DISAPPEARS into the opposite wall.

Suzanna drops the knife.

                    OPERATOR
                    (V.O.)
          9-1-1. State your emergency,
          please.

                    SUZANNA
          Um—yeah. An intruder just...

                    OPERATOR
                    (V.O.)
          Hello?

                    SUZANNA
          Never mind.

She hangs up. Scrambles for her clothes.

EXT. DRIVEWAY - MINUTES LATER

She slips through the gate, stuffed overnight
bag over her shoulder, and jumps in her Saab.
SCREECHES down the road.

INT. THREE PALMS VILLAGE GARAGE - DAWN

CONSTRUCTION MEN set up for morning repair work
at one end of the condo complex garage.

INT. SAAB

Suzanna is asleep in her car at the opposite
end. A JACKHAMMER wakes her. She groggily
sits up, her face and hair a mess. Tries to
unscramble her disturbed thoughts. A couple
of the WORKERS spot her car and begin walking
towards her. She starts the ENGINE and rolls
out the exit.

                                        CUT TO:

INT. BURTON REALTY RECEPTION - MORNING

Suzanna marches in, still unkempt and obviously
on too much coffee.

                    SUZANNA
          Hi. Monty Burton, please.
          He's around, right? Because
          if not, I don't—

                    SECRETARY
          And you are?...

                    SUZANNA
          Suzanna Bristol. I just
          rented that guest house on El
          Mesa two days ago.

> SECRETARY
> Right. I remember. You were
> very sweet.
>> (checks something
>> on her computer)
> I'm afraid that Mr. Burton
> is in Tahiti all this week,
> though. If you want to leave
> a—

> SUZANNA
> What do you mean he's in
> Tahiti?

> SECRETARY
> On vacation. He rents an
> overwater bungalow at the
> Intercontinental—

Suzanna SMASHES her fist on a stapler sitting atop the counter. One of the ejected staples whizzes by the secretary's cheek, startling her.

> SUZANNA
> Oh God—I'm so sorry....But
> really. Yeah. If Monty checks
> in you can give him a message
> for me: I want out of the
> lease.

The secretary doesn't bat an eye.

> SECRETARY
> Oh, you can speak to our
> attorney about that. Should I
> text you his number?

> SUZANNA
> No. I would rather talk to
> Monty about this, not some
> attorney. Can you please give
> him the message?

> SECRETARY
> I'll do my best, Ms. Bristol.
> Umm...May I ask why you want
> to leave?

                    SUZANNA
              Yes. Because the place is
              fucking haunted.

She storms out.

EXT. SIDEWALK - MINUTES LATER

Suzanna looks weirdly happy when she exits
the office building door. It doesn't last. The
sidewalk has many PEDESTRIANS and TOURISTS
going past her, and she gets turned around for
a moment. Forgets where she parked. Starts in
one direction, then does a 360 and goes the
other way.

INT. SAAB

Finally gets to her car and drops behind the
steering wheel. Her mind tries to unscramble,
but her panic is winning. She clutches the
wheel with both hands, looks down at the floor
and DEEP BREATHES some more. Then a new thought
hits her and her head rises again.

                    SUZANNA
              Attorney...leases...
                    (her eyes narrow)
              Owners...

                                        CUT TO:

INT. SANTA MONICA HALL OF RECORDS - DAY

A CUTE YOUNG GUY working the information desk
squints at Suzanna.

                    GUY
              Property records for what
              address?

                    SUZANNA
              849 El Mesa. In the Canyon.

                    GUY
              You could do this online, you
              know.

                    SUZANNA
          Well, I'm here, so...

                      GUY
            (points to a computer
          terminal across the room)
          Go ahead and use that. The
          home page pretty much walks
          you through it.

                    SUZANNA
          Thanks.

INT. HALL OF RECORDS - MINUTES LATER

Suzanna types 849 EL MESA into the search
window. There's a pause, and then a series of
names come up:

Montgomery Burton (1985-present)
Burton Realty (1960-1985)
Leland Burton (1930-1958)
Woodrow Burton (1920-1929)

                    SUZANNA
          Nice, Monty. Keeping it in
          the family...

She takes out her phone and SNAPS a photo of
the screen.

Collects her things, heads out past the info
desk and the cute young guy gives her a flirty
goodbye wink. Suzanna smiles back at him, then
pauses for a second, a new thought triggered.

EXT. SORRY MAN TAVERN - DAY

Suzanna pulls into the lot. There's a few more
cars there this time.

INT. TAVERN

She enters, looks around at three or four
unfamiliar PATRONS. Walks up to the bar and the
BARTENDER nods.

                    BARTENDER
          Howdy. Another Zinfandel?

                    SUZANNA
          Umm, sure. You remembered me!

                    BARTENDER
          Part of my job.

                    SUZANNA
          Listen. Last time I was here
          there was this young guy
          sitting over in that booth
          in the corner. Slicked-back
          hair, white denim shirt. You
          remember *him*?

                    BARTENDER
          Can't say I do. Get a lot
          of one-timers and tourists
          passing through. Excuse me—

He sets her wine down on the bar and ducks
into the back room again. Suzanna picks up the
glass, gets off the stool and wanders around the
room a bit. Spots a row of framed photos on the
far wall that she missed last time and heads
over to them.

The usual signed Hollywood celebrity pics. She
recognizes ones of Arnold Schwarzenegger, Dyan
Cannon, Michael Landon.

The next row over has some lesser ones.
Including one of a young handsome man in a
white denim shirt with his hair slicked back.
The man who was watching her from the booth and
appeared naked in her guest house. His name is
TYLER WORTH.

Stunned, she plucks the photo right off the wall
and gazes at it. The bartender comes back out
and she quickly walks it over to him.

                    SUZANNA
          This guy. You've never seen
          him?

                         BARTENDER
              You kidding? He was on a
              TV show or two back in the
              1950s, I think. A little
              before my time, hon.

She's mystified. Starts to take the photo back
to the wall, then changes her mind when the
bartender's back is turned. Stuffs it in her bag
and leaves without drinking her wine.

INT. MAR VISTA COFFEE SHOP - DAY

A low-key place with mood lighting, DOWNTEMPO
music playing and a small amount of HIPSTERS.

Suzanna hunkers with her laptop at a back
table, going deep into the IMDB site to dig up
a short TYLER WORTH page.

            BORN: 1933   DIED: 1957

                         SUZANNA
              Jee-zus. He was 24?

He played "GAS STATION ATTENDANT" in Wake Up
and Smell Murder (1955), and "SAM DRISCOLL" on
The Young and the Reckless daytime drama (1956-
57).

There's nothing else there, so Suzanna hits up
Google, scrolls down a few pages until she finds
a link to a Los Angeles Herald Examiner article
entitled "YOUNG ACTOR FOUND DEAD ON CANYON
PROPERTY".

It's a very short item from May 4, 1957, and
her eyes zero in on a couple of lines:

              "Cause of death has yet to be
              determined."

and

                    "'He was a smart, up-and-
                    coming kid,' said his manager
                    Sy Goldman of Star Talent,
                    'My heart goes out to his
                    friends and family.'"

She goes back to the Google page and scrolls
some more, but sees nothing worth clicking on.

                         SUZANNA
                    Sorry, Tyler. Guess that's
                    all you get...

INT. HALLWAY, SUZANNA'S OFFICE - AFTERNOON

Suzanna races up to her office door. RACHEL, a
highly stressed client in her 60s, is leaning
against the wall and looking perturbed.

                         SUZANNA
                    I'm so, so sorry. I was in
                    the middle of something and
                    the time got away from me.

                         RACHEL
                    This is very unprofessional,
                    you know.

                         SUZANNA
                      (unlocking the office door)
                    I know it is. And I promise
                    to give you a full session.

                         RACHEL
                    You better!

She follows Suzanna inside.

EXT. EL MESA DRIVEWAY - DUSK

The property is quiet, the main house and trees
painted in an orange glow from the setting
sun. Suzanna gingerly unlocks the gate, swings
it open and starts up the driveway, toting a
Trader Joe's bag.

INT. GUEST HOUSE - MINUTES LATER

She enters, immediately puts some CLASSIC JAZZ
on her bluetooth speaker. Sets the bag on the
floor and slides out a baguette, a pre-mixed
salad, and a new bottle of Zinfandel. Puts
the bottle on the kitchen counter and sees
something.

Every one of her newly potted plants on the
windowsill have had the soil knocked out of
them. The seeds ejected and strewn across the
counter.

                    SUZANNA
          What in hell?

She wets a sponge and cleans up the mess the
best she can, sweeping the seeds into a trash
basket.

Then sees Yolanda's backpack, still under the
sink.

                                   CUT TO:

EXT. CAMULOS STREET, BOYLE HEIGHTS - NIGHT

Small lots, fences and bars everywhere. Spanish
GANG GRAFFITI scrawled on a number of alley
walls.

INT. SAAB

Suzanna re-checks the address on Yolanda's
backpack in her lap. Follows the numbers until
she sees 575, a vanilla-colored, two-story
apartment building. Backs the Saab into a tight
spot across the street.

EXT. APARTMENT BUILDING

Suzanna goes up a flight of stairs to the second
floor, carrying the backpack. Different kinds of
LATIN MUSIC from at least four apartments fill
the air. She follows the numbers to #37 and
KNOCKS on the door.

An exhausted-looking WOMAN in her 50s opens
the door. Behind her, three or four TEENAGERS
are eating at a table. It's obviously a very
crowded tenement.

                    SUZANNA
          Hi. I'm looking for Yolanda
          Perez?
            (the woman shakes her head)
          Do you speak English?

                    WOMAN
          Who are you?

                    SUZANNA
          I'm Suzanna. And Yolanda is
          maybe your daughter?
              (holds up the backpack)
          She left this in the Santa
          Monica guest house I'm
          renting—

                    WOMAN
          She doesn't want that.

Starts to shut the door on Suzanna. Suzanna
stops it with the toe of her tennis shoe.

                    SUZANNA
          Please. There might be a
          problem with the place, and
          if I could just—

                    WOMAN
          What problem?

                    SUZANNA
          I'm not exactly sure yet.
          That's why I need to talk to
          her. What's your name?...

The woman GRUMBLES a little. More agitated.

                    WOMAN
          Lupé.

                    SUZANNA
          Okay. It's good to meet
          you, Lupé. Anyway, it's a
          problem with the lease. And I
          desperately need to talk to
          other people who have lived
          there.

Lupé grips the side of the door. Something
seems to be bothering her. Finally she swings
it open.

                    LUPÉ
          Okay. But quick.

                    SUZANNA
          No problem. Gracias.
               (steps inside)

                    LUPÉ
          Be nice to Yolanda. Her head
          is no good now.

Suzanna mulls that over while she smiles and
EXCUSES herself past the crowded dinner table.
Lupé leads her down the narrow hall to a shut
door at the far end. KNOCKS lightly once and
opens it for Suzanna.

INT. YOLANDA'S ROOM - NIGHT

All the lights are off except for three candles
glowing on a night table. Suzanna inches
inside, closes the door behind her. Waits for
her eyes to adjust and sees YOLANDA sitting up
in bed, fully dressed and a wool blanket draped
over her head like a hood. She's around 20
years old, with a delicate face, sorrowful dark
eyes and black, matted hair sticking out of the
wool hood.

                    SUZANNA
          Hi Yolanda. I'm the woman who
          called you the other day.
          Suzanna?

Yolanda just stares at her with a blank

expression.

                    SUZANNA
          I brought your backpack...

Again she doesn't respond. Suzanna places it on
the floor at the foot of her bed.

                    SUZANNA
          Your garden seeds didn't take
          to my pots too well.

She tries a smile but it also has no effect on
Yolanda. Suzanna walks a little closer to the
bed, notices that three or four crucifixes have
been hung on the wall over her pillow.

                    SUZANNA
          Do you...mind if I sit for a
          minute?

Yolanda slowly shakes her head but brings her
knees up to her chest defensively. Suzanna sits
on the edge of the bed.

                    SUZANNA
          I've had a couple of strange,
          restless nights at the guest
          house on El Mesa you were
          renting, so I wanted to
          ask...if you heard or saw the
          same things I did.

Yolanda pauses, then shakes her head very
rapidly.

                    SUZANNA
          Well, you apparently moved
          out very fast. At least
          that's what Monty Burton told
          me—

                    YOLANDA
          I WAS ATTACKED!!

                    SUZANNA
          What? You were—

                    YOLANDA
          HE CAME FROM NOWHERE! WAS ALL
          OVER ME!

                    SUZANNA
          Okay, okay. Was his name
          Tyler?

                    YOLANDA
          HE WAS FROM HELL!!

Lupé opens the door behind them.

                    LUPÉ
          You must go now!

                    SUZANNA
          Just a minute, please. I have
          to know—

                    YOLANDA
          IT IS EVIL! NO ONE CAN SLEEP
          THERE!

She POUNDS the wall with a fist and two of the
crucifixes drop off and nearly hit her.

Lupé rushes in, grabs Suzanna's arm and yanks
her off the bed and out of the room.

                    LUPÉ
          I told you quick...

                    SUZANNA
          I know. I'm sorry! Yolanda
          should talk to someone about
          whatever happened.

                    LUPÉ
          No. Home is good for her.

She ushers Suzanna back through the kitchen and
past the staring family members to the front
door. At the last moment Suzanna whirls and
drops one of her business cards in Lupé's hand.

                    SUZANNA
          Just in case...there is
          something else to tell me. I
          can help her.

Lupé looks at the card and nudges Suzanna
outside.

INT. SAAB - NIGHT

Suzanna heads west on the 10 freeway. She's
rattled, using the slower right lane. Dials a
number on her car speaker phone.

                    DENISE
                    (V.O.)
          Well hello.

                    SUZANNA
          Hi Denise. I um...

                    DENISE
                    (V.O.)
          How's your new digs? Waiting
          for that first pool party
          invite.

                    SUZANNA
          Actually, it's not the best.
          I was wondering if I could
          take you up on that drink you
          offered.

                    DENISE
                    (V.O.)
          You mean now? Sorry, lady. I
          got younguns to put to bed
          and a show to watch on Prime.
          How about breakfast tomorrow
          at John O'Groats? I'll text
          you early.

                    SUZANNA
          Umm...Okay sure.

                    DENISE
                    (V.O.)
              You doing alright?

                    SUZANNA
              I'll manage. I mean, I'm
              fine. I'm fine...See you at
              breakfast.

She hangs up. Instantly looks anxious again.

EXT. GUEST HOUSE DRIVEWAY - NIGHT

It's pitch black and quiet, with absolutely no
wind. Suzanna slowly walks up the drive with
her phone light pointed in front of her.

INT. GUEST HOUSE - NIGHT

She enters, shuts the door and puts her back up
against it. The JAZZ MUSIC she left on is still
lightly playing.

She switches on every light she can, looks
around the small space, her senses sharper.

                    SUZANNA
              I can help you too...

She goes to the counter, opens the Zinfandel
and pours herself a very large glass.

INT. GUEST HOUSE BATHROOM - MINUTES LATER

She enters the room, turns the shower facuet to
get it going. Shuts the curtain and starts to
undress, then pauses. Opens the front of the
curtain and looks down at the water circling
the drain.

                    SUZANNA
              Maybe not this.

Turns off the shower and runs hot water in the
sink instead. Grabs a wash cloth and soap and

starts cleaning her face.

INT. GUEST HOUSE - A HALF HOUR LATER

She's washed up and changed into her nightgown.
Puts some EARTHY AMBIENT MUSIC on her bluetooth
speaker beside the bed and is about to climb
in. Gets a thought and walks back to the
counter.

Opens her silverware drawer and contemplates
her small collection of steak knives.

                    SUZANNA
          Really, Suzanna?...

Starts to close the drawer and hesitates.
Finally grabs one of the steak knives, takes
it to the bed and lays it on the night table.
Climbs under the futon sheets. Changes her
mind, takes the knife and tucks it under her
pillow instead. Lies back, deep breathes, and
tries to focus on the relaxing music.

                              DISSOLVE TO:

EXT. GUEST HOUSE - A FEW HOURS LATER

We can hear CRICKETS chirping through the
canyon. The far-off WHOOSH of a wave hitting
Santa Monica Beach.

Something SCRATCHES on the lower wall of the
empty pool. We want to look down into it but
maybe we don't.

Instead, we MOVE to a glass window on the guest
house, which slowly begins to crystallize.

INT. GUEST HOUSE

Suzanna is asleep and lightly SNORING. With
every breath, we see more condensation "steam"
coming out of her mouth.

She wakes up, absolutely shivering. Reaches for
a bottle of water on her night table and its cold
to the touch, the water inside FROZEN SOLID.

She sits up in bed. Wraps her blanket tighter.
The ambient music on her bluetooth speaker
suddenly fades out.

She looks over at the speaker. Rolls up on her
side to grab it and

                    TYLER'S VOICE
          Suzanna...

She GASPS, jumps away from the speaker and gets
up on her knees. It's the same chilling, half-
crying voice he's used each time. She catches
her breath.

                    SUZANNA
          Is that you...Tyler?

She can hear his SLOW BREATHING, slightly
amplified.

                    SUZANNA
          I'm sure that you're in pain
          of some kind...and I'm here
          if you want to talk about
          it...Or anything, actually.

                    TYLER'S VOICE
          Suzanna...

She leans back over, drops the bluetooth
speaker volume, and his VOICE EXPLODES from her
cell phone—

                    TYLER'S VOICE
          Suzanna!!

She jumps out of bed. Snatches the knife from
under her pillow and backpedals to the middle
of the room.

                    SUZANNA
          I mean that when I say it,
          Tyler!...I help troubled
          people for a living. Maybe
          you knew that.

Now, faintly, there are SOUNDS OF A STRUGGLE, a
WOMAN'S CRY, then a MUFFLED SCREAM. Suzanna's
thoughts sharpen.

                    SUZANNA
          What happened, Tyler? Back in
          1957...Did you do something?
          You can tell me.

The sounds fade away. It suddenly warms back
up, the water bottle's ice melting inside. And
the yellow light from the main house's turret
returns.

                    SUZANNA
          Oh wonderful...

Along with the light comes the ghostly CREAKING
sound she heard on her first night. It gets
louder and louder, seems to echo off the guest
house walls. She opens the door and ducks
outside.

EXT. GUEST HOUSE

The CREAKING is everywhere, drowning out the
birds and crickets.

Then it seems to get quieter, and concentrate
on the area past the pool.

Where the formerly locked shed door is now wide
open and still. The weird CREAKING coming from
inside.

                    SUZANNA
          Hello?

Keeping the steak knife gripped in her hand,
she inches toward the shed.

Reaches the open door. The black maw within.
The moon slowly emerges from behind a cloud
and illuminates what's inside.

Tyler, wearing his jeans and nothing else,
swings back and forth with the awful, CREAKING
rope tied around his neck.

Suzanna drops the knife in horror. Backs away.

                    TYLER'S VOICE
          Suzanna...

                      SUZANNA
          NO!!

She turns and runs past the pool, down the
driveway.

Gets to the gate. It won't open. She rattles
the thing.

                    TYLER'S VOICE
          Suzanna...

She whirls around. In the yellow turret light,
Tyler is gliding down the driveway towards her.

She struggles with the gate again. No luck.
Turns and Tyler is TWO FEET AWAY. No rope
around his neck and he's SOBBING.

                      TYLER
          Help me...

His ghostly body MERGES INTO HERS. Suzanna's
mouth sticks open and she slides to the ground
in front of the gate. Her body trembles.
Feeling every ounce of his horrific pain. Then
her eyes go up in her head and she passes out.

                              DISSOLVE TO:

EXT. GATE

The yellow light is gone. A woozy Suzanna opens
her eyes, raises herself up on her elbows. How
long was she out?

EXT. GUEST HOUSE - TWO HOURS LATER

A normal desk lamp glows through the guest
house window.

Through the glass, we can see Suzanna, now in a

bathrobe and fully awake with a cup of coffee,
sitting at her desk and pounding away on her
laptop.

EXT. DENISE'S BEDROOM - MORNING

A wired Suzanna paces back and forth in
Denise's massive master bedroom while Denise
folds the family laundry on the bed.

                    DENISE
          I think they call this
          "jumping horses midstream".

                    SUZANNA
          But it's a brand new horse. A
          much better horse!

                    DENISE
          What happened to The Newer
          You? I've got Viking on the
          hook, Amazon and Barnes
          & Noble on board for pre-
          orders—

                    SUZANNA
          This will blow that away.
          Just listen...

Denise waits for Suzanna to stop pacing, then
looks up from the laundry pile.

                    SUZANNA
          Why does a person commit
          suicide? There's all sorts
          of studies and books, right?
          But no one has ever asked the
          person who actually did it.

                    DENISE
          Probably because...they're
          dead?

                    SUZANNA
          Yes! But I have an
          opportunity here.

She resumes pacing.

> SUZANNA
> I know this sounds crazy, or
> ridiculous, but listen: I've
> made contact, as they say,
> with a young guy who took his
> life over sixty years ago,
> and I'd like to write a book
> about our sessions.

Denise looks up at her from a pile of kids'
overalls.

> DENISE
> I can't believe I'm hearing
> this.

> SUZANNA
> We can put The Newer You on
> hold for now. This guy is in
> pain, Denise. he needs me.
> And I need to find out what
> happened to him and write
> about it.

> DENISE
> O-kay. So...Why not make it
> a magazine piece for Psychic
> Phenomena Monthly?

> SUZANNA
> Denise, I'm serious about
> this.

> DENISE
> Oh, I can see that.

> SUZANNA
> And I was hoping you'd get
> behind it.

Denise reaches for Suzanna's pacing arm, but
misses.

                    DENISE
          Listen to _me_ now. I have a
          professional stake in your
          career, Suzanna. I just want
          to be sure this haunted guest
          house thing is the right
          move at the moment, and not
          you...I don't know, working
          something out from your past.

Suzanna stops with her back turned. Stares
into space. She heard Denise's words, but they
passed through her head like a ghostly cloud.

                    SUZANNA
          This is about Tyler. Not me.
          Thanks for listening, Denise.

She walks out of the room, and then the house
without saying another word.

INT. SAAB - MINUTES LATER

Suzanna gets back in her car on Denise's nice
Brentwood street and SLAMS the door shut.
Gathers herself again, but seems to do it
quicker this time. Takes out her cell phone and
dials a number.

                    ROBOTIC WOMAN
                      (V.O.)
          To listen to your voice
          message, press 2...To record
          a new message, press 3.

She presses 3, waits for the recording BEEP.

                    SUZANNA
          You've reached Dr. Suzanna
          Bristol. I will be taking a
          leave of absence for personal
          reasons for the next two
          weeks. If you are a client, I
          will be contacting you soon
          after that to resume regular
          sessions. Thank you.

INT. GUEST HOUSE - EVENING

Suzanna affixes her iPhone to a small tripod
atop her eating table, then turns it
horizontally and checks the viewfinder to make
sure it captures the entire main room.

Places a fresh legal pad and pen beside the
tripod...

                    SUZANNA
          Ready for you, Tyler...

Stands there and listens to the canyon quiet
through the half-open windows. Nothing but a
few CHIRPING birds.

She goes to her little stove and starts to boil
a large pot of water. Opens a box of pasta on
the counter. Looks around again, then gets
another thought and shuts off the flame.

INT. BATHROOM - A MINUTE LATER

She hesistates a moment, staring at her open
shower stall.

                    SUZANNA
          Oh screw it.

Starts the water, shuts the curtain and begins
to undress.

                                        CUT TO:

INT. SHOWER

Suzanna soaps and rinses herself. It feels
fantastic. Pauses to peek out the curtain at
the shut bathroom door. Listening.

Then grabs a shampoo bottle and begins washing
her hair faster than she ever has.

INT. GUEST HOUSE - TEN MINUTES LATER

Wearing fresh sweats and rubbing her hair dry
with a towel, she returns to the stove and
lights the pot of water.

INT. GUEST HOUSE - TWENTY MINUTES LATER

Sits at her little table, eating pasta with
marinara sauce, a small salad and a piece of
bread. She's put an empty chair across from
her, about six inches away from the table as if
to give her "guest" room to sit.

She fidgets with the tripod a little to confirm
it's pointed at the shadowy corner where Tyler
first appeared.

Takes a sip from a water glass and resumes
eating.

The bird noises outside have subsided, and a
few CRICKETS have taken their place.

Suzanna lays her fork down and stares at the
corner of the room. CLEARS HER THROAT.

                    SUZANNA
          Tyler?...Are you here?

A few CRINKLING oak leaves sound in the light
breeze outside, but otherwise the place is
silent.

INT. GUEST HOUSE - FIFTEEN MINUTES LATER

She washes her plates off in the sink. Glances
around the still-quiet room. Picks up her phone
tripod and water glass and takes them outside.

EXT. GUEST HOUSE

Sits on one of the lounge chairs, facing the
pool shed, which is now padlocked shut again,
as if it never opened. Sets up the phone tripod
beside the chair. Gazes around the pool area.

                    SUZANNA
          Tyler? I'm here to listen to
          you...

No response. The ocean breeze gets a bit
stronger and the temperature suddenly drops.
She rubs her arms.

                    SUZANNA
          Damn it.

Gets up and ducks back into the guest house.

INT. GUEST HOUSE

Goes to her futon and grabs a sweater off the
floor beside it. Pulls it on over her head and
turns back to the open door.

The door is closed. Its glass crystallizing
before her eyes. She shivers, spins—

And Tyler stands in the middle of the room.
Wearing jeans and the white denim shirt he
had on at the Sorry Man Tavern. Seems to be
barefoot but it's hard to tell because his feet
are transparent and appear to be hovering off
the floor.

Suzanna stares at him, in both elation and
terror.

                    SUZANNA
          Okay...Please don't move.

She throws the door open, grabs her phone
tripod. Ducks back in and hastily sets it on
the table. Starts to RECORD without even making
sure it's working.

Tyler is still in the center of the room. His
head cocked a little, gazing at her with a
deeply sad expression.

Suzanna delicately takes her seat, nudges the
chair across from her out a little more with an
outstretched toe.

                    SUZANNA
          Can you sit?

He doesn't move. Atop the main house, the
yellow turret light begins to glow again. Tyler
doesn't seem to notice it. Suzanna motions to
the main house.

                    SUZANNA
          Do you know why that
          happens?...Is someone you know
          up there?

                    TYLER
             (weak, barely audible)
          Once was.

She reaches for her legal pad and pen. Quickly
jots a note.

                    SUZANNA
          Okay. Can you tell me who?

                    TYLER
          Night after night...

He shakes his head ever so slightly.

                    SUZANNA
          Night after night what?...What
          happened night after night?

He begins to fade in and out. His voice becomes
garbled.

                    TYLER
          They h-ted me...

                    SUZANNA
          They hated you? Who did?

He raises his transparent hands, SOBS into them.
Then DISAPPEARS.

The yellow light fades. The room warms back up.
Suzanna GROANS frustratingly. Drops her pen on
the open pad.

INT. GUEST HOUSE - DEAD OF NIGHT

She tosses and turns on the futon. Sits up and
checks the time on her phone. 2:47. Glances
around. Tyler's shadowy corner is still empty.

She SIGHS. Then reaches into a drawer on her
night table. Takes out half of a pre-rolled
joint and lights it up.

INT. GUEST HOUSE - MORNING

Suzanna trudges over to the counter, groggy
beyond words, to get some coffee going.

Out of the corner of her eye, notices that her
legal pad is turned around, facing the opposite
direction. She leans over and picks it up.

Five words have been scrawled on the open pad
with her pen:

                TELL ME WHY THEY DID

EXT. WILSHIRE BLVD., SANTA MONICA - DAY

Suzanna exits a dry cleaners toting three or
four shirts. Answers her RINGING cell as she
walks to her car.

                    RECEPTIONIST
                      (V.O.)
            Dr. Bristol? It's Marlene
            again from Star Talent/
            Cullen/McGee?

                    SUZANNA
            Yes!

                    RECEPTIONIST
                      (V.O.)
            I was able to speak to Howard
            Bloom, our oldest partner,
            and he actually worked with
            Sy Goldberg back in the day.

                    SUZANNA
            Yes?

                    RECEPTIONIST
                      (V.O.)
            Mr. Goldberg is in his 90s
            now and living in a group
            home in Los Feliz. I can get
            you the facility's name and
            address if you hold on...

                    SUZANNA
          Great. Thank you.

EXT. SUNSET RETIREMENT OASIS - DAY

Tall palms and lush grounds at the base of the
Hollywood Hills. Suzanna drives past a GUARD at
the gate and into the lot.

INT. RECREATION ROOM - DAY

An ORDERLY walks Suzanna to a card table in the
back corner, where SY GOLDBERG sits alone in
his pajamas and bathrobe, working on a jigsaw
puzzle. 95 years old with a small oxygen tank
on his wheelchair and tubes running into his
nose, he has thick glasses, hearing aids in
both ears and is somewhat emaciated.

                    ORDERLY
          Sy? This nice woman is here
          to visit you.

He stares at the puzzle piece in his hand that
goes somewhere in a barely-begun landscape.
Suzanna slides over a chair and sits beside
him.

                    SUZANNA
          Hello Sy. I'm Dr. Bristol,
          and I wanted to—

                    SY
          No more pills. Just tell me
          where this goes...

                    SUZANNA
          Actually, I'm here because I
          understand you used to work
          at Star Talent? The agency?

                    SY
               (ignoring her)
          Maybe it's in this part...

                    SUZANNA
          And you represented a young
          actor named Tyler Worth?

Sy's hand freezes. His eyes squint. He slowly
looks up at the far wall, mining a memory. A
little smile touches his dry lips.

                    SY
          "Fast Track" Tyler...He hated
          my cigars.

                    SUZANNA
          Right. And I also just
          learned he took his own life
          when he was only 24. Do you
          remember why?

                    SY
          Too many problems, that
          boy...Mother died in
          childbirth...Father a well-
          off schmuck who thought acting
          was a waste of time, would
          barely talk to him. Then
          all the trouble with that
          girlfriend.

                    SUZANNA
          A girlfriend?

                    SY
          Knocked her up right when I
          got him two call-backs...
                    (spins the puzzle
                    piece in his hand)
          Had a big fuckin' breakdown
          over it, too...Poor "Fast
          Track"...Loved his plums but
          hated my cigars...Maybe this
          section...

                    SUZANNA
          So Tyler had a lot of fans...
          And they didn't hate him?

                    SY
          You kidding? They all
          would've married him. Even
          a few guys. Half a dozen
          hotties would sneak into
          every one of his pool parties
          at that place.

                 SUZANNA
          Interesting...Can you tell me
          more about this girlfriend he
          got pregnant?

                    SY
              (shakes his head)
          Never said her name. Don't
          know what happened to her...
          Pressure sure ate him up
          though...I was on the 15th
          hole with Mel Baum when I
          heard he packed it in. Can
          you help me with this piece?

Suzanna glances at the puzzle box nearby. A
gorgeous autumn shot of Lake Tahoe. She winces.

                 SUZANNA
          Uhh, I'm really not good with
          these...
              (standing)
          Thanks so much for talking to
          me, Sy.

She walks past the orderly to the hallway, her
mind spinning.

EXT. GUEST HOUSE - NIGHT

The turret window on the main house glows
again, painting the pool, oak tree and guest
house in yellow.

INT. GUEST HOUSE

CLOSE ON

Suzanna's cell phone. It says RINGER OFF, and

also: YOU HAVE 18 NEW MESSAGES.

Suzanna sits at her table beside it, her
notepad and pen out again. In the middle of the
room, Tyler hovers a few inches off the floor.

The air is chilly, and Suzanna has a small
blanket draped around her.

                    SUZANNA
          Again. Why did you take your
          life?

Tyler says nothing.

                    SUZANNA
          Please, Tyler...You'll feel a
          lot better and may be able to
          move on if you talk to me.

Still no response.

                    SUZANNA
          I spoke with the man who
          managed you. Sy Goldberg...
          He says you had <u>many</u> fans and
          they did not hate you at all.

Tyler's face pinches a little. As if confused.

                    SUZANNA
          He told me about the girl you
          got pregnant...Can you tell
          me her name?

He fades out a little, but then comes back, a
few inches closer to the table. Suzanna sits
up, spins around the notepad and pen.

                    SUZANNA
          If you want, you can write
          her name...

He lowers his ghostly gaze to the notepad. He
glides a few inches closer—

And a MASSIVE AFTERSHOCK VIOLENTLY SHAKES the
guest house! The foundation CRACKS, dishes

SMASH on the floor, pictures fall off the walls.
Suzanna dives under the table, clings to one of
its legs but the entire table falls over. She
SCREAMS, covers her head.

The shaking lasts a good twenty seconds, then
dissipates. When Suzanna wobbily stands back
up, the yellow light is off, the air has warmed
up, DOGS BARK everywhere in the canyon, and
Tyler has vanished.

A MINI-SHOCK hits seconds later. Delirious,
Suzanna stumbles out the door. Crawls across
the deck in the darkness, the lounge chairs
RATTLING, both houses CRACKING. Rolls up in a
fetal ball and loses consciousness...

EXT. POOL - DAY

She opens her eyes and sees a blinding,
cloudless sky. Hears WILD SPLASHING around her,
KIDS LAUGHING and SHRIEKING.

Realizes she's on her back, on the pool's
diving board which has been put back together
with masking tape. The SPLASHING sound
continues, but she's not getting wet. She sits
up on her elbows, nervously peers down.

The pool water is dark green and churning. A
pair of pale, clammy BOY'S HANDS reach up at
her. Suzanna opens her mouth to scream but
nothing comes out—

                                        CUT TO:

INT. SAAB - MORNING

She wakes in the front seat when a POLICE
OFFICER KNOCKS on her window. She still has the
blanket around her. Can't find her keys so opens
the door instead.

                    OFFICER
          You okay, ma'm?

                    SUZANNA
          Yeah! I um...the
          aftershock...Couldn't get
          back to sleep, you know?

                    OFFICER
          I hear you. But there's an
          ordinance about sleeping in
          your car on these streets.
          You'll need to go back in
          your house or put the car in
          the driveway.

                    SUZANNA
          Fine. No problem. I just need
          a couple minutes...Thanks.

The officer nods and goes back to his cruiser.
Suzanna sees him still watching her and grabs
her keys off the floor, starts the ENGINE. The
cruiser drives off.

She has a NEWS RADIO STATION on.

                    REPORTER
                    (V.O.)
          ...with most reports giving
          that large aftershock a 5.8,
          centered in Van Nuys...

                    SUZANNA
          Shit.

She pulls on her seat belt and turns the car
around.

INT. SUZANNA'S VAN NUYS OFFICE - MORNING

She cautiously enters. Books and papers are on
the floor, and a tall indoor fern has fallen
over. But no serious damage.

She props the plant back up, then the fallen
chair behind her desk and drops into it.

Stares at a blinking red message light on her
phone. SIGHS and plays the first message over

the speaker.

                         WAYNE
                        (V.O.)
            Hi Doctor, it's Wayne, for
            like the fourth time. I know
            you said you're taking a
            leave and all, but I just--
            It's really the worst time
            you could do this. At least
            for me. Floppy's been sick,
            and she won't eat one piece
            of lettuce I put in her cage.
            Anyway I just really need
            to have a session with you.
            Maybe on the phone?
                    (DEEP BREATHES)
            Sorry to bother you—

CLICK. She sits there. Looks around at her
shaken office. Emotions spinning and her brain
in a fog.

EXT. GUEST HOUSE - AFTERNOON

Still wearing her clothes from the previous
night, Suzanna stands at the foot of the
outside deck.

The entire guest house has been unmoored from
its foundation, and tilts down to the left at a
five-degree angle.

                         SUZANNA
            Christ...

She goes up on the deck, walks to the right
side of the house to inspect the damage.

There's a six-inch gap now between the
foundation and the dirt below the house.

She frowns, is about to head for the door when
something catches her eye.

A dull piece of cloth protruding from the dirt.

She goes back to the gap and crouches.
Carefully pries a small object out of the
loosened soil.

It's a CHILD'S DOLL, many years old, with small
buttons for eyes and red thread for a mouth,
a lot of withered black thread for hair, and
wearing a cloth dress that was once white and
is now a decrepit yellow.

INT. GUEST HOUSE - NIGHT

Suzanna has propped the table and chair back
up, and has secured her pen and wine glass to
make sure they don't slide off in the slightly
tilted house.

Tyler has returned, hovers again in the middle
of the room.

> SUZANNA
> What happened to your child,
> Tyler?...

He doesn't respond. Suzanna reaches into the
pocket of her dress, takes out the old child's
doll and places it on the table.

> SUZANNA
> Did this belong to your
> daughter? The woman you got
> pregnant gave birth to a
> girl, right?

Tyler stares at the doll. His transparent form
shakes a little.

> SUZANNA
> What happened to her, Tyler?

> TYLER
> (softly)
> Not mine...

> SUZANNA
> Not yours? Okay. Who did this
> doll belong to?

Now his head is shaking.

                         TYLER
                       (booming)
              NOT MINE!—

And with that, he vanishes again. Suzanna
POUNDS the table in frustration and the wine
glass nearly slides off. She grabs it in time,
splashing some on her hand. Reaches for the
bottle and re-fills the glass.

INT. GUEST HOUSE - DEAD OF NIGHT

Suzanna SNORES on her back, having drunk
herself to sleep. Wears a sleeping mask and
earbuds.

The yellow turret light re-fills the room. The
bedcovers on Suzanna's legs ever so slowly
slide down.

She stirs, grabs the covers and pulls them back up.

They slide down again. She yanks off her
sleeping mask.

Tyler hovers horizontally above her. Naked
again.

                         TYLER
              Help me, Suzanna...

She tries to get up but a powerful, unearthly
force pins her to the futon.

                       SUZANNA
              You have to get off, Tyler.
                 (pushes at his "chest" but
                 her hands go through him)
              Can't talk to you like this—

                         TYLER
              Embrace me...

                       SUZANNA
              I can't—

                              TYLER
                    Embrace your ghost...

She tries to scream but his body MERGES INTO
HERS on the bed. His sorrow paralyzes, then
overwhelms her. Suzanna's stiff body slowly
relaxes and Tyler's WRACKING SOBS come out of
her mouth, followed by his voice.

                              TYLER
                    Only you can help me,
                    Suzanna...

                             SUZANNA
                    I know that...I know.

                                        FADE TO BLACK

INT. WEST SIDE MARKET - ONE WEEK LATER

Suzanna strolls down an aisle with a half-
filled shopping cart. She looks thinner and more
tanned than when we last saw her, and has a
relaxed but vacant expression on her face. She
picks out two canned soups and two packets of
stovetop ramen and puts them in the cart.

Looks up as Denise rounds the corner with a
hand basket and nearly collides with her.

                             DENISE
                    Whoa! Is this weird or is
                    this strange?

She notes the change in Suzanna's appearance.

                             SUZANNA
                        (with a dreamy smile)
                    How are you, Denise?

                             DENISE
                    Uhh, fine. And you?

Suzanna looks away with the same smile. Chooses
another item for her cart.

                    DENISE
          Haven't heard from you in
          weeks, so I assumed we were
          taking a break from each
          other. Or at least you were—

                    SUZANNA
          Look what I have, Denise.

She reaches into her purse and takes out the
old doll she found.

                    SUZANNA
          Isn't she sweet?

                    DENISE
          Definitely.
                    (hides a laugh)
          Been hitting up yard sales?

Suzanna admires the doll a few more seconds,
then puts it back in her purse.

                    SUZANNA
          He says it wasn't his
          daughter's, but I'm not
          convinced.

Denise gently touches Suzanna's arm.

                    DENISE
          How's that new book project
          of yours going? I mean...if
          you have an outline worked up
          or some sample chapters I'd
          be happy to look at them.

Suzanna cocks her head with an odd squint. As
if unsure what Denise is even talking about.

                    DENISE
          Right...I was afraid so.
          Do me a favor and call me
          when you come out of this,
          Suzanna. I'll be there for
          you.

She gives Suzanna a friendly peck on the cheek,

starts to walk past her.

                    DENISE
          Oh, and that doll of yours?
          It may be worth something.
          I've seen people selling
          those on eBay and that one
          looks over a hundred years
          old. Take care.

She leaves. Suzanna thinks for a beat, glances
down at the doll inside her purse, then keeps
walking.

EXT. GUEST HOUSE DECK - DAY

The plum tree is so withered now it looks in
danger of falling over.

Suzanna lays back on one of the lounge chairs,
gazing up at the massive oak tree, partially
shading her from the sunny sky. She's dressed
down into a T-shirt and dungaree shorts.

                    SUZANNA
          I can't imagine what it must
          be like to be an actor, with
          all that rejection...

Tyler climbs out of her, hovers on the deck for
a moment, then "settles" onto the other lounge
chair.

                    TYLER
          Weren't you?...

                    SUZANNA
          Weren't I what?

                    TYLER
          Rejected...

His question catches her off guard. She flashes a
little smile.

                    SUZANNA
          Wasn't everyone? In high school
          especially, there's so much
          bullying...

Tyler lets out a drawn-out, mournful SIGH.

                    TYLER
          No mother...And no one cared...

                    SUZANNA
          I care now, Tyler...
                    (gets up on her elbow
                    and faces him)
          Whatever happened to you must
          have been very painful. I hear
          it in your voice...I can feel
          it. But again, I need more
          details...Please don't be
          afraid to share anything with
          me, okay?

                    TYLER
          Share with me too...

                    SUZANNA
          Well, I'm helping you,
          remember?
                    (turns and glances up
                    at the dark turret)
          Who was up in that window?

Tyler's legs fade in and out as he gazes at the
main house.

                    SUZANNA
          Who was watching you, Tyler?

He slowly shakes his head and DISAPPEARS. Suzanna
GROANS, swings her legs off the chair to get up—

And Tyler is crouched on the OTHER side of the
chair. Startling her.

                    TYLER
          Tell me about Suzanna...

Words catch in her throat. She folds her arms

defensively.

                    SUZANNA
          Um, I don't like where this
          is going.

This time he COMPLETELY VANISHES. She stands up
and paces a little, as if trying to shake off
the conversation.

                    SUZANNA
          Fine...Actually, I could use
          a walk—

EXT. CANYON ROAD - LATE AFTERNOON

Suzanna has donned socks and tennis shoes and
grabbed a bottle of water. Heads down one of
the neigborhood's prettier streets, away from
the house.

Feels her phone VIBRATE and takes it out of her
shorts pocket.

It reads VOICEMAIL MESSAGE FROM DEB

She frowns, puzzled. Plays it back.

                    DEB (V.O.)
          Hi Suzanna, got your message.
          Um, not exactly sure why you
          needed to ask me that, but
          as far as I remember the
          name you're thinking of is
          Whispering. Hope you're doing
          okay out there.

Suzanna stares into space a long second, as
if trying to recall even leaving her sister a
message. Stuffs the phone back in her pocket.

EXT. DEEPER INTO CANYON

It's still a hot day, and even though the road
is under a canopy of trees, she has to stop to
drink from her water bottle.

                         TYLER
                    (V.O., faint)
          Suzanna...

She whirls around. The road behind her is empty.

Screws the cap back on the bottle and tries to
shrug off what she might have heard.

Twenty yards ahead, at the next corner, Tyler's
ghostly shape hovers slightly above the
sidewalk. Suzanna's heart stops. It could be a
mirage from the heat, but she can clearly make
out his bare feet.

                         TYLER
          Suzanna...

He glides around the corner and vanishes.
Suzanna takes a deep breath, then picks up her
pace and follows him.

The road he took winds down into deeper shade,
but aside from a few gardeners' trucks and trash
barrels, there is nobody on it.

Suzanna takes it anyway. Walks a bit faster.

The next corner eventually comes into view. And
there's Tyler again, this time hovering beside
the sidewalk with half of his body visible
through a mailbox. The street is SAN ANSELMO RD.

                        SUZANNA
          Where are you taking me?

He turns and moves out of sight down San
Anselmo. Suzanna takes another belt from her
water bottle and follows him.

San Anselmo is a little wider, but still purely
residential and more in the sun. Suzanna gets
about halfway down the block but doesn't see
Tyler anywhere. She stops, polishes off her water
and looks around.

Across the road, Tyler hovers over some grass

near a white adobe wall and metal gate. By
the time she waits for a pickup to go by and
crosses to the other side, he's gone.

Gorgeous red bougainvillea and purple wistertia
drape themselves over the wall. Suzanna
approaches the gate, which has a chain around
it and a sign:

                    BURTON/RODRIGUEZ
                    FAMILY CEMETERY

                     NO TRESPASSING

Suzanna's mouth drops open. Large expensive
homes flank both sides of the thing, with a
handful of others across the street.

She backs away, peers over the wall. A patch of
neglected grass and embedded stones lead to a
second, higher wall under some spreading oaks.
She can make out a large wooden cross in the
cemetery, but nothing else.

She goes right, looking for another entrance or
way inside, but the place seems impenetrable.

Then she spots a private security vehicle
across the street, a few houses away. A MAN
sits behind the wheel and appears to be dozing.

She walks determinedly over to his car, and up
to its open window.

                     SUZANNA
          Excuse me!

The man snaps awake. A cell phone and half-
eaten breakfast burrito are in his lap. He
quickly puts the burrito aside, wipes some
crumbs off his trousers.

                     MAN
          Hello. Yes.

                     SUZANNA
          Do you know anything about
          that little cemetery across
          the street?

                    MAN
          It is private.

                  SUZANNA
          I figured that. I'm just
          curious about its history,
          and um, who might have the
          keys for the gate.

                    MAN
          I don't know. I am just here
          to watch—
          (checks clipboard on the seat)
          McManus and Clevenger houses.

                  SUZANNA
          Okay. Sorry to bother you.

He nods, looks back at his phone. Suzanna keeps
walking down the road, away from the cemetery.
Comes to a patch of shade and glances back.

The man is still looking at his phone, paying
zero attention to her.

She goes another few yards, then quickly re-
crosses the road and doubles back toward the
cemetery, keeping in the shade and behind
parked vehicles as much as possible.

Reaches the right side of the low first wall and
vaults herself over it. Hurries around the back
of the higher wall.

It borders a little cliff, with a drop leading
to a lower canyon road.

There's a small locked maintenance gate on the
far side. Suzanna looks around to make sure
no residents are at windows, then wedges her
tennis shoe into a grating in the center of the
door and climbs over the top.

INT. CEMETERY

Drops onto the cemetery grass. It's a very
small space, overgrown with weeds, remains of

dead flowers scattered around. The large wooden
cross she saw from the road is termite-infested
and slightly leaning out of the ground, but
still lords over the cemetery. Smaller wooden
crosses and a dozen or so headstones poke from
the high grass.

Suzanna takes out her phone and begins snapping
photos of every headstone she sees:

          WOODROW BURTON...LELAND BURTON...ENRICO
             RODRIGUEZ...MARIA RODRIGUEZ...
               JOSE & LUNA RODRIGUEZ...

A handful of newer crosses don't even have
names on them, only dates.

Suzanna hears a DOOR OPEN and CLOSE from a
nearby house. She quickly finishes her photo-
taking.

INT. SANTA MONICA COFFEE SHOP - EVENING

Suzanna is back at her familiar table and glued
to her laptop screen. On a Web site titled
SANTA MONICA ORIGINS, she's reading a long
paragraph called A FAMILY FRIENDSHIP.

                    SUZANNA
                (reading softly)
            "The development of Santa
            Monica Canyon increased
            after Woodrow Burton formed
            a friendship with Enrico
            Rodriguez, a young Mexican
            farmer who showed Burton how
            to clear difficult land and
            wrap new houses with native
            vegetation."

We see a faded, turn-of-the century photograph
of overweight, mustachioed WOODROW posing
beside suspendered, humble ENRICO on a wooded
hill.

                    SUZANNA
                  (reading)
          "To show his gratitude
          following Enrico's premature
          death, Woodrow Burton used
          a small plot of his canyon
          land to construct a private
          cemetery to forever honor the
          bond of the two families,
          which still stands today."

                                        CUT TO:

INT. SAAB - FIFTEEN MINUTES LATER

Suzanna drives away from the coffee shop,
looking more wired than we've seen her in
a while. She's on a bluetooth call off her
dashboard.

                    BURTON REALTY SECRETARY
                         (V.O.)
          ...away from our desk right
          now. Please leave us a
          message.

BEEP.

                    SUZANNA
          Yeah, it's Suzanna Bristol.
          Again. I desperately need to
          talk to Monty Burton, and
          if he doesn't get back to
          me in 24 hours, I will be
          filing my lawsuit claiming
          psychological damages. Thank
          you.

She jabs the hang-up button.

Rounds the next corner and her phone RINGS. She
doesn't recognize the number, with a 323 area
code. Answers.

                    SUZANNA
          Hello?

                         LUPÉ
                    (V.O., nervous)
               Is this...Suzanna?

                         SUZANNA
               Yes?

                         LUPÉ
                      (V.O.)
               This is Lupé...Yolanda's
               mother?

                         SUZANNA
               Oh right! How is she doing?

          We can hear Lupé softly CRYING.

                         SUZANNA
               Hello?

                         LUPÉ
                      (V.O.)
               I told her to call you. But
               she wouldn't!

                         SUZANNA
               What happened, Lupé?

          The crying is now SOBBING. Suzanna pulls over
          to the curb, raises the call volume.

                         SUZANNA
               Talk to me...What did she do?

                         LUPÉ
                      (V.O.)
               I told her to stay home—

                         SUZANNA
               Lupé. Please tell me what
               happ—

                         LUPÉ
                      (V.O.)
               She walked in front of a
               car!!

The SOBBING increases. Suzanna shuts her eyes
a long moment. Waits for Lupé to calm down a
little.

                    SUZANNA
          I am so, so sorry...

                    LUPÉ
                    (V.O.)
          I <u>knew</u> she should not have
          rented there. And sorry
          Carmenita ever mentioned it.

                    SUZANNA
          Carmenita? Who's that?

                    LUPÉ
                    (V.O.)
          My mother's old friend.
          Carmenita Salgado...She was
          nanny to a boy there long
          time ago.

                    SUZANNA
          A boy?

                    LUPÉ
                    (V.O.)
          And I knew you should not
          talk to Yolanda! You bring
          her backpack and the awful
          thing comes back to her.

                    SUZANNA
          What awful thing?...
               (Lupé CRIES softly)
          Lupé? What exactly happened
          to Yolanda?

                    LUPÉ
                    (V.O.)
          He attacked her! Raped her!
          Didn't you know that?? I am
          going—

                    SUZANNA
          Lupé!

Too late. She's hung up. Suzanna idles at the
curb, centering herself with DEEP BREATHS. but
an inner rage is taking over. She SCREECHES
away from the curb.

INT. GUEST HOUSE - NIGHT

It's ice cold again, but this time Suzanna
doesn't bother with a blanket. Paces back and
forth on the slanted floor and addresses the
empty room while she talks.

                    SUZANNA
          You haven't been honest with
          me, Tyler...And you need to
          be honest. What did you do to
          Yolanda?

A shadow across the room undulates. As if
trying to form a more solid shape.

                    SUZANNA
          Trust me. You will not be
          able to rest until you admit
          what happened....until you
          admit what you did...Both
          in 1957 and in the last few
          months.

The shadow thickens. We hear Tyler's MOURNFUL
SIGH.

                    SUZANNA
          Tell me what you did to
          Yolanda, damn it!

Tyler appears RIGHT BEHIND HER and she jumps
out of the way. He's transparent, but we can
clearly see tears sliding down his cheeks.

                    TYLER
          They made me do it...

                    SUZANNA
          What? Attack Yolanda? Who
          made you do that?

                    TYLER
          Hang myself...

Suzanna frowns, puzzled.

                    SUZANNA
          O-kay...But you had many
          fans, Tyler. They flocked to
          your pool parties. I don't
          believe it when you say they
          hated you.

Tyler slowly looks up at her with his chilling,
wet eyes.

                    TYLER
          No...They haunted me. Why
          did they haunt me??

He buries his face in his transparent hands
again. Suzanna takes a step toward him and he
VANISHES. The room warms up.

Suzanna gets a sudden thought. Takes out her
phone and thumbs through the recent recordings
she attempted. Plays the very first one.

The visuals are blank, but we can hear Tyler's
half-garbled VOICE.

                    TYLER
                    (V.O.)
          They h-ted me...

She rewinds it a bit. Plays it again and gooses
the volume.

                    TYLER
                    (V.O., clearer)
          They haunt-ed me...

Suzanna lowers herself into a chair at the
table. Dwells on this. And something else.

                    SUZANNA
          Carmenita...Salgado.

She grabs her purse, then her wallet. Plucks
out the business card for SALGADO MOVERS. The
address is in El Segundo.

EXT. MAIN STREET, EL SEGUNDO - NIGHT

Clammy fog pours off the bay, rolls through
the quiet, hilly town just south of the L.A.
airport.

INT. SAAB

Suzanna has an address punched into her GPS.
Turns down a narrow street with smaller homes
and even smaller yards.

Sees the pickup truck for SALGADO MOVERS backed
into a driveway at the end of the block. Behind
it is a cluttered, dimly lit open garage.

Suzanna climbs out, goes up the driveway and
steps into the garage. Sitting on a stool
trying to patch a truck tire is MANNY SALGADO.
Late 50s, with long, ratty hair, a greying
moustache, and nervous eyes. He wears dirty
jeans, an old Santana concert T-shirt and has
religious tattoos on both bare arms.

He squints warily at Suzanna. Recognizing her.

                    MANNY
          Problem with the mattress? We
          take it to storage.

                    SUZANNA
          That's not why I'm here,
          Manny. We need to talk about
          something else.

                    MANNY
          No. There is nothing else.

He looks away. She steps closer, then crouches
in front of him.

                    SUZANNA
          A boy named Tyler. He became
          an actor and then committed
          suicide. Carmenita Salgado
          was a nanny to him many
          years ago. Was she your
          grandmother? Your aunt?

Manny abruptly stands, walks to a workbench and
grabs a bottle of cheap whiskey. She follows
him.

                    SUZANNA
          What did Carmenita tell you
          about the guest house on El
          Mesa Road? It had to be bad.
          You couldn't even deliver a
          bed there.

                    MANNY
                (mumbles)
          We don't go near that house.

                    SUZANNA
          No shit. Why?

He swigs from the whiskey bottle, then SLAMS it
down on the workbench. Startling her.

                    MANNY
          You are right, smart lady.
          It is bad. Bad to even talk
          about!

                    SUZANNA
          I was in the little cemetery.
          Where generations of the
          Burton and Rodriguez families
          are buried. But many of the
          names are missing from the
          graves. And I think maybe
          Tyler was also—

                    MANNY
          Missing because some are not
          there!

He takes the bottle, goes back to the stool and

sinks onto it.

                    MANNY
          Some of us heard the story.
          For a long time...Enrico
          Rodriguez was a good family
          man. A religious man. And he
          trusted this Burton who he
          helped too much.

                    SUZANNA
          You mean...Woodrow Burton?

                    MANNY
          Si. A lying son-of-a-bastard,
          people said.

Behind them on the driveway, the fog has gotten
so thick it's hard to see the street they're
on.

                    MANNY
          Enrico and his wife...and his
          son...and his daughter lived
          in a shack next to his house.
          Burton used to visit Enrico's
          wife Maria when Enrico was
          farming. And one night...one
          night they all disappeared,
          and nobody found them.

                    SUZANNA
          You mean never?

                    MANNY
          Si, never. That is why Burton
          built graveyard for the
          families. To honor them. But
          it was _mierda_. Many did not
          believe his sadness. They
          believe he did something
          terrible to Enrico and his
          family there.

                    SUZANNA
                 (thinking)
          The boy in the pool...

                    MANNY
          What?

                   SUZANNA
          Nothing. I thought I saw
          someone in that pool...
          But what about Tyler, who
          Carmenita took care of?

                    MANNY
          Not for long I think. She
          heard same stories about
          Woodrow Burton.
                    (leans closer)
          He planted _evil_ there, smart
          lady. I wish I did not see
          that gate.
                    (touches her arm)
          And I pray for you to move
          away.

The fog has seeped into the garage and become
bone-chilling. Suzanna doesn't answer him, just
backpedals out of the garage.

INT. GUEST HOUSE - NIGHT

The floor is even more tilted now. Suzanna
enters, has to grab hold of the table to get
across the room.

                   SUZANNA
          Okay Tyler. No more games...I
          need to know who was haunting
          you.

No answer. She looks around, zeroes in on the
old photo of the main house, hanging askew on
the far wall.

She walks over, comically tries to straighten
it in the tilted room. Looks at it a bit
closer.

The photo of the house's backyard is dated
1925. The pool is under construction, and in
the rear corner, we see a small shack. but

there is no guest house to be seen.

                    SUZANNA
          Huh...Monty said they both
          went up in '25...
            (backs away from the photo)
          Bullshit. The guest house was
          built <u>later</u>.

She turns, spots the old child's doll sitting
on the counter. Right below the empty pots she
attempted to plant seeds in.

She suddenly looks stricken. Goes to the
cupboard below the sink. Finds a garden trowel
and rushes outside.

EXT. GUEST HOUSE - NIGHT

At the back corner of the house, the gap
between the raised foundation and ground is
wider than it's ever been. Suzanna kneels,
turns on her phone flashlight and props it
against a rock so that it points at the gap.

Grabs the trowel and frantically begins digging
into the soil.

She's at it for many minutes...

Until the trowel makes a weird CLICK sound.
She pauses, then carefully digs down a little
more. Wedged between the dirt and a few roots
is a HUMAN BONE. She widens the digging area,
and hits a second bone, then a third. Pulls out
more dirt with her fingers.

Uncovers two small HUMAN SKULLS. Both of them
appear to be crushed in.

                    SUZANNA
          Good God...

She rises and backs away from the hole. Grabs
the cell phone and dials 9-1-1 with her dirt-
caked fingers.

                    SUZANNA
          Yes! I'd like to report a
          murder. Murders, I mean...No.
          Maybe a hundred years ago.

EXT. GUEST HOUSE - HOURS LATER

POLICE and a FORENSICS TEAM are on the scene.
Suzanna is sitting on the curb outside the
property gate, a police-issued blanket around
her shoulders even though it isn't cold. A few
yards down the cul-de-sac, we can see a curious
NEIGHBOR or two watching in the flashing red
lights.

An OFFICER approaches Suzanna.

                    OFFICER
          We're still trying to locate
          Monty Burton, but having no
          luck yet...Did he tell you
          how long he'd be in Tahiti?

                    SUZANNA
          I don't remember...If he did,
          it probably was a lie.

                    OFFICER
          Well, forensics says there
          appears to be four victims.
          At least three of them killed
          by a blunt object. You said
          you had some idea who they
          might have been?

Suzanna just stares into space.

                    OFFICE
          Dr. Bristol?

                    SUZANNA
          Yes. Umm...Enrico Rodriguez
          and his wife and two
          children.

                    OFFICER
               (jotting on a pad)
          And you know this how?

                    SUZANNA
          He showed me the cemetery
          with the fake graves.

                    OFFICE
          What fake graves?...And who
          showed you?

                    LOCAL REPORTER
               (V.O., shouting)
          Dr. Bristol! What can you
          tell us?

The officer steps toward the first of THREE
REPORTERS who have just arrived.

                    OFFICER
          Back up, please. She's not
          answering questions right
          now.
               (to Suzanna)
          You have another place to
          stay tonight?

                    SUZANNA
          I think so...

                                        CUT TO:

INT. DENISE'S GUEST ROOM - MIDDLE OF NIGHT

A still-rattled Suzanna sits on the bed beside
some spare blankets. Denise quickly enters with
a cup of hot tea and closes the door behind
her.

                    SUZANNA
          Whiskey might be better
          actually.

                    DENISE
          Celestial Seasonings doesn't
          make that flavor, hon. You
          need to calm down.

                    SUZANNA
          Please don't tell me what I
          need.

Denise sits on the bed next to her.

                    DENISE
          We just saw the breaking
          news item on Channel 5. The
          remains are maybe a hundred
          years old, they're saying.
          Just like that doll!

Suzanna takes one sip of the tea and gazes into
the cup.

                    SUZANNA
          Woodrow Burton did it. Enrico
          walked in on him with his
          wife and Woodrow killed them
          all. Buried them in the
          ground, told people they
          disappeared and then built
          the guest house right on top
          of the bones.

                    DENISE
          Shit...

                    SUZANNA
          Poor Tyler had no idea.

                    DENISE
          And neither did that backpack
          girl.

                    SUZANNA
          Right! Yolanda. Her mother
          called me. Said she was
          raped.
                    (frowns)
          But if it was Woodrow's
          spirit who attacked her it
          would make more sense. Tyler
          didn't do it.

                    DENISE
          Oh...And Tyler told you this?

                   SUZANNA
          Yes, Denise. In so many
          words.

She stands, sets the teacup on a nearby night
table and turns back to her friend.

                   SUZANNA
          Look. I know you think I've
          lost it, but I need you to
          take me seriously right now.
          Because I'm not ready to
          bring up the supernatural
          with the police, or certainly
          reporters. At least until I
          know what really happened.

                    DENISE
          Okay so...Why would these
          spooks have been haunting
          your spook?

                   SUZANNA
          I don't know. But it was
          so awful it drove him to
          suicide.
               (gets a brainstorm)
          Unless they thought...he was
          somehow related to Woodrow.

                    DENISE
          Was Tyler buried in that
          cemetery you mentioned?

Suzanna thinks on that a beat, then pulls out
her cell phone. Starts scrolling through her
photos.

                   SUZANNA
          Some of them had no dates,
          but some had only names...

Denise stands to look through them with her.

                    DENISE
          I don't see any Tyler.

Suzanna stops on a photo. Uses two fingers to
zoom closer on it.

                    SUZANNA
          Look.

Behind a few weeds, we can make out the dates
1933-1957.

                    SUZANNA
          It has to be him.

                    DENISE
          But that was way after
          Woodrow's time.

                    SUZANNA
          Exactly. Because someone else
          buried him.
             (pockets her phone, looks
              around for her bag)
          I have to go back, try and
          talk to Tyler again.

                    DENISE
          You're not going anywhere,
          lady. If you want whiskey I
          can find some to knock you out
          with. But you need a good
          night's sleep.

She pulls back the bedcovers, sits Suzanna down
again and kisses her cheek.

                    DENISE
          Coffee and French Toast a la
          Denise in the morning.

She heads to the door and turns off the overhead
light.

                    DENISE
          Sleep, Suzanna.

Leaves the room. Suzanna EXHALES and lies back

on a pillow. Her thoughts tumbling.

EXT. BRENTWOOD STREET - HALF AN HOUR LATER

Suzanna sneaks out to her car in her bare feet,
carrying her shoes.

                                        CUT TO:

EXT. EL MESA ROAD - FIFTEEN MINUTES LATER

A new wave of clammy fog has made its way into
the canyon. Suzanna's Saab reaches the end of
the cul-de-sac and parks.

The police and press and forensics have left
for the time being. Even from the gate, though,
Suzanna can see the first wall of yellow police
tape.

She opens the difficult padlock on the first
attempt and starts up the driveway. The police
tape leads up to the guest house, which is
practically wrapped in a yellow police tape
ribbon.

The further Suzanna goes, the slower she walks.
Because she's looking up at the heavily-vined
side of the main house, and at the dark turret
on top.

Halfway up, she cuts left toward the barbed
wire fence. Fights her way through some thick
hanging vines.

Reaches a section of the fence she hadn't seen
before. At its base, a small flap of barbed wire
has been either pried open or badly attached.
She drops to her hands and knees and slips
inside.

Makes her way around the side of the house. The
only door she comes to is boarded shut, but
past the door, a stained glass window has been
broken open. Making sure not to cut herself,
she hoists herself through it.

INT. BURTON HOUSE - NIGHT

Pitch black. Suzanna COUGHS from the musty air. Waits for her eyes to adjust a little, then inches across a hall to what looks like a large room.

Hits a wall switch around the corner just for the hell of it. No luck.

Takes one step into the big room and a chandelier above her flickers, then TURNS ON.

                         SUZANNA
          Well, now...

She stands in a high-ceilinged dining room. A long table stretches before her, covered with dusty sheets. Animal skins and trophy heads of deer, a moose, a tiger, and a bear are mounted on two of the walls. On the left side of the room, above a long-inactive fireplace, a huge oil painting of a BEARDED, WELL-DRESSED MAN lords over the room.

Suzanna approaches the painting to look at it closer. A gold name plate affixed to the bottom of the frame says WOODROW BURTON. He seems to be in his fifties, overweight and dressed in an early 1900s waistcoat and ruffled white shirt. Sits in a dark green armchair with a fat cigar between two of his fingers. His beady eyes are both confident and penetrating, and Suzanna has to turn away from them after a few seconds.

She glances around the room briefly, then turns back and exits. Sees a grand staircase leading up. Doesn't see any wall switches here so puts her phone flashlight on and begins walking up.

INT. BURTON SECOND FLOOR - NIGHT

She comes to a wide, dark hall. And a light switch, which also works, though the wall sconces SIZZLE as they come on.

She passes a couple of open bedrooms, all the furniture still inside but covered with dusty sheets.

Slowly walks to a door at the end of the hall.
Opens it onto a bigger, dark space. Locates the
light switch.

It's a combination office/billiard room.
Mahagony walls, long-dead plants, a huge desk
raised in front of a stained glass window at
the far end. The pool table is covered with
dusty boxes of papers and file folders, and an
old bar near the entrance door is covered with
spider webs.

She moves around the pool table to the desk.
A series of framed photographs are on the
wall beside it. Various shots of Santa Monica
office buildings from the 1930s and 40s. A
handful of ribbon cutting ceremonies, with a
stooped, impeccably-dressed man in each one who
resembles Woodrow and is labeled as L. BURTON.

On the oppsite side of the desk, a small table
contains six or seven spent candles arranged
around a portrait of an attractive YOUNG WOMAN
from the early 1930s. The table appears to have
once been a shrine.

As Suzanna stares at the table, a light TAPPING
SOUND comes from the window. It makes her jump,
but she quickly sees it's just a branch hitting
the glass.

But then the FLOOR CREAKS. She whirls around.
No one else but her is in the room.

                    SUZANNA
          Tyler?

There's another, smaller window without stained
glass back near the room's door. She creeps
over to it, peers outside.

She can see the police-taped guest house. And
an oddly thick mist filling the empty pool.

She backs away from the window, trying to calm
herself.

The CREAK sounds again, this time louder. And

it's coming from THE FLOOR ABOVE.

She hurries back to the hall.

Retraces her steps, stepping into each open
door with her phone flashlight on.

Passes a narrower side hall she'd missed the
first time, with a heavy black curtain drawn at
its far end.

Hears the CREAK again above her head. Inches
toward the curtain.

Slowly pulls it back to reveal a narrow stone
spiral staircase. She turns off her flashlight
and carefully starts up, trying not to make a
sound. Feeling the walls as she goes.

A dull yellow light begins to illuminate the
staircase. She moves up a little more and sees
a shut wooden door at the top, a sliver of
bright yellow light shining out the bottom.

She tiptoes the final few steps. Puts her hand
on the doorknob and slowly turns it.

INT. TURRET - NIGHT

Monty Burton sits in an old, dark green
armchair in the center of the round turret
room. He wears a pair of wrinkled tennis
sweats. A single bed that has definitely been
slept in recently rises beside him. His legs
are crossed, and he has a mixed drink in his
hand and small, open bag of cocaine on a little
table in front of him.

Sees Suzanna and a wry grin splits his face.

                    MONTY
          Hi, Doctor. Shoot a rack
          of balls on your way up?
          Grandpa Leland loved it when
          strangers used his table.

                    SUZANNA
          It was you up here? Watching
          me??

                    MONTY
          Of course. It's a family
          tradition. And congrats, by
          the way.

                    SUZANNA
          For what?

                    MONTY
          For lasting far longer in
          that house than the last girl
          did, or the two before her.
                    (sips his drink)
          You might actually be my
          perfect tenant.

                    SUZANNA
          You attacked <u>two</u> other women?
          What the hell is wrong with
          you??

                    MONTY
          You tell me. Aren't you the
          psychiatrist? Anyway, I
          prefer to call them surprise
          visits. As you know, I can
          be pretty peruasive when I
          desire an outcome.

                    SUZANNA
          Nice, Monty. But now you're
          in deep shit.

She turns to leave and he yanks a .38 revolver
out of his waistband.

                    MONTY
          I don't think so, Dr.
          Bristol.

                    SUZANNA
                    (stunned)
          You're kidding me.

                    MONTY
          Get away from the stairs...
          As Woodrow first proved, you
          never refuse a Burton.

                    SUZANNA
          Oh, you mean like Enrico's
          wife?

                    MONTY
          Tsk tsk. Poor dumb
          Enrico made the mistake
          of disrupting Woodrow's
          surprise visit, so my great-
          grandfather took care of the
          situation like the genius he
          was. All the Burtons have had
          a knack for that.

Monty manages to sip some more of his cocktail
while keeping the gun pointed at her.

                    SUZANNA
          I'm curious...Who told you
          that awful Enrico story?

                    MONTY
          Grandpa Leland. We were
          tight. At least before the
          day he keeled over in front
          of me. Yep, he filled me in
          on the whole family history.
          Every nook and cranny of
          Burtonology, as I like to
          call it—

                    SUZANNA
          What about Tyler?

                    MONTY
          What about him?

                    SUZANNA
          He was Leland's son, wasn't
          he? The one Burton who
          couldn't handle a situation.

Monty finishes his drink, sets the glass down,
reaches into the plastic bag in front of him
and puts a thumb and fingerful of cocaine up his
nose.

                    MONTY
          Very insightful, Doctor. His
          mother died while having
          him, which I think made him
          a little needy. And very
          insecure, like most actors
          I've met.

The yellow wall sconces on both sides of the
room begin to FLICKER. The temperature drops,
and Suzanna suddenly shivers.

                    SUZANNA
          Tyler?...
                  (listens for him)
          I think he's coming.

                    MONTY
          I don't think so. He knows he
          isn't supposed to be up here.

                    SUZANNA
          Why's that?

                    MONTY
          Because it was Grandpa
          Leland's private room! To spy
          on him. Why do you think he
          gave him the guest house?

                    SUZANNA
          I'm not sure Tyler cares about
          those rules anymore. No one
          told him about Enrico and his
          family, and suddenly they were
          haunting him to death. And now
          you've terrorized these girls?
          He might even hate <u>you</u> now.

                    MONTY
          Oh no. My father would never
          hate me.

Suzanna does a double take.

                    SUZANNA
          I'm sorry. What?

                    MONTY
          I said MY FATHER WOULD NEVER
          HATE ME!!

He kicks over the cocaine table in a rage.
Suzanna lunges at him. He raises the gun but she
knocks it out of his hand, into the corner. She
dives for it but Monty's knee lands on her back
and pins her to the floor.

                    MONTY
          Oh, I tried to track down the
          skanky slut he got pregnant...
          Seeing she was my mother and
          all. But that got me nowhere.

She squirms in pain and he presses harder on her
spine.

                    MONTY
          Then one day...I go into a file
          cabinet at the foster home...
          and learn my real name is
          Burton. That I'm from one of
          the wealthiest real estate
          families in town.

                    SUZANNA
          Let me get up, Monty. We can
          talk about this.

                    MONTY
          Oh sure. For what is it, fifty
          minutes?
                  (laughs to himself)
          Sorry, but I'm the doctor now.

She struggles to get up. He drives his knee down
even harder.

                    MONTY
          It took me years, but I finally
          found out about my father...
          How weak he was. Thinking pool
          parties and sex could replace
          the money-making Leland
          expected of him.

                    SUZANNA
          Not everyone's a businessman,
          y'know—

                    MONTY
          He should have been! It was
          in his damn blood. Like it
          was in mine. That's why I
          legally changed my orphan
          name back to Burton, studied
          real estate like a bastard
          and bam!!

He motions to the house around them.

                    MONTY
          Eventually raised enough cash
          to get control of this place
          and the family business from
          some greedy cousins.

                    SUZANNA
          Good for you...And now you're
          a liar, a peeping tom, and a
          rapist—

He SMACKS the side of her head. She GROANS in
pain. He starts to get off her but both yellow
sconces FIZZLE out.

                    TYLER
                    (V.O.)
          Don't...hurt...Suzanna...

Monty stops, looks around at the darkness. Fear
touches his face for the first time. He lets up
on Suzanna's back just a little.

                    MONTY
          I'm real glad you're here,
          Dad. Been meaning to
          introduce you to Suzanna
          myself, but didn't get a
          chance.
                    (to Suzanna)
          Neither of us had mothers,
          Dr. Bristol...Isn't that what
          you call an emotional bond?

                    TYLER
                   (V.O.)
          The bodies...

                    MONTY
          Thought maybe one of those
          girls I brought in would make
          a good mother for you, Dad.
          But they were just nervous
          nellies that I had to scare
          off. And then what do you
          know? Dr. Bristol shows up.

Tyler appears a few feet away. Hovering in his
usual white denim shirt, jeans, and bare feet.
But this time with a livid expression on his
transparent face.

                    TYLER
          The murders...You knew...My
          father knew...Said nothing.

                    MONTY
          That's where you're wrong,
          Dad. I didn't know about them.
                   (Tyler's expression
                   contorts even more)
          I _swear_ I didn't know—

                    TYLER
          LIAR!!!

His booming voice shakes the walls of the
turret. An aftershock in itself. Monty slips off
Suzanna. She struggles to get up but falls back
down, Monty's cocktail glass SMASHING on the
floor beside her. She crawls away.

Monty makes a run for the open door and
staircase. Tyler ROARS with rage, MERGES
HIMSELF INTO HIM.

                    SUZANNA
          Tyler no!

Too late. Monty's entire face turns yellow and
caves in with a ghastly HISSING sound. He loses
his balance on the top step, tumbles down the

hard stairs with sickening THUDS.

Suzanna gets to her feet, rushes down to the
bottom.

Monty lies dead at the bottom in front of the
black curtain, eyes bulging out, his neck
twisted horribly and broken.

We hear a final long, mournful SIGH from Tyler.
His wispy form rises out of Monty's body and
vanishes into the yellow glow from the turret
lights that have come back on. All is quiet
again.

EXT. MAIN HOUSE - FIVE MINUTES LATER

Dawn is breaking as Suzanna trudges up from the
main house. Physically and emotionally bruised.
Passes the mist-less pool and stops when she
gets to the guest house's outside deck.

Behind the yellow police tape, the old plum
tree is sprouting new white flowers.

EXT. VENTURA BOULEVARD - ONE WEEK LATER

Another hot day in the valley. Suzanna's Saab
exits a Coffee Bean drive-thru line.

INT. SAAB - DAY

Coffee cup in hand, a far more rested-looking
Suzanna cruises along, on her dashboard phone.

                    SUZANNA
          It's got a nice balcony view
          of the Sherman Oaks hills,
          and the deposit was very
          reasonable. Thanks so much
          for the tip, Denise.

                    DENISE (V.O.)
          My pleasure. You've been
          deserving normalcy for quite
          a while.

                    SUZANNA
          You got that right. And The
          Newer You outline is back on
          my laptop, by the way.

                    DENISE (V.O.)
          Wonderful to hear.

A second call from WAYNE comes in on the dash.

                    SUZANNA
          Listen, I need to take this.
          My clients are back in full
          force.

                    DENISE (V.O.)
          Also wonderful. Talk later.

She punches in Wayne's call.

                    SUZANNA
          Hi Wayne.

                    WAYNE
             (V.O., a bit shaky)
          Can I see you a day early,
          Doctor? Have to leave town...

                    SUZANNA
          Uhh, not really, Wayne. I
          have other sessions lined up.
          Is it important?

                    WAYNE
             (V.O.)
          Yes...Just for five minutes.
          We can meet in your office
          garage.

Suzanna EXHALES. Sips some coffee.

                    SUZANNA
          Fine. But I have a 10:30, so
          how about 10:15?

                    WAYNE
             (V.O., after a long pause)
          Okay.

He hangs up. Suzanna moves into a faster lane.

INT. OFFICE GARAGE - TEN MINUTES LATER

Suzanna sits in her assigned space, facing the
entrance. Checks her watch, which says 10:20.
Already getting irked.

Begins scrolling through some of her recent
photos and deleting them. Comes to the graveyard
series. Finds the one for JOSE AND LUNA
RODRIGUEZ and uses her fingers to expand it.

Jose's grave is dated 1921-1923.

                    SUZANNA
          Wait...He was only two?

While she mulls this over, she finally sees
Wayne walking into the garage from the street
and puts her phone down.

Wayne looks winded, out of sorts. Suzanna
flashes the Saab headlights at him and he heads
toward her. Suzanna starts to climb out.

                    WAYNE
          No. Can we talk in your car?

She nods, unlocks the passenger side for him.
He gets in, all jumpy. Perspiring heavily.

                    SUZANNA
          Are you okay?
                    (he half-nods)
          You park on the street?

                    WAYNE
          I walked...

                    SUZANNA
          From Woodland Hills? Wow. Is
          something wrong with your
          car?

He twitches. Looks out the windshield, then at
her. But doesn't answer.

                    SUZANNA
          Listen I need to get
          upstairs, so if this can
          wait—

                    WAYNE
          It can't.

He twitches some more. Then Suzanna's PHONE
MESSAGE ALERT goes off. She GROANS, picks it up.

               ONE NEW VOICEMAIL
               FROM WAYNE B.
               2 MINUTES AGO

                    SUZANNA
          That's strange. Hold on a
          second.

She plays back the voicemail.

                    WAYNE
               (V.O., exuberant)
          Hi Dr. Bristol, it's Wayne!
          Glad to hear you're seeing
          clients again. Just want
          to say I'm looking forward
          to our session tomorrow
          afternoon. I'm doing much
          better, but I'll wait to tell
          you about it. Later!

She puts the phone back down. Slowly turns and
looks at Wayne beside her.

His twitching has stopped, but his complexion
darkens. Wisps of hair sprout up on his nearly
bald head. Turn sandy. His face is changing,
becoming weirdly handsome before her eyes.

                    SUZANNA
          Wayne??

                    TYLER
               (in Wayne's body)
          Time to embrace your ghost,
          Suzanna.

                    SUZANNA
          Oh my God...What are you
          doing here??

                    TYLER
          You helped me...find mine.
          Now...for yours.

The car ENGINE STARTS by itself. Suzanna's seat
belt buckles, straps her in, and the Saab roars
out the entrance.

INT. SAAB - DAY

They weave through traffic on the busy
boulevard. Suzanna frantically tries to get
control of the steering wheel and brake pedal
but it's hopeless.

                    TYLER
          Don't fight him, Suzanna. He's
          been winning for too long...

                    SUZANNA
          Who are you talking about?
          Where are we going??

Her GPS switches on, and a destination types
itself in: WHISPERING PINES LAKE

Suzanna looks at the name, and her eyes glaze
over for a second. Something clicks in the
deepest chamber of her soul. While the car
comes to a 5 FREEWAY NORTH sign and turns up
the ramp, Suzanna grabs her cell and manages to
dial a number.

                    DEB (V.O.)
          Hi Suzanna. This isn't the
          best—

                    SUZANNA
          Deb! Listen to me. I need
          you to tell me about a place
          called Whispering Pines Lake.

                    DEB (V.O.)
          You're kidding. Again with
          this?

                    SUZANNA
          Yes! What happened there?

There's a long pause.

                    DEB (V.O.)
          I honestly thought you'd
          moved on from that, Suzanna.
          Mom and Dad spent many years
          and thousands and thousands
          of dollars to get you the
          best treatment, and help you
          out of your guilty, self-
          destructive head while they
          were paying no attention to
          me—

                    SUZANNA
          I'm asking you what
          happened!!

                    DEB
                    (V.O.)
          Suze. I'm sorry you're having
          some kind of bad flashback,
          okay? But I'm probably not
          the best person to talk you
          through this. If you want
          the details of the incident
          again, I suggest contacting
          Tommy Dunnerston's parents,
          assuming they're still
          around.

                    SUZANNA
          Deb, please—

                    DEB
                    (V.O.)
          I gotta go.

The call disconnects. Suzanna stares out at
the 5 freeway whizzing past them. Then over at
Tyler, still fidgeting in his Wayne body, some
drool leaking from his mouth.

                         SUZANNA
                   Tommy Dunnerston?...

He slowly turns to look at her. The Tyler
inside his head nods.

                                        DISSOLVE TO:

EXT. 5 FREEWAY - DAY

Wind blows dust across the lanes and dark
clouds billow up over the parched low mountains
on the left side of the road. Suzanna's car
exits and veers west onto Route 126, a four-
lane highway.

                                        DISSOLVE TO:

EXT. ROUTE 126 - DAY

By the time they've turned onto a narrow two-
lane road toward Whispering Pines Lake, the sky
has darkened considerably.

INT. SAAB

Suzanna leans back, helplessly pinned by her
seat belt, almost in the same erratic dream
state as Tyler while the car drives them up the
twisting road.

After passing under a half mile of oak trees, a
good-sized, dark green lake comes into view on
the right. The car begins to slow.

They turn into what looks like a dusty parking
lot, unused for years. Tyler sits up straighter
in Wayne's body, gazes out the windshield.

                         TYLER
                   You're here...

The ENGINE DIES. Suzanna's seat belt pops
off and the driver door flies open. She looks
confused, terrified. But something is drawing
her out of the car.

An old wooden sign lies in the nearby weeds.

Suzanna walks over to it. The post the sign
once stood on must have rotted away maybe
twenty years ago.

                    CAMP WHISPERING PINES
                       SUMMER FUN
                    FOR BOYS AND GIRLS

Now <u>Suzanna</u> begins to twitch. The truth of
where she is seeps into her like ice cold
syrup. She peers up at the shimmering lake.
Slowly begins to walk toward it.

As she nears the water, a long wooden dock
materializes. The SPLASHING and LAUGHING of
KIDS having a good time swimming.

Suzanna is nine years old again, wearing a
bathing suit and yellow swimming cap. Walking
out onto the dock with six or seven other
CAMPERS.

The wind is as fierce as it gets, and the lake
is dangerously choppy, splashing against the
dock.

At the far end, TOMMY DUNNERSTON, another nine-
year-old and her best friend at camp, stands
a few yards in front of the other kids at the
edge of the dock wearing a yellow bathing suit,
smiling at Suzanna and beckoning her to join
him.

She nods and hurries past the other kids. Gets
a few feet away and a rogue lake wave rises
out of nowhere and SLAMS into the dock. The
dock CRACKS and splits open beneath Suzanna's
feet. She SCREAMS. The entire end of the dock
collapses into the water, taking Tommy with it.

Suzanna grabs hold of one of the fallen
beams. Tommy is just a yard away, yelling and
splashing like a maniac.

                        TOMMY
                Help me!! Can't swim—

Suzanna clings to the beam, terrified and numb.

A plank floats by. One she can easily grab and
hold out for Tommy.

But she doesn't. The wind and waves pick up
even more and carry Tommy out into the lake.
Until he suddenly disappears beneath the water.

                    SUZANNA
              (in her current voice)
          I was scared! I didn't know
          what to do!!

The wind and water calm down, and what's left
of the dock disappears.

Suzanna lays on her back at the edge of the
lake, SOBBING into her hands.

                    SUZANNA
          Please forgive me, Tommy.
          Please...

She hears a low CHIMING SOUND from the parking
area. It's the Saab, reminding her that the
keys are in the ignition and the door is open.

She sits up again. Sees Wayne climbing out the
passenger side and looking around in complete
bafflement.

                    WAYNE
          Dr. Bristol? Is that you?

Suzanna stands, dusts herself off. Wipes the
tears from her eyes and gives him a weary wave.

                    SUZANNA
          Yes, Wayne...

Shuts her eyes for a long, meditative moment.

                    SUZANNA
          This time it is.

And starts back to the car.

                              FADE TO BLACK

ONE EYE OPEN

A Novel

❧ ONE ❧

I gazed down at the Santa Monica Freeway rushing under my legs and wondered how big a mess my falling body would make. The overpass I stood on was the highest around, but the late afternoon traffic below was tight and fast as it whizzed toward the ocean, and I was sure I'd be ripped apart between cars like a tomato in a blender.

I was shuffling out to the 14th Street bridge once a week at that point, especially with the holiday season approaching. I meant to visit the overpass on Monday but 48 hours of balmy rain from a Mexican hurricane scrapped that plan, and the one thing I was good at was rolling with adversity. It was hard to be homeless and not be.

My name was Leo, and I'm much better now. Mining a lost soul requires getting your hands grimy in a deep suitcase, so sit back while I unpack everything that happened to me and a few others in that strange, freaky week. I can still hardly believe it.

I sensed I'd been homeless for over fifteen years, the same way I sensed I was in my late-30s. I was through expecting charity from anyone, especially in a place where Porsches, Beemers, and Jaguars grew on trees and celebrities were more concerned with starving people on the other side of the planet.

But I wasn't a beggar. I found that beneath me and knew it pushed people away. Not that I wanted anything to do with people, but to beg for money meant interacting with them. I was far more comfortable in my "natural bedroom" in the Centinela cloverleaf, plowing through a discarded book, venturing out to check for lost change in newspaper boxes or public toilet stalls. I was never much of an eater, and had the nightly meal in front of City Hall to keep me going in between found snacks.

But Thanksgiving was a week away, a day that never failed to spiral me into depression. Was it the birth of the holiday season, its focus on home, family, and comfort I might never have? Or just the promise of impending rain and colder weather? I knew being homeless in L.A. couldn't compare with a frigid, snow-clogged doorway in New York or Minneapolis, but Southern California wasn't twelve months of sunshine and bikinis, either. There were floods, fires, or mudslides nearly every year. Sometimes Malibu homes spilled into the sea.

My homeless cohorts were always getting miserable colds. I would never forget Bullfinch, a crusty Vietnam vet who slept on the Santa Monica cliffs in a wheelchair, sneezing violently one night and giving himself a fatal stroke. I had pegged myself as a candidate to die sad and alone one day, but had no desire to go out in an explosion of snot.

Anyway, back to the 14th Street bridge. The cars behind me were multiplying. I could tell by the sound. I imagined a few of the drivers were slowing down to take their brief, semi-caring glance at me, this poor unkempt waste with ratty beach bum hair, contemplating ending it all in a soiled yellow Hawaiian shirt, torn corduroy pants and holey sneakers, before a light turned green ahead or their radio station needed switching and it was on to their warm homes and warmer dinners. ("You should've seen this guy, honey. If I passed him on the sidewalk I would've given him a buck, but the car was moving too fast, and y'know…Hey, whatever you got in that oven smells great!")

I hadn't eaten anything since the remnants of that Burger King mushroom burger five hours ago, and the speeding cars below were suddenly blurry. What was this now, my eyesight going? Christ, why not just climb the damn rail and get it over with?

I peeled the frayed, ten-year-old backpack off my shoulder. Zippers rusted and useless. I undid the three safety pins holding the thing closed and dug inside. Slid out a small bottle of Wild Turkey and helped myself to a final swig, then propped the backpack against the bridge wall and raised my right ventilated sneaker into the first open slat beneath the rail.

I'd memorized the fatal sensations before, and was convinced they'd match my prediction: *short hop with both feet, cool wind in my face and up through my hair, clamp my eyes shut and wait for the windshield smack on the truck I'd picked out and that's that.* I was more prepared than a Marine on Guadalcanal.

The second sneaker was the tricky one, because I had to grip the rail with both hands to secure my balance. Ancient surfing days would benefit me here, assuming I actually had some. I inched my feet apart slightly, raised my torso and gazed at the rushing lanes coming at me. One moving truck, a roach coach, and a Winnebago were in play, but no semis. Nothing with the right finality…

A young couple was watching me from the nearby embankment. They were pale, in dark dress clothes for some reason, standing in the undergrowth at a strange, impossible angle. Almost like they were *hovering.* They were at least fifty yards away but I could make out their stunned, vapid expressions.

"What's that man doing, Mom?"

The little boy's voice in the car behind me was followed by a ripple of shrieking brakes and metallic crunches. I whirled, saw the multiple accident I just caused and lost all selfish desires. Hopped back on the sidewalk, stared at the mother's Volvo wagon with its disfigured rear, at the angry Latino contractors behind her climbing out of their smashed van, at the old lady behind them slumped over her steering wheel in horror, at the two or three bridge commuters yanking out their cell phones. I stepped off the curb, reached the mother's window to apologize and got shoved out of the way by a contractor yelling "Get lost, loco!"

I lost my footing and landed next to the curb. Heard a police siren cleaving through the air and quickly scrambled over to my backpack, pinned it shut and hurried off the bridge in the quieter direction.

The young, staring couple on the hillside had vanished.

✽ TWO ✽

Roxie down at the pier landed in a jet one time and said the Los Angeles Basin looked like an endless bathtub of putrid air, with cars and palm trees floating in it. I called it the Land of Invisible Worms. Pick up any moist rock in a garden and you'd find an assortment of slimy creatures ducking for cover. Out here, the rocks were bigger and drier and the worms impossible to see. I only traveled by foot and had reduced my amblings to the perimeters of Santa Monica, but I'd lived here long enough to know that the area had a buried, unspoken past that was forever being paved over and redeveloped. I'd been to most of the libraries and knew about Father Serra and Olvera Street and did see *Chinatown* a long time ago, but there was so much more to uncover. I felt it.

For as long as I could remember, I had what some people call a third ear, a way of picking up details of nature and sound others apparently missed. Like stepping aside moments before a gob of seagull crap hit the sidewalk. Or looking at a businessman three seconds before his cell phone rang. Or God, that Northridge quake in '94, which had me tossing and turning hours before it hit. I had heard of dogs and cows doing stuff like that, and most of the time it amused me. When I was on a brandy binge the strange radar would fold up on its own and leave me alone for days or maybe weeks.

Willful amnesia also plagued me, and ten minutes after the bridge incident I'd forgotten about it. Golden, benevolent, late afternoon light was everywhere, and my personal freeway beckoned to the sea. I heard once that the secret of getting around L.A. by car was knowing the short cuts, and I'd applied that theory to my feet. My favorite alley was the one two blocks north of Wilshire that began around 26th and went straight down to the cliffs, quiet and shady with a minimum of barking dogs and police cruisers and a stretch of bougainvillea that took me out of my woeful world and put me in one more exotic and life-affirming. On a languid summer day with lizards darting up and down the fences and seagulls wheeling above, I was tempted to start singing.

This day was far cooler, and spits of rain hurried me along. I detoured south a few blocks to visit my favorite public toilet inside a Rite-Aid. I avoided a scrawny orange cat that sidestepped me near a dumpster. Dogs were mere guardians doing their jobs, while cats were demons in disguise, forever watching from shadows and sneaking up behind me.

Iggy struggled by somewhere around 10th Street, pushing his three-cart train of clothes, recyclables and neatly folded cartons. He never changed his clothes or did anything with the stuff in the carts, just rolled them around town and barked vulgarity at the sidewalk and gloried in holding up traffic at crosswalks. I sometimes wondered how Iggy became this way, but thinking too much about that might get me dwelling on my own bottled-up past.

Midnight Star Books with its old fashioned couches and musty secondhand offerings spilling off every shelf would take care of me another few hours. Old Jerry, the half blind and mostly deaf owner, nodded at me as I entered and I went down a back aisle looking for a title to fall into a nap with. On this day *A Short History of Dams* by Darbus Koonce, published in 1958 and originally bequeathed to a Columbus, Ohio library by a T. SLEDGE would do just fine.

"Mr. Koonce?" I muttered, "Welcome to Leo."

I found my favorite green antique couch and secluded myself with the volume. I always believed you could write a book about a fingernail and keep it interesting if you knew how to really write, and dams were hardly fingernails. I had no idea, for instance, that the first recorded dam was on the Nile River at Kosheish around 2900 B.C. Dams made of timber across the American frontier also intrigued me, espeically the old photos of them. The problem was that I was exhausted. The lack of food, combined with a briskerthan-usual walk to get there and the psychological burden of the bridge incident had my eyes dog paddling by Chapter Three. I knew I could fold over the page at any time, stick it back on the shelf and resume it next time, but Koonce's descriptions of rushing water made me groggy, and before long the headwaters were flowing over my scalp and dunking my mind...

...and I was back in the house. The cozy suburban one I'd been finding myself in lately. Every room a kitchen with crackling fire and festive table set for four. Then a bell would ring, louder than a church's. I heard the tapping of shoes on the front doorstep, but the quicker I ran to answer it, the deeper my feet would sink into the linoleum. I'd throw the door open and no one was ever there—only the same postcard lying on the front step. Always addressed to LEO, a photo of a cemetery on the front and no message on the back. And it was always the same cemetery: deep, rolling lawn, a high stone entrance gate with an angel carved into each side.

The postcard was there again. I picked it up, turned it over. This time words had been scrawled in magic marker on the back:

WISH YOU WERE HERE

A ghastly chill went up my back. I crunched the card in my hand and something gripped my left shoulder. I gasped—

It was Old Jerry, standing behind me.

"Closin' up early today, Leo."

I shook myself awake. Folded over the page I had left a bit of drool on and shut the book. "Thanks, Jerry. Gimme a minute, okay?"

I got to my feet, shouldered my backpack and found the slot for it on the shelf. I was a nervous wreck.

* * *

By the time I reached Santa Monica City Hall, the meal line was wrapped around two palms. I was never concerned about them running out of food, but I was very weak with hunger, and if I sat down in the line I could lose my place three times over. They hadn't even opened the door yet, and guys were jockeying for position at the entrance, eager to eat or fight.

"Wassappenin', Leo?" It was Duce, an angular black guy in his 50s with salty hair and a signature yellow pillowcase stuffed with his bedroll and clothes.

"What's up, Duce?"

"Blood pressure, no doubt. There was some creepy white boys scopin' around the cliffs last night, but me and Dagwood scared 'em off by acting crazier than them. You was in the cloverleaf?"

"Yup. Little bit of rain woke me once, but that was it."

Duce nodded, motioned me a bit closer and dropped his voice. "Wanna grab us some bills tomorrow? Jobworks offerin' cart-wranglers at Ralph's again."

I scratched a bite under my arm, laughed a little. Good old Ruby. She really dug deep for job possibilities. Or at least scraped.

"Yeah, maybe…Not sure what I'm doing yet."

"Oh. I see. Like what? Your tennis game with that supermodel again? Trust me, homie-less, there ain't nothin' better you could be doing than showin' up on Ruby's doorstep at 7 a.m."

The door to the food hall opened briefly, then closed again. Angry shouts filled the air.

"Hey Leo!" The frantic, guttural voice behind us belonged to Coolie, a white guy with red dreadlocks who carried a stuffed gym bag he never let anyone see the insides of. "Need more Sunday picks! You won me 30 bucks last week!"

"He did?" asked Duce.

"Butt out, brother," said Coolie, "Me and Leo got our own arrangement." He tried to lay a friendly arm around me but I shook it off.

"Not really in the mood today, Coolie."

"Just once more, Leo. I need that money."

I turned away for a moment. Put two fingers to my temple and shut my eyes.

"Falcons…Chiefs…Giants…Raiders…Bears…Niners…and Falcons. Start with those."

"You already said Falcons!"

"Okay, then Steelers."

"What about the Monday night game?"

"Buccaneers. Happy?"

"You do this for him every week?" asked Duce. A few other transients had wandered over to listen in.

"No. And that's it. Think I'm gonna find grub somewhere else." I shouldered my pack again and headed off to the street.

* * *

The rain was a tease, but damp enough to keep me ducking into doorways all the way up Wilshire. It was dark now, Santa Monicans returning from downtown jobs, happy hours, dinners, and yoga classes. The few on the sidewalk swerved or picked up speed to avoid my path whenever possible. I fished a half-eaten muffin out of a trash can around 10th Street which kept me going for a little while, but I still had two hours to kill before Jack-in-the-Box dumpster time.

More than anything, I liked the location of this Jack, directly across the street from nice little Douglas Park, a long rectangle of shade and rocks and water and during the day, serious lawn bowlers in their prim whites and soft shoes. The police patrolled there regularly, but if I had a newspaper or book with me I could spend hours at a picnic table or on the sloping lawn without being bothered.

Night was a bit trickier. I had my regular secluded spot in a shadowy gulley beneath a pine tree. Patrol cars shining their lights always missed me here if I dropped my head a notch. Tonight with the misty rain, I didn't see one cruiser. Any kind of weather in

L.A. seemed to keep the city workers and the law in hibernation; I often fantasized about the madness that'll occur in this place when we finally get a freak blizzard.

Torty Shell and his family were out on the rocks tonight, craning their scrawny necks around. I always looked forward to these visits, maybe because I felt a kinship with the box turtles. If they could find their little patch of serenity outside, why couldn't I? There was a time when people who chose to leave society and live up in remote caves were called hermits; their eccentric independence and resourcefulness even commanded some grudging respect. True, many homeless today were lazy, crazy, drugged or drunk, but lots had just fallen through the cost-of-living cracks, while others had actually chosen their wayward path. I knew I was in the second category, even if the reasons for my choice had gotten fuzzy and sort of disappeared.

I grew weary of watching the turtles after a while, and meandered over to a dark picnic table to stare at a house across the street. It was one of my favorite pastimes. Most people kept their blinds or curtains drawn at night, but I could always count on a house here and there without fear, and it always comforted me to study what I could see of an ordinary life—even from a distance. Tonight's offering was a very Americanized middle eastern family with a big screen TV in their living room. The dad read a magazine and smoked a cigarette while the mom and teenage son watched some detective show on a plush couch beside him. It was just nice that they were all together.

I breathed deeply, glanced over at the Jack-in-the-Box. Its sign had finally gone out. I made my way back across the park, keeping an eye on the giant brown dumpster behind the restaurant. I parked myself against a pine and waited. A police cruiser rolled by, seemingly uninterested, but I did a slow rotation behind the tree just in case.

Fifteen more minutes went by, and then Jack's back door opened. It was the chubby little Latino girl tonight carrying trash.

Thank God, I thought; that goony white kid with the pimples came back out to shoo me off last time. I waited for the girl to dump three giant plastic bags and disappear, then crossed the street and lifted the dumpster cover.

I opened one of the bags, saw a couple of Ultimate Cheeseburger wrappers in the light of the streetlamp, but there was nothing left on them but grease and a sliver of cheese. I went for a half box of onion rings, used it to collect a handful of uneaten fries, then nabbed ninety percent of a chicken sandwich some mom had probably forced on her non-hungry kid. I shoved everything into a used paper bag I also fished out, then stuffed the bag in my backpack and quickly walked off. I would feast that night.

* * *

My cloverleaf residence was a circular ocean of ivy, tucked under the I-10 westbound exit ramp at Centinela Avenue. I liked living in a cloverleaf because I could count on the whoosh of the cars circling around my head to put me to sleep. This one had the added feature of being directly under the southbound flight path of incoming planes traveling down the coast. You could look up in the night sky on any clear evening and see a dozen aircraft approaching or taking off from the local airports; when I lay on my back and faced the southbound jets, I felt like a gatekeeper or host, welcoming them to safety from the scary skies.

I sometimes heard rats scuttling through the ivy patch, but after beating one to death with a shoe one night, they never seemed to venture close. They also stayed away from my "bureau," a discarded leather suitcase filled with old clothes, items, and questionable toiletries I kept hidden behind a concrete freeway piling, and whatever dry food scraps I kept buried in plastic bags around the area. The ivy was actually dense enough to hide a good-sized record collection, and I had made it my closet over the years.

Thankfully, the rain had stopped by the time I reached the cloverleaf. I picked my way through the ivy to the freeway piling. Dropped my pack and forged to the lower struts of a billboard sign that loomed over the freeway high above me. I reached into a gap between the struts and slid out a long, flattened cardboard box. Carried it over to the piling, where I quickly re-shaped it into a high-back chair. Set myself into it, opened my backpack, and gleefully extracted the Jack-in-the-Box dinner. The chicken sandwich tasted like prime rib, and I savored every chew, then washed it all down with a warm can of Bud I'd hidden in a hole five feet northeast of the piling.

Satiated, I listened to the steady hum of cars over my head while I finished the beer. This really was a cozy little spot, I thought. It was hard to believe I was teetering on that dumb bridge only hours ago. This is how it was with dark, depressing waves: one minute they're rolling over you, the next they're receding. The holidays just had more high tides.

I re-flattened the box when I was done and dragged it to my accustomed sleep spot, an ivy-draped dip in the earth right under the lip of the freeway. In bad weather it was just a short drag to total cover. I fished an army blanket and soiled pillow from the bureau, then laid myself down on the box. Overhead, a good-sized jet floated down from Malibu, cutting its engines, wingtip lights blinking. Welcome back to Earth, people. Welcome…

* * *

I was at a high school prom and none of the kids had faces. A band was onstage and none of them had faces either, and then I was standing behind the drummer all of a sudden and for some reason wearing a pajamas and bathrobe. They were playing a super slow rock ballad I couldn't place and young dancers on the floor were moving slowly to it. The curtain kept closing and opening and every time it did I had less and less clothes on.

Then a sledgehammer appeared in the faceless drummer's hand and metallic, muscular sounds replaced the music. Gruff, male shouts that got louder every second—

I woke up on my cardboard box. Light beams from above flashed over the ivy in all directions.

"Can't use one of those, dufus!!" yelled some guy.

"Says who, asshole?" yelled another.

I quickly sat up. Heard clangs and thuds and small motors. Got to my feet and peered up at the freeway.

There was a night crew of road workers up there, dressed in orange vests and yellow hardhats. Moving slowly down the ramp. One guy in a small jeep was rolling ahead of them, dropping plastic cones. *Shit. No bedroom here tonight. And they better not be doing any ivy gardening.*

I stayed in the shadows, quietly folding up my bed, and slipped my sneakers back on. Waited until the crew was out of sight behind a big dead bush, then shouldered my pack and made my way through the lower part of the ivy to Pico Boulevard.

* * *

I moved east on Pico for many blocks, then turned north and east again. My destination was an unguarded parking garage with a faulty gate, just past Sepulveda on a quiet residential street. It was one of my three emergency bedrooms, and certainly not my favorite. The place was clammy, there were gas fumes, frequent sirens on Olympic Boulevard, and people who lived in the apartment complex over the garage occasionally saw me huddled in the corner and called the police. Still, it was mine and mine alone, which always counted for something.

By the time I neared Sepulveda, misty fog fingers were reaching in from the sea. I especially liked fog because it made everything so still and silent, and easier to improvise a shelter. I also knew the city didn't get a fraction of the fog San Francisco was known for, so when it came it was a treat. The vapor invigorated me, and I walked a bit faster, thoroughly enjoying my time in the cloud. After about four blocks, though, the fog lifted a bit, and I was a little sad and distraught.

I first saw them as I crossed Sepulveda. All three dudes were pale, wearing black leather jackets. They were outside a cheap Thai restaurant and seemed to be either waiting for a bus or loitering. As I approached the light, I got a better glance. One guy had spiked hair in assorted colors, another wore a black T-shirt with the words PEACE SUCKS on it, while a third had a black cowboy hat and carried a giant shoulder bag. The three of them had lifeless, druggy eyes, and they were all staring at me.

"What d'ya think?" said Spikey to Cowboy.

The WALK light was taking forever to change. I shuffled nervously, saw the Cowboy slowly nod. "I think he's our star."

I turned away, jumped the light by about three seconds and nearly got hit by a honking cab. Moved briskly in the crosswalk, peering once and only once over my shoulder. The three guys were following me.

"Hey shitbag!" yelled one. I didn't react, just picked up speed. Ducked left into a hidden short cut, past a long row of mailboxes leading to an alley. They were still behind me.

"You can run, asswipe, but you can't hide!"

By the time I reached the alley, I was nearly out of breath. I knew nobody driving on a main street would stop to help me, but there were often people parking their cars back here. Not tonight, though.

"Where ya off to, shitbag?" The voice was right behind me, sharp and nasty, and a hand grabbed my shirt collar, spun me around. There was one garage security light on, but it was three buildings away, and I could barely make out Spikey's pale sneer.

"Please…" I shuddered, "I don't have anything…"

T-Shirt let out a stupid giggle. "Aw, that we know!" He yanked off my backpack, tossed it in a nearby puddle. Spikey cocked his head at me, like an iguana sizing up a fly.

"We don't want anything you got, Shitbag. We just want you."

"'Huh?"

"HHUUUHHH??? WHAAAA???"

They all laughed now. Spikey glanced up and down the alley, then looked at Cowboy.

"How's the light here?"

Cowboy had his shoulder bag open. He reached in, extracted a camcorder and switched it on. "We've had worse."

Spikey motioned T-Shirt over. The guy spat a loogie at the pavement, then clamped a hand on my shoulder and shoved me to the ground.

"What the hell are you doing??" I blurted.

"Makin' a movie!" said T-Shirt, as if the answer was obvious. Spikey pulled on some black leather gloves he produced from a hidden pocket.

"Ever hear of bumbeaters.com?"

I froze. I of course had heard of sickos doing this kind of thing, but thought it was contained to Florida, Texas and other redneck haunts.

"You nuts, fool?" said Cowboy, moving closer and crouching for a better angle. "This loser never uses the Web."

"Bet he's never seen a computer!" added T-Shirt.

"Anyway, they pay decent money for gripping home video." He stood over me with his legs apart, grinning. "Such as...the following presentation...And ACTION!" A red light appeared on Cowboy's camcorder, and Spikey punched me in the jaw. I fell back on the asphalt, stunned. Tried to get up but Spikey and T-Shirt were both kicking and punching now. As I desperately tried to ward off the blows, I thought I saw a face peering out an apartment window, but the curtain was quickly drawn.

Headlights appeared in the alley. The camcorder went off and the three guys dragged me away by the ankles, into an empty carport. Held me down, hands over my mouth, until the car rolled by, then resumed beating and filming.

I felt sharp pains everywhere. Tasted blood in my mouth. Tried with all my might to believe this wasn't happening, tried to imagine a peaceful jet floating overhead. Nothing was working.

"Fuck you guys!" yelled Cowboy, "Gimme a slice." He tossed the camera to T-Shirt and reared back with one of his work boots. I waited till the shoe was airborne, then snagged Cowboy's ankle before it hit my face, quickly shoved him backwards. Cowboy slipped on a grease patch and slammed into Spikey, knocking them both over.

I seized the moment. Got to my feet, stumbled out of the carport like a madman. Scooped my backpack out of the puddle and tore straight up the alley toward Wilshire.

"GET BACK HERE, SHITBAG!" yelled Spikey. "WE GOT TWO MORE SCENES!!"

I reached Olympic, panting and wincing. Darted straight across the wide boulevard before a wave of cars and tripped on the opposite curb. Thankfully, the fog had returned. When I got to my feet and turned, I could barely make out the bastards squirting from the alley. I wasted no time. Raced around the corner and up a dark, residential street.

These were the high-priced homes of what they called Beverly Hills Adjacent. Not one person would open the door for me if I even rang a bell, but that was okay. More bucks meant more security guards and cruisers, and if I saw one I'd finger the bumbeaters, maybe even get myself a ride down to the Santa Monica shelter.

As I hurried up the winding, tree-laden street, wiping my bloody lips, the fog completely swallowed the neighborhood. I stopped and turned. Thought I heard a far-off creepy howl in the rolling mist, but wasn't sure. I kept moving.

There were blisters on both of my feet by now. I needed to find a place to hide, but had no idea which direction I would find one. I cut through a vine-covered alley to the next street, which had even bigger trees. Moved up the sidewalk, keeping an eye for a driveway of some kind.

About ten yards ahead, an ethereal orange light glowed in the mist. I couldn't tell whether it was due to the fog or not, but the light appeared to pulsate. Almost as if it was beckoning me. A siren cut through the fog, and I spun around for a moment. When I looked back at the orange light it had vanished.

I was standing at the mouth of a curved brick path, which wound its way past a hedge and into a dark, ungated cavity between a pair of lushly manicured ranch homes. The bricks were slippery, and I nearly tripped twice. Past the hedge lay an inviting wedge of grass, tucked between a pepper tree and bougainvillea. Most likely in shadow by day, it was the perfect place to sleep.

The fog subdued every sound from the street. I barely heard a passing car. I opened my pack and dug out a flannel shirt I'd pre-rolled into a pillow with pins and masking tape for such an occasion. Set it on the ground, tugged off my wretched sneakers and collapsed on my back.

A gauzy backyard porch light from the adjoining house glowed in the mist, and comforting jazz piano tinkled from a window. The house straight ahead of me was just a looming horizontal shape with no lights on. The night's disturbing events still had me jittery, and I drifted off with one eye open, like I'd been doing for as long as I could remember.

* * *

Pulsating orange…pulsating orange…A sick neon heart pumping in the fog.

And now I smelled smoke, and sat up. The entire brick path was awash in the same orange, and pungent fire smoke had blended into the fog. A woman was yelling for help. Then a man was. Then the woman again.

I heard crackling, and saw fire—leaping through the windows of the house in front of me. The yelling intensifed. I closed my eyes, covered my ears, and rolled into a ball.

The sounds evaporated as quickly as they'd begun. I opened both eyes and saw the orange light was gone. Stood back up and glanced around.

The house was dark again, and this time I noticed that half the windows were boarded up. In the thick fog just minutes earlier I had not been able to see that. Neighbors had not rushed out of the house next door. I couldn't even hear a dog bark. I smacked the side of my head. *Is this one of those spooky and crazy nightmares I've been having lately?* Sure didn't seem like one.

A car whooshed by in the street, and I thought I heard the distant long honk of a fire truck. *Well, whatever the hell it was, it went away.* Cozy spots to sleep were tough to find, and fatigue soon washed over my fears again. I dug into the backpack, fished out a crusty pint of Hiram Walker that was two-thirds empty. I laid back down in the soft, grassy wedge, drained the thing, and let my mind empty.

❧ THREE ❧

Morning dew leaked into my nose at sunrise. I got to my feet, groggily gathered my things. The fog had lifted, and the sounds of sparrows and jays were more than welcome. I looked at the boarded-up, abandoned house as I exited the path. Passed an old mailbox out front that was leaning over, and was about to look for a name on it when the blast of a metallic horn made me jump. A black and white L.A. police cruiser idled at the curb, a blonde crewcutted cop in its open passenger window.

"What the hell were you doing in there?"

He waved me over. I hung my head like I was accustomed to, sauntered out to the sidewalk. "I'm lost, actually. I was just heading back to the shelter…"

"You mean Santa Monica?" piped in his partner behind the wheel, a muscled black guy wearing shades. "You're over the border, pal. L.A. begins at Centinela."

"Right, right. It was pretty foggy last night. Listen—I heard a whole mess of screams in there that woke me up. I think a man and woman might've gotten hurt."

The cops shared an amused glance before Crewcut looked at me again. "No shit, Sherlock. Just start moving, okay?"

"Aren't you gonna check it out?"

"Hey! If you aren't five blocks away from here in a westerly direction by the time we circle back around, you are the one who's gonna check out. Now MOVE."

The cruiser rolled away. I stood there, mystified. My third ear had always been a benign gift, almost playful. It had never crossed a dark line. But suddenly, like the recent recurring nightmares, like the sadistic creeps last night, my shell of aimless innocence was being cracked like a walnut. I gave the property a final shivered look, then hurried south and west toward Sepulveda.

* * *

I hated waiting around for Victor. The corner of Purdue and Tennessee, like Colorado and 7th, or a dozen other corners in the area, was crawling with Latino job seekers, scruffy, cold men with donut house coffee and *La Opinion*, some in animated clusters, most alone, perched on curbs or against walls or parking signs, eyeballing every passing pickup or van with an inmate's optimism, hoping for that rare, full, tax-free day uprooting trees or hauling stones in a millionaire's backyard.

I did admire these souls, but knew they were a closed group and didn't exactly relish seeing me anywhere near their concrete turf. Often I'd have to make myself a little more disheveled and pretend to talk to the air so they'd figure I was just some crazy white dude who'd wandered into the neighborhood. Not that I wouldn't mind a day of work like theirs on occasion, but I was also aware of the dangers involved, like when that Juan Corona guy in the 70s raped and murdered a whole bunch of migrant workers he lassoed from corners. I also knew about six words in Spanish, and wouldn't feel comfortable riding around in a flatbed filled with joking Salvadorans.

Victor finally appeared after a half hour wait, hopping off the Pico bus in his ripped jeans, stained sweatshirt and backwards Dodger cap. He had come to my aid one morning down on Colorado when I was especially hungover and foul-mouthed and a score of corner guys threatened to beat me up. Victor had skirted me away, bought me a muffin, and we'd become part-time friends. I won him a few dollars now and then by picking ballgame pitches, which Victor was very grateful for, seeing that he lived over an hour away by bus in Boyle Heights with his wife and three hungry kids.

A chubby guy and his grinning pal were giving it to me now from the opposite sidewalk. "*Oye perdedor! Ir robar el trabajo de alguien más!*" they yelled over and over. I just smiled, shook my head, threw up my hands with incomprehension, but was clearly feeling irritation growing on my neck.

Finally I spotted my friend strolling up from Pico and waved him across the street.

"Shit, Victor! Two more minutes and they would've rolled me in a burrito!"

"What you doin' here, man?"

"Hoping you were getting breakfast today."

Victor gave me a tired shrug. "Wasn't planning to. Drank a little too much Cuervo last night. And I don't know if Jesús is working today—"

"I need to talk to you about something."

He stared at me. I had a serious, shaken look he was familiar with.

"Okay…let's go see."

* * *

Marlene's was an ancient Santa Monica diner of stone and glass and pointy roof wings straight out of the 1950s that served four-dollar breakfasts and famously horrible coffee and always seemed to be packed with laborers and drunks. I could almost afford to eat there on occasion but opted for the free route when Victor was around: his friend Jesús was a busboy.

We waited in the alley behind the eatery, keeping an eye on the back door. The diner was close to the ocean, and we shivered.

"Okay, dude. Spill it out."

I hesitated, glanced around. Our only company was a pair of seagulls pecking at a trash bin.

"C'mon, dude. You been asking about my kids the last half hour and you never do that."

I took a deep breath. "Okay. Kind of afraid to tell you this, because I know that supernatural shit freaks you out."

Victor gave me a sketchy look. "This about demons?"

"Er, no. Has more to do with ghosts. At least I think—"

"Demon ghosts?? 'Cause those are the worst. My sister in El Paso lived in this house once where they had an old wooden Jesus in the garage and blood was dripping out of its eyes—"

"Goddamn, Victor! Let me talk!"

He shrank a little, hung his head. "Sorry…"

"This gang of crazy assholes tried to film and beat me up last night, okay? So I ran into a fancy neighborhood east of Sepulveda. Off of Olympic, I think. Ended up in the backyard of this ranch house. And I heard…at least I think I did…a guy and a woman screaming for help in a burning house."

"What??"

"Except they weren't. I smelled smoke and saw the fire for a second but then it was all gone. Like a haunted vision or some-thing."

"Shit..."

"Yeah. And when I woke up in the morning I could see the place was all boarded up with smoke damage on the outside walls, and it looked recent. So someone had to have died there lately."

Victor wiped his runny nose with a hand. "Wait. What street was that on again?"

"Aw, I don't remember."

"Was it Carden?" He thought another moment. "No, no. I re-member. Camden!"

"It might've been. I'd have to go back and—"

"Because that sounds like that tech dude Jason Ordway's house."

"Ordway?"

"Yeah. He owned like three of them, and I think it was his wife's place. They were broke up—"

"What happened??"

"Chill a sec, okay? There was definitely a fire, and the wife died in it, and Ordway got burned a bit but he escaped. Think it was one of those house invasions but the guys who did it got away.

You didn't hear about this?"

I squinted hard, as if it would help the cause. "Sort of…"

"Shit, it was on the news and in the papers for weeks!"

"I don't read newspapers, Victor. And I don't have a TV, re-member?"

"Yeah, but everybody on the streets was talking about it!"

"And I don't talk to everybody. Sometimes anybody."

The back door opened. Jesús appeared with a bulging styro-foam container. Victor gave me a resigned look and headed over. "Right, I forgot. Graçias, amigo!" He took the container from his friend, who waved and ducked back in. Victor popped it open: three hunks of uneaten French toast, scrambled eggs, two sau-sages and four pieces of slightly burned toast, only one with a bite out of it. We dug in ravenously.

"You ever hear anything like that before, man?" Victor asked. Like…someone screaming for help who wasn't really there?"

"Nope. Wish I knew why I did this time."

"Think it might happen again?"

"How the hell do I know?"

"I mean if you went back there tonight, think you'd hear the same shit?"

I wiped my fingers on my pants, looked down the alley at the nearby street. A showbiz type in a Benz convertible was stopped at a light. "I-I don't know. Why the hell would I want to?"

"Okay, man. Here's the deal. This Ordway dude? He's big news around here because he also bankrolled a couple movies once. See what I'm sayin'?"

"Uhh…no."

"People might pay grande bucks for a scoop on him. So if you went back with a tape recorder—even just a camera, and spooky shit from the Ordway wife came out on it, you could eat real nice for a month. We both could, maybe."

I studied him. "Yeah…maybe. Be nice to have a witness this time, too."

Victor ignored me by flossing between two teeth with a finger-nail. "Anyways, you just go ahead with it. Meet me over on Tennessee in a couple days with the pictures—"

"Are you whacked, man? I need help with this."

"Aww, I can't. Elizabeth is gettin' over a cold, and I gotta—"

I jabbed a finger in his chest. "You come sit with me over there tonight, or you don't get paid jack shit."

Victor slowly nodded. Shaking.

* * *

The Drugs-4-Less on Barrington was a big, disorganized discount house. It was mid-afternoon. Victor combed his hair around the side with a fair amount of spit, then entered and occupied the store manager with a few inane questions while I slipped in through an open delivery door. The place was always short of help, and I had no trouble locating a display of cheap throwaway Kodak cameras without being seen. Caught Victor's eye while the manager's back was turned, then slipped the camera into my pants pocket and hurried out the way I came in.

Victor hooked up with me down the adjoining alley. "You better hope no video camera saw that. I can't afford another arrest."

"No chance. The only one they got is pointed at the register. I snuck out of that place once with a lounge chair."

Victor was picking up speed, glancing behind him. "I don't know, man. I got many bad feelings about this."

"What are you scared of?"

"Huh? You think I'm scared? I'm worried, maybe, but I ain't fuckin' scared, okay?"

An hour later we were parked on crates behind Jo-Jo's Liquor, sharing a fresh pint of Hiram and dining on McDonald's refuse. The drink made Victor even more jumpy. As the daylight began to fade he had the look of a baby chinchilla on the edge of a prairie.

"Last scary movie I saw was *13 Ghosts*—the old one. They had it on Channel 13 one Saturday and Javy wanted me to watch it with him. I know it's like fifty years old with bad acting and suckass effects, but that part when the dad is trapped in the room and the round fire thing is goin' around and it burns a 13 into his hand and he's screamin' and shit? I almost pissed myself! You ever see scary movies, man?"

I smirked, motioned for the bottle. "Haven't seen a movie since forever."

"Yeah? What was it?"

I just sat there in a blur. Victor knew better than to press any further, so stood up and went behind a dumpster to piss.

We spent the next hour or two trying to find an open paint can. Victor's wife had been told he was on an all-night painting job at a restaurant, and he wanted to dab some on his jeans, but the search was fruitless. I talked him into a house watch off Barrington to calm his nerves, though the sight of a budding 14-year-old girl practicing guitar through the den window got him all worked up and mumbling obscene things in Spanish.

Sometime after ten we headed east. Fog wasn't an issue this time, which only made our journey more harrowing. Twice we had to duck behind cars or trash cans when police cruisers went by, and a private security car dropped us on our bellies once we were north of Olympic.

It was close to midnight by the time we slipped down the brick path on Camden. Lights in almost every house were out, and I guided us to the backyard grass, directly across from the boarded-up Ordway house. Victor was freaking out again.

"Get comfortable, man," I whispered, "It's a long night." I dug out my makeshift pillow, leaned back against it in a half-sitting position. Took out the throwaway camera and set it on the grass beside me. Victor took forever to locate a spot, then hopped back up and pissed again on one of the bushes.

"Christ," I said, "Trade your bladder in, would ya?"

"Sorry…I can't help it."

"No shit."

He scratched his hands. He was even afraid to look at the house. "There's no fuckin' way I'm sleeping."

"Good. You can wake me up when something happens."

"But I might not see a damn thing. Right?"

"It's possible."

"Possible that I'll see and hear shit?"

"Just relax, man."

"But what if his wife's become a demon bitch? Ever think of that? She looks in my eyes once and I get bad luck for ten years. My kids'll come down with polio and shit—"

"Victor. I don't wanna be rude. But shut the fuck up."

He opened his gym bag, pulled out a sweatshirt even more filthy than the one he had on. Rolled it into a tube and laid his head down on it, his back to the house. The brandy was still warm and sweet on my breath, making it hard to keep my eyes open. I thought I heard a jet passing overhead but couldn't see it through the overcast night sky. Someone opened and closed a trash can a few houses away, a dog or two barked, and I was able to send my mind down a cozy alley of imaginary comfort.

* * *

"NO! GET THE FUCK OUT OF HERE!!"

My eyes snapped open. Everything was orange, and smoke was in the air again. Victor had bolted. And the woman I heard last night was shouting again.

"WHAT ARE YOU DOING??"

Glass crashed. Fire crackled. I fumbled for my camera. Her horrible shrieking resumed moments later, echoed through the yards. I pointed the Kodak at the house, fired off three flash pictures in a row.

This time I didn't hear Ordway yelling. Only his wife. I got to my feet, raised the camera a second time but it jammed on me.

I cursed, shook the thing. No luck. Was about to throw it on the ground, then stopped myself. Stuffed it back in my pocket.

The orange light faded, along with the smoke and unearthly sounds. I was tired and shaken, and furious at Victor. That was the last time I'd ask that loser for anything. I collected my things and trudged out of the yard, in search of a warm, comfy carport until dawn.

* * *

I was first in line when the Santa Monica Library opened its doors at 10 a.m. Rutledge the security guard who'd seen me off and on when Midnight Star Books was closed nodded and steered me toward the periodical section.

It took a few minutes of doing, but I found a couple of *Los Angeles Times* stories on the Ordway fire.

TECH MOGUL INJURED, WIFE PERISHES IN BEVERLY HILLS HOME INVASION BLAZE

(Beverly Hills *Adjacent*, I thought. They left out that word.) Apparently, Ordway was returning from an "interface seminar" in Santa Barbara and stopped on Camden to see his wife Jo, unaware two assailants had broken in, robbed the place, and set fire to the house. He suffered slight burns trying to rescue her, but was unable to.

There was also a little uncertainty about why he was coming to the house, and what part his relations with a young programmer in his office may have played. The media, as they often do, raised questions for days before the next local scandal replaced it.

I left the library feeling the weight of the camera in my pocket—and knew right away who might help me.

Maybe it's a good time to tell you a little about this person...

❧ FOUR ❧

In Ruby Mellon's view, e-mail was the best and worst thing ever invented. It eliminated ninety percent of the cloying long distance phone calls from her mother, but simultaneously created a flood—no, a tsunami of daily blatherings that throttled her inbox and made it a chore to even boot her computer up in the morning.

Jobworks was on the first floor of a nondescript office building down on 2nd Street. Ruby had trained herself to breathe through her mouth as she crossed the odorous, often packed reception area, but the early arrivals were minimal today. She peeked in her office and was more bothered by the sight of Chloe noodling through paperwork on the desk instead of fundraising in her cube like she was supposed to be.

"Need something?" Ruby asked her in a tight voice.

"Nope. Thought maybe you had the new *Vanity Fair* in here."

"I don't read that stuff, Chloe. And I don't like you snooping at my desk."

"Fine. Whatever." She batted her blue eyelashes at Ruby and retreated to her corner of the room. Chloe had only been fundraising for them two months, but Ruby already had a half dozen issues with her. She was one of those spoiled USC kids who took a part-time job until her screenplay sold or Daddy got her a development gig, and was more apt to make small talk with the celebrities she called than ask them for money. Ruby never considered herself an uptight or punitive boss, but she knew a shit work ethic when she saw one, and had an occasional urge to rip out Chloe's tongue ring.

Ruby took some time to pour herself a black coffee, switched on her Mac and got annoyed all over again. Her mother's IQD (Insane Question of the Day) was waiting for her: *Should I let Dr. Boles ask me out or surprise him with a barbequed tofu dinner?*

Ruby stopped giving her mother romantic advice about ten years ago, after an affair with a Coos Bay whale migration expert went south and Lila blamed Ruby for every shred of its heartbreak. But Lila Mellon was too deep into her crystals business now, and too enamored with her homegrown pot to even notice that Ruby had stopped listening. Lila's last three psychic consultants had run screaming from her, and there was really no one left for her to communicate with.

Not that Ruby had anything against people who dabbled in the beyond. Grandma Flora had made an acceptable living as a psychic healer all over Oregon—she even made house calls. Ruby could still remember the taste of her oatmeal cinnamon cookies, happily devouring them and listening to stacked '45s on Flora's old record player, while Flora would sit at a table in the next room with various strange men and women, holding their hands and whispering. It took a while before Ruby realized she wasn't having love affairs with any of them.

Lila poo-poohed her mother's practice every chance she got, but after she drove Ruby's father into the arms of one of his psychology students at Oregon State when Ruby was 11, she submerged herself in new "alternative" professions twice a year. Detached from her mother and forever untrusting of men now, Ruby cloistered herself in the grunge scene until she was about 21—the night her older brother Erik was found dead in a Portland alley, loaded up on ludes and Guinness.

Ruby tried her best to cry at the funeral, but anger wouldn't let her. She'd been worried about her wayward brother ever since he dropped out of high school, and neither of her parents had the capacity or time in their selfish lives to care about him. Ruby drove past Erik in Eugene one night, caught him wobbling on a street corner beside a fat homeless girl he was slumming around with. The girl had her pants down, big white ass in view as she peed on the curb, and Erik signaled Ruby with a fuzzy wink before hanging his head in shame. Ruby had never seen a sight more pathetic, and couldn't even muster the courage to tell anyone.

After Erik died, though, Ruby sharpened her wits, her drive, her heart. She left Oregon for the North Beach section of San Francisco, realized it wasn't far enough and headed down to L.A. She talked herself into a downtown job in a small human services office and reviewed cases for two years before hooking up with Jobworks.

The homeless population was growing like ragweed, as lower middle class Americans everywhere were slipping through the cracks and joining the ranks. It was little comfort to know this would always guarantee her a job. Ruby wanted a magic wand to be waved that would provide food, shelter and employment for the transient masses, or at the very least cast a spell to make them feel worthy. Was that too much to ask?

The work came natural to her, gave her an undeniable boost every time one of her clients' success stories went up on the office wall. Ruby didn't care as much for the yearly fundraisers, mainly due to the influx of phony, patronizing celebrities they attracted, but she understood their place in keeping the operation running.

She took to me the first time she met me, maybe because my beach-bummy nature and buried good looks reminded her of her brother. The first few times I flaked on her she was unusually upset, and had to keep reminding herself to keep the personal distance required, but I always managed to resurface—especially around the holidays—and she recovered from her mother's IQD instantly when she looked up and saw my furtive face and scraggly locks in her office doorway.

"Nice to see you, Leo."

I wrinkled a smile, took a plastic seat in front of her desk. "You too, Ruby." She looked a little more hefty than usual, I thought, and there were bags under her pretty eyes.

I hadn't befriended many social workers over the years; either I didn't like them or they changed too often. But Ruby was different. For one thing she was genuinely caring, not a phony earth mother or lame student looking for an after school job. As it happened, I met Ruby years ago on her first day at Jobworks. I was fighting through a cheap wine jag, couldn't stand the puke smell on my clothes anymore, and had decided to try employment. Ruby had nothing to offer that first day, but I didn't care. I liked guiding her through the list of questions on her pad, slicing away a layer of unease with each answer.

I also liked her face. Sometime long ago in some forgotten high school I learned that legs and butts and tits were nice but wildly overrated, that the core of a woman's beauty was her face. Eyes, cheekbones, the magic of a smile—nothing could entice and arouse me quicker. Ruby was short, chunky in places, opted for baggy wool sweaters and dopey clips in her boyish red hair, but by God, even though she was probably in her early 30s her face reminded my of a young 18th century duchess I saw once in a painting in Pasadena before the museum guard tossed me out. Ruby had snowy white skin, evergreen eyes, and a smile as warm as a down comforter.

I watched her clack away on her keyboard, something she never failed to do when I sat down.

"Where you been sleeping lately? The cliffs?"

"Naw, I kind of like it in the cloverleaf these days…You look tired."

"Tell me about it. Been up working on a psych paper for almost a month."

"Oh…Doing that grad school thing?"

"Trying to." She hit a button and finally looked at me. "I got cart-pushing work on the Promenade, trash pickup on the PCH, maybe a sandwich costume by the end of the week. What's your fancy?"

I hesitated, then extracted the throwaway camera from my pocket and set it on the desk in front of her.

"If you get this developed for me, and there's something on it we can use, I'll cut you in on the profits."

She gave me a baffled look. "I really think you need to elaborate, Leo."

"I can't right now. Let me just say that something weird's going on."

"Weird?"

"Yeah. Like strange people watching me, attacking me. Other shit, too."

"What other shit?"

I got my sudden feeling, and looked at her phone for a couple of seconds. "Better get that."

She frowned. Two seconds later, the phone rang. She rolled her eyes at me and grabbed the receiver.

"Ruby Mellon, good morning…Uh-huh…Okay, but I'm with a client." I smirked. *Loved* being called a client. She hung up the phone and stared at me.

"I wish I knew how you did that."

I smiled a little, but Ruby could see I was still jumpy.

"C'mon, Leo. Tell me what's going on."

"Okay…It has to do with Jason Ordway. That famous tech dude who's wife died in that fire?"

"What about her?"

"It's kind of tough to explain—"

"Try. Unless it was just another nightmare."

"Come on. Ruby. You think I'd walk all the way here and make this up?"

"No, but you come see me like once a month if I'm lucky. How do I know where you've been or what stuff you've been taking—"

"So you don't believe me."

"Leo, I barely know what you're talking about. And I can smell the booze on your breath." This quieted me down. "Put yourself in this chair for a minute, okay? Homeless coming here in day and night, half of them with crazy stories—"

"Forget it then!" I jumped up, knocking my chair over. Turned to leave.

"Wait, Leo! I'm trying to help you—"

"If you wanna help, develop that damn thing. It's a job possibility I came up with all by myself, Ruby. Thought you'd actually like that."

I put the camera on an adjoining file cabinet and walked out.

* * *

I felt strange after leaving the camera with Ruby, kind of like leaving a possible rare coin with a hot dog vendor. On the other hand, maybe "cashing in" on any of those photos was just another stupid dream in a town filled with them.

I knew celebrities were all over the place in L.A., but to me they dwelled in some unseen parallel universe, a netherworld quietly tucked into the sprawling city quilt. Regular citizens had a far better chance of intersecting this magic plane, though I did have a few brief sightings of my own. Back in the 90s while wandering in Hollywood, Bruce Springsteen walked past me on Melrose Avenue, luring enamored salesgirls out of trashy boutiques behind him like baby ducks.

But that was decades ago. Now it was easy to forget normal, non-homeless people lived there, let alone famous ones.

I found half a slice of pizza in a Wilshire garbage can, and enough change in a gutter for a can of soda. A house watch off Pico from the shade of a pine kept me occupied for a few hours, and it was mid-afternoon by the time I got back to the cloverleaf. I welcomed a nap. The road crew had finished whatever the hell they started the other night, and it wasn't long before the circle of whooshing cars lulled me to sleep.

* * *

A deep chill woke me after dark. Damn fog again, I thought, as I opened my first eye.

Yet there wasn't any fog, and the road crew must have installed a new freeway light because the cloverleaf was bathed in an eerie, orange glow.

An orange glow. I sat up with a start. Sweating. The ivy patch sharpened, faded, pulsated like a heart.

"Help…"

The woman's voice was right behind me. I whirled.

And saw her standing in the ivy, maybe twenty feet away. At least I thought she was standing. The ivy sloped at about ten degrees in that spot, but her feet were still level. No, no—she was *hovering*. She wore a plain white dress that was partly burned off her. Her once pretty face was half-scorched, skin replaced by fleshy moon craters.

I was petrified, but somehow able to open my mouth.

"Jo Ordway?" I croaked, hoping for either verification or salvation. She let out a long, pained sigh, hung her head.

"What's wrong?" I feebly asked.

Her head twisted to the left at an impossible angle, and the sigh rose and rose and became a loud, manic shriek. Cars zoomed up the freeway ramp behind her, their headlights shining straight through her nightgown.

"What's wrong??" I asked again. I had the urge to run up and hug her, but was afraid she'd either vanish or possess me.

"Please…help…" Other parts of her face were now melting away from invisible heat.

"Help you HOW??"

"Help…Leo…" The last piece of her face turned to burned pulp, and she faded away, taking the orange glow with her.

Thirty seconds went by before I resumed breathing. I tossed the bottle I'd been drinking and bolted down Pico Boulevard with my pack.

* * *

The Human Heart Mission was another non-profit operation about five blocks from the Santa Monica cliffs. In cold weather their beds were usually full and doors shut by 8 p.m., but I was counting on the clear, balmier night to help my chances.

I had to knock three times. A scraggly college kid with a goatee opened the door, reeking of mint tea and hostility.

"Sorry, no new beds after—"

"Yeah, yeah. I need one bad, though. Kind of an emergency."

The kid looked me up and down. "How so?"

"Like—someone coming after me."

The kid smirked. "Really?"

"Hey man, don't give me a hard time, okay? I've been living in town for years, I know the streets, and I fucking know I need to be indoors tonight."

The kid raised a clipboard and pen. "How long do you plan to stay?"

"I don't know. Hopefully just overnight."

"Got any laundry?"

"No."

"Looking for work?"

"Yeah, yeah. Every goddamn day. Can I please just go in?"

The kid sniffed, tore off the bottom half of the form. "Bed 31. Fill out the rest and sign. There's pencils inside. And don't make a habit of this."

I grabbed the slip and huffed through the door.

As usual, nearly every cot was taken, and many of the shelter-dwellers were already asleep. It was the usual potpourri of drunks, wayward teenagers and immobile regulars, a handful of them gently rocking or babbling. As I picked my way through the odorous maze, though, I only recognized Daniel Jack and Angel Dust Annie, a homeless couple from Playa Del Rey who always seemed to be curled up like doomed possums. The shelter had a lot of out-of-town guests.

Bed 31, identified by an index card taped to the front bar of the cot, was in a far, dark corner of the cavernous room. I was relieved; I hated feeling surrounded. A snoring old woman with drool on her pillow and pee dripping off her sheet was in bed 32, my only neighbor within three feet. I slipped off my shoes, tucked them under the head of the mattress. Crammed my pack between the pillow and the wall and rolled up on my side.

Some guy across the room was cussing in his sleep until another guy told him to shut the fuck up. Otherwise there were only coughs and labored breathing. I may have been floating in a sea of troubled souls, but at least they were living ones.

I was sitting against my favorite palm, down by the Venice lifeguard station at Westminster. I knew it was a dream because they'd cut that palm down from disease three years ago. A little girl in a pink two-piece bathing suit had wandered away from a parent and was standing directly in front of me, munching a batter-wrapped hot dog on a stick. There was mustard on her face and a dab in her short, nut-brown hair. I was groggy from a brandy binge, happy to see a friendly face. I said hello but she didn't respond and just munched away. I asked if she was lost. She only stared, eyes wider than buttons. I asked if she could get another hot dog for me and a woman's hand clamped on her shoulder from nowhere, yanked her away with a biting, "Don't look at him!"

I snapped my eyes open, furious. Remembered the little girl being real once, maybe in my early, blurry homeless days, but I'd comfortably drowned it in alcohol long ago. Why was she bubbling to the surface again?

And what was that drooling, pissy old woman doing now, whispering in her sleep? I had rolled onto my back at some point, but without even turning my head knew that she was sitting up and staring at me, curious and judgmental at the same time. The little girl and her horrible mother combined—

"…Believed in him…"

It was a strange thing for a drunk old woman to say. I raised my head, dared myself to look at her.

Oh shit. She was levitating.

Two inches above the cot, fresh urine dripping off her ankle. Her head had an orange aura behind it, so I could see every inch of her face, which inside an explosion of dirty white hair was clearly dead.

"I believed in him…" She was addressing someone above her, or beside her. It was hard to tell.

"HE STRAPPED ME IN…" she suddenly blurted, pained and pleading, eyes blank and hollow. I was paralyzed. Watched as she reached into the air with a glowing, bony hand. A putrid stench came with it, and I glanced at her dirty scalp line, now laced with wriggling worms—

I shouted, sprang off the bed. Grabbed my shoes and pack and tripped over someone's leg. Voices told me to shut the fuck up but I was out the door in seconds.

* * *

I figured there was at least a week to go before the next police sweep and I was right: The cliffs at the end of Broadway were riddled with sleeping shapes. I hurried to the well-known patch of flat grass, a spit away from restroom no. 3, and thankfully saw Swifty there on his rolling board.

Swifty had no legs and jackhammer arms, slept in the daytime and kept himself up all night with Bolt Colas. After being discharged from the vet hospital, he took on Dracula hours, likely residue from the Iraqi tank shell which took off his legs one night at Medina Ridge in '91. Swifty didn't say much, but he was a lighthouse on wheels, alerting the cliff crowd of impending weather, psychotics, and lawmen.

He nodded as I approached, instantly caught the panic in my eyes.

"You on somethin'?"

I shook my head. "Can I stay here?"

Swifty almost grinned. "You got a reservation?"

"Don't mess with me, Swifty. Not tonight." I dropped my belongings on the grass, glanced in every direction as I sat. Swifty looked at me a long time, then handed me the remnants of a pre-rolled joint. I thanked him with a nod, smoked it up and stretched out with the pack under my head. Fronds rustled overhead, waves shushed on nearby sand, but the soothing sounds were no comfort.

"I believed in him…"

"He strapped me in…"

The mystery of Jo's appearance now boring into my mind, I wasn't sure I would ever sleep again.

❧ FIVE ❧

The Jobworks door was locked. Assorted homeless sat or paced on the sidewalk, but none that I recognized. "Thought they opened at 8:30!" I screamed to whoever would listen. One guy checked the time on his ancient iPod, peered up through sand-crusted eyes. "It's 8:24, dude!" I rapped on the glass doors anyway. The pavement gathering grumbled, stirred to life in case I got results.

After three volleys of raps, a supple young woman in jeans and a yellow Radiohead shirt appeared on the other side of the door. She had blue eyelashes and didn't seem pleased.

"Sorry, not open yet," Chloe mouthed.

"I need to see Ruby! Tell her Leo's here!"

"Ruby's in at noon. I'll tell her—"

"No please! She has something of mine, and I need it back!"

Chloe squinted with her mouth open. The morning sun glinted off her tongue ring. "It's an emergency!" I continued. Finally she rolled her eyes, unlocked the door and I slipped inside. The sidewalk people hooted and jeered.

"Thanks!" I said, moving quickly through the empty waiting area. Chloe seemed to be the only person around. "I would've waited till later but I really, really need this—"

"Tell me what it is and I'll look for it."

"A camera. One of those cheap throw-out ones. I was hoping she'd go develop the pictures but I'll try to do it myself."

"Pictures of what?"

I fidgeted, looked at the floor. "Oh…just a place. I can't really—"

"You're Leo, right?" She smiled coyly. "I've seen you here a few times."

"Yeah. Just trying to get through the day. Think you could look for me now?"

"Sorry, I can't. Ruby loses it when I go in her office. She'll definitely be here at noon if you wanna come back—"

"No! I mean—I can't wait that long." Chloe frowned, ready to either call 911 or boot me out herself. I paced nervously around in a small circle. Scratched at things in my hair.

"It was Victor's idea, see, to take the photos at the house. 'Course he didn't wanna be there, but how was I supposed to know, right? So we get there for an all-nighter and he freaks and he splits, and now I got Jo fucking Ordway haunting my ass because her husband may have helped kill her!"

Chloe was stunned. "You mean Jason Ordway?"

"I'm sorry, I'm sorry. I'm making no goddamn sense right now. Know what? Let me try something else and maybe I'll come back for it later. Tell Ruby I was here."

"Okay, sure." I turned and headed for the door. She ran over to unlock it for me. "Have a good day, alright?" I nodded faintly and was quickly up the street. The other homeless swarmed the door and she fended them off by pointing to her watch and putting up five fingers.

After I left—I heard what happened between her and Ruby from the both of them in the next few days—Chloe walked to her cubicle, churning my words through her brain. Phillip, one of the new caseworkers, came in the back door and waved. "Did you make coffee?"

"No," Chloe said, " Go for it." She waited for him to duck into a small kitchen area, then made a beeline for Ruby's office.

The camera was right there on a filing cabinet. She pocketed the thing and left the room.

"Phillip? I forgot I got this quick errand!"

"Now??" he said from the coffeemaker, "We're opening the door!"

"So stall them a little. See you in a half hour!" She grabbed her bag and keys and ducked out the back exit.

* * *

The library wasn't open yet, so I bee-lined it to the Apple Store on the Promenade. I rarely went in there but when I did, it was important to wedge my pack somewhere outside or around the corner in an alley and put my hair under a cap and wipe any stray dirt off me. Apple had at least a dozen employees on the floor at all times, and all of them seemed to be looking at me.

I cruised past the new iBook laptops and found one I could access the Internet on. Googled *Ordway Fire* and found at least seven or eight headline stories from various online news places. The first one that caught my eye was PLEASANT PAST LED TO STORMY PRESENT in the *Orange Country Register*. Jo Shaw had a comfy, uneventful childhood in Cincinnati, moved to Southern California when she was sixteen. Her dad was a reputable surgeon, her mother a piano teacher. Horse riding filled her time, along with communication studies.

When she met Jason Ordway at a software convention in the Bay Area, everything changed. She gave up school and became Ms. Ordway, traveled the Caribbean and ski resorts with him and her photo appeared in *People* on occasion, happily on Jason's arm. When Ordway scored a few box office hits with two produced action thrillers, she relished their new upper-scale lifestyle for a while until she got bored, busied herself and carved out an image with various charities and global hunger projects.

Ordway's immersions into the tech world created distance between them, caused a few affairs, and to keep their sanity they divorced with Jason buying her the ranch house on Camden.

A second article I clicked on with a large Apple guard staring at me and inching closer was mostly concerned with Jo's parents' coping strategy, but it ran with a two-column photo of them, posed in front of a magnolia-shaded Tudor, or something close to that style. Mr. Shaw had his arm around his wife in a half-clutch, both of them wearing forced smiles. I read the caption, which referred to their "new Sherman Oaks home", and a thought sparked in my head. I scanned the entire story again, then the caption. Then the picture again.

There was a space between the Shaws' house and their neighbor's, with a patch of green hill clearly visible through the gap. There seemed to be a tree house up there, except it was round, and didn't seem to be made of wood. What the hell was that? I tried putting my eyes closer to the screen, then stood back for the wider effect as the guard came up behind me.

It was a water tower.

"Can't be browsing in here," said the guard, a line I doubt he repeated to non-homeless individuals.

"Sorry. I um, got what I needed. Thanks..." And quickly left.

On the Promenade I was able to beg for enough change to make a call at one of the last pay phones on the west side. I didn't know if Ruby was in yet but thought I'd leave her a message anyway.

* * *

The one-hour photo place was on Santa Monica, two doors down from a Coffee Bean. Chloe was stoked about that because she'd skipped breakfast, and the Bean had these new low-fat cinnamon raisin muffins that were beyond sick. While her mocha brewed, she stood in the back with her muffin bag and an inner smirk, pleased with her latest ploy to mess with Ruby's mind.

That bitch never liked me, she thought. *People up north have sticks up their collective butts about L.A. She probably resents even being here. Forget the fact my dad's rich and I got more industry contacts than her, she's too much of an arrogant puke to even look at me. Twenty to one she has hair under her arms.*

"Decaf percent mocha latte for Chloe?"

She sat with her coffee and muffin, surfed the net and watched a half hour sitcom on her iPhone, then returned to the photo place.

The Korean lady behind the counter had a weird guilty look about her. "Something happen. Not my fault."

"What happened?"

The lady spread out a half dozen of the glossy prints on the counter. I had taken one flash photo after another of the Ordway house, and in practically every one, a weird, swirling orange fog was visible through the windows.

"First I think it's developer, but I check and it's okay. So maybe camera broken. It cheap one—"

"No wait. Let's see the rest of them."

The lady frowned, then spread out the whole batch. Chloe stared at each print with growing excitement. One of them stopped her cold.

It was a closer view of one of the windows. Maybe it was the light, maybe it was the angle, but a terrified Jo Ordway was clearly sitting sideways in a chair, right in the midst of the orange fog.

Chloe slumped against the counter, clutching the print.

"I only charge you half—

"No, no. They're perfect. Make another set." Her hand was already fishing into her bag for her wallet. She plucked out a twenty and dove back in for her cell phone.

* * *

There was a time when I used to love the heat. I knew this because whenever Santa Ana winds kicked in and blew all the exhaust fumes and acid smog out to sea and made my hair crinkle, foggy memories of laughter and pretty girls' faces came with them. I once knew a homeless guy from the Midwest who said an August day in St. Louis could knock you over. L.A.'s heat was never like that. It was dry, deceptive, drilled its way into your eyes and brain and sinuses until you screamed at a driver while using a crosswalk, or flopped down for a 4:30 nap with your head splitting.

Santa Anas were especially bad because they often brought

wildfires. New arsonists emerged from apartment cocoons, fruit flies of hell who struck their matches and masturbated to the resulting news coverage. I never forgot the Malibu fires of '93, when the sleepers on the Santa Monica cliffs were overwhelmed at night with local residents watching the distant inferno, the same way I imagined Washingtonians watched the Battle of Manassas from their carriages.

The one good thing about Santa Anas was that they rarely lasted three days, but as I trudged up Barrington, turned right on Montana and a hot breeze slammed into my cheek, I knew they were just beginning. Normally, if I were choosing to walk to the San Fernando Valley I would take Sepulveda the entire way, but for obvious reasons I wanted to avoid the giant Veterans Cemetery just north of Wilshire. Jo Ordway was still groping at my soul, and the last thing I needed were a hundred dead soldiers pitching in. Besides, this stretch of Montana had far more shade.

My plan was simple enough: Walk over the Sepulveda Pass, straight into Sherman Oaks. I knew it would be ungodly hot, knew I might not get there till dusk, but thoughts of meeting Jo's parents and finding out if their daughter had some connection to me would keep me going. I snuck around the side of a house just before Sepulveda to load up two discarded water bottles from a coiled hose. Packed away my jacket, then dug out a soiled, adjustable Angels cap I found in Venice once and secured it on my head. There was no sidewalk on Sepulveda, but the shoulder was wide and there were plenty of bushes in case I needed to piss. The freeway snaked up and over the pass on my left, and the sight of the Getty Museum, stunning and lordly on its baking perch, filled me with hope for mankind, though if I ever tried to enter it I would probably never even get past its gate.

* * *

Chloe was aggravated already, and Hunter Drake hadn't even arrived. It took three calls before he returned one, then insisted on meeting for dinner. She really had something he wanted this time, though, and managed to whittle him down to a late breakfast at the Overland Cafe. What the hell, she wasn't going to eat anyway.

Chloe met Hunter, star producer/reporter for The Buzz Channel, at some movie premiere after-party in Los Feliz, and they got it on for three weeks until he went to Vegas to cover a porn convention and slept with an actress named Allura Vivaldi. Chloe stalked him a while and left dead flowers on his doorstep, until he apologized and agreed to an occasional friendly fuck. It was actually a better arrangement for her. She didn't have the patience for a true relationship and really just liked being seen with him. And if she ever gave him a great scoop, something he craved more than life itself, well, who knew where that could lead.

He finally walked in the congested eatery and dropped into a chair across from her. The points of his bleached spiky hair looked sharper than last time she'd seen him, though the deep tan and dimples hadn't changed.

"Hey. Sorry. Two actors left the same rehab clinic on the same day and I got footage up to my throat." He grabbed the menu, bounced his khakis. "What's the word?"

"Well…I think I have something incredible for you."

"Incredible is good. Do they still have those fresh raspberries?…"

"Are you listening?"

"Don't I always, babe?"

Chloe had to pause and brace herself. Hunter was in his usual overdrive, reminding her once again why they were incompatible. "Okay. Jo Ordway?"

"I've heard of her."

"She might be back."

It was his turn to pause. "Back. As in family lawsuit?"

"As in supernatural."

He stared at her, befuddled.

"Her house, Hunter. In Beverly Hills Adjacent. It might be haunted. Check these out—"

She glanced around, then handed him one photo at a time, saving the best for last. "Is that not Jo Ordway?"

"Who took these?

Chloe hesitated, cherry-picked her words. "This guy Ruby Mellon knows. He was over there the other—"

"A homeless guy?"

"Yeah, a homeless guy. Big deal. He was crashing in her backyard and snapped them off."

"You don't think he Photoshopped them?

"I just had them developed, Hunter. And I doubt he even knows what Photoshop is. He's just a nice, normal homeless guy—"

"You seeing him?"

"Don't be a prick."

"Sorry. Hard to resist sometimes."

A gum-chomping waitress arrived and Hunter ordered a poached egg on lightly browned wheat toast, herbal tea and fresh raspberries. He checked a number on his vibrating phone.

"You're dreaming…Okay, so what's your ransom for these? A finder's fee? A weekend in Rancho Mirage?"

"I was thinking more along the line of…co-producing the segment."

He smirked, ready to explode in laughter. "You must be high. A segment?"

"Jo Ordway haunting her boarded-up house is not a segment?"

"Not when the lead comes from a Santa Monica bum pushing a shopping cart."

"He doesn't have a cart. And you're not supposed to call them bums."

"Come on, Chloe. You know what my life is like. If I don't come up with something sexy, druggy, or scandalous once a week, my stock goes in the crapper. And five precious minutes about a *homeless individual* who may or may not be a psychic scam artist is not exactly moist-see TV."

"It isn't about him, Hunter. It's about Jo Ordway. Can't we just leave him out of it and air the photos?"

"Why do you keep saying 'we'?"

Her eyes went volcanic. She grabbed the pictures back, then her purse. "You know what? Fuck you, and fuck your raspberries. I'm sorry I tried to help you out."

"Chloe—"

"Have a shit day!" She stormed out.

He rolled his eyes and ran out after her, caught her on the sidewalk.

"Okay, you win. Leave the photos with me, and I'll talk to Gortner, see what I can do."

"You mean what *we* can do?"

He sighed with some effort. "Right."

* * *

Ruby walked in the Jobworks back door, immediately noticed a packed waiting room. Phillip darted across with a couple application forms, obviously overwhelmed.

"Where's Chloe?" she asked him.

"Hell if I know. Called an hour ago, said she had another errand. Left me with the frickin' Alamo here."

"Great. Let me just get settled, and I'll jump in."

She ducked into her office, checked her voice mails. The first one had a hollow, outdoor pay phone sound. And my raspy voice.

"Ruby? I came by to get the camera but you weren't there! Some girl was but she wasn't much help…"

Chloe entered from the parking lot in mid-message, out of breath. Heard my voice and lingered outside Ruby's door.

"Anyway, I wanted to tell you something else…Jo Ordway was haunting my ass all last night, and I heard her say 'He strapped me in.' Not sure what that means, but it doesn't sound good. I um… I'll call you back–" I hung up. Chloe let my words ferment in her brain. Ruby was already whirling around to her cabinet. Saw that the camera was gone. Chloe started for her cubicle and Ruby spotted her.

"Chloe?" The girl paused, came back to the doorway. "Did you see a camera in my office?"

"I don't go in your office. Remember?"

Phillip poked his head in. "Can someone please take Midge?"

"I will in a second," said Ruby.

"I can take her—" said Chloe, trying anything.

"No, Chloe. You stay right here and tell me what you did with that camera."

"You think I'm lying?"

"I don't know. Should I?"

"You should try trusting me for a change."

"Trust you? You're gone the whole morning doing God knows what when we're stuck with a full waiting room. How do I trust that?"

"Ruby, come on. What the hell would I want with a cheap Kodak throwaway camera??"

Ruby smiled. Chloe suddenly realized why she did and fumbled for her next words.

"Oh…Well, I'm sorry. Leo was here and told me about it, and I knew you were busy and just thought I'd help you out by getting the photos devel—"

"So why did you lie?"

Chloe wanted to melt into a puddle like the witch in that famous old kids' movie she saw once. "I don't know, I…I knew you'd be mad if I was in your office—"

"Alright, enough. Just give me the photos."

"I can't. See, that's the other problem. The dumb lady at the photo place ruined them. Or maybe Leo did. They were all over-exposed."

"No kidding."

"Yeah, it really sucked. So I just…threw 'em out. Anyway, I'm gonna go check my e-mails." She exited, headed for her desk. Ruby clenched her fists, then her mind, and walked after her.

"Don't bother, Chloe."

"Huh?"

"Just keep walking out the door. You're fired." Phillip looked up from his desk, where he was interviewing a ragged black man. The entire waiting area stared. Chloe stood there in a frozen fog bank.

"Why?? Because of a stupid camera?"

"No, because I don't like you!"

"Well, isn't that fucking news." She threw open one of her drawers, grabbed a makeup bag. Snatched a bottled water off her desk and marched out. Ruby calmed herself, turned to face the waiting area and worked up a smile.

"Midge? Why don't you wait in my office." An enormously fat old homeless woman made her way past, mumbling to herself. Ruby exhaled, leaned over Chloe's computer to shut it down. Saw she had five new e-mails and got a thought. Clicked on the mail icon to bring them up.

One was from Hunter Drake: GORTNER BIT ON THE PICS. CALL ME WHEN YOU CAN.

Ruby wanted to scream.

❧ SIX ❧

I could feel the wall of valley heat a half mile from the top of the pass. Thankfully I was in shade, but going uphill neutered that perk in a hurry. It was also early rush hour, meaning a slow parade of exhaust and throbbing urban music to add to my headache. Nobody was hooting at me, yet I could feel the sting of obligatory glances, could smell the stench of indifference.

What I really wanted to do was shrink myself and follow a lizard under the nearest concrete slab. Normally I would just pick up my pace, establish a cardiac rhythm to screen out the world, but not on this hill, not in this ungodly heat.

Sockless, I could feel every pebble through my paper-thin sneakers, and knew a blister on my small left toe had already ruptured. I was halfway through my last water bottle, with no garden hose in sight.

I came upon a hollow wedged between two large bushes, and ducked into the cool, dark space to catch my breath, watch the northbound cars crawl by. Maybe if I just took a nap here it would be night when I emerged, and the traffic would be gone. But that would mean sleep and a possible dream, maybe even Jo's cadaverous face or clammy hands—

No. This would be a quick breather, and nothing more.

It also gave me time to mine my troubling thoughts. *What if that water tower was gone? What if Jo's parents had moved away or died? If I even found them, what the hell would I say?*

On the other hand, I'd created an actual mission for myself, a goal, and I couldn't remember the last time I had one that didn't involve food or shelter. I stretched out in the hollow, leaned back on my elbows, shut both eyes. What I wouldn't give for a tall glass of lemonade and one of those phones that played music. I was in the mood for something tropical, maybe even Brazilian. One of my favorite afternoon pastimes in the last twenty years had been to hike up to the third floor music section in the old Borders chain or at Amoeba Records in Hollywood to sample their musical wares. I remembered a rainy day once when I must have stood in the same spot, lost in Gregorian chanting for a full hour, before some executive type flipping through the female vocalists complained about my body odor to the teenager at the register. I circled the block a few times and gave it another try, but the store security goon was stationed out front and that was that. I knew about turnover, though, and a month later a new sleepy guard that I could walk by had replaced the old one, and the teenager was probably off to Pepperdine.

Lying in the thicket now, I conjured up a twangy, bass-driven reggae beat to fill my head. The whooshing cars morphed into sea waves, the hard, thorny ground beneath me into a swaying hammock. I kept the beat going and almost dozed off, but a slow whisper filtering through the coconut trees jerked me awake. I sat up, turned. The whisper was soft, more like a long sigh, and moving through the bushes behind me.

"Jo?"

No reply. A twig snapped, one of the bushes moved. My heart pounded blood into my throat. The whisper became a hiss, and a four-foot-long Mountain Kingsnake slithered from the undergrowth. I yelled, grabbed my pack and dove out of the bushes in a cloud of dust. A few of the drivers threw their brakes on, rolled ahead when they realized they weren't threatened. I shook myself off and kept walking, sleep and reggae booted from my mind.

* * *

Down in Santa Monica, the Buzz Channel corporate offices occupied the entire top floor of a green-glassed mini-high rise off Cloverfield, a budding west side corporate neighborhood that mainly packaged entertainment products for the masses and clogged traffic for locals.

Hunter Drake demanded the best corner office on the floor some time ago, and was constantly perturbed that his ocean view was more and more blocked by construction cranes and new buildings. Not that he was even in the office that often, but when he was, with his coffee and bowl of fresh raspberries, he liked to see water.

"Hunter? There's a Ruby Mellon here to see you."

Willy's voice never failed to annoy him, but this was unexpected and made him grit his teeth. "Tell her I'm in a meeting."

"She says it's an emergency. About some photos?"

"Christ…Okay, send her in." He quickly collected the photos at the edge of his desk, tucked them under some papers. Stood up and moved out to a plush leather seating area as Ruby entered the room. He narrowed his gaze and snapped a finger.

"I know we met once."

"Only once. The Mission Relief benefit."

"Right, right…So I gather Chloe sent you here?"

"I sent myself here. Chloe was just sent packing."

He tightened his expression. This was obviously news. "Oh. I wasn't—"

"Can I have the photos please?"

"Photos?"

"Cut the bullshit, okay? They belong to one of my clients who's going through a lot right now."

"Hey. I'm sorry. But I don't—"

"I saw your goddamn e-mail, Drake."

Hunter turned away, returned to his desk. Rearranged a few items on it.

"I wasn't really going to do much with them. Chloe's the one who thought they were newsworthy."

"Didn't sound that way."

The phone buzzed, with Willy's voice again. "Hunter? Chloe on line 1."

Ruby glared at him. "Don't you dare…"

"I probably should."

Ruby mouthed the words "I'm not here" as he lifted the receiver.

"Hey…" He listened for a beat. Drummed his fingers. "You're kidding…Well, I guess she had her reasons." He worked up a silent yawn. "Chill, okay? I didn't mean anything by that." He rolled his eyes at Ruby, who declined to react.

Then his fingers stopped drumming. He leaned forward on the desk. "He heard what?" Now Ruby was engaged. Watched Hunter grab a pen, jot down some words. "Well, it certainly waters the tree…Yeah…Sure, I should be home by ten. Later." He hung up, looked at Ruby with a barely-contained smirk.

"Don't tell me," she said, "The 'strapped me in' bit?"

"You gotta love it. May not amount to shit, but it sure makes the story pop. How about this—" He sprang from his chair, sat on the front of his desk facing her. "Your client, face kept in shadow, his name unused. Telling his story for five minutes. No longer, no shorter."

"Don't you people have enough other lives to ruin? This is a homeless man."

"I know what he is. Trust me, he will be an anonymous homeless man. We can do this thing with his voice, too. Make him sound like a homeless space alien."

"I don't think so—"

"He'll be a few thousand dollars richer."

Ruby's eyebrows hopped. She settled into a chair. "So that's how you do these things?"

"What do *you* think?"

She exhaled, contemplated a tall, rustling palm outside his window. "How many thousand?"

"Two. Three. Standard rate."

"In cash?"

"If that's what it takes—"

"Up front?

"Partly. How much are you going to want?"

"Nothing. I work non-profit." She stands. "But if Chloe gets within two inches of this arrangement, it's history. I'm the one who's going to find him, and convince him. And keep his head on straight while it's happening. When are you thinking of filming this?"

"Soon as possible. We're way past Halloween, but supernatural celebrity stuff always flies."

"Well…Guess I better start tracking him down." She turned to leave, came right back. "Oh—and you might want to fork over his advance."

❧ SEVEN ❧

I hadn't been in the Valley for a long time—maybe even since the weekend with Violet. I met her picking through a dumpster behind the library one day, and we talked about books and places to sleep as we shared a Wild Turkey bottle across the road from Santa Monica Canyon. We made it through some sloppy screwing that night and the next, before she insisted on bringing me to her "luxury crib" out in Tarzana. Violet was maybe 25, a runaway from Nebraska ten years earlier, with cute sunburned cheeks, sandy hair sprouting from her armpits and the kind of braless, droopy boobs I always liked. She also screamed at imaginary persecutors in her sleep and peed in public, but I was going through a severe loneliness phase at the time and put up with her craziness for some company.

She lured me in the free back door of a bus one morning and got me out to the Valley, but we were drunk on a pint of something else before long, stumbling around a grid of commercial strips in Reseda. Violet wandered into a mall while I took a leak in a nearby alley, and that was the last I saw of her. Spent the next three hours getting lost, eventually forgot who I was looking for and ended up sleeping off a trail in the Santa Monica Mountains.

Today would be a more successful trip; I was sure of that. Basked in some cool air walking through the tunnel atop the pass, took the heat punch when I emerged, then descended through a pretty Sherman Oaks neighborhood with plenty of garden hoses to slurp from and trees to duck behind when police cars passed. By the time I reached Ventura Boulevard I was actually invigorated, and scaled some parking garage stairs to its roof to scope the hills around me.

Daylight was fading, and a smoggy haze still choked the trees, but I could make out telephone poles, the spire of a church or synagogue off to the right. A ribbon of headlights snaked down the 405 just to my left, balanced perfectly by the glowing red tails climbing beside them. I narrowed my gaze and studied every inch of hill on both sides of the freeway, searching for anything that resembled a water tower. There were dark shapes here and there, but all of them were houses or extensions of houses or clumps of sneaky pines. I scratched my head, moved to the stairwell on the far side of the roof.

Which is where I spotted the water tower, re-painted in grey but the obvious match of the one in the article's photo. It had been blocked from my view by a small high-rise, and now winked at me in the setting sun, a shabby industrial siren luring me closer. I hustled down the parking garage steps.

* * *

I should have known: Things seen from a distance in L.A. often take forever to reach. The maze of curvy foothill streets didn't help, all without sidewalks, and before long a new blister on my right heel was splitting open and my throat felt like tree bark. I lost sight of the water tower at least twice, retrieving it both times accidentally by randomly choosing a direction.

The residences here were squat but lush, and beautifully vegetated. If I wasn't hurrying to find one in particular, I might've leaned against a tree for an extended house watch. Except here, I was the one on display. A young homeowner bouncing his baby stared at me from his living room window before drawing the shades. A woman in her garden grabbed pruning shears and ducked in her back door. I tried my best to nod or smile at the judgmental ones, hoping it would avoid a 9-1-1 call, but it was never a sure bet.

The third time the water tower vanished I thought I'd lost it for good, suddenly finding myself at a high wire fence, a steep, scorched hillside and a NO TRESPASSERS sign riddled with B-B dents. But a break in some tall, nearby pines revealed a flash of bulbous grey, and as I inched closer the full bottom of the structure revealed itself— only a couple hundred yards away. I rounded another corner and the house from the library photo appeared like a Tudor fairy castle.

It was larger than I anticipated, though rundown in places. The white stucco exterior was in need of a paint job, the lawn a good mowing. There was no mailbox with a name on it, though; knocking on the door would be a crapshoot. Worse, I'd forgotten about my appearance. Checked my reflection in the side window of a Chrysler parked across the street, and it was enough to make the glass crack: filthy hair, sweat drenching both armpits, pants that could have been tugged off a Khmer Rouge dragging victim.

I went to work immediately. Cupped water in my hands from a nearby lawn sprinkler and soaked my scalp, then fabricated a ponytail with a slice of recycled adhesive tape from my pack. Hurried around someone's garage and turned my tropical shirt inside out to dull the pit stains, then tucked it into my pants. I crouched, rolled up the cuffs three times to hide a hanging garden of rips. The decrepit sneakers would have to do.

I returned to the Chrysler window for a final check. The end result sure wasn't gorgeous, but a drastic improvement nevertheless. A neighborhood security car rolled past a block away and I straightened my posture, shouldered my pack and ambled across to the stucco-framed door.

I lifted my knuckles to knock, changed my mind and pushed the doorbell instead: a church-belly two-toner. Ten seconds passed before I heard any sound at all, a blue jay yelling at me from a nearby tree. *Was anyone home?* There was no car in the drive, though there might have been one or two in the giant closed garage. I hadn't bothered to look.

Suddenly there was a dull click, and a short, attractive woman in a flowered pants suit swung open the door. It was clearly Jo Ordway's mother, despite her aged face and slightly stooped posture.

"Yes?"

I remembered I needed to talk, and twitched first. "Hi. I'm looking for Glenda Shaw?"

She squinted. "I'm Glenda. Who are you?"

I put out a sunburned hand. She stared, and I retracted it. "Leo. I'm an old friend of your daughter. Jo."

Glenda took a quick, deep breath. "She passed away, you know."

"Yeah. I just found out. Like a week ago. I've been out of the country a real long time. Traveling. Backpacking."

"Oh. So you do know how she…"

"I heard a couple of the details. Is um, Mr. Shaw here, too?"

"Yes, but he's not fit to see visitors—"

"WHO'S AT THE DOOR, GLENDA?" His gunpowder-filled voice boomed from a nearby room, and Glenda rolled her eyes.

"A young man! Says he knew Jo!"

"WHAT'S HIS NAME?"

Glenda touched my arm. "I'm sorry. What was…"

"Leo. Smith."

"Leo Smith!"

There was a long pause. "DON'T REMEMBER THAT ONE!"

"We worked together, actually," I said, speed-thinking, "On one of those hunger projects she did."

Glenda looked impressed, turned to the dark hall behind her. "He says they worked on one of her hunger projects!"

"SO GIVE HIM SOME MONEY!"

Glenda began to retreat. "I'll get my checkbook—"

"Wait!" I said, suddenly desperate, "I just want to talk about Jo a little. Actually I need to. She um…meant a lot to me." I wiped a convenient drop of sweat off my cheek with a wrist. Glenda stood there, softening.

"Maybe you should come in. I made a pitcher of Arnold Palmer—Raymond's favorite—and you look awful thirsty."

"I am, actually. That would be great—"

"HOW MUCH DID YOU GIVE HIM?"

Glenda rolled her eyes, swung the door wide open. I stepped inside. It was a high-ceilinged foyer with buttery walls, and I instantly felt at home. A fragrant tomato aroma wafted down the hall.

"Stay here. I'll get you a glass."

"WHAT'S HE DOING?"

"Having an Arnold Palmer, that's what he's doing!"

"WHAT??"

She shook her head irritably, disappeared down a long hall.

I didn't move right away. Then a dagger of hot sun hit my face through an overhead skylight and I took a few brave steps around the foyer. After staring through windows of dwellings like this for so long, it was surreal to be walking on a polished hardwood floor, to pass directly in front of a watercolor desert landscape. To hear an icemaker rattle.

"Tell me if it needs more sugar." Glenda had returned, handed me a tall, frosty glass with golf clubs on the sides. I sipped it, nodded my delirious approval and drank half the glass right there.

"My! Glad I made a pitcher!"

"Me, too…Whatever you're cooking, by the way, smells real good."

"Oh, just an old family spaghetti sauce. Thank you, though." There was a quiet, awkward moment. I looked at the floor. "I might have some extra angel hair if you're hungry."

"Really? I mean, are you sure it's okay?"

She nudged me toward a dining room. "Go sit with Raymond and I'll be right in with your plate." I turned down a short side hall, paused to inspect a row of framed family photos. There was Jo, age thirteen or fourteen and apple-cheeked, on a ski trip. Seventeen at a senior prom. Then a photo from the last few years of her life, with her mom and dad at some Hollywood dinner. Jason Ordway nowhere in sight.

"WHAT ARE YOU WAITING FOR?"

Raymond Shaw's voice startled me, and I stepped into a sunken, Tudor-style dining room. Most of it was taken up by a long, mahogany table with wood so dark it was nearly black. Raymond sat in a wheelchair at the far end of it, twirling spaghetti. He was more shrunken than Glenda, as if any discernible joy had been squeezed out of him like an old washcloth. He was wearing a bib and gazing at me.

"I don't remember you at all." His voice had calmed, thankfully, but still retained its tenor. I attempted a smile, walked over and dropped into a side chair a few feet away.

"You probably wouldn't. We just worked on a couple of things together. Before she died." The old man grumbled something, took in a clump of pasta. "I bet you still miss her," I said.

Raymond drank a bit of *his* Arnold Palmer. "Every damn day."

I had a sudden thought. "Sorry I wasn't around for the funeral," I said, "Wasn't it in that cemetery with the angels over the gates?"

"Nope," said Raymond very matter-of-factly, "She burned to death so they just burned the rest of her."

"Here you go!" Glenda reappeared and set a rapturous plate of food in front of me. Golden angel hair smothered in sage, diced tomatoes and real parmesan. I felt like I wanted to cry but restrained myself.

"Thank you…I haven't eaten like this in a while. When you backpack everywhere it's mostly soggy sandwiches and trail mix." I plowed into the pasta like a desert island escapee. Glenda watched me, a bit curious.

"Now which project was it that you met my daughter on?"

I paused to swallow and think. "The big one. For the hunger?"

"The Uganda Relief Fund."

"Yeah, that one. Lots of people. A real success." I polished off my Arnold Palmer and reached for the pitcher. Glenda grabbed it, poured me some more. "And then there was this one for homeless people we worked on."

"There was?"

"Yeah. It was a while back and only for a week so she probably never got a chance to tell you about it. And I left to travel abroad around then, too."

"Hmm. You're right. I don't remember—"

"It was called Mission for the Mission. We met lots of destitutes." Raymond had cleaned off his plate and was dozing in the wheelchair. "I've actually been trying to get in touch with some of the people we met on that. Did she ever mention any?"

"Any what?"

I was lying myself into a corner, but couldn't stop now. "You know. Homeless people. Thought maybe she kept a notebook or something that would have some of their names in it."

"Hmm. I suppose she might have."

There was a long, silent pause. I was afraid to look up from my plate. "Do you have a lot of her stuff?"

Glenda looked at me oddly. "Some things. Personal mementos, mostly."

I nodded, ripped off a hunk of nearby garlic bread and mopped my sauce with it. "But you don't remember any kind of notebook or address book?"

Glenda saw Raymond was asleep, reached over and wiped his soiled mouth with a napkin. "I don't believe so. If we did it would be in a box in our second floor attic...Why do you need to know?"

"Well, there was one guy I really need to get in touch with again."

"Who was that?"

"I uhh...I'll recognize it if I see it."

Her expression twisted like an old croissant.

"Hmm...Before I forget though—"

She reached around to a side table and grabbed her purse, pulled out a checkbook and pen.

"Another $100 for the Uganda Relief Fund should help, right?"

"Uhh...right. Would you possibly have that in cash?"

She wrinkled her nose at me. My facade was crumbling.

"Oh don't be silly. They'll be happy to take a check and you can tell them hello for us. And I'll tell you what—"

She tore off the fresh check, handed it to me. I slid it into my pocket. Then she reached back into her purse, took out a notepad and slid that over. "Write down your phone number for me. I'll snoop through Jo's things when I can and call if I find what you're looking for."

I stared at the notepad. It was from the Two Palms Country Club. My hands were suddenly clammy.

"Phone number?"

"Yes, or just put your address down. In case there's anything I can mail to you."

I picked up the pen. It was an expensive ballpoint that felt heavy in my hand.

"I um, kind of don't have a real address right now."

"Oh! So you're in a hotel? Just write the name—"

"No. I'm not. I mean I can't."

She was clearly puzzled. And then I smelled smoke.

"Is something burning in your kitchen?"

She sniffed the air. "I don't believe so. Why?"

"I just—"

And then I heard its accomplice: crackling fire. I quickly stood up, knocked my chair back.

"WHAT'S HE DOING?" yelled Raymond, suddenly waking back up. A misty orange glow slowly filled the hallway behind him.

"Are you alright, Leo?"

"No! I mean—I'm sorry, gotta split!"

Grabbed my pack and ran to the front door.

"WHERE'S HE GOING??"

* * *

The streets that were lush and comforting on my way there were now pine-infested spike pits, poisoning me with hidden eyes. Poplar Glen? Ardmore? Still fucking Oak Terrace? I knew that the more lost you thought you were, the more lost you became, but panic was in my DNA and even if it began as a slow leak it was a ruptured hydrant in no time. I had been keeping my homeless feelings under wraps all day, but now they were throttling me.

I was no stranger to ghastly, punishing shame. But the panic I felt at the Shaw house was a darker hue. I'd gone there looking for an answer and bolted in terror from a home-cooked meal. *Why did I think I'd be able to fool these people? What the hell was I thinking?*

Then I suspected the police may have been called. Twice I crouched behind hedges when I heard approaching cars or saw headlight beams. If I could just find that damn commercial strip.

I finally did, lured by the sound of a bus, an aura of blue neon behind a rooftop satellite dish. I really needed to piss out some of that Arnold Palmer, and hurried into an alley behind Ventura Boulevard. I chose a space between two dumpsters, a few yards from the back of a kosher meat market, and let loose. The stream was so loud and my relief so profound I didn't see or hear a bulky, curly-haired shop worker walk out to the alley with two plastic bags of trash. One was flung into the open dumpster beside me, the other smashed over my head.

"Scumbag fucker!!" the guy yelled in a strong mid-eastern accent, "I teach you to pee on my store! Moshe!"

A second worker nearly identical to the first ran over.

"Hold this asshole while I call someone."

I made one weak attempt to stand and was slammed to the pavement face first, a knee lodged in my spine. Tried to raise my head and someone knocked off my Angels cap, grabbed my hair and held fast. The police were already cruising the neighborhood and appeared in less than a minute. I peered up from the asphalt and caught their shiny boots, fit physiques. Their hands yanking on tight black gloves.

❧ EIGHT ❧

Elsewhere, Ruby was having what she liked to call "an evening to dismember." It was difficult enough to track down a homeless who wanted to be found. Many of them were nomadic, their habits tough to predict, and acquaintances often too inebriated or self-absorbed to be helpful. Besides, I had left her office earlier in a state of angry, anxious confusion. I could literally be anywhere.

She had ever-shifting files of "residences" of homeless clients who came through Jobworks, and much of the info was unreliable days or hours after it was entered. I was what she called a "semi-monogamous dweller," someone who favored two or three regular spots, so it didn't take long to jot down what she needed and go out again.

She naturally started with the Centinela cloverleaf, but my cardboard bed was unoccupied, and there was a faint dead animal smell she chose not to investigate. The Human Heart Mission and Ocean Avenue cliffs were the next obvious choices, but no one in either place had seen me, though Swifty did promise Ruby some info if she let him feel her boobs. Ruby politely declined.

She had a plate of black pepper chicken and bottle of Singha at a reasonable Thai place off the Promenade. The sun had long dropped into the Pacific and she was about to give up for the night when another possibility occurred to her. I once mentioned crashing in a pedestrian tunnel that ran under the coast highway at the foot of Santa Monica Canyon. She thought it had been a one-night stay caused by a sudden February downpour a few years back, but who knows? If I was trying to get away from people today I could very well have gone "underground".

She drove down the California Incline to the PCH. It was close to 10 p.m. and a fog bank was tucking itself into the canyon. She parked her Accord on a side street next to a closed liquor store and rickety apartment building and made sure to double-set her car alarm. Residents here were largely well-off, but the canyon had a sticky bohemian feel close to the water that brought out the paranoid in her. She had two friends in Venice on the same street whose cars had been broken into, and this neighborhood was only slightly better than that one.

The tunnel stairs were at the end of Entrada, just past a tacky row of darkened souvenir and beachware shops. She walked briskly toward them, the fog so thick she nearly bumped her knee on a parking meter. Naturally, she hadn't worn the right shoes, and had to clutch the rail to keep from slipping on the damp steps.

The tunnel was lit by a blinking bank of fluorescent lights close to the stairs. Beyond, except for a cloud of moon-tinted mist barely visible at the far end, the passage was dark. Unseen drips echoed, overlapped. There was a dead, salty aroma. Ruby waited for her eyes to adjust, took a few steps.

Her foot hit a large, soft clump and she gasped, jumped back. When the thing didn't come to life she crouched, groped into the darkness—and touched a discarded, sopping wet beach towel. She took a deep breath and kept moving.

The fog bank at the far end gave the tunnel an otherworldly feel, like a corridor into one of those parallel universes she used to see on old *Twilight Zone* episodes. What made this bearable was the faint whoosh and pound of ocean waves, muted through the thick air but present nevertheless. Her mom always loved the sea, and used to sleep on the Oregon coast next to campfires when she was little. She once told Ruby that waves were really the voices of Neptune's daughters, singing her lullabies in a strange oceanic tongue only they could understand. Ruby firmly believed this, and was found in the local library one day asking for a non-existent reference book of oceanic words. She wished the wave sounds in the tunnel were louder, but they were better than nothing, and kept her moving onward.

Then she froze. Just ahead, she could make out another dark

shape, curled against the wall. This one was breathing.

"Leo?" The booming echo of her own voice startled her. The dark shape twitched. She inched closer and could make out a tattered blanket.

"Leo, is that—"

The stray dog lept from the blanket with a ferocious bark. Ruby recoiled, swatted the air with a hand. The mutt growled once, scampered into the mist. Ruby collapsed against the tunnel wall, shaking. She'd prepared herself for a snarling, boozy transient, not a wild-eyed fuzzy creature, and her whole metabolism needed re-alignment.

Listen to the waves, Ruby. Just listen to the waves…

She tried that, but for some reason they were getting softer when they should have been washing over her ears. The flickering tunnel light suddenly went out, and she was left in near darkness.

A wave finally did break on the shore, but it was light and ethereal and almost sounded like speech.

"Tell himmmm…"

Her forehead felt clammy. The circle of mist at the far end was spilling into the tunnel. She held her breath, sharpened her hearing for the next wave.

"Tell him for meeee …"

Did she really just hear that? No. Impossible. A third wave broke, but this one was loud and sounded like pure water. The lights behind her sputtered back on. Her forehead felt cool again.

She hurried out the far end of the tunnel. Gave the near-empty parking lot a cursory check, then darted up to a ghostly traffic light to wait for the walk sign.

* * *

I knew I was dreaming again, because no jail cell had a bed this soft. Hell, the room those two Valley storm troopers threw me into didn't even have a bed. I was lying on my back in an al-

ley between two 50-story buildings, so that the wedge of bright blue sky looked more like the end of a tunnel. Still, birds chirped and darted in the sky patch and a breeze hit my face and there was a fragrant jasmine odor (which was strange because I never smelled things in my sleep) and even trickling water somewhere.

I couldn't see the bed I was on because I was so comfortable and had no interest in raising my head, but I knew it was some kind of undulating fabric that molded itself to my body and cradled each of my limbs with a separate dollop of care whenever I moved one.

Who gave me this bed, and why did I deserve it? I'd gotten so used to flattened cardboard that I'd forgotten what a real bed felt like. This one was like laying on heaven-scented pudding, and the thought of having to eventually get off it frightened me.

Overhead, the blue sky had turned grey, and the birds were growing dark and fat. Their chirps were now caws, and they soared down the shaft, multiplied. Hovered in front of my face with their talons flexing, beaks unhinging, Spanish words spewing out in the same raspy, human tongue...

"Wake the fuck up, cholo!"

An unclipped fingernail poked my rib, and I was wrenched awake. In the dim, dank holding cell I could see two Latino thugs crouched in front of me. The one who jabbed me wore a backwards Lakers hat and boa constrictor tattoo up one arm and around his neck.

"There a problem?" I groggily asked.

"Fuckin' right there's a problem! Pumpin' out shit clouds while you sleep!"

"I'm sorry. I didn't—"

"Sorry's no good, cholo." He motioned to his looming buddy, who was twenty pounds heavier and chewed on a toothpick. "We need you in that fuckin' corner before Hector here rips out your kidneys, comprende?

"Yeah, yeah. Sure…"

I rose, hobbled my way around a handful of other shadowy losers, and hunkered in the far corner. The two thugs strolled over anyway, sniffing the air.

"Know what, Hector? It's no shit clouds. This piece of gringo just stinks like my uncle's port-o-potty. Know that one at his Pomona site? When you open the thing on a hot day and you can't breathe 'cause there's ten pounds of old turdcakes down there and you dare yourself to not look but you do anyway? I think we're lookin' down that hole right now." He blurted out a chuckle. Hector didn't laugh, just raised one of his size 16 basketball shoes and nudged me in the shoulder.

"Leave me alone, scum," I muttered. Hector's expression turned from stolid to psychotic. He raises his shoe again, poised to flatten my nose. I shut my eyes, ready for the crunch and the pain, ready to be through with this sick, uncaring world…

"Que pasa?"

The shoe retracted. Both men stared down at me, turning pale, then backed into the darkness. An eerie orange light had filled my corner of the cell, wrapping around me in misty swirls. I felt the undulating softness again, but this time I was sitting up. And wide awake.

"Shit…"

Tried to get to my feet but the orange mist wouldn't let me. A woman's voice grew in my ear, a voice I'd heard at least twice now.

"Help me…"

"Jo?" My voice echoed across the concrete floor, and two of the sleeping inmates stirred.

"Who's he talking to?" asked Hector.

"Who cares? Stay the fuck away from him!"

I looked up at the ceiling in anguish. "I can't help you if you don't tell me how!"

The woman in my ear sighed. "Help me and I'll help you."

The orange mist pinned me in the corner. My chest hurt, like it was being squeezed from behind. I struggled onto my knees and two sections of mist half-solidified in front of me—both of them women's hands.

I shouted in horror. A guard clanged his keys on the cell bars. "Shut up in there!" I sprung to my feet somehow.

"Hey, let me out! I gotta make a phone call!"

"Sorry, jerkoff. You had your chance last night and you passed."

"I changed my mind, okay? It's an emergency!"

"Let him do it, man!" yelled the first thug, "Get him out of here! He's crazy!"

The guard turned away to exchange words with a cohort. There was a pause, and he returned to the cell door. Yanked out his key ring.

It took 90 minutes for Ruby to show up; to me they seemed like hours. I didn't have her home phone or cell, and had to resort to leaving an hysterical message at Jobworks I was certain she'd never get. When the watch commander announced she was on her way, a massive weight was lifted, but I still couldn't look at my cellmates again without expecting them to knife me. Actually, the two Latino guys wouldn't come within a yard of me now, even though the orange aura disappeared the second I was let out to make my call. I was as baffled as they were by the event, but was glad it got me out of trouble—and that the spectral hands were gone.

Ruby was bleary-eyed but happy to see me. After some private words with the watch commander, she paid the public urination fine while my face turned red and we were on our way.

"Your message said Sherman Way, not Oaks. I was driving in circles for half an hour." I muttered sorry, and she took my elbow, guided me out into the cool dawn air. "What the hell did you go to the Valley for?"

I hesitated. "I don't know. Just...needed a real long walk."

"To the Valley??"

"Just open the car."

She unlocked the passenger side of her Honda and I rolled in. The freeways were jammed already so she opted for Coldwater Canyon instead.

"Did you get any sleep in there?" she asked, watching my eyes try to stay open.

"Some. Wasn't all that helpful."

"Well, grab some while we drive. We're having breakfast with this guy and you need to shower at my office first."

"Breakfast? With what guy?"

"Just a friend, okay? Someone who might be able to help you."

"With what? A job? A shower?"

"Close your eyes, Leo. Please?"

"Will you settle for one?"

Ruby smirked a little. "One's fine."

She felt strange being at Jobworks at the crack of dawn, and waiting for someone to take a shower was even stranger. The building used to be a paint store, and still had a plastic shower stall off the rear supply room. Ruby offered to let their clients use it if the odor in the waiting room ever proved unendurable.

I gave myself a natural alley shower a month or two ago during a downpour but a passing police cruiser cut it short before I could wash my armpits with a gob of dish soap. This one was a true luxury. The water hammered the plastic basin at my feet and I constantly put my head in the way to muffle it and massage my temple. There were no weird sounds in my ears, no weird light filling the room, just bliss, a hot waterfall gushing down from points north and through these pipes and over my scalp...

Except the water was cooling off. The bathroom's mirror had fogged up. I suddenly felt very alone, and vulnerable.

"Ruby??"

I could hear her pacing outside the closed door. "I'm here! Wrap it up, okay?" I killed the shower, slid open the curtain and opened the door, my face dripping.

"Have I met this friend of yours?"

"Uh-uh." She handed me a navy T-shirt with a snappy Job-works logo. "Try this on."

"What's his name?"

"Hunter. Let me see if there's a pair of sweats—"

"Don't."

"What's that?"

"My pants are part of me. My identity. Your friend will have to…y'know, accept them."

"Fine, just get dressed."

I closed the door again. Could hear Ruby drop into a nearby chair. "I didn't know you had an identity, Leo. At least one you'd like to share."

I stared at my foggy reflection in the mirror for a long moment. "Leo?"

"Can I pick where we eat breakfast?"

"Well…sure. Not too fancy, though."

"Okay…"

Marlene's was stuffed with commuters, laborers, and yawning beach punks. I sat in a big circular booth with Ruby and Hunter Drake, wolfing down a Big Daddy special. Hunter, already uneasy from the clientele, sipped a glass of pulpy juice, shot Ruby an impatient look. She nodded and tapped my arm.

"Need anything else? Got enough butter? Syrup—"

"I'm cool."

"Okay. So let's talk about why Hunter's here."

"He wants to become a homeless person?"

Ruby snickered. Hunter rolled his eyes.

"Good one, Leo. No, Hunter works in television. He's a producer, and wants to put you on the Buzz Channel."

Hunter's chest puffed out a bit. "Ever watch *Celebrity Soup*?"

I gave him a vacant, slightly hostile stare. Ruby jumped in.

"It has news tidbits about famous people—"

"Tidbits?" sniped Hunter, incredulous. "Try segments."

"And he knows about your ghost thing with Ordway's wife, and wants to do an interview with you. A short one."

I stopped chewing my pancakes. "You mean put me on TV? I-I don't know."

"No one will see your face," said Hunter.

"Yeah, but what am I supposed to say?"

"Nothing personal, I promise. You can even change your name—"

"I like my name." A wedge of pancake fell from my mouth. "Don't go changing my goddamn name!"

The other customers turned, stared. Ruby clutched my arm. "Sssh…it's okay, Leo. We don't have to. First they're going to show those photos you took, then—"

"You developed them? Why didn't you tell me? Are they here?"

"They're at my office," said Hunter, coolly. "Trust me, they're spooky."

That made me nervous, and I returned to my meal. "I don't think I want to see them, actually."

"Anyway," continued Ruby, "all you need to do is tell your story. About the other night at Ordway's house."

"Which night??" I dropped my fork. "She's haunting the FUCK out of me every time I close my eyes!"

"Leo! Please keep your voice down. And keep eating, you'll need it."

I took a deep breath, picked up the fork again. Slipped Ruby a glare.

"Why did you tell him? And show him the pictures—"

"It wasn't me, okay? It's a long story I can tell you later."

"You said this guy here wanted to help me. I don't see how putting my shit on the air is gonna help—"

A pair of hundred dollar bills left Hunter's shirt pocket and landed on the table in front of my plate.

"That's your advance. You'll get the rest after the interview."

I stared at the bills, then at Hunter. Picked one up and inspected it. Caressed one of Ben Franklin's cheeks with a finger.

"Shit. I um…I think I need to talk to my agent first."

They gazed at me for an awkward moment before I snorted and gave them a big, toothy smile. Jesús, the busboy who fed me scraps in the alley two days previous, passed by the booth with a tub of dirty dishes. I waved, held up my drained water glass.

"Señor? More aqua, por favor!"

Jesús kept walking.

In the parking lot outside, Hunter pulled Ruby aside.

"Have him at the studio 4 p.m. sharp. He's going to need serious prep time."

"No problem. Where's the phone?"

He nodded, fished out a cheap maroon cell phone still in its plastic sleeve. "It only comes with 100 minutes, but he probably has no one to call."

"Yeah, except me."

I was leaning against a newspaper box, still gazing at one of the bills. Ruby walked the phone over to me.

"Yours for the day, so we can reach each other. Do not lose it."

"Where *you* going?"

"I have a job, remember? I'll pick you up at 3:30 on the Promenade. At the dinosaur fountain."

"We can't do it earlier?"

"No." She saw I was anxious, fidgety. "You'll be fine, Leo. I really think talking about this stuff will help. You're also making a little dough here, and that's a great thing." I half-smiled, pocketed the bills. "What are you going to spend it on, anyway? "

"Not what you think, I'll tell you that."

"What am I think—oh, never mind. I trust you." She leaned in and gave me a friendly peck on the cheek. "See you this afternoon. And put the phone on!"

She walked off to her car. I found the phone's power button

after a few failed attempts and it made a melodic chirping sound as it lit up. Stuffed it in my pants pocket with the money and headed toward 3rd Street.

❧ NINE ❧

It was a dazzling morning on the Promenade. Moms and Latino maids with strollers, slackers, skateboarders and a handful of fast-walking businessmen enjoyed the sea-cooled air. I passed the gaudy spitting dinosaur fountain where I was due to meet Ruby later, a few clothing chains, burger places and that useful Apple store. There was a spring in my shuffle, a heavy burning sensation in my right pants pocket, a feeling I belonged in public. Crossed Arizona with a gaggle of pedestrians, unafraid to actually smile at a few, and headed over to the window of a Starbucks. There were maybe half a dozen people in line for drinks. I licked both hands, slicked back my hair the best I could and opened the door.

The sweet, nutty java aroma nearly flattened me. A Coffee Bean around the corner had given me water cups a few times, and I remembered liking the smell of that place, but it couldn't compare to this. The dark, stylish décor, soft Billie Holiday on the sound system, scattered books and newspapers, the reading and writing and laptopping coffee drinkers filled me with instant warmth, with belonging, with a love for pure sanity and civilization. Two women at the rear of the line managed to turn and eye me, but for the time being I didn't care.

"Good morning!" I said.

"Hi," one of them uttered, and turned back around. They edged a bit closer to the guy in front of them.

"Can I start something for you?" It was a barista, a pale young girl with her purple hair tied up.

"Yeah! I'll take a big size coffee with some stuff in it."

"Like what stuff?"

"Oh, um…espresso or cappuccino would be cool. What's good here?"

She blew a strand of purple hair out of her eye. "Take a look.

It's all good."

I glanced up at the menu board but it was too overwhelming. "You pick for me. I've never been here."

"Fine. How about a caramel spice mocha latte with extra foam?"

"Awesome, yeah."

I moved up to a register and the beaming register guy already had the drink rung up. I groped in my pocket, took out the crumpled hundred dollar bill and the guy stared at it.

"Anything smaller?"

I shrugged. "Sorry, man."

"Well, we're sorry, too. We can't take anything bigger than a twenty."

The hair on my scalp began to itch. Maybe not every person in the place was looking at me, but it sure felt like they were.

"Hold my drink."

I snapped the bill off the counter and marched out with my head down.

I had to flash one of the hundreds at the corner bank to get the security guard to open the door for me. Two old ladies were in line for a teller, and my neck bristled with the guard's stare the entire five minutes I was waiting behind them. The teller inspected both hundreds with everything but a metal detector, before reluctantly breaking them into twenty ten dollar bills.

Minutes later, I strolled down the Promenade with my mega coffee drink. Sat on an empty bench to relax, to take in the air and a nearby banjo player, but a homeless girl I didn't recognize dropped on the bench across from me after a few minutes and I felt too self-conscious to sit there.

The lower part of the Promenade had more restaurants and the entrance to the Santa Monica Mall. I stopped at a row of kiosks to buy cheap sunglasses and replace my lost Angels cap with a new old-fashioned one with the halo on top. Then I crossed Broadway and entered the mall.

A couple of homeless loitered at food court tables, and I hurried past them to avoid eye contact. My coffee was delicious but the buzz intense, and as I rode an escalator to the second floor the skylights and colors and weird indoor sculptures and trees made me dizzy and I needed to grip the thick rubber rail to keep from tumbling back onto shoppers.

I had been in this mall a handful of times but never made it past the food court. I always imagined the mall beyond as a wondrous assortment of shops and stores that could better my life if I ever had a real one, but seeing this sad collection of pet toys and boot barns and light bulb emporiums firsthand filled me with disappointment. There wasn't even a bookstore in the place.

And all the walking was starting to make me hungry again. The array of eateries on the lower Promenade had many cute hostesses perched out front toting menus, drawing me in like food sirens, but I still wasn't entirely comfortable being normal and wanted a place where I wouldn't be judged.

There was a low-key Italian café called Frankie's a half block up from Broadway. It had a striped awning and some empty outdoor tables in the shade. I helped myself to one after exchanging nods with a server and got comfortable. Every item on the menu looked delicious; the cheesy sauce smell wafting out to the patio was enough to knock me out.

After a minute or two a thin, pony-tailed waiter appeared, pad and pen ready.

"Yes, I will have the chicken and mushroom pasta. With extra penne."

"The penne is the pasta."

"Oh. Right."

"Soup or salad? Today we have minestrone."

"No," I said, handing him the menu back, "just bring me the soup."

The waiter sighed, jotted something down. "And what would

you like to drink?"

I paused. I'd promised Ruby I wouldn't indulge. Hell, I'd promised myself. But this was a special day for me, the sky was blue, and I still had three hours to get things together.

"Give me a wine with that."

"Red or white?"

"Oh…whichever tastes better."

The waiter's mouth tightened and he went inside.

After a few minutes basking in the sunshine with my eyes shut, the waiter brought me a glass of superb white wine and I drank it down in no time, ordered another. A middle-aged affluent couple joined me on the patio and I smiled at them until they looked away. I was finally relaxing, there was a cell phone in my pants and all was heavenly.

Then the pasta arrived, a modest but scrumptious portion garnished with herbs and lightly tossed and a breadbasket included and I didn't want to be anywhere else. I took my sweet time drinking the second wine, took out my cell phone and poked around with its buttons…

"Leo? What the fuck—"

I looked up and saw Duce at the railing, armed with his overstuffed yellow pillowcase. I flashed that I could probably just ignore him and pretend to be Leopold, Santa Monica man of leisure, but didn't have it in me.

"Hey Duce."

Duce's mouth nearly unhinged. "I was right! You did become a big-ass executive!"

"No, no. I just got a little check in the mail from an old relative. Decided to give myself a real day out, if you know what I mean."

"Hmph. Thought you didn't have no relatives."

"Yeah, well…this one was distant. It's kind of like a belated birthday gift."

"Uh-huh…That's cool." There was a long, awkward silence. I dug back into my pasta and Duce studied every chew. The waiter reappeared, saw Duce and leaned over the rail.

"You need to keep walking, sir."

"Yeah," replied Duce, "and you need to suck my big dick."

"It's okay, man," I said quickly to the waiter, "I know him."

The waiter gave us both squinty looks and went back in while the young couple stared. Duce kept his killer sneer on.

"Fake Italian fuckface faggot…"

"Hey. Duce. You should really let me finish my lunch. I would do the same for you."

"Oh. That's good. And when's that gonna be? When Bill fucking Gates puts me in his will?"

I stared at Duce until he began to pace a little and scratch his head. "Okay, okay. Shit. Enjoy your gourmet lunch." He walked away a few feet, then moseyed back. "Say, now that you're one of them elite people, you got a couple bucks I can borrow?"

I fished in my pocket, handed him a five. Duce grinned and gave me a dazzling wink. "Thanks, brother. Catch ya later." I grabbed my wine, drained the rest of it in one gulp as Duce finally left. Raised the empty glass for the waiter through the window, but when the guy reappeared he was carrying my check.

"I'll take that when you're ready."

"Oh. I was thinking I'd…" I read his irritated face and set the glass back down. "Nothing. Thanks." When the waiter left again I looked at the $28.40 on the check and started dropping cash on top. I had no idea whatsoever how much to leave for a tip, counted the bills out until they reached thirty dollars, then collected my things and stood up, a bit tipsy from the good wine. The affluent couple still eyed me, and I climbed over the rail instead of walking past them.

Duce's surprise visit put me out of sorts. The wine didn't help, its buzz-demons merrily poking their pitchforks into my temple. I was used to drinking Mateus or Big Daddy Merlot, a cheap bottle from Argentina, when I drank the stuff at all. Crossing 2nd Street

I nearly got hit by a bicyclist, and had to stagger back against a light pole to keep from falling into the gutter. The cliffs were just a block away, and I focused on their rustling palms to keep myself moving.

Damn that Duce! Here I was feeling good about myself for the first time since whenever, and the bastard had to show up and smash it all, like taking a golf club to an ice sculpture. Well screw him, I thought as I weaved across Ocean Avenue, I still got a few hours here, and Leopold ain't dead yet.

It was refreshing to be on the cliffs in daytime, when it wasn't a homeless sleepaway camp. Toddlers and roller bladers and wealthy middle eastern families were among the folk drinking in the sea breeze and lush walkways, and I smiled at most of them as I passed.

There were still a handful of homeless, though, sprawled on the grass or propped against trees, and after averting my eyes a few times, I began to feel awkward again. I turned, walked a few blocks to the neon archway at the end of Colorado, and headed down the steep ramp to the Santa Monica Pier.

I normally stayed off this congested wooden protrusion; tourists and Pomona residents fleeing inland temperatures flocked to it, meaning the homeless were a lot less tolerated. Leopold belonged, though. Leopold would blend right in and enjoy the sparkling afternoon.

I walked into a giant arcade, bought myself five dollars worth of tokens and used them all playing Skee-ball. I missed badly with the first few tosses, but a black boy in the lane beside me offered a few pointers to spare me total embarrassment.

The boy then dropped into the seat of a hyper-realistic driving game called Long Beach Grand Prix. "Wanna race me?" he asked, motioning for me to take the empty seat and wheel next to him. I froze, staring at the demo view of whizzing city streets, hairpin turns, cheering crowds lining the route…

"No," I said bluntly, "I get dizzy." Shut my eyes for a long moment, snapped them back open and abruptly left the arcade.

I walked to the far side of the pier, and the salty breeze revived me. A handful of scruffy Latino fisherman leaned against the rail to my left, adjusting their long poles, cleaning their catches. A few had their boys with them, and I marveled at the silent, methodical way they went about feeding their families.

The fish aroma wasn't helping my condition, though. My stomach suddenly tunbled like a dryer, and I ran to a nearby trash can to make myself throw up. Then I slid to the opposite rail and focused on the breaking waves below. Boogie-boarding kids and surfers bobbed in the water all the way up the coast like cormorants, and the sound of the surf calmed me again. I made my way to a wooden staircase that led down to the beach.

I didn't spend a lot of time on the sand, even though the beaches here were vast and clean and picturesque. I knew a few homeless down in Venice that had been badly beaten or arrested while trying to camp out, and the beach patrol guys did their best to keep "riff-raff" away.

Venice was sort of a freak show, though; I had a better chance of solitude if I walked north of the pier. I found a virtually empty stretch of sand below the cliffs and close to the water, and removed everything but my cords. Rolled up the cuffs, bunched one of my shirts into a pillow, and laid on my back, dark glasses in place, to let the sun put me to sleep.

With the alcoholic poison now out of my gut, I felt wonderful. Relaxed. The satiny sand under my back beat any cardboard box, and the waves whispered in one ear, out the other. In one ear…out the other…

I am part of this earth, I thought…part of this earth…

I was in a marshy field. Blue sawgrass all around me, growing so high I couldn't see over it. Breathy voices called to me, or was it the wind-blown grass, the fluttering of bugs, a loud hum of a bumblebee…

Something throbbed on my thigh. Throbbed again. I sat up in a daze, yanked the cell phone out of my pants pocket. A lit message in front said CALL FROM…UNKNOWN. I flipped the thing open.

"Hello?"

I heard mostly static, but a garbled woman's voice was in there somewhere.

"Ruby? Is that you?"

The static cleared. The voice sounded far away.

"There you are…" she said.

"Ruby? You gotta speak up. I can hardly—"

"There you are…"

I froze. It didn't sound anything like Ruby.

"Who is this?"

More static. Than a desperate, but even fainter "There you are…"

I closed the phone, shoved it back in my pocket. The sun had moved in the sky, and the tide must have retreated because the waves were strangely quiet. I had a terrible headache, and had the sudden inescapable feeling I was being watched.

I glanced around, peered up at the cliffs. People strolled along, oblivious, admiring the view in conversations I couldn't hear. But none of them were looking at me. I turned back to the ocean, a murky shade of grey despite the brilliant sunshine. The waves were white and foamy and cresting right in front of me, but for some weird reason I could barely hear them, like the voice I just heard on the phone.

Low whispers came from my left now. I looked in that direction, slightly behind me, and saw the same young couple I'd seen watching me the other day at the 14th Street bridge. They stood on the beach about ten yards away, facing me, but their feet were below beach level, as if the sand was up to their calves. Standing at the same impossible angle they shared on that embankment.

They were still in dark dress clothes, gaping at me with stunned, vapid expressions. I raised my sunglasses and squinted, trying to make out more detail on their pale faces, but there was a fuzzy quality to the air, like a desert mirage, that wouldn't let me. All I knew was that a horrible queasiness came with the vision, and I felt faint.

The cell phone vibrated again. I knew who was calling now. Yanked the thing out and flipped it open—

"WHAT THE LIVING FUCK DO YOU WANT FROM ME??"

"Leo?"

This time it was Ruby. Kind, fully alive Ruby.

"Oh Jesus. Oh shit—"

"Are you okay? Where are you?"

"On the beach. There's this creepy couple—"

I spun around. They'd vanished again.

"Great. You're getting a tan and I'm sitting next to a dinosaur in a red zone."

"I'm sorry. Forgot to check the time—"

"Never mind. Just meet me up at the pier entrance. Five minutes."

I nodded instead of saying goodbye, closed the phone, then put the ringer back on in case she called again. Grabbed my bunch of clothes and hurried off the beach without raising my eyes.

Ruby was cool on the surface, but her obvious irritation leaked into her driving. Twice she came within an inch of slamming the car in front of us. My story about the ghostly phone call and couple in black only made her more anxious.

"I can smell the wine on your breath from here, Leo."

"That had nothing to do with it."

"Really. Positive it wasn't just heat stroke?"

"It wasn't hot on the bridge that day. And it doesn't explain the phone call."

She blew a strand of hair off her face. "Pretty freaking weird, Leo. Might as well throw it on the fire for Hunter Drake, right."

I bounced my leg like a madman. "How long's this gonna take?"

"I told you already. Two hours. Max."

"No, no. The drive!"

She shrugged. "Who knows? Forty-five minutes? It's in Hollywood, and traffic there usually sucks. Need a bathroom?"

"No…Just drive."

❧ TEN ❧

The Buzz Channel studio was on Cahuenga, on the seventh floor of a steel and glass "media center." I sat with Ruby in a bright waiting room filled with minimalist furniture, feasting on a lush, mystical view of Hollywood's hills and lordly sign.

The vista was certainly a peaceful distraction from the manic vibe of reception. Tart young women and oil-slicked guys whizzed through with clipboards, dry cleaning, go cups of coffee, half of them chirping into headsets.

A mannequin-faced blonde in a jean mini-skirt finally arrived to escort us down a blinding hall filled with the same hyperkinetic energy. I had taken a moment to tuck in my Hawaiian shirt, but my pants were too low and it was spilling out again. Ruby nudged me to leave it alone, so I fussed with my ragged hair instead.

"We meet again!" It was Hunter, greeting us at the door to Studio D. I shook his hand sloppily, eyes downcast, and we were ushered inside. Rolling cameras and sound booms and grips and another army of wired mayflies skipped around them and I had to drop into the first chair I saw.

"You okay?" asked Ruby.

"I don't know. A little queasy."

"Here then." She gave me a peanut health bar and bottle of lemon mineral water from her bag. I ripped the bar open with my teeth and began devouring it.

"Okay Leo," said Hunter, crouching down after being careful not to crease his pants, "Ready to do this?"

"Yeah. I just—"

"Great. Then we need you on this chair over here for makeup."

"Makeup? I thought people wouldn't see me."

"True, but even a silhouette needs a touch-up. Over here please."

I grumbled and stood. Followed Hunter to a lonely stool propped in front of a giant blue screen. The moment I sat a mousey girl with an eyebrow ring appeared and began combing my hair. Or tried to.

"Jee-zus," she said, mashing the implement into my molten collection of sand, lint, dead bugs and hair. I grimaced as the girl tugged a few times, then gave up and tied the whole mess back with a rubber band. Hunter dropped a hand on my shoulder.

"Now all you have to do is sit here, relax, and answer a few questions. Take your time, and say anything you want to. We'll pick out the best stuff later in post."

I nodded, still overwhelmed, and was left alone. Took a deep breath, squinted as a spot lit up the blue screen from behind and plunged me into shadow. I could make out an elaborate video camera on wheels a few feet away, a drooping sound boom and faceless gathering of crew members.

"Keep your eyes on me, Leo," said Hunter, parked in front of a nearby monitor with a headset and clipboard.

"Okay."

"Speed!"

"And we…are…rolling."

A red light blinked atop the camera. "Leo?" asked Hunter, "Tell us what happened the other night. At Jo Ordway's death house."

I shifted my bottom atop the stool. Scratched my face.

"Well…I needed an emergency place to crash—I mean sleep that night. It was kind of foggy out, and I couldn't—"

"Foggy? That's great. Start again, but this time describe the fog. You know, get into it a little."

"Yeah…It was super foggy out. When you can't see a block away. Real spooky. And I needed a place to sleep and found a way into their backyard. Not knowing it belonged to Mrs. Ordway. The house, I mean. Was that enough about the fog?"

"Perfect. Keep talking."

"So…I fell asleep, and woke up again in the middle of the

night. Victor had already freaked out and split like hours ago. Left me with the camera—"

"Time out. Who's Victor?"

"Oh wait. That was the second night I was there. When I took the pictures."

"Leo? We need a little help here, okay? Please try and tell the story in the order it happened."

"I *am* trying. Think this is fucking easy for me?"

Ruby leaned over Hunter's shoulder. "Can you just let him tell it his way and fix it later?"

"Are you telling me how to produce my segment now?"

"No, I'm telling you how you're going to get through this damn thing. In case you haven't noticed, Leo isn't real good at taking direction."

Hunter stared at the ceiling a long moment, then hissed. "Fine. Say it the way you want, Leo." He nodded at the assistant director.

"Speed!"

"We're rolling!"

I took a deep breath, fussed with my hair again. Hunter gave me a gleaming, patronizing smile from the shadows.

"Okay. Now tell us what happened…in the middle of the night."

"Everything was orange. Not a bright, fruity orange but like a fire orange, and I heard crackling. Smelled smoke."

"Go on…"

"Anyway, I took the camera and just started clicking. No, wait. That was the second night. With Victor. The first night I just woke up, and there was a man and woman screaming. And then the woman—least I think it was her—appeared in my cloverleaf the next night and asked for help—"

"Your cloverleaf?"

"Where I've been sleeping, yeah. Then she possessed an old woman at a shelter and said 'He strapped me in.'"

"Who did? Her husband Jason?"

"I don't know! Maybe—"

I shivered violently.

"Can you crank the heat up a little?"

"You're cold?" asked Ruby. "With that spotlight behind you?"

"Yeah. Could you just—"

I paused again. Something in front of me wasn't right. The air moved. Or did it? I shifted my butt on the stool, tried to sharpen my gaze. Then wished I hadn't.

Misty clumps of orange fog were rolling in from the shadowy corners, swirling around the legs of the crew members.

"What's with the special effects?" I yelled. "Think this is funny?"

Ruby nudged Hunter's arm. "He's flipping out a bit."

"Leo?" asked Hunter, "Do you need to take a break?"

His words echoed, then faded in my ears, as if he were suddenly being rolled away from me in a wheelchair. The fog thickened, became fire smoke, formed unrecognizable shapes.

"No..."

It seemed to swallow everyone in the room except Hunter, who continued to sit with his legs crossed, though his face was turning pale, his hair lengthening.

"It's allll righhht..."

His voice changed, became higher and raspier. I leaned forward for a better look, saw his cream-colored shirt sprout saggy breasts, his eyes go dull, the skin around his mouth cracking and dissolving as if from fire heat, skeletal teeth giving him a ghastly dead grin—

"He strapped me in..."

I howled, knocked over my stool and bolted from the room. Ruby shot Hunter a dirty look, then futilely went out the door after me. I lost her easily in the maze of hallways.

* * *

A tour bus packed with leering out-of-towners nearly hit me as I ran across Santa Monica Boulevard. That would have been fine with me, seeing there was no freeway overpass handy.

I hurried north on Vine, passing a handful of mohawked punks heading toward Amoeba Music. The crowd I would lose myself in was approaching, and it was guaranteed seven days a week.

Hollywood Boulevard used to be a place I would avoid, but with the arrival of the Kodak Theatre and gaudy shopping complex at Hollywood and Highland, the street had been steam-cleaned and facelifted. Global tourists mingled with the local riff-raff and Darth Vader impersonators, and I felt relieved right away because people were paying far less attention to me.

I lingered in front of the Chinese Theatre a good half hour, marveling at the camera-snapping folk, the ones crouched on the pavement trying to fit their hands and feet into grooves left by dead actors, unconscious attempts to touch their souls. I was grateful Jo wasn't a famous actress, because I didn't need a pair of rotting hands grabbing my legs from the cement.

I wasn't sure how long I'd been leaning against the theatre wall, but my feet were starting to hurt. I fished in my pockets, dug out a ten, then walked to a corner stand, took a stool and bought myself a pastrami burrito.

I felt bad about ditching Ruby and the interview, but I had no choice. Jo Ordway didn't want my help; she was trying to drive me crazy, and I wasn't going to give in without a fight. Should I have just sat there in the studio and held a conversation with her putrifying corpse? I was the only one who could see it, and thirty seconds more they would've been fitting me for a strait-jacket!

The burrito relaxed me a bit. The faces I passed on the sidewalk were happy and curious and certainly not morphing into death masks. The evening breeze which often cooled the city at sunset had vanished, and a sticky warmth took over. I strolled east, then west, then east again, crossing the Boulevard at nearly every light. As I passed the ancient Roosevelt Hotel I felt a bit light-headed, peered up at a third floor window and thought I saw a Marilyn

Monroe look-alike gazing out at me, but wasn't quite sure. I needed to find a restroom and located a pristine one in the shopping plaza after evading a nosy security guard for a few minutes.

The cell phone in my pants pocket chirped repeatedly while I was using the stall, but there was no way in hell I would answer it, not wanting to hear from the living or the dead. It chirped once more as I hit the sidewalk, so I yanked it out and turned it off.

"Hey! What TV show have I seen you on?"

I spun, found myself looking at a handsome young guy in sunglasses, khaki shorts and an olive madras shirt.

"Umm, I don't think so. Unless it was the Buzz Channel—"

"No, no. I know the head of programming there and he would've told me about you. I'm guessing I saw you on *Cold Case* once, or maybe it was *My Name is Earl*."

"You got the wrong guy, man."

"Okay, maybe I do. But I'm casting for a CBS pilot right now, and you have the look I've been after." He handed me a creamy business card. "Gus Bennett, Discovery Talent."

I stared at the card. "Oh…What look is it that you're—"

"Streetwise! Someone who's been around the block and won't take crap. Ever done any acting?"

"No. Except like I said, the Buzz Channel just interviewed me. If you can believe that."

"I believe everything, friend. That's why I live here. Anyway, speaking of being around the block, that's where my photo studio is. Right down this street here. If you can spare a couple minutes I'd really like to do a quick screen test. Free of charge."

"Shit, man, I'm not really an actor—"

"Didn't I just say you have the look? What better start do you need?"

I smirked, tried to turn away from the guy but couldn't shake him. "Do you have any idea how much money you can make from one recurring guest role on a hit TV series? From syndication alone?" He lifted his shades on a pair of brown, friendly eyes.

"Come on. Five minutes max."

I stared at him. The guy certainly seemed legit, and maybe it would lead to easier cash than the route I just endured.

"Okay…"

"Good call. This way."

He led me one block east, then up Rampart Street toward the Hollywood hills. There were old office buildings here, but a few of them had FOR LEASE signs.

"Where's the studio?"

"Chill, dude. Right down here."

We made another left down a dim alley. I could make out a narrow doorway approaching, but it seemed to have a padlock on it.

"You mean that—"

WHACK! It was hard, and it was metal, and hit the back of my head with enough force to knock me against the nearby wall. The guy seized me by the shoulder, spun me around and planted the cold nose of a grey revolver against my cheek.

"Give me that cell phone, douchebag. Wallet, too."

I groggily felt in my pocket for the cell, handed it to him. "I don't have a wallet, you asshole."

"Aw. Too bad." He flipped the gun around and smacked my forehead with its butt. I hit the pavement like a beanbag chair. "Gus" crouched, rifled through my pockets and found the last of my cash. Then snatched his business card back from my shirt pocket.

"No sense wasting these, right?" He stuffed the gun barrel into one of my nostrils. "Go to the cops and I'll track you down for another screen test. An R-rated one. Got that?" I half-nodded and the guy stood up, hurried away.

I lay there for I don't know how long, smothered in pain. Could taste my own blood as it leaked into my mouth from the head wound. A handful of people walked by the alley, caught a glimpse of my wheezing, prone shape and picked up their pace.

I used the wall to pull myself to my feet, then careened out of the alley and turned north. A family in matching Universal Studios shirts saw me coming and cut across the street the way they would for an unleashed Rotweiler.

A trickle of blood found my eye. I rubbed it out with a sleeve, then tore a strip of fabric off the bottom of my Hawaiian shirt and tied it around the head gash.

A jumpy man with a goatee came out of a vintage LP store and looked at me with actual empathy. I grabbed his arm.

"Somebody mugged me…Where's a hospital?"

"Umm, I'm not sure…Wait—yeah! East of here. On Vermont, I think. I'd drive ya, dude, but I don't got wheels. Sorry!" He ran off. I stumbled across the street without looking for cars and headed east.

* * *

The East Hollywood Medical Center was nine stories of nondescript concrete. My twenty-minute trudge there took me on a section of Sunset Boulevard far from the chic eateries and hipster nightspots. Latino discount stores and ethnic markets were the norm here, decapitated chickens hanging in windows that made me look away, and the sidewalks teemed with immigrants. I asked two or three people if I was near the hospital, got no English back, then found the place with the help of an ambulance siren.

When I entered the emergency waiting room I thought I'd mistakenly walked into a welfare office or circle of hell. People were standing six deep at three separate windows, and every seat was filled with sneezing, bleeding or wailing souls. I took a spot in what looked like the shortest window line, right behind a Korean dad toting his miserable, runny-nosed three-year-old boy. The kid stared at my head wound in quivering horror, forcing me to work up a smile and wave to try and soothe him.

The line crawled, every patient in front of me with some apparent crisis. I felt faint after the first fifteen minutes and helped myself to a seat on the cold, dirty floor. I was afraid to look at the people in the real seats, afraid I'd see nothing but dripping cadavers sitting there. So I kept my head down, sliding forward whenever I was nudged from behind.

When the dad and kid finally left the window, I stood and took their place. The 40ish black admitting nurse chomped gum at me from her computer terminal.

"I.D. and insurance card, please."

"Right…Um, I don't have them. I got mugged, y'see, and everything got taken."

"Did you contact police?"

"No! I was bleeding and couldn't see! I need a doctor!!"

"Yes, sir, but we need some form of I.D. and proof of insur—"

"OH FUCK THAT! LOOK AT MY HEAD, YOU WITCH!!"

"Sir. Please keep your voice down. I can see you've been injured but we have procedures here that need to be followed—"

"Like FUCK you do! If I bleed to death you've got a roomful of witnesses here and the county will shut you down!"

The nurse popped a giant, angry bubble. A guard stirred in a hallway behind her.

"Think we can avoid a big old mess here, sir? The last thing you want is a big old mess."

"And I bet the last thing you want is to be out of a job." I kept my eyes locked on her. The nurse resumed chewing, whacked around a few keys at her computer for pure spite.

"Your name, please."

"Leo."

"Last name?"

I blanked. This was always the hard part. "Jones."

She typed it in, eyeing him. "Address?"

"15434. Santa Monica Boulevard. Los Angeles—"

"Phone?"

"I don't have one."

"Mm-hmm. Take a seat over there, please. I'll see if someone will look at you. Next!"

I was bumped out of the way. Moved into the stuffed waiting area, wedged myself into a standing spot between a feverish old man and water fountain and tried to blend in. Even with a delta of dried blood on my head and shirt it wasn't hard to do.

Minutes passed. Accumulated. The feverish man left his seat, but I was busy staring at the floor and missed a chance to replace him. I felt dangerously groggy; whatever ventilation system the room was using was practically sucking oxygen out.

A fuzzy TV in the corner was showing headline news, and my dull eyes fixated on the endlessly repeating crawl at the bottom of the screen. 39 PAKISTANI REBELS ARRESTED…TROPICAL STORM ROBERT FIZZLES WEST OF BERMUDA…POP ICON TEESHA SPARK ARRESTED FOR DRUG POSSESSION AND CHILD ABUSE…I let my legs buckle and took another seat on the floor. Should I try and sleep? Probably not wise, especially if they called my name. I wished this was like a private doctor's waiting room, with stacks of magazines and maybe even a coffeepot. A nice article or pictorial on some Wyoming national park would transport me to a safe place in no time. I could even read the thing twice.

"Shut up or I'll make you even sicker!" It was a sloppy, low-income mom in a nearby chair, threatening her crying toddler. I had the urge to do the world a favor and smack her, but was too weak to stand. I checked the TV again and the crawl had finally changed: USC TROJANS DEFEAT OHIO STATE 30-3 FOR 38TH CONSECUTIVE WIN…"HE STRAPPED ME IN," SAYS BURNED WOMAN FOLLOWING TRAGIC DEATH…

I blinked. What was that? Raised my back up the wall for another look.

…INSISTS DEAD, TECH MOGUL'S WIFE FOLLOWING NOTORIOUS TRAGEDY…

"Shut up…" I uttered, and shook my head furiously, trying to rid it of the vision. A few patients glanced my way.

A USC running back weaved through tackles but the field under him was turning into sand, and he was sinking, groping… "HE STRAPPED ME IN, HE STRAPPED ME IN—"

I jumped to my feet, lunged over the legs of three patients and ripped the TV plug out of the wall. "Hey!" yelled the sloppy lady. I staggered back to my spot, unable to look at anyone, but a nurse with a clipboard had already opened the admitting door.

"Leo Jones? This way please."

I exhaled with relief, detoured into the adjacent hall—where the security guard was waiting. "We need to get your blood pressure and temperature," said the nurse, "so if you'll follow Douglas here to our mobile unit…"

"Mobile unit?"

"Down here, friend," said the guard, taking me by the arm. I was bewildered, but so happy to be out of the waiting room I didn't even resist. In seconds we were down a short hall and out the door, where two muscular paramedics helped me into the back of an ambulance.

"What the hell's this?"

"Mobile checkup," said the paramedic who was bigger and uglier, "And it's on the house." The other one hopped back out, slammed the door, and went around to get behind the wheel. The first paramedic buckled me into a side-facing seat, yelled "We're good!" to the driver, and the ambulance screeched off. The guy then wrapped a blood pressure sleeve around my arm, making me jumpy.

"Be cool, alright? This won't take long."

"Since when do they do this while moving?

The paramedic wouldn't look at me. "Since whenever we need to. Take a deep breath."

I did. The sleeve tightened. We swerved around a corner and my behind nearly slid off the chair. "This is fucked—"

"Quiet, please." He stared at the pressure reading, then unwrapped the sleeve. "140 over 87. Good enough."

The vehicle's siren went off, and we lurched forward. The paramedic stayed calm, slid open a nearby drawer. I was wild-eyed.

"What are we doing??"

"Temperature."

"Fuck that, I need something for my head!"

"Temperature first. Open wide."

I sat with my mouth clamped shut and the paramedic stuck the thermometer in anyway. I clamped on it even harder and almost cracked a tooth.

From where I sat, clinging to the sides of the seat, I could peer out the small back windows. Caught a whizzing glimpse of the Silverlake neighborhood we barreled through, lofty hills perched above a winding strip of markets, Mexican food places and old Hollywood scenic shops, but the recognition was little comfort. Something was very wrong here.

The paramedic yanked the thermometer out prematurely, shrugged at the reading but didn't say anything.

"Where are you taking me?"

"Across town."

"I can see that, asshole. Where??"

"We're transferring you, okay? Hospitals do that sometimes."

"I don't want to be transferred! I need first aid!"

The paramedic rolled his eyes, pulled a walkie-talkie out of his back pocket.

"We close?" he apparently asked the driver. There was static, and then the driver's responding voice: "Twelve blocks."

I panicked and started to unbuckle myself. The paramedic seized my arm.

"I need you to keep that on, sir."

"Fuck you."

"Don't make me sedate you."

I stared at him, toyed with the possibility of a nice soothing shot, a brief release from this madness, this pain…

And then the siren was cut. The ambulance made a sharp left, then a right, and we were in a dark, bumpy alley. The brakes hit.

"Where are we?"

The paramedic said nothing, unbuckled me. His partner threw the back door open. The smell of garbage and human urine hit me like a truck.

"You fuckers..."

The first paramedic stuffed an aspirin packet and wad of band-aids in my shirt pocket. "You'll be fine, pal. Just get some sleep." He pushed me out the door. I whirled, stumbled over a garbage can lid and landed in a filthy puddle.

"And bring your insurance card next time!" yelled the driver, cracking up with his buddy as they got back in the cab and roared away. I staggered to my feet, unleashed an insane blue streak of obscenities at them that echoed off the decrepit buildings on both sides of the alley. Someone equally insane yelled back from a street away, and I collapsed in a heap, band-aids spilling out of my shirt.

❧ ELEVEN ❧

I knew exactly where I was. Could tell by the fecal stench, by the distant, dancing glow of crack pipes at the edge of the alley, by the hellish symphony of cursing, shouting and crazy-ass preaching that echoed off the tenements. I had been tricked, abducted and dumped like a turkey carcass just off San Julian, the worst homeless street in America.

I had been fortunate enough to steer clear of this pit. My only visit was years ago, when I rode a bus down here with a buddy who was trying to find his wayward, heroin-devoured girlfriend. After two days of evaporating leads, of sleepless, futile walking and a handful of near-brawls, we learned she had hitchhiked to Arizona and overdosed in a Blythe gas station toilet before she even got there.

Skid Row L.A. was actually fifty square blocks, but San Julian was all you needed to see. It was a wretched street fair of homeless drug dealers, users and whores, endless rows of makeshift tents, gutters caked with clothing and discarded food and human shit. There had been recent police sweeps to help clean up the scene and make the nearby neighborhood of high-priced condo complexes more desirable, but from the looks of things on this night, loft prices weren't rising any time soon.

I crossed the street at a light, something no one else seemed to be doing, and headed for a pay phone outside a liquor store. Four crack-wasted black guys congregated around it. One actually used the phone while the others argued and jabbed and made sour, frightening faces at me as he approached, so I kept walking.

A scrawny Vietnamese girl with needle road maps on her arms emerged from an alley, sashayed up to me.

"Feel like a party, handsome?"

"Get lost..."

"Come on. Only twenty dollars for a cock-suck—"

"You fuckin' deaf?"

I gave her a violent shove. She hit a parking meter with her ribcage, bounced off it like a pinball. Darted back across the street and nearly got pancaked by a speeding BMW. The hooker screamed at me and I picked up speed, took another alley and ran until her screams dissolved.

The sticky warm air thickened. I thought I saw a lightning flash, then heard a rumble and knew I was right. I would have to find shelter soon, but was weak and thirsty and had double blisters and knew I could end up in a piss-filled doorway if I wasn't careful. My first plan had been to scrounge up change and call Ruby; now I'd settle for any kind of roof.

I found a half-eaten chicken breast in a Pollo Loco bag but it tasted like a salty shoe and made me gag. Rinsed my mouth with the warm, watery remnants of a fast food soda cup, then found myself on Seventh Street, which was far less teeming than San Julian but no more safe. There was another liquor store or two, a couple of bars, the same shady hodgepodge of characters but also more homeless camped out for the night and a fair amount of peace being kept. I saw another hooker, this one Latino and younger than the first, exit a Port-o-san behind a sheepish, long-haired businessman zipping up his fly. A decrepit brick structure called HOTEL CLIFFORD had become a flophouse, lost residents perched on its front steps, fire escapes and in its open windows, scratching arms or regaling the night with their blatherings.

Another lightning flash lit up the sky, was followed by a sooner and louder rumble. I felt rain spitting on my head. Hurried across to the endless line of homemade shelters, hoping for a tiny, unoccupied space between cardboard, maybe even an invite from one good soul. But this was a tightly packed collection of filth and human cordwood with no entry point in sight.

Then the rain spits became gobs, and a bank of rogue clouds opened. Howls and curses filled the air, and the stretch of sidewalk campers compressed and folded in like dark red rose petals at dusk.

I was soaked in seconds, and ducked down a side street. Every doorway was filled with limbs or unfriendly eyes. At the corner three drunks fought over space inside a dumpster. If I paused for five seconds, piss and rotten French fries would wash over my shoes, so I kept moving.

The Los Angeles River was nearby—that much I knew—and with a river came storm drains and overpasses. I crossed Eighth Street, avoided the splash of a passing cab, and headed toward a distant spot where the buildings seemed to drop away.

Another flophouse appeared on my right, KELVIN CASTLE, this one bigger and sadder, filled with pale faces gazing out its broken windows. One of the inhabitants on the second floor whistled and waved me up, a lit cigarette stuck to his lip. I hesitated, then darted up the building's steps and through the open front door.

It was incredibly dark inside and smelled worse than death, but it was dry. Doomed, motionless men and a few women watched me mount the stairs, which were rotting away and mined here and there with collapsing boards.

The guy with the cigarette sat in the window of the first room, surrounded by a dozen silent, drifting roommates. I walked over, avoiding a large hole in the floor. The guy had an old-fashioned butch haircut and wore a torn, soiled cowboy shirt. The right side of his face was covered in soot or grease; it was too dark to tell. He nodded at me with a tiny smile, as if recognizing an old friend.

"Just so you know…it wasn't my cigarette."

"What's that?"

He leaned forward, plucked the butt off his lip and held it aloft. "I had one just like this, but so did Stinky. And he's the idiot who slept on newspapers."

"Not that night!" echoed a pathetic voice behind them.

"You sure goddamn did!"

I was already backing away. "Hey, I have no idea what this is about—"

"You do now," said the guy, and the right side of his face exploded in flame. I shouted, leaped back. Fire licked around the walls, ignited every resident in sight. Awful screams pierced through my head and I turned, fell through the floor—

—and landed face first on a wet, grassy mound, each of my knees in a separate puddle.

The building had vanished around me.

"Have some respect, dumb ass!"

A foot slammed into my thigh. I rolled over, caught a glimpse of an old homeless guy wearing an egg carton hat pointing at something. I peeled myself off the mound, saw that a plaque had been screwed into it:

IN MEMORY OF THE 46 WAYWARD SOULS
WHO PERISHED IN THE "KELVIN CASTLE FIRE"
JULY 7, 1953

Horror seized my throat. I got to my feet, slipped on the wet grass, tumbled back and flattened another man's sheet-draped dwelling. The man squirted out of it like paste from a tube, half-naked, wild-eyed. He swung at my head with a large chair leg.

"Hey, I'm sorry!" I yelled, but a line of death had apparently been crossed. The man charged me again and again. Other homeless were there, but no one intervened and a few urged on the leg-swinger. I tried to grab hold of the weapon but the man was quick, and landed a blow in my side. Winded, I fell off the curb, waited for two pairs of headlights to approach, then darted in front of the cars. My attacker froze on the curb, raised the chair leg and howled in twisted triumph.

I took the nearest alley and paused under a fire escape to inspect the latest wound. The chair leg had a splintered end, and had put a long, ugly scratch in my side next to the bruise the blow had made. It stung like a paper cut, and when I dropped my shirt again I sank to the wet pavement in utter hopelessness.

How could God have let me sink this low? True, I wasn't a famous believer in the Big Guy, but there were certainly forces in nature, there was karma, and even though I'd forgotten the better life I must have had once, I knew I was still good in this one, that I cared for others, that I appreciated the small blessings I occasionally received, the hummingbird I saw once drinking out of a backyard swimming pool. What did I ever do or say to bring me to this torturous moment?

"Please, Jo…" I muttered, unsure who else to conjure, face buried in my wet hands. Tears formed, and my body shook. "I'm really trying to help you…I am…but I need some FUCK-ING GUIDANCE HERE!!" I smacked my hand in a puddle and sobbed away.

Then there were light footsteps, and I looked up. A boy of about nine in a T-shirt and saggy cargo pants stood at the edge of the alley beneath a ratty umbrella, staring at me. He had a small plastic grocery bag in his other hand. I squinted, slowly rose to my feet.

"Are you a goddamn ghost, too?"

"Huh?" asked the boy.

"I said are you alive?"

The boy walked over, rather fearlessly. He was pale and underfed, but had quick, intelligent eyes.

"We have room if you need a place to sleep tonight."

"No shit…You live around here?"

The boy nodded. I raised an eyebrow, saw a loaf of Wonder Bread sticking out of the plastic bag and decided to follow him.

His name was Sam, and he led me a half dozen blocks to a cul-de-sac wedged between a vacant warehouse, a patchwork wire fence, and the L.A. River. A peeling, 20-year-old Dodge van was parked there, its back wheels gone and the rear bumper propped on black plastic crates, making the vehicle look slightly airborne.

"Cops never come down here for some reason," said Sam, folding up his umbrella. The rain had finally tapered off; down below, the river was in a hurry to get somewhere.

The van had Michigan plates, a UAW decal and bumper stickers from every conceivable state and national park and roadside attraction from the Mississippi to the Pacific. There were odd, sticker-free black windows on the side and the back.

"Melanie usually takes the air mattress but she can sleep with my mom." He rapped twice on the back door, then three more times. The van shook with inner movement and the door swung open.

Sam's mother was equally pale, with unwashed blonde hair and eyes like dying embers. It looked like she hadn't slept in a week.

"You here to judge me?" she snapped, raising a camping lantern to look at my face.

"He's okay, Mom," said Sam, "They were giving him the business on Eighth Street for no good reason. He just needs a bed. I glanced at the boy, unclear how he knew all that.

"Sammy likes to wander. Send him out for bread and he might end up at the Rose Bowl. Come on in, you two. I'm Danielle." I worked up a smile and climbed in back.

Danielle shifted the light, giving me a good look at the interior. Plastic bags filled with clothing were neatly masking taped to the van's walls. A discarded file cabinet had been turned on its side and covered with a plastic flowered tablecloth. Neatly divided toiletries covered the dash, the steering wheel and rear view mirror serving as towel racks. A Styrofoam board plastered with family photos hung on the back of the passenger seat. Most were faded, curled up. A sleeping little girl—Melanie, apparently—was wedged into a crevice below that on a small air mattress, her bare dirty feet sticking out from under a Grand Canyon blanket. She mumbled and twitched while she dreamt.

"It's real nice of you to do this," I whispered. Danielle poured me a glass of water without asking from an overused plastic jug. "How long have you been here?" The woman blew a strand of hair off her face. I could tell she was probably attractive once, but who wasn't?

"A year. On the road for two before that."

"Jesus…"

"Dan losing his assembly job was hard enough. Then the department store I was managing went under. The whole chain, in fact."

"What happened to Dan?"

She looked into space. "Shot himself."

"Oh God! Sorry—"

"Please don't be. When you're drunk and unemployed for five years it's definitely an option." She threatened to smile. "But don't get any ideas."

"Believe me, I have."

Sam handed me two pieces of buttered Wonder Bread. I nodded my thanks and wolfed them down.

"Must be tough for your kids."

Danielle's eyes glazed over as fresh raindrops pelted the van's windshield. "They're in a better place now."

I stared at her. "You don't mean that."

"He was going to take them, so I had to."

"Really? How could he have done that? Without a job, I mean."

"They were starving out here…He told me he would take them."

"Yeah, but you didn't have any family members in Michigan who would—"

"They were starving out here."

I studied her suddenly blank face. A chill jetted up my spine. "I don't…know what you're—"

"The Lord said he would take them and He meant it. So I did it for Him. On a night like this…"

The rain water was in sheets again, making an odd swirling sound on all sides of the van. Melanie's sleeping mumbles rose into tiny shrieks. I turned, caught a glimpse of Sam bound with cord in a rear seat, eyes frozen open in shock as water bubbled up through the floorboards. Then the lantern fizzled.

"MOM, NO!!!" His awful cry made me cover my ears, seconds before the windshield exploded in a shower of glass and river. I screamed, went under. Fought for air. The family van that was once there dissolved around me and I kicked my legs upward like a madman. The current was vicious, carried me ten yards and slammed me against a tire that was caught on a broken concrete slab. I climbed up and over the thing, gasping. Peered up at the huge break in the wire fence I must have tumbled through. Clawed my way up and along the slippery embankment until I found a dry, unoccupied burrow beneath an overpass I could safely pass out in.

❧ TWELVE ❧

By the time Ruby found a classical station in her car, I had already fallen back asleep. There was nothing calmer or saner for a disturbed passenger than a soft background sonata, and whatever 19th century pianist this was even had her making slower, wider turns around corners.

After hitting up every Hollywood hospital and urgent care facility, strange reactions to her questions at East Hollywood Medical Center made her follow a nasty hunch and cruise over to skid row. She was well aware of the dumping practice, and knew that recent rumors of its being stopped were most likely bullshit. San Julian Street was the usual nightmare, especially in the rain, so she parked a few blocks from the river and spent a good hour on foot.

I didn't recognize her at first when she nudged me awake. When she told me I'd fallen through the wire fence at the very spot where that homeless woman drove her van into the drink with her kids a year ago, I lost it again. She outran me across a vacant lot, held me from behind, then had to talk me down for five minutes to get me into her car.

We reached her block in Mar Vista around 2 a.m. She shook me awake again, walked me up the stairs to her neo-Spanish apartment. Ruby rarely saw her single, terminally-busy neighbors, so wasn't concerned what they'd think, but she knew she was crossing her organization's line. Taking a homeless client into your home violated every Jobworks regulation she'd once helped draft.

Yet this was me, more of a friend than a client, a man she'd always cared about a little more, a man whose current predicament was partly her doing, so crap—she had no problem letting the rules slide.

I was fine with crashing on her couch—I would've slept in a dog bed if it were dry enough—and she made me a cup of herbal plum tea to calm me further. I spent the first ten minutes sitting upright on her refurbished down Chubbuck, taking in every inch of Ruby's once-hidden domain.

"Can't believe how quiet it is here," I said. "How do you sleep?" Ruby laughed. She'd come to accept the midnight sirens on Lincoln, the rapmobiles, the frequent weekend parties in the complex, and figured she'd have to move into a canyon to find real peace.

"Not too well, actually. For lots of reasons." She smiled, but I didn't really get the joke. "Anyway, you should try and sleep. We both should."

"Not sure I can do that."

"Leo. You're in my apartment. Nothing but living, breathing people around us—"

"It doesn't matter. If even one person died in this building its… *thing* will find me! I've turned into this goddamn ghost magnet and I don't know why!" I pounded a pillow with my fist. Ruby came over and sat beside me.

"Sssh…Okay. I hear you. But I still think you'll deal with this better if you sleep—"

"That's when they come!"

"Not always. What about under that bridge just now? You were sawing logs when I found you." I cocked my head, struggled to retrieve this crumb of recent history. "Look. How about I sleep in that chair over there?" She pointed to a beige retro recliner across from us. "Any ghouls show up I'll kick their ass, and if you just have a nightmare I'll be here for that too…I'll even make you a nice breakfast in the morning."

I looked at her. "You'd do that?"

She patted my sun-baked hand. "Of course." The air undulated between us. I never imagined I'd be in a place or a moment this private with Ruby. Hell, I couldn't imagine being this close to any woman who didn't smell of piss. Ruby let my hand go after a few electric seconds and went down the hall, but I was happy. The feeling of her hand could last for months.

Ruby opened a hall closet, crouched to pick out some bedding. "I've already decided to go in at noon. Phillip won't be thrilled but he'll manage. Plus there's a temp who's on call if it gets out of control." She collected her armful, shut the door with a foot. Walked back into the living room and probably stopped.

Because I was already fast asleep.

* * *

His dream the other night had him trying to break into his own building with a butter knife. This time Hunter found a giant pad-lock strung through the door handles and a toothpick in his hand. He peered through the green glass and saw the same two smiling idiots manning the front desk, both in dark suits and toting legal pads. Neither of them had ears.

"Open the fucking door! I'm late!!" Hunter screamed, but the men just kept on smiling. Hunter kicked and kicked and kicked the door until his shoe and the foot inside it shattered like glass. He howled—

Hunter sat up in his satin sheets, sweaty and quivering. His cell phone vibrated next to the bed and he lunged for it, squinted at the number, and popped the thing open.

"What's up, Mort?" He listened a moment, then his eyes popped. "You're kidding, right?"

* * *

A recycling truck in the alley woke me the next morning. I sat up, trying to remember where I was. Looked around and saw Ruby in the kitchen, freshly showered with a new outfit on, mixing egg yolks. I could smell greasy meat.

"Shit…What time is it?"

"Eleven, if you can believe that. You've been Sleeping Beauty over there." The truck finally went away and she dropped a CD into a portable player. "You good with Gerry Mulligan?"

"He's okay. Kind of prefer that acid jazz stuff."

"No comment. Wanna shower?"

"Not yet. Too hungry."

"Come on then. I'm making kick-ass Denver omelettes."

I stretched and rose. Sunlight filled Ruby's place and everything seemed new, after the first real good sleep I'd had in a year. I walked to her small table and sat. A tall glass of orange juice and buttered sourdough toast were waiting for me.

"Wow…I could get used to this."

"Well, the idea is to get you in the right direction so you can."

I took a bite of toast, let it resonate. "So…That mom from Michigan…"

"Yup. Plowed through the fence. Bacon or sausage with yours?

"Both." I took a prolonged sip of juice. "She felt like she had to unload on me. You know, guilt. Same as that guy in the burned-down building."

"I don't know who or what you're talking about, Leo, but I'd rather not get into that stuff right now—"

"Why? Isn't this a good time? We're relaxed, having some food—"

"Because it's making you crazy, that's why. And I know I talked you into that stupid TV thing, so it's partly my fault. But we need—you need—to get back on track with normalcy as soon as possible. *Bon appetite.*" She placed the steaming omelet in front of me, adorned with three bacon pieces and three sausage links. Took the seat across from me and began to eat. I stared at her.

"I can't help it, Ruby. This 'craziness' isn't going anywhere until I figure out where it's coming from. Why do you think I walked out to the Valley the other day?"

"I don't know. Did you tell me—"

"To visit Jo Ordway's parents."

Ruby's mouth halted in mid-chew. "Are you serious?"

"I'm not kidding. Their last name is Shaw and they live in Sherman Oaks. Looked them up on a computer—"

"What the hell did you bother *them* for?"

"Wouldn't you? And I wasn't bothering them at all. Matter of fact Jo's mom invited me in for dinner."

"Is that so?"

"Yeah. Thought maybe I'd learn something about some connection Jo might've had to me, except I didn't really. "

"Huh...." Ruby ate some more of her omelet, visibly irritated. "Did they know you were homeless?"

"Nope." He dropped his eyes. "They were very polite to me. More than the damn cops over there, that's for sure."

"So they believed whatever tall tale you told them."

"What do you mean?"

"Leo, please. You show up at their house in what I assume is a nice neighborhood. You probably stink after the walk. And they just invite you in for dinner."

"Yeah. It happened. Christ, I've had dinner in a house before. What do you call this?"

"Breakfast."

I rolled my eyes, kept eating. Ruby traded her fork for her coffee mug, cradled it while she gazed at me. "I wish you would tell me about yourself already."

"You know all there is."

"I don't know crap, Leo. Never have. You come to my office one day looking like a shipwreck survivor, and when I try to take your information you go into a self-induced coma. How do you expect me to fix your life if I don't know how or why or where it's coming from?"

"I'm not asking you to fix my life. Just to..."

"Bail you out? Rescue you from dark alleys over and over? It's starting to get old, Leo."

"So don't fucking do it!" I shoved my chair back and stood up. "Thanks for the couch and fancy omelette."

"Wait! Don't leave yet, okay? I'm not mad at you. I'm just... real, real frustrated. I take Jobworks very seriously. And I'm proud of what I've done for my clients, so this whole thing with you is kind of throwing me. I've never worked with anyone so…mute about their past."

I stared at the pretty flowered tablecloth she'd laid out. At the mostly eaten sausage. Grabbed another link and munched on it.

"Think back to the first night you ever slept outside" she said, "Was it on a camping trip? Your backyard?" I wolfed the rest of my sausage, slowly sat again with a contemplative face. Ruby leaned forward, let Mulligan's mellow sax draw in her own past. "My dad set up a tent next to our barbeque pit one night. For me and my brother…He joined us, armed with a big flashlight and copy of *The Hobbi*t. It was great…Until these two possums showed up around 3 a.m. and got into the jerky my brother left out—" She chuckled to herself. I smiled but remained quiet.

"After that it was a long stretch. Until me and Cyril Porter camped on the beach at Coos Bay. The stars were incredible… Ever camp with a girl?"

My face seemed to cave in on itself, like an oyster shell. "Nope. Never done much of anything with any girl."

"Aw, c'mon. I don't believe that. Handsome guy like you?"

I blushed, closed my posture even more. "Where's your bathroom?" Ruby leaned back, deflated. Pointed down the hall. I quickly left the table.

Ruby's bathroom was done in a spare, Japanese style, but it didn't make me feel any calmer. I sat on the shut toilet seat, rocking slightly. Exasperation throttled me. Camping and kisses on a beach…Why did they sound so good, so damn encompassing? Because I never did them? Or because I'd forgotten I had? The cloud bank that routinely swallowed my memories showed no signs of drifting north. Maybe I would just stay in this bathroom until Ruby left for work.

As long as I didn't look in the mirror. Dark things lurked in mirrors.

Ruby's doorbell rang. Great, I thought, probably her boyfriend. There was no way she didn't have one. And he was just in time to find her fantasy lover hiding on the toilet.

"Hold on, hold on!" Ruby cried, then rapped on the door. "You okay Leo?"

"Yeah. Did someone just—"

"Hunter. He's coming up."

"Shit…Don't tell him I'm here."

But she was already back down the hall. I groaned, shook off my latest willies and stood.

Hunter was jacked up on five cups of coffee or something worse. He paced around the living room, rifling through his open leather shoulder bag. His eyes smoldered, and the rest of his face lit up as I entered.

"There he is! Star of the show!"

"Hey," I returned sheepishly, "Didn't mean to run out—"

"I'm not kidding, pal. Your next production is going through the roof."

Ruby wasn't amused. "What kind of shitburger are you trying to sell us now, Hunter?"

He plucked an unmarked DVD out of his bag, held it aloft like a sacred jewel. "Play this."

Ruby simmered for a moment, then snatched it out of his hand, took it to her TV cabinet. Hunter walked me to a prime viewing spot and sat me down. "Gotta be honest. I was just as pissed about that last show as you. Prep time was too short and abysmal, and we barely sunk our teeth into the good stuff when you walked."

The DVD started up: a series of silent takes of me in my interview chair, shot from a number of angles.

"What's the big deal?" asked Ruby.

"Just watch. I went straight home after we wrapped, didn't even see this stuff, and then Mort called me in the middle of the night."

A strange orange fog billowed along the studio floor in the next medium shot. "What the hell's that?" asked Ruby.

"Exactly," said Hunter. I leaned forward on my knees, stunned. The fog swirled around Hunter in his chair, hid him from view.

"No one saw this? When they—"

"It wasn't there, Ruby."

The next close-up shot of me, awkward and restless and ready to bolt, featured a clump of the orange fog drifting around behind me. Reforming. Shaping itself into a woman's tormented, half-burned face and upper torso.

"Oh my God..." Ruby had to sit down.

"The weird thing is that no one could see this on the live feed. It wasn't until Don did the 35mm transfer later that it showed up."

"It's her..."

"Fucking-A right it is. I fired this off to programming, got the cash wheels spinning and we're booked for a live broadcast Wednesday night at her house."

"To broadcast what? Lawn sprinklers?"

"The séance, baby, the séance!" Ruby knew this might be coming but turned away in disgust anyway. I just stared at Hunter, desperately trying to conjure hope.

"It's all cool, man, believe me. We are going to get to the bottom of this Jo Ordway shit for you once and for all."

"You think so?"

"I know so. And here's some proof of insurance." He reached back in his bag and took out a fat envelope of cash. I nearly fell off the couch.

"What the hell is that now?" barked Ruby.

"What does it look like? We've got people buying commercial time left and right—"

"Didn't you learn a damn thing last night? Leo can't handle this!"

"He doesn't have to."

"Then what are you doing here with your fucking money clip? Leo, you are not going to carry the ball for his next psychic masturbation hour!"

"She's right, Leo. You're not. Know why? Because we have none other than Simmons Hempwood on board."

I drew a blank. Ruby didn't. "Hempwood? The guy with that BBC series?"

"*Spectres from Beyond*. Only one of the highest rated shows in the UK for 25 years. The guy is amazing. He once spent two hours in the North Drawing Room of Kensington Palace talking to Queen Victoria!"

"How the hell did you—"

"Meant to be, kid. Just so happens there's a paranormal convention in San Diego this weekend with none other than Sir Hempwood as featured speaker. A little extra cash wired in advance, a room booked at the Hotel Bel-Air, and poof! He'll be warming up with us."

Ruby was speechless. Hunter killed the DVD, ejected the disk and kissed it. "I got this stuff in the promos, cutting as we speak. Trust me, people, this will be the highest-rated paranormal production ever broadcast."

"Excuse me, but I think Leo needs to assess this—"

"Exactly. Leo does. Not you." He turned to me. "Assess away, big guy. Assess the fact that after I give you the next envelope of cash, the only place you'll be sleeping at night is on your own apartment futon."

"You mean that?"

"I don't fuck around, Leo. I don't have time to. If you want proof, take a look outside."

Curious, I got off the couch and went to the window, followed closely by Ruby. Parked right in front of the building was the teal Buzz Channel van, side doors rolled open, three bulky guys in sleeveless black T-shirts and shorts hanging out of it like irritated crows.

"That's a full prep crew, waiting to take you away. Just like that magical mystery tour song."

Ruby nudged her way in for a view. And saw someone unexpected, someone truly ghastly in the passenger seat, sucking on a mineral water: Chloe.

"What is that bitch doing here?"

"Chloe brought me the original photos, remember? I owed her one." Ruby just turned and glared at him. "Actually, she threatened to sell them to the *Enquirer*, but that had nothing to do with it. I love her energy and she makes a great P.A."

"Get out of here," said Ruby. "Now."

"You sure? Always room for another body. As in, Leo's coach—"

"I've never been more sure. I don't want anything to do with this abomination, and I'm hoping Leo doesn't either."

I looked at her, then back out at the van. At the cash still in his hand. "I don't know, Ruby…Sounds like this English guy might be able to help—"

"Fine. Great. Have a nice time."

"Hey, don't be mad at me."

"Mad? Who's mad? Just because I'd rather find a real solution to your problem instead of being whored out to a freak show? Go on. Both of you. I need to get to work and rejoin the living."

"Ruby, I—"

"JUST GO!!"

Hunter shook his head and went to the door. Held it open for me. I stood in the middle of the living room a long moment, then pocketed the money, found my tennis shoes and carried them out. Ruby retreated to the kitchen area. Grabbed her coffee cup and drained it, then tossed it in her sink and let it smash.

∾ THIRTEEN ∾

I rode in the van's back seat beside Chloe, because Hunter had replaced her in front. Which was just fine with me. The Jobworks office had been dark when I saw her the other morning, and I was too frazzled to even notice how supple her figure was. Today she wore a tight creamy T-shirt from a Lady Gaga concert over black, stylishly ripped jeans, and smelled like raspberries.

"Remember me?"

"Yeah. Guess you don't work for Ruby, huh?"

"Onward and upward." She pointed at my pack. "Got anything in there that doesn't stink?"

"Probably not…"

She nodded, then poked the driver's shoulder. "Makeover detour. Melrose Ave."

"You got it."

"We have time?" asked Hunter, skimming through his phone texts.

"If we don't we should make some. Give Hempster one nostril of Leo in this state and he could bolt."

"We're going to see him? The séance guy?"

"Tonight we are," said Hunter. "Maybe stop at Ordway's house on the way to take light readings."

I nodded, not thrilled about that idea but not wanting to make waves. I could scarcely believe I was taking the plunge into another Hunter Drake production, but a true psychic was involved this time, someone who maybe could shed sane light on my insane predicament. Maybe even save me.

We got onto Pico heading east. I gazed out the window as we passed my Centinela cloverleaf, and it suddenly looked so remote, so belonging to someone else, especially now that I'd tasted the alternative. I didn't like the way yesterday unraveled, but there was no mistaking how much I loved strolling down that Promenade with cash in my pocket. I wanted to do it again, and quick.

I remembered Melrose Avenue as being a decidedly hip street about ten years ago during my deep stoner days, but it apparently had peaked ten years before that. Stores like Retail Slut and Vinyl Fetish had closed, the goofy knick-knacks of Soap Plant and Wacko had moved to Hollywood Boulevard, and mostly everything that was interesting had been replaced with upscale eateries, chains, overpriced boutiques and the ever-present java chains.

The noontime traffic was expectedly sluggish due to signals at every intersection, and Hunter squirmed in his seat like a six-year-old.

"Would it be too much to ask to build a fucking parking structure here? Half of this traffic is from assholes backing into metered spaces."

"Just relax," said Chloe, never one prone to, "Scalp is on the next block. Pull over and we'll get out." The second the driver braked, she slid the rear door open and helped me out. "You'll love Rayanne" she said.

I didn't even like Rayanne. Shrill, anorexic and devoid of humor, she pinned the barber collar around my neck as if fitting me for a noose. When she announced my "new commanding look" would begin with a ten-minute "deep shampoo," my chest tightened. I'd already dropped my gaze to avoid the multiple mirrors in the loud beehive of a salon, and I'd be damned if I was going to let this harpy's bony fingers morph into Jo Ordway's the moment I shut my eyes. I pulled Chloe close to me, dropped my voice.

"Somebody else."

"Huh?"

"I need somebody else to shampoo me. A guy. Even a fag's okay. Like that one over there." He motioned to a mutton-chopped barber in a silk shirt and tight peach pants. Rayanne sensed trouble.

"What's the problem?" asked Hunter.

"Nothing," said Chloe, "He's just—"

"I want a guy to do the shampoo. It's um, really dirty in there and needs stronger hands."

Rayanne raised hers. "These aren't exactly meat hooks, but I could probably wring your neck with them." I grumbled something. "Come on dude, we're squeezing you in, doing Chloe a big favor—"

"Then forget the goddamn shampoo." Rayanne chewed on her lip and Chloe pulled her aside.

"Look, he's got his reasons. I don't understand them either, but we have got to clean and cut his hair. Just this time, okay?"

Rayanne rolled her annoyed eyes. "Siggy!"

Siggy, a de-closeted German whose name had to be Siegfried, had hands that could massage an elephant. The soap and hot water were enough to put me to sleep, but then Siggy did this thing behind my neck where he wrapped hair strands around both thumbs and squeezed out the grime like a garlic press. I didn't want it to end.

When Rayanne got me back she sculpted my wet hair with a sour face while Chloe paced beside her, texting, dropping teaser-bombs to her about the show.

"All I can tell you is if we pull this off, Leo's story could be a bonafide rags-to-riches thing in 24 hours."

"So why's he hooking up with this limey psychic? Leo some kind of ghostbuster?" I just sat and took it; how nice to be talked about in the third person.

"You're just going to have to tune in and watch, Rayanne."

Twenty interminable minutes later, my head was reborn. Gone were the long, ratty shanks, replaced by a neatly layered half mullett with the sideburns squared off at mid-ear. My clean-shaven face was even more shocking.

"George Clooney? Meet your match" said Chloe with a coy

wink as they hit the sidewalk, "New threads, pair of shades, and those Venice Beach hotties will be rollerblading after you."

She guided me west a few blocks. I felt like there was an air conditioner pointed at my neck. I couldn't remember the last time my hair had been this short, certainly not since I'd begun this homeless existence. I had a hard time recognizing myself in Rayanne's mirror, and now noticed a major difference in the way pedestrians viewed me. The homeless force field I'd gotten so used to had utterly dissolved. Hipsters, models, even moms with their impressionable kids had no problem looking me in the eye without even the thought of diverting their path. I knew my daily life had been like this once, even if I'd forgotten where or when it was. All that mattered now was reclaiming and keeping it.

We reached a DON'T WALK light at the corner of Curson, and Chloe held my wrist to keep me from jaywalking. "Hot Duds is just ahead. Killer thrift store." It sounded great. A new wardrobe could keep the force field away indefinitely. Except the light was taking forever to change.

And there was a quivering bend in the air. Someone stood on the curb diagonally across Melrose from us, gaping at me as if I were encased in museum glass. Two people, actually—the pale, young couple dressed in black I'd already seen twice. They hovered amidst a gaggle of oblivious shoppers, their shoes either inches above the pavement or lodged within.

"Light's green, Leo."

I couldn't move. The couple stared at me and I stared right back.

"Leo!" She grabbed my arm and I ripped his gaze away, marched off the curb.

"You don't see them, do you?"

"See who?" I glanced back, and naturally they were gone.

"Fuck it."

The next half hour in Hot Duds felt like a day. I kept my eyes trained on the store window for a sign of the Omen Couple, while a skanky salesgirl carted out cheap herringbone blazer after cheap retro shirt and Chloe wasted everyone's time by settling on nothing. Hunter and the crew picked us up out front, me the indifferent owner of a hundred dollars worth of clothes I had no say in. The important thing was that no one dead was waiting on the sidewalk, but this latest apparition had still shaken me to the core. When Hunter announced we were going to swing by the Ordway house, I went ballistic.

"What are you doing to me, Leo?" he blurted, "I thought we were on the same page."

"Yeah, but I need to see this psychic guy right now."

"Well I don't think he's available yet. He probably hasn't even checked in."

"So call and find out."

"You're antsy to do this," added Chloe, "We get it. But the show isn't until tomorrow night. In the meantime we got you a nice room at the West Tower in Brentwood, so how about we check in, you can relax—"

"No! I want to talk to the psychic!"

Hunter hissed, yanked out his phone.

* * *

Ruby had a mid-afternoon meeting with Melissa, a cadaverous homeless woman who wore a nightdress, shower cap and smelled like cheese. She was also one of her more exasperating clients, famous for smiling and saying yes to every suggestion Ruby made before going back out to get drunk, stoned and ignore them all.

"The Culver City Pet Clinic. Remember them? They needed someone to sweep the floors two weeks ago." Melissa smiled and nodded. "Did you ever go over there?"

"I sure did!"

"O-kay…And what did they say?"

"They said 'we're closed, come on back tomorrow.'"

"And did you do that?"

"Do what?"

"Go back the next day."

'I sure did!"

"And what happened?

"Nothing happened, because they were closed already."

Ruby's thoughts just packed up and left at that moment. She suddenly didn't care whether Melissa ever earned a day's pay again in her life. Whether she rolled off the Santa Monica cliffs at midnight. The incident with me had bothered her more than she thought it would, and she needed to escape.

The moment Melissa smiled, said thanks and waddled out, Ruby checked with Phillip about which temps were available the next few days, then shut her office door. Picked up the phone and dialed her mother's number in Oregon.

It rang seven times—her mother had never believed in answering machines—before the other end was answered.

"If you're a Sagittarius, happy birthday! Mellon Crystals, Lila speaking." Ruby was real sick of her mother's organic syrup greeting; it was one of the reasons she'd begun e-mailing her. But this time Ruby needed a quick, clear answer.

"Ma? I need to come visit."

"Why didn't you e-mail?" Enya or some other ethereal vocalist sang in the background, and Ruby was stressed already.

"Please, Ma. Don't make this difficult."

"Something happen? If you call I figure it has to be something happened."

"No, nothing. I've just been working too hard and need a few days off." There was silence on her mother's end for a few seconds. "You have a guy there?"

"No. Do you?"

"That's funny, Ma. Assuming I can still get a flight to Portland, will you pick me up in Eugene?—"

"When have I not?"

"You always have. And you probably always will. I'll call you right after I land, okay?"

"Guess I'll need to buy more fish then."

"Whatever you want. See you tomorrow."

Ruby hung up before the next volley of guilt was launched, and began to think about packing.

* * *

Simmons Hempwood had indeed arrived, but he was tied up with the press, a 5 p.m. massage and 7 p.m. dinner reservation at the Palm, meaning he had a fifteen-minute window to meet us around 6:30. Hunter told me to take this or leave it, which pretty much ended further talking.

The Buzzmobile slogged through rush hour traffic up to Sunset and headed west. I was still a nervous mess, and asked to ride in the rear of the van with the crew so I wouldn't have to look out the window. The camera and sound guy dueled each other in some action game on matching hand-held consoles, pretending I wasn't even there. Chloe occasionally turned in her seat to ask if I was okay or wanted a water bottle, actually seeming to care about me.

The Hotel Bel-Air was tucked into a quiet, tree-choked canyon off the winding west segment of Sunset Boulevard, reached by a quick, hidden turn that didn't want to be found, like a secret trap door on a racetrack. The structure sprawled across eleven acres of secluded natural beauty and was proudly pink, its Tuscan main building flanked by gardens, fountains, swan pools and a line of lush private bungalows fit for royalty.

It took me a minute to collect myself and leave the safety of the van. I knew this was an old hotel, meaning all manner of weird things might have happened here. Wasn't there some *Shining* movie about an old hotel these Buzzheads had seen?

"Can we do this now, please?" snapped Hunter after the van's rear doors were swung open to reveal me still sitting there. "You made us drive you the hell over here—"

"I know! Just a second..." I took a deep breath, pried loose a wedge of underwear from my butt crack and stepped out. Chloe was there to take my arm and walk me up the heavily vegetated path to the hotel entrance.

"I look okay?" I asked, desperately trying to distract myself.

"Like the TV star you're gonna be." She winked again, and I began to fantasize where she might be taking this.

The modest lobby was ripe with fresh flowers and antique furniture, and classical piano music briefly put me at ease. Then Hunter strode ahead to the reception desk, leaving me and Chloe standing just inside the front door, and something shifted. Maybe it was in the flickering light thrown from the lobby fireplace, or a cool draft from outside they brought through the door. But I was certain someone else was in the lobby with us, and couldn't see whoever it was. I shuddered a little, and Chloe looked at me.

"You okay?"

"Yeah, let me just…" I dropped onto a nearby pink couch, and she joined me.

"You look like you're coming down with something. Let me get you a water bottle—"

"No. Stay with me, okay? I'm fine. Just need to rest."

Hunter came over from the front desk, flustered again. "His Hempwoodness bumped his dinner date to 7:30, but he still can't see us for fifteen minutes. So I'm going to the bar for a quick whiskey. Anybody?"

"We're good, Hunter. Thanks."

A regal-looking older couple with sweaters tied around their shoulders walked in and took the couch across from us. They smiled thinly and sat with arms locked, apparently waiting to be served in some way.

"They have a magnificent quail here," said the man in Chloe and my direction.

"Excuse me?" Chloe responded.

"In the restaurant. Have you tried it?"

"Actually, no. We're just meeting someone."

"Ah!" said the man, "So you don't have a room here."

"Uh-uh…Little out of our price range, you know?"

The man's wife had taken out a fat designer magazine to leaf through. Sniffed once and buried her eyes back in it. "Yes, I imagine it would be."

Chloe smiled back. She would rather have said go piss up a rope and kicked over their couch, but no, she was a professional, and unlike her last job, she actually enjoyed this one and preferred to keep it.

I was immobile beside her, completely unfazed by the snotty lady. Maybe even comforted. The odd feeling of not being alone in the lobby hadn't gone away, despite the new couple's presence. Chloe was communicating with them, so at least I knew they were alive. Yet the light piano music, the occasional shoe sounds on the stone paths outside were mixing with something else, not rustling leaves but human hushes, carried through the air and swirling around the lobby, never failing to bypass my ears.

"Let her take you…"

It was a whisper, so faint it was hard to tell whether it was male or female. The tone of the voice wasn't pleading, or mean-spirited. It was more like a commonplace statement. I heard it once, then five seconds later a bit louder, and then it was gone. I was already stressing about it.

"She's not taking me anywhere…" I mumbled to myself, just loud enough to get alarmed stares from the quail-lovers. Chloe shot to her feet.

"I think we're going to find our friend in the bar," she announced, "C'mon, Leo." I stood up right away, nodded at the older couple to be polite, and left the lobby with my chaperone.

Hunter had drained two Johnnie Walkers, so his balance was a bit off as we made our way to Bungalow 12 five minutes later and knocked on its French doors. Chloe, who had applied some lip gloss when no one was looking, fussed with her tart outfit while we waited for admittance.

An elderly manservant in a forest green vest swung open the door.

"That would be Hunter, Chloe and Leo?" He sounded like Alec Guinness with a head cold, and moved about as fast.

"Bingo," said Hunter, trying to peer over the man's shoulder, "and you're Rawlings?"

Rawlings nodded. "Mr. Hempwood is finishing his early evening tea, but he's ready for you, if you'll just..." He stranded the sentence in mid-air and motioned them inside.

Simmons Hempwood rose from his Edwardian armchair, folding the *Wall Street Journal* that was in his lap. He was well into his 60s, with an open, beefy face, purple velvet smoking jacket and perfectly coiffed shock of silver hair. His eyes were as sharp and blue as the Mediterranean, and seemed capable of hypnotizing you at any moment. He shook Hunter's hand, then Chloe's, words spilling out of his mouth in a buttery baritone.

"Delighted and charmed, delighted and charmed." I stepped forward and readied my hand but Hempwood held back, gave me a cautious smile.

"Leo, is it?"

I nodded, shuffled my feet while I spoke. "I hear you're real good at this kind of thing, Mr. Hempwood. Hope you can help me."

"Yes, I do have my merits. Shall we sit?" He retreated to his armchair. I exchanged odd glances with Chloe and Hunter, followed them over and took a large couch across from him.

"Can I get anyone..." It was Rawlings with another vanishing sentence, but no one was listening this time. All eyes were trained on the famous psychic who seemed wary of shaking my hand.

"So what's this San Diego event like?" asked Hunter to break the ice. "I should send a crew down there sometime."

"I wouldn't. It's basically a lot of paranormal peacocks strutting about, displaying their wares. I enjoy the weather, naturally, and the society pays a decent wage, but it's become so invaded by fringe dwellers and horror film fanatics it's all getting a little pointless." He continued to stare at me, and finally leaned forward in his chair. "Is it really true you are a homeless fellow?"

"Yup…It really is."

"I ask because I'm sensing an aura about you that is quite thick. Which is the reason I didn't shake your hand, you see. I prefer my initial contact with inflicted subjects to be non-physical."

"What did you mean it was thick?"

"My apologies. Thick is my term for …heavily populated." He leaned forward even more. "You have many spirits about you, sir."

"Really? Well, guess that's no surprise. I've been seeing a lot of these dead creeps around town."

"Of course. Yet from what I gather, Ms. Ordway is the one on point, so to speak. The one whose predicament must be the spark that has launched this psychic dilemma."

"Yeah, okay. she was the first, but what do these other things I'm seeing have to do with her? They show up when I'm asleep, when I'm awake, it's getting so I can't shut my eyes or leave 'em open, and I'm starting to go fucking NUTS so you gotta stop feeding me your snobby bullshit and tell me why this is happening already!!" I caught a glimpse of Hempwood's shocked face, Hunter and Chloe frozen on the couch, and dropped my head shamefully. "I didn't mean to…I'm real sorry."

"He's had a rough few days. Been running on fumes," said Chloe, and gave my shoulders a cursory rub. Hunter squeezed out a smile while Hempwood merely sat there, finishing off the rest of his Earl Grey.

"Yes, well…I'm sure we'll be able to make some headway tomorrow evening. For the viewing audience's sake, we'd better. Until then?" He rose, expecting everyone else to follow his lead—which we did.

Rawlings appeared from nowhere, eyed me furtively. "Are

you sure he's going to be…" he started to ask, then walked away. Hempwood seemed annoyed by the entire visit, lagged behind us as we moved to the door. I hesitated, turned back at the last moment and put out my hand again. Hempwood sighed, maybe feeling the weight of this destitute man before him, and this time shook it.

A ghastly pallor painted his lips. He looked at his hand, wriggling weirdly inside mine. "Good lord…" he uttered, and stared at it as if it were suddenly some exotic reptile.

"What's wrong??" blurted Chloe. Hunter's first instinct was anger for not bringing his cameraman, but he stood transfixed, equally baffled beside them.

The wriggling quickened, shot up Hempwood's arm until his entire upper body fell into line, and then the smoking jacket opened, a button popped on his fancy linen dress shirt beneath and his already reddish face turned beet.

"Her heart…too strong!" he yelled, and the wriggling finally abated. The color in his face drained and his whole body seemed to shrivel before them.

"Let go of him!" cried Hunter.

"No, shut up!" I said, "He's getting somewhere…"

Hempwood's eyes closed and he lowered his head. A labored, raspy breathing wafted from his mouth.

"Take her…with you…" I was stunned. The words I'd heard just before in the lobby! The voice was an octave higher and clearly not Hempwood's, but one choked by dirt and roots, drowning in anguish, the voice of a tortured, departed woman. Chloe was too scared to even scream, while Rawlings stood a few feet away with the empty teacup, a fascinated but oddly patient expression on his face. "She wants…you to…" he said.

I was dying to ask Hempwood's possessor something, but was afraid to break the connection. Sweat from our fused hands dripped on the plush carpet. Rawlings exchanged the teacup for a pen and pad of hotel stationery, held it out to his employer.

"Sir! Do you need to write?"

Hempwood knocked it out of his hand. "TAKE HER! WITH YOU!" he yelled in his channeled voice.

I squirmed in place. Perspiration flooded my shirt. I couldn't let this moment pass, not with my sanity at a ripping point. I had to say something.

"Do you mean Jo?" My voice cracked as I uttered the question. Hempwood stood there, bushy eyebrows twitching, eyes still closed.

"Yes..." was the response, "I am Jo..."

Hunter and Chloe shared a puzzled glance. I narrowed my gaze, letting the words chart a course through my brain.

"If you're Jo, then...who are you talking about?"

Hempwood's lips crinkled. His mouth opened again but this time said nothing.

"Who do I take, Jo?"

The psychic's hand began wriggling again, spread upward. The lights in the room flickered, then went out. Hempwood's breathing quickened, gurgled; something thick was clogging it.

Rawlings looked panicked for the first time. "Sir? You need to come back to us now." He reached for Hempwood's arm, grimaced and sprung back as if he'd touched an exposed power line.

"I'm getting a cameraman!" said Hunter, and started for the door. There were two loud knocks on it at that moment.

"Housekeeping!" The cheery girl's voice with its Spanish accent seemed to evaporate the psychic tension. Lights flickered back on. Hempwood's hand loosened its grip on mine, and he staggered back into Rawlings' arms. Hunter threw the door open on the bewildered maid, standing there with a fresh armload of towels.

"Nice fucking timing," said Hunter, and grabbed them from her. Rawlings had lowered Hempwood back into his armchair, ran to pour him water. Chloe leaned over him.

"Holy-oly shit," she said, "You okay?" Natural color had returned to his face. His laser beam eyes had snapped back open, and came with an ecstatic smile.

"Did I say who I was?"

"Y-yeah. Jo Ordway."

Hempwood clenched a fist in triumph, rose again and patted my shoulder. "We've done it, young fellow. We've done it."

I was out of sorts. "Done what?"

"Breached the astral plane, of course! We're wired! Tomorrow night at her death site we will put on a show no one will ever forget."

"But who was she talking about? Someone she wanted me to take—"

"We will probe further. All answers tomorrow night, my good man." He turned to Chloe and Hunter. "I've never had a talent for predicting, but if you milk this event properly you will have a long-running sensation on your hands." He took his water glass from Rawlings and raised it to me. "Because this is the most haunted bloke I've ever met."

❧ FOURTEEN ❧

Lila was a good twenty minutes late arriving at the Eugene bus station. Ruby had already endured an hour delay on the LAX runway, a couple hours of turbulence and a bus ride next to a teen-age boy with grunge punk blasting out of his ear buds, so she was in no mood for further annoyance.

"Is it my fault all the good gas stations are closed Sunday night? I had to go into North Bend to find one that didn't look like a rapist lair." She slid across the seat of her ancient Monte Carlo to let Ruby behind the wheel. "You look pale. How can you live down there and never get sun?"

"Do you really need to ask me this every time, Ma? I told you. Because I don't have the time, or the skin for it. Now can we please have a nice, stress-free drive?" Lila made a screwy face and sat with her arms folded.

Silence filled the car the first five miles through winding pines. Ruby tried to tune in a classical FM station but was having no luck and gave up.

"So how are the crystals doing, Ma?"

"Slow as usual…I figure three more months before I start look-ing into solar therapy."

"Up here? There's isn't enough sun to get a worm exposed!"

"Who said here? There was this nice man who came in the store last week that has his own solar therapy clinic in Tuscon, and he invited me down to check it out."

"You mean check him out."

"Oh be quiet."

"It's way too hot down there, Ma. Trust me, you'd hate it."

"Better than going into bankruptcy up here. And at least we'd be closer to each other."

Ruby didn't even respond to that one. She had a habit of checking the odometer every time her mother picked her up in Eugene, and knew there were only twelve miles of agony left.

"Something wrong at your job?" Lila asked.

"Oh…nothing specific. Just been an awful week. I had to let Chloe go. Remember her?"

"Of course I do. The one with the lesbian lover."

"No, that was Margaret. And they were actually married with an adopted kid. Chloe was the insufferable USC grad."

"Whatever. You've always known how to pick 'em."

Ruby tightened her grip on the wheel to keep from swerving, or shoving her mother out of the car.

"I really need to get some exercise the next few days, Ma. Shore Acres would be good, maybe even Cape Arago. If you're not up for it, I can do it alone."

"Why wouldn't I be?"

"Okay, then you are."

Silence re-filled the Monte Carlo. For Ruby it was absolutely preferable.

* * *

Chloe drove me over to the West Tower Hotel, a straight shot down Sunset from Bel-Air. Hunter had booked adjoining rooms for both of us, because his trust in me had diminished considerably and wanted someone nearby in case of another freak-out. He'd thought about having us share a suite, but that would have been way too much to ask of Chloe.

As it turned out, Chloe was looking at me in a new, saucy light after my encounter with Simmons Hempwood. The old medium was correct: ratings for the Buzz Channel had a good chance of skyrocketing, and here she was, suddenly the budding celeb's personal escort. She'd helped re-shape my hair and dress me like a homeless Ken doll, and she was pretty damn proud of her job. Throw me into a nice long shower and who knew what would emerge?

The hotel was perched beside the Sunset overpass of the 405 freeway. Chloe and her friends had been calling the overpass the O.J. Bridge ever since his slow speed chase neared its climax over it back in '94, and it was still a bit chilling to cross the thing. I didn't remember what I was doing that day when Chloe asked me, and seemed focused on the odd round shape of the hotel. At least it wasn't too many decades old, I thought, meaning it wouldn't be wall-to-wall with ghouls yet.

Our rooms were on the 17th floor, each with a stellar view of the 405. Even at night, the freeway was terminally busy, its tail and headlight ribbons snaking in and out of the Sepulveda Pass. Chloe ordered me a $20 room service cheeseburger and fries, then spent a good ten minutes showing me how to work the TV remote. Once I seemed to get the hang of it she lingered, leafing through the program guide.

"CNN, MSNBC, ESPN, HBO, the usual alphabet…Check it, they even have the Buzz Channel!" I skipped around a bit, then switched the set off, tossed the remote aside and stretched out on the bed.

"Jesus…"

"Comfy, huh? They got Jacuzzi tubs, too. Can't wait to hop in mine…Bet you never stayed in a place like this."

"Can't say if I have."

She stared at me until it seemed awkward. "You sure you're okay being alone?"

"Hope so."

She tapped the wall behind my headboard. "Well, I'm right on the other side here, so…don't be afraid to knock."

"Thanks." I glanced at a wedge of bare belly peeking over her jeans. "Wish we could've gotten this thing over with tonight."

"Yeah, but you heard Simmons. We need a full day of promos, and it takes that long to set up all his stuff."

"What stuff?"

"What d'ya think? Cameras, lights. Plus all of his ghost-hunting shit."

"Right…" Fresh anxiety crept into my face. "So what the hell do I do all day?"

She shrugged. "Stay here. There's a pool downstairs. You can order room service and watch soaps for all we care. It's paid for, remember?" I sighed, gazed at the cottage cheesy ceiling. She gingerly reached down, took one of my large tanned hands and squeezed. "See ya in the morning?"

I nodded. Waited for her to go out the door, then rose and drew the curtains shut. Went to the door and bolted it. Returned to the bed, removed my shoes and laid down again. Shut my eyes.

I was tired, but my mind was far too charged to sleep. The Simmons Hempwood handshake may have energized the famous seer and the Buzz Channel, but it had only left me more befuddled. Jo Ordway had been trying to talk to me for days, but there was apparently another spirit involved now. Or maybe Hempwood was wrong and it was really this other entity speaking about Jo. I was also mad at myself for not bringing up the young couple in black. Who the hell were they, and did Hempwood sense them in any way? I made a mental note to "look" for them the second tomorrow's séance began.

I killed the lamp beside the bed, watched a dull, liquefied version of the car lights flow up a small section of wall. Found the remote and put the TV back on to channel-surf and dull my mind. It didn't take long. The Golf Channel replayed a seniors tournament from Orlando. American Movie Classics was showing *The Best Years of Our Lives* with Fredric March and Dana Andrews. An old black-and-white movie was as good as a tranquilizer to me, and my eyes were in deep flutter until the scene where the young Navy guy arrives home from World War II, and his family and girlfriend next door get spooked when they see his hands have been replaced by hooks. The tragedy of the moment disturbed me so much I chose to kill the TV and plunge myself back into near darkness. The hot sun and waves of Will Rogers State Beach would be my sleep-aid memory tonight, and I revved them up the moment I closed my eyes.

I woke in a lathering sweat just after dawn. I was used to not being exactly sure where I was, but something about this hotel room wasn't right.

I sat up. Sunlight filtered through the light brown curtains. The air conditioner hummed softly. A door or two opened and closed down the hall. Nothing strange there. So what was bothering me?

Then I knew: the traffic noise on the 405 freeway was missing. I even thought I heard a couple of chirping birds. I slowly got up, went to the curtain drawstring and yanked it open.

The freeway was still there, but every car on it had stopped and killed its engine. Doors were wide open on most of the vehicles, and the drivers and passengers stood outside them, staring up at me.

"What the fuck—"

I jerked the curtain shut, wedged myself into the corner. Deep breathed a few times to keep my insides from imploding. Collected my wits, then turned and reached for the drawstring again. Rose and reached up. Re-opened the curtain.

The drivers and passengers were hovering above the road, closer to the window, as if fitted with invisible jet packs. They were still a bit far away, but I could make out splotches of blood on a few faces, oddly twisted limbs on others. A handful of the cars below were either smashed together or on fire. I knew the young couple in black had to be among the airborne apparitions, but I didn't want to look for them, not now. Not ever—

The ringing room phone saved me, and I was back in bed with the curtains drawn, the daymare gone like evil fairy dust that had been blown away. I lunged for the receiver and heard Chloe's cute voice before I had a chance to say anything.

"Leo?"

"Yeah…"

"Shake off the webs, dude. Got us a field trip."

"A what?"

"Hunter proved his worth for a change and swung us parking reservations at the Getty. Ever been up there?"

"Uhh…nope."

"Cool then! I'll be over to get you in fifteen."

"Can we make it a half hour? I have to shower."

"Oh. Right…Good call."

While I waited for the shower to heat up, I found a tiny complementary shampoo bottle on a tray. I left the room a moment, inspired, darted down to a maid's cart and grabbed five more.

The water was soothing, heavenly, and the three shampoo bottles I used on my hair gave me a soapy afro to be reckoned with. I'd convinced myself the nightmare was just a nightmare—no psychic connotations, no deep symbolism to keep my mind scrambling all day—and I would forget all about it the moment we got to the Getty.

I opened the door for Chloe. She was surprised to see me still in my boxers, one of my new shirts thrown on over them, but she blew into the room regardless, hair freshly spiked and murdering some gum.

"Quick! Where's your remote?"

I wasn't quick enough and she found it for me, switched on the TV.

"What is it?"

"Wait'll you see…"

Chloe tuned in the Buzz Channel to a distorted wide angle shot of the boarded-up Ordway house, complete with a swirling CGI fog bank. The voice-over guy had an obligatory lurid baritone.

"…to mark the two-month anniversary of the gruesome event with paranormal disturbances. Now, with the help of a mysterious drifter, Simmons Hempwood puts his worldwide psychic reputation on the line."

"Oooooh," said Chloe, squeezing my arm, "Mystery man!"

"Watch *Séance for Jo*, live and exclusive on the Buzz Channel. Tonight at 10 Eastern, 7 Pacific."

Chloe beamed brighter than the TV screen. "Pretty damn cool, huh?"

I shrugged. The word "drifter" was certainly better than "homeless guy", but the whole thing felt unclean.

"What does Jason Ordway think about this? And Jo's parents?"

"All on board. Or at least handsomely paid to act like they are. Believe it or not, the towelhead couple that lives next door were the worst to deal with. Anyway…"

She clicked off the set. I just sat there on the bed, picked at an old scab on one of my raised legs. Chloe couldn't help but notice one of my hairy, good-sized balls peeking out from the boxers, and was certain that if I hadn't been in dark, slovenly places for who knows how many years, she probably would've jumped my knob by now. With my scraggly locks washed and trimmed and about ten hours from being on national TV, I was close to being a real catch.

"Better get some pants on there, Leo. Got a woman present."

I dropped my leg, sheepish, and reached for my new pair of jeans. "Think I'll be warm enough?" I asked, turning my back to finish dressing.

"Sure, if you button your shirt. You live outside, so you know. I'll be in the hall."

She darted out, and I found a full-length mirror for my final inspection. Nothing shadowy lurked in the corners, my new rayon shirt looked positively sporty, and a pretty girl waited to escort me to a beacon of culture.

Death, be damned.

* * *

Ruby slept reasonably well, aided by nearby waves crashing on the Coos Bay shore. Lila kept every west-facing window open at night, regardless of temperature, one of Ruby's childhood curios forever encased in the Oregon museum. Add to that the incense candles burning in both bathrooms, the kitchen table seat under the driftwood clock she instinctively dropped into on visits, and the lemon wheat germ hot cakes her mother served the first morning.

Today's were exceptional, and for a good hour Ruby enjoyed hearing Lila's usual Coos gossip. They dressed, packed bottled waters and trail mix and hit Cape Arago State Park by 10:30, and it wasn't until they huffed their way onto the old steep wagon road that the brief morning sun went into hiding.

"So what's bothering you?" Lila suddenly asked, as if on cue with the darkening sky.

"Didn't I tell you already?"

"Come on, dear. I may be a bit loony in the bin, but I still know my daughter. And I'm not buying this work stress crap."

"Can't we just have a nice hike for once?"

"It *is* nice. Nature sees to that without being asked. It's also the best time to spill our beans. I was up here with Felicia once and she told me about her breast cancer and gambling addiction in the same hour."

"Well, sorry if I can't be that dramatic, Ma." She took the lead around a steep bend, grimaced from a nippy sea gust that shot through an opening in the pines and struck her face.

"Who's the guy?"

"Ma!"

"Oh Ruby, grow up and talk to me, will you? You're not fifteen and hiding your tampons anymore. And I can see that sad blue aura around you from a mile away."

Ruby paused to catch her breath and take in her mother's stabbing gaze. Though it was often hard to take Lila seriously, Ruby had always respected her intuitive talents. The way she used to stock up on cold medicine the day before her son and daughter came down with one. The time she called her old college room-mate and implored her to leave an Oakland freeway moments before the '89 earthquake collapsed it. Ruby wasn't even sure how much Lila valued her unique skills. The fortune telling business had been allowed to dry and up and blow out to sea with the rest of her whimsical experiments.

"It's really that noticeable?"

"Sad and blue. Like one of those '50s jazz albums."

Ruby walked another yard or so, staying mum. Lila sidled up to her.

"Where'd you meet him?"

"Okay. It's not anyone I'm seeing. Just…a guy I work with. That I care about."

"Really? You've been hiring? I thought you just let that girl go—"

"No, this is a temp. Someone we've used a few times actually."

"Oh. Did he used to be homeless?"

"Hell, no. Though he could be if he isn't careful…He's made a few bad decisions recently."

"You've gone out with him?"

"Are you kidding? He's a little, um…old for me."

"Not the worst move you can make. Your father was certainly no duckling when I met—"

"No Dad references, please," snapped Ruby, and her mother clammed up with a perturbed expression. They passed a crop of ancient grassy bunkers used as defense posts during World War II, and Ruby paused to gaze at them.

"They still get transients sleeping in these?"

"Occasionally," said Lila, swigging from her water bottle. "At least they have enough respect to not use them for toilets…What bad decisions did this friend of yours make?"

The question snapped Ruby out of her meditation, and she resumed walking. "Oh, I don't know…Career stuff. Then I steered him somewhere that made it all worse."

Lila sighed. "You can only do so much for people, you know." She poked Ruby playfully. "How many psychiatrists does it take to change a light bulb?"

"Just tell me."

"One. But the light bulb has to want to change." She snorted a laugh.

"I think I've heard that."

"Well, it's true."

"No it isn't. Shit, if I believed that I wouldn't have a job, would I? Some people actually need to be forced to change."

"Come on, dear. I'm just—"

"Could you stop please? You're kissing my boo-boo again and hoping it goes away. But sometimes boo-boos are festering fucking sores that don't."

"Nobody's a miracle worker—"

"But you have to try! You don't think Erik could have used one before he went off to die in an alley?"

That did it. Lila froze in place as if crazy glue had just been poured into her hiking shoes. Her face hardened, nearly cracked. She dug out a handful of trail mix, pulverized it with her dentures and pushed past Ruby to take point on the trail.

* * *

As the Getty's long tram car flanked its way up the sun-baked mountain, I flashed back to a hot afternoon on a similar train. There were parapets and banners of a magic castle out the window that day, odd jungle growth and a haunted mansion. Why was this coming back to me, I wondered? Had I stumbled drunkenly into Disneyland once, or was I taken there long ago?

"Check it, Leo."

Chloe was pointing at the spacious entrance plaza we were rolling into. She was wearing some kind of spicy perfume that reminded me of cinnamon drops, and for the first time I noticed a delicious little beauty mark perched on her bare shoulder.

We went up some wide steps, through a building and into a central courtyard that was like no place I had ever been, certainly not in L.A. Stunning glass and stone buildings surrounded us, yet there was a spaciousness to the area and the city and ocean views beyond that made it feel like an airport runway you could just soar out of.

"This is so cool," said Chloe, obviously a first-timer herself. "Let's get a brochure." She grabbed one off a nearby stand, walked me to a bench and unfolded it for both of us. I suddenly noticed she wasn't wearing a bra, and angled myself perfectly over the unbuttoned portion of her blouse to take in one of her perky goblets. "Awesome!" she cooed, "they have an outdoor café. And gardens."

"And art, I guess," I said.

"Oh, right. You like paintings? I don't have a lot of patience for staring at pictures of crucified guys."

"They're okay. Sometimes they're kind of peaceful. "

"Well here—" She handed me the map, bounced back up. "Pick whatever you want and I'll keep you company."

I studied the thing while Chloe slipped away to a kiosk to peruse Getty Center coffee mugs. I remembered liking Impressionism for the brief time I was at that museum in Pasadena, and eventually found the correct building on the map that had some. Chloe passed on a mug but quickly paid for a T-shirt and joined me for the start of my art walk.

The East Pavilion had some Dutch and Flemish landscapes I was fond of. I was also drawn to *The Musicians' Brawl* from 1625 by a painter named Georges de La Tour, a strange, detailed depiction of a lute player squeezing lemon juice into a blind man's eyes. But as I entered a room with a couple of religious scenes, Chloe hissed and rolled her eyes.

"See? This is what I meant. Crucified dudes a go-go."

I nodded to placate her, moseyed on ahead. A room of Rembrandts drew us down a connecting hall into the South Pavilion, where Chloe yawned after twenty seconds in a gallery of tapestries, vases, and 18th century clocks. From there it was west, and through a fine upstairs display of Impressionism. A Millet gave way to a Monet, which gave way to a Courbet. Natural light filtering in through skylights bathed each room in a comforting glow. It was also a weekday, and thus uncrowded. A gaggle of Japanese teenagers swarmed in front of Van Gogh's *Irises*, but there were few paintings I didn't have easy access to.

"Non voglio essere qui…"

The husky foreign voice came from behind me, and I turned to look at the speaker.

Only Chloe was standing there, checking something on her cell phone. She looked up.

"What?"

"Nothing. Just that…" I peered around the room. The Japanese kids had moved on, and only two old ladies remained, eyeing a sculpture with their audio tour headphones on.

"I thought I heard something," I said. Chloe shrugged and popped her gum, followed me into the next room.

This one featured a Renoir and Pissarro and the same animated Japanese teenagers, squirming in front of each other to get better looks at things.

"Non voglio essere qui…"

I stopped in my tracks. This time the voice echoed behind my ear, as if I had suddenly entered a deep grotto. I listened for it again, but all I heard were the scuffing shoes of a watchful guard.

Chloe touched my sleeve and I jumped.

"Whoa—sorry! You okay?"

"Yeah. Fine." I really wasn't at all, but with all the guards watching this was the last place in the world I wanted to flip out in.

"I'm about ready to hit the old snooze button. Wanna go to the gift shop?"

"Um…not really. Maybe some lunch, though. I never ate breakfast."

"I can ride with that. And I do have the magic Buzz card."

We stood in line a few minutes. I opted for an oven roasted turkey and swiss cheese sandwich and sparkling cranberry juice. Chloe chose a crunchy vegetable wrap that she proceeded to barely touch at our sun-splashed patio table.

"Hunter can be such a nimrod," she said, texting him for the third time in a minute. "He puts me in charge of talent, then treats me like a six-year-old. 'Yes, ass-clown, we'll be there by 5:30. No problem, I'll make sure he stays sober.' Can you believe him?"

"He's nervous. Seems like a big show."

"Hey, there's nerves, and there's Nazis. Hunter won't even fart if he can't control the fumes."

The remark made me chuckle, the first time I'd done that in a while. I gazed at the gumdroppish nipple points on Chloe's blouse, trying to remember if I'd ever had relations with a girl this cute. I figured I hadn't.

"How's the sandwich?"

"Oh, good. Great, actually."

The turkey was fresh and warm, very unlike the cold, processed turkey slabs I was used to. The sultry breeze crinkled my hair, soothed my face, and I wanted to file the moment away so I could retrieve it whenever I wanted.

"Odio questa! Si prega di voler liberare me!"

The tortured voice shot through the hot air and straight into my skull. I dropped my sandwich, stood and scanned the patio with a queasy look on my face.

"Leo? What's wrong?"

"I um…I need to find a rest room. Definitely."

"Oh! Well…go for it. Know where they—"

"Yeah."

I hurried away. There was a bathroom sign around the cafeteria to the left but I strode right past it, bounded up the stairs to the main level. I had the urge to jump on the next downward tram and flee, but how could I escape this new goddamn voice? I heard it bubbling up inside my head again, paused in the middle of the courtyard to let it come.

"Non voglio essere qui!!"

Shit, what the hell language was that? I whirled, looking for a sign, even a cadaverous shape to go with it. The hot sun drilled into my scalp and I felt dizzy, dropped onto a bench and held my head.

"Vi prego di aiutarmi…"

The man's voice was quieter now, almost pleading. I slowly looked up. Caught an odd glow bouncing off the upstairs window of another pavilion on the left that we'd skipped. Was it the angle of the sun? I stood, inched toward it.

No. The glow was clearly inside the gallery. And it was orange.

"Non voglio essere qui…"

I moved toward the gallery doors. I had to. The courtyard around me was filling up, and if Chloe was trying to spot me from the patio I might have been out of view. Either way, I was going to follow this voice.

The North Pavilion housed their earliest European art, and I wove around patrons in search of the nearest staircase.

"Vi prego di aiutarmi…"

The orange glow seemed to fill much of the second floor. My eyes darted about frantically, but tried to keep my walk slow to keep the guards unaware. The first room had mostly crucifixion scenes, and I moved into the second, which was much larger and had blood red walls that were now tinted orange.

"Non voglio essere qui…"

The voice was clear and sharp now, because the man called me from the opposite wall. Even from this distance I could see his long beard and melancholy expression. I drifted toward the painting in a liquid, hypnotic state.

The nameplate said *Portrait of a Bearded Man* by Jacopo Bassano, Italian, painted in 1550. The man wore a black tunic, had huge, watery eyes and was clearly disturbed about something.

Was it the mysterious shadow he or something else cast on the wall to his right?

"Non voglio essere qui…"

The words barked from the painting. I leapt back, colliding with a middle-aged man and his wife.

"Mi pare che sia cosa spiacenti!" said the man, followed by "I am sorry." I stared at him, recognizing the similar language and cadence.

"You're Italian?"

"Si! Do you speak?"

"No, but someone just told me something in Italian and could you tell me what it means? *Non voglio…essere qui.* Something like that—"

"Please say again?"

"Non voglio essere qui…"

"Did the person have a problem?"

"A problem?"

"He said he does not want to be here."

I looked up at the painted man. His eyes were looking off to the left, out of the frame. *"Vi prego di aiutarmi!"* he shouted in my ear.

"Vi prego di aiutarmi??" I repeated.

"What?" said the foreign visitor, "You want me to help you?" I shook my head, turned and backpedaled from the room.

Loud, torturous screams boomed around me. I was in the room of crucifixion paintings, and Christ-blood spurted from every canvas. I closed my eyes, covered my ears and ran. By the time a guard raised his walkie-talkie, I was out the nearest exit.

Chloe had waited on the patio a good five minutes before getting antsy. She pocketed her phone, left the unfinished lunches on the table and headed up into the courtyard. It was then that she saw me dart out of a North Pavilion door, race across the far end of the courtyard.

"LEO!"

I didn't hear her. My head disappeared down a ramp leading

to the Central Garden. Chloe raced after me, squeezing around people to keep me in sight. The walkway switched back on itself about five times, and when it was close to the bottom she caught sight of me trying to climb over the rail. A short lawn, service road and harrowing undergrowth beckoned.

"Leo, don't!" I paused, looked at her with wild eyes and threw a leg over the top anyway. She ran up, grabbed my arm at the last second. Pulled me off the thing.

"What the hell are you—"

"I gotta get out! They're talking to me!"

"What?? Who's talking—"

"All of 'em! This freak in an Italian painting, every damn Christ in the place, probably Van Gogh carting around his fucking ear if I went back up there again—"

"OKAY! Calm down. Just stay with me, okay? C'mon, we'll go down to the garden. There's other people, flowers and plants, a waterfall. You'll be yourself in no time."

"How do you know??"

"Try it, Leo, okay? Just try it. I heard there's people who come here and meditate."

"I don't want to fucking meditate!"

"So don't. Just take my hand and walk with me, okay? Trust me, running off into the bushes isn't going to help anything."

She grabbed my clammy hand with both of hers and I let her guide me the rest of the way down the ramp.

The Central Garden wasn't enormous, but was gorgeously designed in a circular shape with multiple serpentine paths and highlighted a water feature cascading over a stepped stone wall. Hundreds of azaleas adorned the walk, and I tried my best to take it all in as we circled around the back. Just above the garden, a couple of families sat on a sloping lawn and watched their children roll their way to the bottom. The sun was blinding here, and I started to feel a savage headache coming on.

"Demeurer avec nous, merci!"

And that didn't help: guttural French spilling down from a gallery. I didn't care what it meant but knew they were words of the Dead. I smacked the side of my head with my free hand, ripped myself away from Chloe. Slipped around a huge potted plant and dropped into a hidden storm drain wedged below the rear paths.

"Leo, no—" She glanced around to make sure no one was watching, then followed me into the dark stone crevasse. It was thankfully dry, and the service road could be seen out its far end. I was on my hands and knees, trying to reach it, but Chloe was on me in seconds.

"I can't do this…I can't…" I babbled.

"Bullshit, Leo. You can. Whatever the hell you're hearing, either listen to it or find a way to tune it out. How do you think Simmons Hempwood became a success? By running away from his voices like a big wuss?"

"I don't care…I want to die…Just want to fucking die…" I was shaking like a dog after hearing an M-80 go off. She put an arm around me, held me close to her.

"Ssshhh….It's okay…" I shook my head, over and over. Chloe leaned in and gave me a soft kiss on my neck. It made my shaking subside. I turned slightly, glanced at her adorable face. This time she kissed my cheek. I had a musky scent that Chloe actually liked. My eyes traveled down to her blouse, where one more button had undone itself, and an entire nipple was in view. She let me look, because it seemed to help, and there was a desperate, little boy sadness in my expression that was probably irresistible. What might be the biggest night of her budding career was less than two hours away, and she knew what she needed to do.

"Ever see one of those?" she softly asked. I didn't respond either way, but shifted myself on the cold stone embankment for a slightly better view. She smiled shyly, opened the last button on her blouse and freed the entire breast. My breathing quickened a bit. She slid her hand onto my pants and quickly found my growing bulge. I flinched.

"No, no. It's okay. Are you hearing the voices now?"

"Uh-uh. Not this second."

"That's good…that's real good…" She unzipped me. My entire body shuddered. I reached in to feel her wonderfully soft breast for a second or two, then laid on my back and let her stroke me. The waterfall sound helped expedite things, and nearly drowned out the occasional footfalls on the pathways above us. Chloe spit in her palm, worked me like the junior pro she occasionally was. I breathed faster and faster in time with her hand, let the living world go, let the dead rot before my eyes rolled up and I gushed into her warm palm in multiple volleys I might've stored for a decade.

"Yikes," she said, wiping most of it off on one of the damper slabs.

"Thanks…" I muttered, and gave her a gentle squeeze on the arm. She looked away, half relieved but mostly ashamed. Buttoned up her blouse and led me out of the crevasse, miraculously unseen.

The downhill tram was packed solid. Chloe and me sat on opposite sides, separated by a standing wall of patrons, which was probably a good thing. She felt weird about what she'd done, and was afraid to make eye contact with anyone, let alone me. I was nearly smiling, though. Ghastly voices were gone from my head, while fluffy clouds and hilltop mansions glided by across the 405. For the first time in ages, I felt non-dead.

❧ FIFTEEN ❧

Lila chose The Sea Catch on South Broadway to have dinner because she said she knew the owner, though it was apparently not well enough. While Ruby stood by the hostess stand with her arms folded, Lila picked fights with at least three employees in a quest for the perfect harbor view table. Ruby got disgusted before long and wandered into the bar for a chablis, and that's when she saw the teaser for *Séance for Jo*. All three bar TV sets were showing it, so there was no place for Ruby to hide.

"I don't know why they keep digging up this Ordway crap," said a blue collar patron sitting at the bar with his buddy, "Nobody gives a shit."

"Yeah, but this ghost guy's pretty good," said his friend. "He did a show on a haunted London prison once that freaked me out for a week." Ruby wanted to say something, but nothing useful came to her scattered mind so she paid for her wine and left the bar.

Lila was encamped at a table maybe three feet away from the row of harbor view ones, and Ruby could tell by the look on her mother's face that it wasn't close enough.

"When Serge gets back tomorrow he's getting a rather heated phone call from me. This is unacceptable."

"It's fine, Ma. Let it go."

"It is not fine. Look at this. You can't even see the bridge from here."

Before the lumber shortage, Coos Bay was the largest timber shipping port in the world, but now there were only occasional foreign vessels coming into the docks. "Ma, we've eaten on the water like 45 times. I know what it looks like."

"Well, that still doesn't make it right."

"You're the one making it wrong!"

Lila snapped open her menu to kill their latest conversation, and Ruby began thinking about her next glass of wine.

* * *

By the time me and Chloe arrived at the Ordway house, Camden Street was blocked off, and Chloe had to park two streets away. Equipment trucks, mobile dressing rooms and security vehicles took up most of the block, Buzz Channel vans and a mob of barricaded onlookers the rest.

Chloe marched us toward the scene. Her eyes bounced around excitedly, but still managed to avoid mine.

"Hope they have a catering tent going. You hungry?" I shook my head, as awed by the commotion as she was. Hunter appeared out of nowhere wearing a makeup bib, already beyond stressed.

"Jesus F. Christ, where have you two been?"

"The Getty, remember?" preened Chloe. "Your idea?"

"Whatever. Leo needs a short makeover and a mic on his shirt. And grab some food before the crew eats it all."

"Is Mr. Hempwood here?" I asked.

"Locked in his trailer. He needs total isolation before each show. I don't know, builds up his psychic mojo or something. Have to go work on my hair." And he was gone again.

I endured a half hour of some butchy girl fussing with my appearance, which seemed strange because the word was that I was barely going to appear on camera. As I left the makeup trailer and crossed to a food tent set up on the neighboring house's lawn, a booming voice hit me from behind.

"You owe me a round, dickhead!"

I recognized the voice right away, and spun around. Behind a row of metal barricades set up in the street, Duce stood there with a bagged bottle, an envious sneer on his face. I gave him a helpless, apologetic look.

"Yeah, that's it!" yelled Duce. "Forget about your friends! Enjoy the fame and fortune!" Then under his breath: "Sell-out fuckface…"

I looked away, wounded, then caught a glimpse of Victor stand-ing at the other end of the barricade, flanked by his entire Boyle Heights family.

"My wife wanted to be here for Jo!" he cried out with a feeble wave, though he still looked terrified to be there. I gave him a cool, obligatory nod and kept walking.

I stayed in the tent as long as I could, found a spot away from the crowd and dined on catered enchiladas. Chloe yucked it up at a nearby table with a couple of cute Buzz Channel guys, glanc-ing over at me the requisite number of times to justify her job. I eventually got bored and wandered back out, stayed clear of the watching crowd and passed by one of the open trucks to watch crew people empty it.

A helpful crew guy filled me in on Hempwood's standard ghost-hunting equipment: In addition to the TV cameras, a Pola-roid, digital, and 35mm loaded with high-speed film; an infrared thermal scanner; electromagnetic field meter; thermal video moni-tor to measure temperature change; and audio amplifiers to hear EVPs, or electronic voice phenomena.

In the backyard behind the Ordway house, the crew had as-sembled Hempwood's command post: two parallel tables covered with cameras, monitors, and a giant control board one might have found in Quincy Jones' studio. Floorboards had been laid down between the tables so that Hempwood's signature ghost-hunting chair, a high-back burgundy leather Hekman, could glide effort-lessly from one checkpoint to another.

Two steadicam operators were at the ready, harnesses being tightened while sound and light people scurried around them to ob-tain final readings. I looked at the Ordway windows, their boards removed and lit from below in classic spooky fashion. Thoughts of my earlier visits rushed back to me, and I was suddenly anx-ious. Chloe thankfully arrived at that moment and steered me over to a folding chair.

"Stay put for a second. Hempwood's coming."

"What exactly am I supposed to—"

"Wait for the man, Charlie Chan." She ran off again. I dropped into the chair and watched the worker bees. Sound and light men were at a fever pitch. A camera guy shot a good two minutes worth of the windows from four different angles, one while lying on his stomach. I had walked by movie and commercial shoots several times in Santa Monica—usually on the cliffs—and never failed to marvel at the number of crew people it took to produce so little footage. If anything, it seemed recklessly wasteful.

"Ripe for phenomena, are we?"

Hempwood circled around from behind, an impish smile on his ruddy mouth. I began to craft a response but the aging celebrity was already bent over, in my face.

"You are here, and you are not. You see, young fellow, I am normally quite alone when speaking to the departed, but with a spectral event of this import, our combined psychoenergy might very well alter public perception of the afterlife from this day forth."

"Christ…"

"No, He is not participating, only you." Hempwood flashed a grin for all of one second. "When the cameras roll you will sit beside me, completely still, your face always in shadow. You will not make a sound. When I make contact with the Lady Ordway I will take your hand, and let her speak to our joined entities. No matter what she says, no matter what happens, you will not let go of my hand. Are we clear?"

I could scarcely breathe, but managed to nod back. Hempwood gave my sleeve a cautious pat.

"Splendid. Now let's solve this big, bloody riddle already." His assistant Rawlings appeared, toting a thick green concoction in a tall glass. Hempwood took it and drank one-third of the thing in one gulp.

"Avocado, carrot, and wheatgrass," he said, dabbing his mouth dry with an embroidered napkin, "To stimulate the perceptory glands. Care for a taste?"

"No thanks," I said, my stomach already in nervous knots and somewhat weighted down with enchilada.

Crew members swept into position for their final checks. Hempwood parked himself on his leather throne and a grip slid me into his royal psychic court, maybe a foot or two away.

Hunter walked into the courtyard from the left and stood with his back to the stairs, makeup bib removed, hair fluffed, looking like the entertainment news whore that he was. A Tungsten Fresnel light found him, and a camera dolly rolled in close.

"Quiet please!" yelled an unseen assistant, and the area sucked itself into a mute, motionless vortex. "And we're live in 5...4...3...2...1." A red beacon topped the camera. Hunter gazed into it, wild, fabricated excitement in his eyes and a ghostly hush to his voice.

"Two months ago today, Jo Ordway, the wife of noted tech giant and Hollywood producer Jason Ordway, lost her life in a fire started by home invaders that have yet to be found. Her estranged husband, who refused to participate in this event, escaped with minor burns. How did Jo die? Well, all evidence points to her being tied to a chair in the bedroom before the house was set ablaze. Yet in the past week, thanks to apparent psychic visitations and spirit photos obtained by a mysterious local homeless drifter we will call 'Leo,' new riddles demand to be solved.

"I'm Hunter Drake, and tonight we are devoting our entire hour program to a live séance at the Ordway house, conducted by England's—possibly the world's—top psychic investigator, the esteemed Simmons Hempwood. Join us after these messages, and prepare yourself...for anything."

The light was cut and Hunter sneezed violently. "Fucking night jasmine," he said, "Smells great but the shit kills me." An assistant was there in seconds with a Kleenex box but Hunter brushed it aside, hurried back to the trailers.

Hempwood put on his wireless headset and rolled his regal chair up to the control board. He studied the house across from him for a few moments with cocked head, a gothic painter before his canvas, then attacked the controls, twirling this knob, raising this level, checking every meter he could find. The row of cameras were next, and he looked through and adjusted every one with extreme fussiness. Finally satisfied, he unwrapped a thick marker and set it atop an enormous, erasable white board.

"Live in twenty, people!" yelled an unseen A.D. I locked my hands together in nervousness and near-prayer. All lights in the courtyard dimmed. The crew and watching crowd hushed itself, zeroed in on the closest monitor. The A.D.'s voice dropped to a whisper, "and 5…4…3…2…1."

Hempwood addressed one of the TV cameras with his best smile, then closed his eyes and breathed deeply. And breathed again. He leaned back in his chair, let his hypnotic, velvety voice fill the yard.

"We speak to those who have left us yet are still present…those taken from our lives and cast adrift in the unearthly sea…I am calling the wounded spirit of Jo Ordway, shockingly and unfairly deprived of her life in this very location, and now floating among us, thirsty for the comfort she deserves. Jo? If you are with us… please give us a sign."

No one moved. My hands and armpits were so sweaty I could almost hear them drip. Hempwood's batallion of cameras stood at attention, poised to whirr and click.

"Again," he droned, "we call forth the spirit of Jo Ordway…to join us here and ease your pain."

Silence. A dog yapped two blocks away. A jet cut its engines overhead, but I didn't dare look up. The air thickened, more from the combined anticipation than anything spectral.

"This is not good." It was Hunter, whispering in the wings. Chloe threw out an elbow to shut him up. Hempwood opened an eye, surveyed the still yard for a moment with visible concern, then grabbed my hand with one of his ancient ones.

"I am here with a man named Leo…a man you apparently know. You have materialized for him the better part of a week now, addressing him with private messages about your sudden, horrible passing…If you must speak to him through me, then do so, but for heaven's sake, please speak."

Nothing. No weird fog, no orange glow, just some bored cricket chirping under a corner bush. Hempwood gave me a cold sideways glare that ranked of suspicion and utter blame. I wanted to rip myself free and flee from the scene, but I knew live TV cameras were on us, and I really needed the rest of that money. I turned to the black windows and kick-started my desperate voice.

"Jo, it's Leo! What's the matter?"

Hempwood winced, unfamiliar with this crude approach. Chloe and Hunter and most of the crew came to life. At least something was happening.

"Tell me what happened that night! Remember when you spoke to me through that old woman at the shelter and said 'He strapped me in'? Well…tell me that again!"

"You need to be quieter," whispered Hempwood, "or the entity won't—"

"Shut the fuck up. She's my ghost."

Hunter nearly had a stroke, whirled to the assistant director. "What's our delay?"

"Fifteen seconds. Don't worry, we caught it."

Hempwood still gripped my hand, but more out of anger. He squirmed uneasily on his divan while I leaned forward, staring intently at the windows.

"C'mon, Jo. Cut the shit. You know you have something to tell me so fucking say it!"

"Alright, Leo. Let me continue—"

I dropped my hand and shoved him back. The chair rolled five feet, hit the table, toppled every camera like dominoes and spilled Hempwood onto the wet grass.

"Go to commercial!" yelled Hunter.

Mayhem ruled. Chloe raced up, yanked me aside before I could do more damage. Crew members hauled a livid Hempwood to his feet.

"Get that beastly wanker off my set!"

"Fuck you!" I screamed back, "Think I wanted to do this dumbass thing?" Hunter tried to extract me from Chloe and I planted a quick fist in his cheek.

"Okay, that's it!" Hunter shouted, "Throw him back in the gutter!"

"You still owe me money!"

"I owe you the wart on my ass. You scammed us and you ruined this show, and even if we had a contract you would've breached it. Security!"

A pair of armed behemoths walked up. I spun around to Chloe as they grabbed me.

"Can't you talk to him?"

Chloe turned her eyes away and popped a farewell gum bubble. "Nice meeting you, Leo." The crew and crowd parted as I was escorted from the yard, across the street and dumped once more on a cold, friendless stretch of pavement.

❧ SIXTEEN ❧

Ruby stopped in The Sea Catch's bar again on the way out while Lila was in the ladies' room. An ample crowd watched a live feed of the commotion-filled Ordway courtyard on the bar TV, gossiping animatedly. Ruby slipped in close, nudged a patron.

"What happened?"

"Absolutely nothing. A total farce."

"Hempwood got knocked on his ass by the homeless loser," said his friend.

"Damn it…" muttered Ruby.

"Don't worry, I'm sure you can catch it in an hour on YouTube."

Ruby's mind danced. She saw her mother exit the ladies room and hurried out of the bar to join her.

"What were you watching in there?" Lila asked.

"Just some reality show." She swung open the door for them and they exited into cool, damp air.

"Which? I kind of like that one on the island."

"This was no island," said Ruby, digging out her mother's car keys and trying to hide her worry, "and I missed the name of it."

A half hour after they got back to Lila's house, Ruby finally got off the phone with the airline and saw her mother standing there in a pink kimono, gripping a cup of Yogi tea.

"Did I hear what I thought I heard?"

"You mean overhear? Yes, Ma, you did. I'm flying back to L.A. tomorrow."

"But you just got here!"

"Right, but I really need to catch things up with this guy. It's been driving me crazy and I can't relax."

"Hey, I still know acupuncture." She poked Ruby's rib with an elbow. One hour with Madame Lila and you'll forget all about him."

"Thanks, but…I'd really rather go."

"Shiatsu?"

"MA!!" Lila recoiled at Ruby's bark, left the room with a steaming face. Ruby went into the guest room to begin organizing her things and beat back the guilt already creeping up her spine. I was in a bad way; she felt it in her bones. And this time she would not abandon me.

* * *

I paid no attention to where I was walking. Boulevards and streets and alleys passed under my feet and I barely looked up because I just didn't care anymore. I would flush people from my life once and for all and become one of those cave hermits if I had to, living on squirrels and berries and stream water and sleep the days away without people kicking me awake or shooing me away like some giant mosquito.

Now the dead were even betraying me. What was Jo's problem? Why did she contact me through Hempwood in one place and not the other? After a half dozen ghostly incidents with her I was as lost and confused as ever. But that was fine. I would dive in thickets to avoid passing police cars, I would sprint past every cemetery if I had to, and I would not stop until I reached Ruby Mellon's apartment.

At 3 a.m. I did, and on the verge of collapse. I actually got to her Mar Vista neighborhood around 2, but wandered aimlessly for an hour trying to find her street. There were many vanishing alleys and dead ends and similar buildings bent on confusing me, and twice I stopped at the edge of the same park to get my bearings.

Ruby's Honda was in her carport, thankfully, but no one answered the three times I tried her doorbell. Knocking would only disrupt the neighbors, so I found a way to balance myself on a thin stucco ledge and work my way around her windows until I found one I could gently slide open over her kitchen sink.

"Ruby?" I began with a loud whisper just to be sure, then climbed in somehow without knocking over more than a plastic dish soap bottle.

"Ruby?"

Still no reply. I tiptoed into her bedroom, saw the bed all made, closet open—and had a sudden, strong feeling that she'd left town. I switched on a bedside lamp. The earthy wall tones and Indian rugs comforted me, and the chilling voices had dissipated. I went in the bathroom, ran a warm shower, peeled off my clothes and got in. I knew she would freak if she came home and found me sleeping on the couch again, but I had to chance it. There was nowhere else to go, and no one else alive I wanted to see.

A garbage truck in the alley woke me early. I felt like there were baby possums in my head, clawing to get out, but at least I was in a spook-free place. Yellow dawn light painted Ruby's blinds, dabbled across the carpet here and there. I yawned and scratched my stubbly chin. I would milk this safe situation as long as possible.

I made myself breakfast, or at least a bowl of shredded wheat adorned with fresh blueberries. Sat at Ruby's little kitchen table, most content, admired her ceramic Betty Boop salt shakers for a while, until the TV screen across the room began to stare at me.

What were they saying on the Buzz Channel today? About Simmons Hempwood? Was the weird scene in on Camden even news anymore, or cast into the forgotten abyss like I was? Should I even bother to find out?

No. But a pleasant morning talk show, even a nature program would take the edge off, convince me I was still part of a living world. And eating a bowl of cereal in front of the TV seemed a nice, normal thing to do.

I made myself a second bowl, sat on the couch and clicked the remote. A calisthenics show was on, which I vetoed instantly.

Push-buttoned my way past a cooking program, old sci-fi movie, and landed on the local news—more specifically, Hunter Drake being interviewed on the Camden Street curb.

"Yeah, it's all pretty unfortunate. Mr. Hempwood took time out from his hectic schedule to be here, and this homeless individual we trusted basically went berserk on us."

"FUCK...YOU!" I yelled, after nearly swallowing my tongue. A model-worthy blonde reporter now stood outside the Ordway house. "Spokespeople for Ms. Ordway's ex-husband Jason Ordway would not comment on last night's apparent fiasco, and with the tech mogul still secluded in his Montecito Hills home, it remains unclear whether he even tuned in..."

I tossed my half-eaten cereal bowl on Ruby's coffee table, splashing milk across it as the news cut to a third person. "I waited out here for two hours," whined a weight-challenged woman who was either a Hempwood or Jo Ordway fan, "and not one darn thing happened. If you ask me it was all a big hype and a hoax."

I pounded a fist on the table, then clicked off the set and whipped the remote at it, cracking the screen. A neighbor below rapped on the ceiling. I put my face in my hands, muttered into them. "Hoax and hype my ass...Hoax and hype my ass..."

Then a thought came to me, and I looked back up at the spider-webbed screen.

"Montecito..."

I stood, went into Ruby's bedroom.

There was an iMac on her desk. It took me almost a minute, but I found the little camouflaged button behind it and powered the thing up. It was then just a matter of locating the Internet icon on the desktop and clicking that. And every homeless individual knew what Google was.

I wasn't able to find a site that divulged Ordway's home address, but there were a few photos of Jason addressing reporters outside his modern-looking villa, and a host of map pages to steer me into the Montecito Hills. I grabbed a pad of paper and pen and scribbled two pages of notes before shutting the computer off.

I was galvanized. Why had I been wasting my time down here with these lying creeps when the biggest, possibly the most important piece of the puzzle who could explain everything, was waiting for me in his heavily landscaped palace less than two hours away?

But how to get there? I thought there was a train to Santa Barbara from Union Station, and Montecito was one town south. I certainly had the cash to pay for a ticket. I was weary of finding places on foot, though, and this destination begged for speed. Maybe if I just sat in Ruby's place and waited for her to get home I could talk her into driving me up there.

I stood in the center of her living room for the longest time, juggling choices. Building residents were shutting their doors, leaving for work. An uneasy new thought slid into my mind, skipped about for a few minutes, then toyed with my gut. It should have been the first thing that came to me, but only if I were a normal person, not a lost soul trying to keep memories dead and buried.

I went to a side table, where a wicker basket held a few of Ruby's odds and ends: hair clips, business cards, batteries. There was a narrow drawer beneath it, which I carefully slid open. Two decks of playing cards, pens and pencils and paper clips.

And a spare set of car keys, with a fat black rubber top spelling the word HONDA. I turned them over in my hand as if they were a precious emerald, but one possessing a deadly curse that could strike me dead at any moment.

My hand was shaking. I dropped the keys back in the drawer, slammed it shut. Then couldn't take my hand off the drawer's knob. I knew this was the best solution, I knew if I didn't choose it I could be walking toward Union Station, see another dark vision and end up lost in South Central L.A. for no good reason. I had to get to the root of his haunting, even if it meant stepping off a cliff.

I jerked the drawer back open and snatched Ruby's car keys.

* * *

Mahlon Sweet Field in Eugene was rinky-dink, though in a nice way. Three or four gates, one long runway, but the ticket and security people were friendly and courteous and seemed more in character with a 1950s Kansas City bus station.

They weren't exactly chipper this time, though. One of the outgoing shuttle planes was grounded with a landing gear problem, testing the patience of the besieged counter help, while a multilayer cake of North Pacific fog had dropped itself on the airport at six in the morning and refused to budge, testing everyone else.

"What are you telling me?" Ruby asked the de-chippered Southwest boarding girl, "That my flight is delayed or that it's cancelled?"

"I'm trying very hard to be nice to you, ma'm," the girl replied, which was about as mean as she would ever get, "but there's a lot of passengers here with the same problem—"

"You said that before. All I'm asking for is the correct information."

The correct information was that Ruby's flight to L.A. would leave three hours late, depending on the fog, which made little sense to Ruby because she knew these pilots had radar stuff that could cut fog like a light saber through a storm trooper. Ruby normally rolled with these things, satisfied with a large coffee or good book or even the apple-cheeked Eugene TV news, but this was a different morning. My foray into psychic celebrity was an apparent disaster, and Phillip had told Ruby on the phone that I hadn't shown up at Jobworks yet, meaning I could be anywhere.

To her I was like a lost, flea-ridden loveable sheepdog who kept showing up to soil her carpet. Every time I strayed off she missed me even more, and this time something else had kicked in, something she was never even aware she possessed. Ruby had a sudden burning, maternal desire to draw me in, to apologize for anything she'd ever said, to soothe my every fear, to hold me to her breast, pet my head and say: You're the one I'm going to save.

❧ SEVENTEEN ❧

Ribbons of broken lines both white and yellow, knobby lane di-viders, the occasional flat rodent—everything sailed beneath me while sparkling coast and lordly cliffs passed effortlessly on my left and right as if on rails.

Ruby's Honda seemed small to me, and I couldn't figure out why. She drove me around in this thing twice in the last few days, so it wasn't like I was expecting a bigger car. I certainly wasn't wearing bulkier clothes. It had to be the steering wheel—yeah, that made sense—flat and grey and cutting my space to the dash-board in half.

The difference between driving and just riding are monumen-tal, and I was surprised how instinctive my operating skills were. Back near Topanga I flashed on a large parking lot somewhere, on a man seated beside me who smelled like cologne, a sun-splashed day from the past I had long forgotten about when I must have learned the automobile ropes. I knew for years I wanted no part of driving—feared it, actually—yet suddenly here I was going north on the PCH, letting the dramatic land and seascapes pull me along, and it seemed like a perfectly natural thing to be doing.

It helped to have something fresh to focus on, something that required alertness and responsibility. I even switched on the radio at one point, with the road snaking around rocky bluffs on its way out of Malibu, and let sweet violins fill the air. I didn't feel great about taking Ruby's car, but if she knew I had no choice, if she knew I was serenading myself with Ravel at this moment, she would probably forgive me.

The Honda had no maps, and the car was too old and pedes-trian to have one of those GPS things I'd seen Hunter use in the Buzz Channel's van. I knew that Santa Barbara and Montecito were on the coast and that I was moving in the correct direction, meaning I'd slam into them eventually. From there I would need to get creative to find Ordway's house, but I'd had years of practice being desperately spontaneous.

I nearly ran out of gas in Ventura, and had to get off the freeway to find a station. This scared me a little, being unsure whether the car had been reported stolen yet, and too many people could see my plates. I finally opted for a Shell that was a dollar per gallon more than the others but devoid of customers, and bought a giant bag of pretzels and super-size Coke while I was inside paying. I thought of asking the middle eastern guy working the register where to get off for Montecito, then figured it was better not to drop additional evidence and paid for a California road map instead.

As it turned out, the 101 freeway was taking me there automatically. Strapped to the coastline, with nothing but Amtrak train tracks ducking in and out of view, it was virtually impossible for me to get lost. I had spotted the crouching Channel Islands through the haze off of Ventura, and sentry-like oil derricks were now popping out of the distant water. The hills and peaks to my right were spotted with green from the recent rain, dusted here and there with rolling cloud wisps. I had never seen Big Sur, supposedly the most gorgeous stretch of coast in America, but I couldn't imagine it topping this.

I swapped the violins for a soft rock station and tried to relax. With the road calming my brain I began to wonder why the dead voices had stopped again, and whether there was a pattern to them that made sense. I got off the highway in Carpenteria for a fast-food burger, grabbed a pen and an old Macy's receipt from Ruby's glove box, backed into a corner parking space and began to make notes.

The night I crashed in Jo's backyard was the obvious event that got the psychic ball rolling. She appeared to me in the cloverleaf after the second night I spent there, then in the Santa Monica shelter, then at various other locations, always seeming desperate, wanting my help, trying to tell me something I was too frightened to hear.

Then there were the other dead ones, starting with that creepy young couple in black I first saw on the 14th Street Bridge. What the hell did they want? To me it seemed like maybe nothing, other than to make their dead presence known. Maybe Jo's pleas were so strong that they triggered other tragic victims to my side. Sure, that was it. I was suddenly a haven, some kind of Statue of Liberty for the huddled ghoul masses, and as soon as I got the truth out of Jason it was possible they would leave me alone.

The freeway rose and dipped a few times as I neared Santa Barbara, pines appeared, and I chose the second Montecito exit. Coast Village Road looked like a slow-moving cruise past expensive boutiques and eateries, so I ditched it, hung a right and headed into the hills. The road ascended under dark trees, past forbidden gates as stately as winery entrances, each one taller than the last.

I had no real address for Ordway, but figured he was in the neighborhood, and when I saw a Latino gardener helping his crew unload a truck in an open driveway, I pulled over, got out of the Honda and quickly tucked in my shirt.

"Hey, you speak English?" I asked, and got a nod in return. "Good. Can you tell me where Jason Ordway's house is? You know…the big tech guy?"

The gardener grinned, turned and said something in Spanish to his workers, who grinned back. "Why should I tell you, amigo?"

"Why? Because it's important. See…I work for one of those TV stations that was staking out his house yesterday, but one of the guys dropped a lens outside the gate and they sent me up here to grab it, comprende?"

The gardener just frowned, scratched his droopy grey moustache.

"Come on, man," I said, "Nobody cares." Still getting no response, I fished out a ten and held it out. "Here. For some Coronas later."

"Ohhhh, we like Texcate."

"That works."

The gardener snorted a laugh, took the bill and poked my arm in jest. "Up to East Valley Road, take a right. Left on Para Grande, go half a mile. The Ordway guy has a long black wall with water pouring over the top."

"Great," I said. "Muchos gracias." The gardeners chuckled to themselves, shook heads as I hurried back to my car.

The half mile was more like one and a half, or seemed that way with all the twists and turns. There was a brief stretch of former burn area, a blackened slope and scattered bushes that threatened to sprout new life, before the road plunged under an overhang of sycamores and elms that grew so thick they formed a tunnel. I slowed to a crawl as the road switched back on itself, rounded another bend and approached a stream passing under the road.

Wrong. It was a long black marble wall, with water caressing the top before spilling over it in perfect sheets, some Japanese garden artist's well-financed masterpiece. It was flanked by a slice of driveway, but I couldn't see anything that looked like a gate in front of it. No other houses were in sight, but a final TV news van from Santa Barbara was pulling away as I approached. I drove fifty yards or so past the wall, pulled the Honda into a small, shady turnoff, made sure my window was open and killed the engine.

The quiet here was deafening. Crisp, tinder-ready leaves rustled over my head. Was Ordway even home? Maybe there was a 300-pound bodyguard house-sitting for him. Maybe a team of them.

No, I didn't believe that. The news report said he was home last night. Ordway's thoughts about the fiasco on Camden were no longer newsworthy—which would leave him in peace and solitude. I would wait there in the Honda, eyes glued to the black wall and property in my side mirror, ready to jump at the first shred of life.

I was exhausted, and as I sat there trying to stay awake, grey feathers suddenly floated down from the sky.

What? I peered out the window and straight up. A massive bird of prey was perched atop a telephone pole above me, gnawing away at its dinner of fresh pigeon or morning dove. With every peck of its beak, another flurry of feathers floated down on top of the Honda. It was a natural, somewhat hypnotic spectacle and made me even more drowsy.

I dozed for maybe an hour, before a woman's shrill laugh snapped me awake. It was followed by two doors shutting: the first a house, the second a car.

I climbed out of the Honda and hurried across the road. The long, black barrier ended at a thick oak tree, and I was able to lodge a foot in its trunk and lift my eyes over the top of the wall.

The house was sleek, made of stone and glass on many split levels, grafted onto its heavily vegetated hillside. If that guy Frank Lloyd Wright didn't design this thing his craziest fan did.

A seriously buffed navy town car was parked in its circular drive, and a very large man wearing shades and black sweats held a rear door open for a stunning woman in a teal blouse, cutoffs and expensive sandals. She turned to dip and wave at someone in a first floor window, then glided across the drive and slipped into the car's back seat.

I hopped off the tree trunk, crouched and made my way along the watery wall. There was a low click, a hum, and a chunk of it at the far end slid open like the door to the Batcave. I dropped into some thick ivy at my feet, lay motionless. The town car idled just outside the driveway for a moment, then turned right and headed down the hill. I rose up, heard the gate humming again and raced inside it seconds before it closed.

The house looked much bigger up close, almost confusing with all its jutting beams and sandwiched levels. I did a quick scope for surveillance cameras, didn't see any, and ducked around the side.

A short flight of rock steps wound me up through a small Japanese garden to a side door. I peeked through its glass. All I saw was a kitchen, vast and modern, two drained coffee cups left on a table. I carefully turned the doorknob, which was unlocked, and stepped into Jason Ordway's house.

Except for the table, a beveled glass one with four leather-padded chairs, the rest of the kitchen seemed spotless. A plate of fat homemade cookies was on the counter, covered in cellophane with a sticky note attached: MORE OF DARLA'S DELIGHTS, scrawled inside a large heart.

I figured the woman who just left was Darla, Ordway's latest conquest, so didn't feel shy about sampling her baking wares. And I was pretty hungry. Reached under the plastic, grabbed one and sniffed it: peanut butter. It was devoured in seconds, tasting a bit dry and crunchy, but I helped myself to a milk carton swig from the giant aluminum refrigerator to wash it down.

I then heard water splashing outside, and went to a window by the sink. An olympic-sized pool took up three-quarters of the backyard, which was tucked under a high wall of bougenvillea pressed against the hill.

Jason Ordway was doing perfect laps, quiet as a gator, his tan, fit form barely rippling the water. I stared at him with mounting disgust, wondering what Jason did in his life to deserve this lofty existence. I never desired or expected anything this grand for myself, but imagining what he might have done that night to his poor wife upset me to no end. I backed away from the window, slid open a few drawers and chose the biggest, sharpest steak knife I could find.

I moved deeper into the house, tiptoed around every corner. Ordway certainly seemed to be alone. Every room was light- and plant-filled, adorned with expensive-looking modern art.

I found a flight of carpeted steps that wound up to a half-level, and Ordway's office. On one of its sun-painted walls was an exhibit of framed Jason photos, posing with a collection of software gurus, Hollywood actors and moneymen.

I went up another half flight to the top of the house, and what must have been the largest bedroom known to man. For one thing, it took up the entire floor, had a high ceiling, angled skylights and three rotating fans. In the middle of the plush carpet was a God-sized bed suitable for a bacchanal. I sat on the edge, fell on my back and nearly fainted from the feathered comfort.

A door slid open and closed two flights down. I sprang up, grabbed the steak knife and looked frantically around for a hiding place. A far door opened into a palatial Roman bathroom, complete with open shower you could fit an apartment in.

Feet were coming up the stairs. I slipped into an adjoining walk-in closet. The light was off but there was a solar tube overhead, and I could see row upon row of perfectly tailored suits and slacks. I chose a crop that looked dressier than the others and wedged myself into a crevasse behind them.

The first thing I heard was Ordway's measured breathing. Not labored, really, just expertly managed, as if he'd been exercising since birth. He stepped into the closet for a split second, pool water dripping off his baggy blue swim shorts, grabbed something off a hook. Even from my hiding spot I could see some minor burn marks down one side of his face and neck that were trying to heal.

He went in the bathroom. I heard the shower start, followed by the thunderous opening chords of a U2 song. He apparently had a stereo system in there.

I grappled with what to do next. I could jump Ordway while he was in the shower. There might be soap or shampoo in his eyes, his feet would be slipping, he'd be disoriented and I would gain the upper hand immediately.

Then again, I might be the one to slip or get something in his eyes. And I wasn't really there to attack him; I just wanted answers.

So I waited, through what seemed like half of the *Joshua Tree* album. Through Ordway doing whatever he routinely did in there that was taking fucking forever. My knees and lower back were beginning to ache, and I rose to stretch them out, position myself better behind a plastic-covered tuxedo.

The closet door swung open without warning. Ordway switched on the light, singing in a bad Bono voice, dropped his towel and yanked open a bureau drawer.

I held my breath, knife raised and tightly gripped. Afraid to move. Ordway pulled on some striped boxers, thumbed through a rack across the way and chose an olive polo shirt. I waited for the moment when he tugged it over his head, then jumped out of the suits. Ordway gasped, swiveled, but my left arm was around his collarbone, the knife an inch below his chin.

"Don't move, Jason."

"Are you fucking kidding me? How'd you even—"

"And don't talk, either." I nudged him into the bedroom with the shirt still over his head. Turned a chair around and sat him in it.

"There's no cash in the house," Ordway said calmly. "There's a kick-ass big screen but you'll need help carrying—"

"I SAID SHUT UP!" I lightly poked Ordway's neck through the shirt. "I'm not here to rob you or hurt you, okay? I um…just wanna talk about Jo."

The top of the polo shirt half-turned, as if in thought. "I think I recognize your voice." Ordway's breathing was truly labored now. "But I'm having trouble under here—"

I finished pulling the shirt on for him, mangling his wet hair in the process. He quickly looked me up and down, as if assessing my yearly income.

"You're the homeless guy from the show last night, right?"

"Uhh…yeah—"

"I'm on your side, you know. You don't have to do this."

"That's impossible. Nobody's on my side."

"Listen. I've worked with lots of people who know Hemp-wood. He's a pompous ass who exploits people to keep his ratings up. You were the latest and I'm glad you crapped on his cake."

"I thought you didn't watch it."

"Says who? The Buzz Channel? Hunter Drake's a goddamn Hempwood-in-training. Now can you please put the knife down so we can actually talk?"

"Why should I? You'll call the police the second I do."

"Dude. You got—"

"Don't fucking 'dude' me, okay? Just tell me what I need to know!"

"Tell you what??"

"What the hell really happened to your ex-wife! So I know why her fucking ghost is stalking me!"

"Whoa. Back up, podner—"

"'He strapped me in'?? That's what I keep hearing her say."

"Okay...And what's that supposed to mean?"

"Maybe that you showed up 'late' after the robbery started, then strapped her to the chair so she'd burn to death."

Ordway almost laughed. "I'm not even going to begin to respond to that."

"Admit it!"

"Check the facts, ass-clown. Ever hear of a coroner's report? It's all on record."

"Bullshit. People make mistakes."

"Yeah. They do. Like you right now—"

He seized my wrist with one hand, whacked the knife away with the other. I lunged for it but Ordway tackled me in seconds. Rolled me over, dropped on my chest with surprising strength and pinned both of my shoulders to the carpet.

"Nice try. Dude."

I tried raising my head, futilely dropped it back on the rug.

"What, you think you're entitled to break in my house because you've had some kind of 'visitation'? You're no better than the hundred nutjobs a week that were bugging us or writing about us when we split up."

"I swear I'm not one of them..."

"Oh, I know. You're worse!"

I wheezed frighteningly. The weight of everything in my ruined life suddenly broke me, and my bladder burst, puddling Ordway's carpet.

"Shit!" yelled Ordway, leaping off.

"I'm sorry! I couldn't—"

I wheezed again, choked a few times, then began to sob uncontrollably. Ordway threw up his hands, beside himself.

"Jesus Christ…Go clean yourself up, will ya?"

I rose, hobbled into the bathroom. Ordway went over to grab the knife and stuff it under the mattress, then thought for a second. Opened a bureau, grabbed one of about two dozen pairs of jogging shorts, and tossed it to me in the bathroom.

"Try not to sell them on eBay."

"I've never pissed myself before. Or done anything like this. Honest…" I dropped my wet pants and pulled on Ordway's shorts. Began to cough again and had to steady myself on the sink.

"You all right?"

I took a few deep breaths and walked back out. "Think I just need to sit down." Ordway slid over the chair for me and took a spot on the bed, five inches away.

"Just don't want you dying on me here, okay?"

"Yeah...me neither."

"I mean, that would keep the stupid tabloids in business for at least another year."

I got my stamina back, wiped my eyes dry. "I actually read about the fire for hours on the Internet the other day. Lots of what I saw was nasty or trying to spread rumors."

"Right. And you know why?" He leaned forward. "Because good news and truth don't sell."

"Okay…So what was the truth?"

"If I tell you, will you get the hell out of here and not come back?"

"Depends on what it is."

Ordway nodded, weirdly relishing the moment. "Fine," he

said. Went over to the far side of the bed, reached underneath and slid out a long, flat plastic box. Popped it open. Inside was a multi-layered collection of Jason and Jo items: loose vacation photos, dated albums, legal documents.

"What's this?"

"The truth, man."

"Which is—"

"That I was absolutely, insanely in love with Jo and nobody wants to believe it. What do you need to see? E-mails I wrote her practically every day while I was in Europe on business? Or this–" He held up a lined piece of paper with neat, handwritten lines. "New wedding vows. In case we'd ever get back together."

"But I thought you had this terrible break—"

"Total horseshit. The separation was completely mutual. Both of us were fooling around, and we thought we should split for a while. Hell, the night of the robbery and fire I was stopping by to talk about patching things earlier."

"So you never…strapped her into that chair?"

"Are you nuts? She was tied up with rope on a bed. I thought you said you read about the thing."

"Not every detail…" My mind stewed. "So why is she saying this shit to me?"

"You got me. Maybe you should dig out a Ouija board or do your *own* séance, because you're not going to find squat here."

I peered back into his plastic box. Pointed to a bunch of old photos of Jo, including what looked like high school ones. He handed me one of her in a cheerleading outfit, posing in front of a huge banner saying GO FALCONS. I squinted at it.

"That's when I met her, if you can believe it. Her school had a game with San Diego High and I swooned her on the field at halftime."

"I just don't believe it…" I mused, "Every time she's appeared she's tried to tell me—"

"Hey. Enough. Now I think I'm being pretty cool with you

here, considering what you just did. And if you leave right now, I will not pick up the phone or press charges. Like I said, this shit is best left out of the papers, comprende?"

I nodded and stood up, still fidgety. "No, no. There has to be a connection here…I know it. Like maybe she met *me* once."

"If it wasn't on a hunger mission or at a charity ball, then I doubt it. Anyway, you really need to leave. Julius is back in about five minutes and he will literally take you apart." He grabbed a bottled water off his night table and handed it to me before nudging me into the hall. "Want an apple or something?"

"No…but thanks. Actually, I nabbed one of those homemade cookies in the kitchen on my way in."

Ordway paused at the top of the steps. "The peanut butter ones?"

"Yeah. Why?" I heard him snicker. "What's the matter?"

"My girlfriend Darla? Who you might have seen leaving the house? She just got back from Amsterdam and loaded the things with Turkish hashish."

I looked stricken. Ordway guided me down the steps.

"Don't worry. They take like 45 minutes to kick in, and everyone has a different reaction. You'll be fine."

"Oh no. This is bad. I won't be able to drive—"

"Sure you will."

The rumble of Julius' car sounded from the driveway. Ordway hurried me to a back door by the pool and gently pushed me out.

❧ EIGHTEEN ❧

Halfway along Route 192, a two-lane road leading away from Montecito, all I could think about for some reason were those floating bird feathers.

The road was straight, flanked by vineyards and fields of fruit I didn't recognize while overhead, hawks wheeled around on air cushions, eyeing the landscape for rodent snacks. There seemed to be more of the birds every mile, and was the road now bending in odd ways to try and get me lost?

It was possible. By the time I took a left instead of a right on 150 and headed toward Ojai, Darla's hash cookie had kicked in. I paused at a stop sign and had searing anxiety over a crop of road signs, lashed to a pole, arrows and numbers pointing in three directions. I also hadn't counted on the asphalt turning brown, then purple, the broken white lines flying through the air like punched-out teeth. Each curve of the road brought fresh worry, darker and lower tree branches trying to poke the car. My gut had been tumbling for an hour but now, as the hash infected my brain, I was afraid to keep driving.

Two locals in pickups were behind me, agitated at my crawling speed. There was no place to pull over, but my semi-hallucinatory state was making it necesary.

The honking, cursing pickups roared past on a minuscule straightaway, and I was left alone again. Daylight was fading, and what little was left had turned blood orange. A flattened squirrel just ahead in the road startled me when the top half of its body suddenly sat back up as my Honda rolled over it. I braked the car, yanked the wheel and stopped, the right wheels half off the road and partly in a small ditch.

About fifty yards ahead, a bearded, emaciated guy sat in some tall grass by the side of the road with blood all over him and both of his legs crushed into chalk. There was a loud squawking above me. I didn't dare look in the rear view mirror but had to. A bird of prey, the same as the one plucking its grey-feathered victim in front of Ordway's house, had swooped down to rip the head off the shell-shocked, semi-flattened squirrel.

I knew more wriggling road kills were around every bend in the road now, but as I stared at the big bird something clicked and cleaned out my brain.

It wasn't a crow, or a hawk, or some kind of eagle. That bird was a *falcon*. The photo of Jo I was drawn to in Jason's plastic box suddenly made more sense than anything else on earth.

I had to find her damn high school yearbook. And I had a great idea where it was.

I turned the car around, headed back down Route 150 toward the coast and the 101 South, windows open and brisk night air raking my hair. The ghostly visions had stopped.

"Coming to help you, Jo," I muttered, hunching over the wheel as I picked up speed, "coming to help you."

* * *

It was dark by the time I exited the freeway in Sherman Oaks. I stopped at a light, remembering something, and dug into my pants pocket for an item I was praying was still in there.

It was. The uncashed check from Mrs. Shaw, with their home address on it. There was also something that disturbed me about her name printed on the check: GLADYS KRANSON SHAW. Kranson...Where had I heard that? The light turned green, someone honked, and I kept driving.

I had a tough time finding their street in the darkness, but then I could make out that water tower again and soon was killing my headlights, pulling up across the street from their large house.

Ringing the bell was out of the question; the Shaws would see me, call 9-1-1 and I'd be in a chokehold in minutes. I saw a light in a first floor window, and thought I heard laughter from a TV audience. I crept around the left side of the lawn, peered into a downstairs den.

Jo's mother sat on a couch, cackling to herself at a sitcom, while her husband slept beside her in his wheelchair. It was like one of my house-watching escapades, but this time with a purpose.

I ducked below window level, kept moving around the back of the house. One half of a sliding glass door had been left open beside the Shaws' patio, so fresh night air could blow through its shut screen. I tiptoed across flat stones, past a covered gas barbeque and striped patio chairs, and tugged on the screen door. It wouldn't give. I looked around, picked up a flat, sharp wedge of shale and lightly forced it in the gap beside the door's lock. The thing popped open.

I left my shoes outside, inched my way through the kitchen in bare feet, and passed the hall that led to the den. More studio laughter and another light cackle came from the room. Silently made my way to the front hall, then turned right and went up the carpeted staircase.

I was afraid to put on the hall light, so opted for switching one on in a bathroom and half closing the door. Saw a trap door in the hallway ceiling and a cord hanging down from it. Ever so carefully and silently pulled down the attic ladder.

Something rubbed against my pants leg. I looked down and saw a Siamese cat. The hair on its sinewy back rose, and it unleashed a hellish meow that sounded like a strangled woman. I tried to shoo it away with my foot but it jumped back only two feet and arched its back with an even louder cry. Seconds later, Mrs. Shaw's fingers snapped from the front hall.

"Gretchen! Here, puss!"

The cat slunk down the stairs against her better judgment.

"Didn't I give you dry food yet? Oh, that's a bad mommy..." I waited for Mrs. Shaw's voice to fade away, then quickly started up the ladder.

I reached above me in the darkness, found a string, pulled

it and a hanging light bulb went on. Quietly rummaged around garment bags, boxes of clothes and books until I found a carton shut with masking tape marked JOANNA OLD. Seeing her name spelled that way triggered something deep in my brain, and I paused for a second, then peeled off the tape. Inside were a few layers of grade school photos and underneath those, there it was: FALCONIER'92, the yearbook from Dana Point High. The giant, dark green falcon embossed on the cover both delighted and disturbed me for some reason, and I grabbed the book. In seconds I was down the ladder and quietly raising it back up, but the thing clanged loudly when it retracted.

"Who's there?" yelled Mrs. Shaw from the first floor, and all stealth was aborted. I bounded down the steps, past the gaping and gasping woman of the house, and back out to the Honda before she could even get to her phone.

I parked the car on Pico, ran two blocks to my cloverleaf with the yearbook under my arm and hunkered down in the ivy, in the glow from a white freeway light, to study the thing. Thumbed through the pages, littered here and there with scribbled signings, found the senior photos and went straight to the letter K. There she was, JOANNA KRANSON, perched atop a low stone wall in a creamy silk blouse and jade necklace around her neck. Under the photo it said Glee Club 3,4, Vars. Cheerleaders 3,4 and Art Appreciation Club 4.

I paused breathlessly, then flipped past the senior pictures, past the underclassmen, the sports teams, and landed in a section called ACTIVITIES. There Joanna was in the Glee Club, looking damn gleeful. There she was in the front row of cheerleaders beside a doofy-looking Falcon mascot. I kept flipping. The Art Appreciation Club had to be in there somewhere.

And then I saw *them.*

They stood side-by-side on a raised back row of the school orchestra: Marc Driscoll holding his French horn, Laura Figg cradling her oboe, both of them with the unmistakable pale faces and piercing eyes I had been seeing for a week, hovering on the freeway embankment, at the beach, and above the Melrose Avenue sidewalk.

I was chilled to every bone, yet weirdly ecstatic, because I had found a link to the madness. Dana Point High, in a small town south of Los Angeles less than two hours away, held the key to this haunted riddle, and nothing would stop me from finding the lock. For some reason I had never been more sure of anything.

Nothing, that is, except for the friend I now wanted to share my discovery with.

* * *

Ruby had no use for her neighbor. Meg Weitz sold Rancho Mirage time shares out of her apartment and was home 95 percent of the time, yet somehow never saw or heard me break into her place or walk out of it in broad daylight with the Honda's car keys.

And Ruby knew I was the culprit. I left her bed unmade and one of my trademark holey socks was strewn beside the toilet. Where I took her car and why I didn't leave a note were mysteries, and now she needed a new TV.

She had no idea what a hassle it was to report a stolen car, and worse because she had to take an Uber to work and do it from there. First it took about ninety minutes for a cop to show up at the office, then it was a question and answer session that made her feel more like the perpetrator than the victim. Now she had been on the phone for twenty minutes waiting for someone who didn't sound irritated or fascistic to feed her a progress report.

She realized this wasn't like most car thefts because she had a good idea who did the stealing, but that only led to further questions and veiled accusations and Ruby was in no mood for added stress that day. Half the homeless in town apparently decided to get motivated simultaneously because the line was around the block by 8 a.m. and the waiting area was stuffed to capacity and you needed a gas mask to walk through it.

"No officer, I am not being uncooperative," she began on her third go-round with the minion who answered her call, "I'm just trying to find my car and my friend Leo without getting a first, second, or third degree. When will Officer Gibbs be back?" She listened to his response, then swiveled her chair around, grabbed a hunk of telephone cord and stretched it into a garrote, in search of a neck.

"No, I've been over this five times! If I knew what his last name was, wouldn't I fucking tell you??...Yes. Once again, I will hold."

She swiveled back around to the desk, and saw me standing in her doorway.

"Jesus P. Christ," she said, for lack of a better response.

"Sorry about taking your car, Ruby," I said, a manic but magical gleam in my eyes, "but it was the only thing I could do, actually the best thing I could—"

"Hold on." She waved the phone receiver at me. "Officer? Forget it. He just showed up....That's right, Leo...No, I don't think there's a need to do that...Okay, yeah. Whatever." She dropped the receiver and stood up. "Where the hell did you go? I had the friggin' police in Montecito alerted—"

"It doesn't matter. Let me show you something in the car."

"What are you talking about?"

"Hey, don't freak on me, okay? Just come on out back, so I can show you this." I dangled the Honda's key in the air.

"Give me that."

"First come outside."

I ducked to the rear door, swung it open for her. Phillip peered up from his cubicle.

"What's going on?"

"Nothing, I hope," said Ruby, "Man the fort." She followed me outside.

There were no spaces left in the back lot. I had backed the Honda up to another car's bumper, boxing it in.

"Nice parking job," Ruby said, walking around the front of the car, "How many new dents did you make?"

"Come on, hop in." I was already back behind the wheel.

"Get out of the car, Leo. I've reached the end of my—"

"Look what I got." I held up the Dana Point yearbook, beamed at her.

"Congratulations. You're not just stealing cars."

"I think you should look at it."

"I should? Why? Whose is it?"

"Just get in and you'll find out."

She sighed, rolled her eyes, came around to the passenger's side and climbed in beside me. She opened the book, flipped through a few pages.

"I don't get it."

"You will by the time we get there."

"Huh?"

I started the engine. "What are you doing??"

"What does it look like?"

I zoomed out of the lot. Ruby shrieked, clutched her seat.

"LEO, STOP!!"

"I can't! Joanna went to Dana Point High, and so did this ghost couple I've been seeing! It's all down there and we have to go!"

"What are you, nuts? I can't do this! YOU can't do this!!"

I ran a red light, swerving away from someone's bumper at the last moment. Ruby seized the wheel, stomped on the brake, and the Honda jumped a curb and stalled out. I turned and grabbed her by the arms.

"You don't understand, Ruby! I'm not crazy! It's these damn ghosts! And if I don't figure out why they're all over me then I'm either driving off a cliff or jumping off that 14th Street overpass today, because I can't fucking take it anymore!"

"Okay, Leo, but this just isn't the way—"

"THEN WHAT THE FUCK IS? Another drug? A month in a loony bin so I can see Joanna's rotting face next to my cot every night?" I exhaled deeply, my eyes welling up. "You're my only real friend on Earth, Ruby, and I'm asking you to help me not kill myself…I'm begging you."

My arms were twitching. Ruby shut her eyes a moment to calm herself, to keep from reacting to thoughts of her dead brother, then gently removed my hands from her sleeves.

"Okay…I will give you this one day, Leo. We'll call it a field trip. But I have to drive, and the first second it feels like a wild goose chase we are turning around."

"Fine." I got out of the car, hurried around to the passenger side and stood there. Ruby painstakingly climbed over the transmission stick, dropped behind the wheel and I got back in. She waited until I buckled up, then started the engine.

"First I just need to go tell my people where I went, and—"

"No. Call them from the road. Don't you have your cell phone?"

She felt her pockets. "I think so…"

"Well, we can find a pay phone if not. There's still a few around. Know where Dana Point is?"

"Of course I do."

"So c'mon!"

She grumbled at herself for even walking out the Jobworks door, then carefully drove the Honda off the curb.

✌ NINETEEN ✌

I imagined there was once a time when Los Angeles and San Diego were separated by little more than orange groves and dusty hills. Now, as Ruby drove us south past endless freeway ramps and loops, past car dealerships, shopping strips and tract housing nightmares, I thought of a fungus and the way it can spread between two infected trees.

Ruby had classical playing on her radio, naturally, but it was soothing and ghost-free and filled the vocal vacuum between us which threatened to last the entire two hours. It was going to be a warm day, and the hum of the Honda and stop-and-go rhythm of the 405 made me briefly doze off a few times.

"Shit. I'm going to need a Coke or something pretty soon. I got like an hour of bad sleep."

"Whatever. Let me just get past the Long Beach Freeway because it tends to pick up around there."

I nodded, scratched my face. "Maybe we should find a heavy metal station."

"Maybe you should take a nap."

"Uh-uh. That's all I need is another freaking nightmare or you turning the car around."

"Oh, so now you don't trust me? Who's the car thief around here?"

"Yeah, yeah…"

She glanced at me, still perturbed. "Why'd you do that anyway? And breaking in my place?"

"You weren't home! What was I supposed to do?" I looked out at a distant smudge of ocean. "Where the hell did you go, anyway?"

"It's none of your business, Leo."

I snickered at her, which was an achievement considering my

mood. "Ah-hah. So you do have a guy."

"Shut up, I do not. I went to visit my mother in Oregon, okay?...I just needed to get away from everything."

"From me?"

Ruby sighed. "Can we just listen to the music for now, Leo?"

I looked back out the window. Nervously bounced my leg. "I'm gonna need that Coke soon. Plus a piss."

"You really have to go?"

"Yeah. Hey, if you got an empty bottle I can do it right here."

"Don't be an animal. Hold on, I'll take the next exit."

She picked out a 76 gas station mini-mart just past Carson, and parked the Honda right in front of the door so she could keep an eye on me.

"Want something?"

"No. Just hurry up please."

I got out and ambled inside. Ruby shook her head and seconds later heard her cell phone ring, a slice of electronic Bach. She dug it out of her back pocket and flipped it open.

"Hello?"

"Ms. Mellon. Officer Gibbs from the L.A.P.D."

"Oh, hi! Didn't anyone—"

"We've been unable to locate your stolen car, or the suspect you mentioned, but I wanted to get back to you—"

"No, no. Leo's already returned the car. I figured someone told you."

"I've been out on patrol, Ms. Mellon. No one contacted me regarding that. Did you want to press charges?"

"Oh, no. I've already said this to the officer at the station. It was all just a big misunderstanding. But thanks—"

"We did do a thorough search of his two sleeping areas you mentioned, and we collected what appear to be his belongings. If he wants them back you'll have to bring him down to the station."

"Sure, okay. Maybe in the next few days, though." Something

tugged at her. "Wait. What kind of belongings exactly?"

"A few clothing items. And a sealed box he had hidden in this thick patch of ivy. It was addressed to him at the Human Heart Mission so we opened it."

"Addressed? To Leo?"

"Stay on the line. I have it right here…" There was a low dragging sound, something slid across a floor or table. "Sent by a Lois Leonardo to one Dave Leonardo, care of Human Heart Mission. Isn't that your suspect's name?"

"My friend, you mean. Right…What's inside?"

"Looks like a few long-sleeve shirts. A sweater. Deodorant. Razor blades and a can of shaving cream that exploded on just about everything. Two bags of moldy nuts and what looks like a high school yearbook, from…Dana Point High."

Ruby intended to breathe, but suddenly couldn't.

"Yearbook?"

"That's correct. 1992. Something called…the Falconier."

The inside of the Honda seemed to be swimming. Ruby momentarily forgot how to speak.

"Great…Thanks for getting back. To me." She closed the phone, let it fall in her lap. Then she half-turned and stared at Joanna's Falconier yearbook, lying on the back seat where I had tossed it earlier.

While that was happening, I stood in front of the dirty restroom mirror and cracked open my soda can. Despite my bloodshot eyes and typical slovenly appearance, I was glowing inside, and swigged the Coke until I could cap it off with a triumphant belch.

"Hang in there, Joanna Kranson Ordway," I said in my most calm and content voice. Raised the can again and that's when the light switched off.

Something clammy was in the bathroom with me.

"Joanna?"

A pained woman's sigh came from the open stall. I slowly

backed up, afraid to raise my eyes to the mirror because I knew what I would see there. Softly, I whirled to the exit door and grabbed its handle.

It wouldn't turn.

The next sigh was louder, and that sick orange glow filled the bathroom. I tugged on the doorknob but it wouldn't budge.

"Shit…Let me out!" An invisible force pressed me to the door. I could feel cold, slender fingers up the back of my shirt, onto my neck.

"I knew you'd find me, honey…" said a woman's voice. It was different from Joanna's. I stiffened in shock, then pounded on the door with a fist.

"LET ME OUT!!"

"Don't be afraid, honey…Soon we'll be together…"

Dead, overlapping whispers filled the air. The ghosts were back. I howled, the door burst open and the young guy from the cash register stood there holding a spare key.

"Locked yourself in, huh?"

"Yeah. Wait—" I turned. The bathroom light was normal again, and all voices were gone. I nodded gratefully to the young guy and raced back through the store.

Ruby had the engine running. She leaned over and swung open the door for me as I reached the car.

"Don't say a word, okay?" I snapped, "Just go."

"Definitely…" She looked a bit more alert than she had been. Threw the stick into drive and roared away.

A piano concerto was on the radio and I lunged for the tuning knob. "I'm sorry. Need something that rocks." I spun the dial, got nothing but weird crackly static and odd voices and quickly shut the thing off. "Or nothing."

She nodded, kept her eyes on the road. I noticed she was strangely quiet and weaving around cars a bit more. I buckled myself in.

"Everything okay?" I asked.

"Yup. How about with you?"

"I'm good," I said, trying to stop my nervous leg from bouncing. "Guzzled that Coke down and it got me a little riled."

She nodded again, passed the Long Beach Freeway turnoff and picked up speed.

Each south coast town rolled into the next, visible mainly as exit ramps. Long Beach gave way to Seal, then Huntington, Newport and Laguna. Ruby and me remained quiet and nervous while I gazed out at the hazy vistas, always keeping the Pacific in sight, though whether it was a focus or a distraction I couldn't tell.

Ruby finally nudged my leg when she exited at a steep ramp for Camino Las Ramblas. "Open that yearbook for me, would ya? I think the school's address is on the title page." She watched me carefully as I did so.

"4923 Willow. Know where that is?"

"Not at all...You?"

I flinched, almost imperceptibly. "Why should *I* know?"

"Just checking." I gave her an odd look, then fixated on the view again, or what little there was of one. We had emptied out onto a wide, tree-lined stretch of the Pacific Coast Highway that seemed to be curving into town.

"This is when I need a GPS," said Ruby. "Guess we should just ask someone—"

"Golden Lantern!" I shouted suddenly, "Right turn."

"Really? So you *have* been here."

"No. Just a hunch. I get them a lot, remember?"

She shrugged, passed a flurry of shops and coffee places and reached a stop light at Golden Lantern Street.

"Well, well..." She made the turn, went up into a hilly residential section. Beads of sweat were suddenly on my forehead.

"You okay?"

I nodded, clasped my hands together and grinded them. "I

must've…had a dream about this place."

She reached a stop sign. "Which way now?"

"I don't uh…left!"

She made a left. My flinch had increased to more twitching. Sweat was dripping off my cheeks. The nicely manicured homes gave way to a grove of eucalyptus trees, then a large rectangular building beyond. My breathing increased. Ruby passed the trees, turned into the lot for DANA POINT HIGH SCHOOL and stopped. A large bronze statue of a falcon rose in front of the school's main door.

"It was a dream…Fuck, yeah…I've always been dreaming about it…that stupid bird…this stupid building—"

"There's a reason for the dream, Leo."

I didn't even hear her. Bounced my leg so rapidly it threatened to break off. "Know what I mean? Huh? About having the same dream? I'm not a Freud person but I know about symbols and stuff and what big birds mean and fuck! Cats, too! I hate 'em both—"

"Open the yearbook again, Leo."

"Shit, when I felt Joanna's fingers I bet they weren't even fingers but fucking falcon claws! Know what I mean? Can't even look at that goddamn statue right now, so CAN WE GET THE HELL OUT OF HERE??"

The look in my eyes must have been purely psychotic. Ruby put the car in reverse, screeched backward onto the street. Zoomed two blocks away with me mumbling and babbling the whole way and finally jerked the wheel right. Stopped the Honda in front of a vacant lot and killed the engine. Snatched the yearbook from my lap and opened it.

"Look inside."

"Why should I? There's a falcon on the front. I already told you about—"

"OPEN YOUR GODDAMN YEARBOOK, DAVE!!"

A word lodged in my throat. I stared at her like a little boy refusing his broccoli.

"You mean…Joanna's—"

"I mean yours *and* Joanna's! Look!" She thumbed to a page in ATHLETICS that she'd dog-eared. The Dana Point Junior Varsity Falcons baseball team, all twenty of them, standing in two rows at the edge of their school diamond. Front and center kneeled DAVE LEONARDO, unquestionably me with no facial hair and a slight surfer perm under my cap, tanned and smiling, an outfielder's mitt on one of my hands.

"What about it?"

"Are you blind??" She jabbed the photo. "That's you right there! And your name was Dave Leonardo!" I gazed numbly at the page. "Isn't this fantastic? We've found who you really are!"

I blurted out a nervous chuckle, then shook my head. rapidly "There's lots of people who look like other peop—"

"The police called me while you were getting that soda. Your mother Lois Leonardo mailed you a care package which you never opened and buried in the cloverleaf."

"That's crazy…"

"It was addressed to Dave Leonardo. With this same yearbook inside. What aren't you understanding here??"

"Other people have slept and lived in that cloverleaf, y'know. Once I caught—"

"Okay. I get it. You need even more proof." She started the engine.

"What are you doing?"

"Turn the page. Dave."

I wouldn't, so she did it for me, then jerked the car left to leave the neighborhood. I looked down at a photo of the Dana Point Golf Team, posed in front of the Aliso Creek Country Club. This team had only five members, and there was D. LEONARDO again, right in front with my trusty three-iron.

"Big deal. I played golf."

"Yes, Dave! You did!"

She reached the Pacific Coast Highway again and made a right.

"I thought I saw a sign for that place back there…"

"Which place?"

"Just humor me for a little while, okay? Humor me."

I snapped the book shut, dropped it on the floor. She picked up speed, and clicked on her childproof door locks.

The Aliso Creek Country Club was over the town line in Laguna, up a gorgeous, twisting road that had both ocean and mountain views from the parking lot. Ruby pulled into a space, shut off the engine, and looked at me.

"How about this place? Remember it?"

I peered up from my lap, gave it a brief token glance. "Nope."

"Dave, listen—"

"Don't call me that."

"I'm calling you that because it's your damn name! Look, I drove all the way down here to help you solve this supernatural crisis of yours, and we're a lot closer than we've ever been—"

"It was a mistake…"

"What's that?"

"I didn't know what I was talking about. I'm just so hopeless—"

"Bullshit, Dave! You're a rock star! The problem is that here you are, finally headlining the Hollywood Bowl, and you're having a breakdown!"

"I don't know what that has—"

"Okay. You're one sorry haunted son-of-a-bitch, but guess what? So am I. So is everyone walking the damn planet. Name me one person who doesn't have a ghost in their past, someone they screwed over in a big way or something they wished they hadn't done."

I exhaled deep and hard, like a steam locomotive after climbing a mountain pass. But I still couldn't look at her.

"Now something happened to you a long time ago at Dana Point High, and it might've had something to do with Joanna

Kranson, whose pictures I also found, and maybe it didn't. But if you can't remember what it is, then I got no choice except to help you anyway. And we start by finding someone in this club who remembers when you golfed here."

"I've never…golfed here."

"Maybe you're right. But let's go be sure."

"I said I haven't been here!"

She wanted to smack the crap out of me, or grab my shoulders and wriggle me like in one of those bad cop shows. But she merely bit her lip.

"Good. So there's nothing to be afraid of. Come on."

She got out of the car, reached back in for the keys, then walked around to my side and threw the passenger door open.

"I know you can do this. Leonardo."

"Just go in yourself."

"Are you kidding?"

"I'll stay right here. Promise."

"I don't believe you."

"Where the hell am I gonna go? You already took the keys."

She stared at me. "Okay. I'm closing the door, and I'm going to be watching you."

I shrugged. Ruby put the lock down just for show, closed the door and started jogging the twenty yards or so to the club's main entrance—turning to eye the Honda every five seconds.

Maybe she's right, I thought, slumped there in her stupid car. Maybe everyone does have a private ghost, so why be afraid of the damn thing? Except how many people have versions that come with rotting faces and clammy fingers? Ruby couldn't understand what I'd been going through. How could she?

Still, I felt strange the moment we had driven into Dana Point. It was like one of those moments where someone in a room says something specific and then a glass falls over and breaks and a little terrier dog walks by and you know, you just know you've experienced that same sequence before, but when? I figured it was probably in a dream that I had six months to a year ago, an example of precogception or whatever they call it when you see something before it happens.

Meanwhile, where the hell was Ruby? And what was this "Dave" shit she was peddling? I wouldn't be caught dead with a boring name like that. The photos did look a little like me, though…

I picked the yearbook back up and gingerly opened it. Headed for the SPORTS section again but stopped on the way at the varsity cheerleaders page. Cute blonde Joanna Ordway smirked at me from the front row.

"Why are you doing this to me?"…I muttered, and was about to turn the page when something caught my eye.

It was a scribbled signing in the corner I had missed, done with a red pen that was about to run out of ink. The words were inside a crudely-drawn heart.

Dave and Courtney H. forever
—Your pal, Finner

I stared at Finner's name, as if trying to remember who he was, then at the words inside the heart. Something moved deep behind my eye.

"Well, that was possibly helpful."

It was Ruby, dropping back behind the wheel. She checked a yellow sticky note in her hand before putting it under her seat. She had a noticeable gleam to her. "What'd I miss?"

I wasn't moving. Was barely breathing. Ruby looked over at the cheerleader photo.

"Yup. Joanna was a babe, alright." She started the car. "Don't worry, I think I located someone who can tell us everything we need to know." She pulled out of the lot, headed back down to the Pacific Coast Highway. "All we need to do is find his place…"

I was still transfixed by the signature on the page. Ruby gave me a quick stare, which wasn't too easy with the sharp turns.

"Cheerleader got your tongue?"

"Courtney…"

"Excuse me?"

"Joanna's best friend…Courtney H…"

"You knew both of them?"

"Met you at a beach party, going to a bigger one…"

She looked at me again. I was rocking back and forth, cradling the open yearbook. Something very strange was happening.

"I'm Dave…I'm Dave…and this is Courtney…Met her at a beach party…going to another one…going to another one—"

Ruby reached the bottom of the hill, swerved into a patch of gravel, and turned to face me.

"You knew her friend?"

"A bigger one…a better one…"

"Let's find her picture!" She yanked the book from my shaking hands, leafed back to the senior photos.

"Remember her last name?"

I rocked and shook my head, rocked and shook my head. There was no Courtney to be found in the senior pictures with a last name starting with H.

"Maybe they were in a club together…Art Appreciation?" My eyes widened; I had forgotten to check that one. Snatched the book back from her and plowed through the pages until I found the activities section.

There they were. Standing in a group outside the San Diego Museum of Art in Balboa Park. Only ten kids were in the picture, eight girls and two neatly-dressed boys. I ran a finger along their names at the bottom: P. Driscoll, A. Santos, J. Kranson, C. Hutch—

I flinched so hard I nearly pulled a neck muscle.

"Courtney Hutch!"

I looked back at the photo, found Joanna in the back row, her arm around the shoulder of a thin, pale, dark-haired girl with a spellbinding, angelic face.

"It's you, Courtney…"

"Let me see—" She reached for the yearbook but I jerked it away.

"It's mine!" Frantically flipped through the pages. "Another picture…Gotta be one…" Ruby grinned, as excited as I was, pulled the Honda back on the highway and headed south.

I went back through the sports pictures, the activities, into the book's cheesy sponsor pages. Photos of kids among dry cleaning, in booths at local restaurants, in their dad's sporting goods store.

"This is all crap!"

Ruby glanced over again. "You're in the ad section, that's why."

I slogged through the back pages anyway, checking every photo. Ruby fished out her sticky note and a gust of wind off the sea buffeted the Honda.

"Damn!" She regained control, saw an inky black layer of clouds galloping toward us from the water. "Where's all that coming from?"

I didn't hear her, or chose not to. I had come to the end of the sponsors, and stopped in front of a special grey matte page on the inside back cover.

IN MEMORY

Only two photos graced the page, both with thick black borders. Marc Driscoll and Laura Figg beamed in their junior prom clothes, a tacky disco ball over their heads, not ready for the black clothes and matching cadaverous expressions I had seen them with. Below them was Courtney Hutch, head tilted coyly, mesmerizing green eyes and a killer smile, seated at her home dinner table for some holiday function. Underneath the two pictures were two sentences in lush script:

Taken from all of our lives on May 12, 1992.
We will never forget you…

"Mother's Day…" My voice was almost a whisper.

"Did you say something?"

I gazed hypnotically at the date until the entire book slid off my lap and hit the floor. Then I began to rock again. A second wind gust shook the car and spits of rain hit the windows.

"Courtney…Courtney…Courtney…"

Ruby was suddenly alarmed. She rounded a big curve and pulled into the emergency lane, then grabbed the book off the car's floor.

"Where's the page??" I wouldn't answer. She leafed quickly through the ads and found what I had seen. Her eyes met Courtney's, and she shuddered.

"Oh my God…What happened to them?"

"Beach party at midnight…bigger and better…"

"Tell me, goddamn it! You have to remember this!"

The black squall hit the road. Rain poured on the car and wind rocked it. Ruby grimaced, grabbed her door handle. Looked back down at the yearbook page. Courtney Hutch's eyes were glowing, or at least they seemed to be.

"Leaving at quarter till…Can't be the first ones…" I had a slight smile on my face, one foot back into my youth, oblivious to the weather attacking us. A flurry of hailstones hit the roof of the car, rolled down the windshield, and for a moment I snapped out of my trance, looked at Ruby.

"Hailstones…" She didn't respond for some reason. Her red hair was in her face as she stared down at the photo in her lap. I nudged her and she gasped in some quick oxygen, as though she were underwater.

"Whoa…" she said, then saw icy pellets slide off her car's hood. "Check out those hailstones."

"I just told you about them."

"Oh. Right." The stones had stopped for the time being, replaced by normal rain. She put the car back into drive and started moving. The yearbook slid off her legs and hit one of her feet.

"Wait—" I grabbed it, found the inside back page again. "Where the hell are we going now?"

"To someone's house…" Now Ruby was the spaced-out one, driving maybe 15 miles an hour. There were weird dark circles under her eyes and her forehead looked pasty. "I don't feel too good."

"She's just so beautiful…always was…" I mumbled. And then the car began to lurch, her foot losing control. "You have to take the wheel, Dave!" she yelled, "You have to drive!" I turned but it was too late, because she was toppling over. Caught her with one hand, snagged the wheel with the other and steered the car off the road, where it rolled against a guardrail.

I hopped out, tugged Ruby back over the transmission stick and buckled her into the passenger seat, then fought the wind and rain in my face and ran around to the driver side. Ruby was making a strange gurgling sound in her throat as I got behind the wheel. Her limbs twitched. Panic filled my eyes. Was she having a stroke?

"Fuck wherever we were going, Ruby. You need a hospital."

I reached for the transmission stick and her left hand gripped my arm. It was bone white and viciously cold and made me jump. I turned and saw her head rising, face thinning, eyes turning liquid green. It was still Ruby's short red hair and funny little body, but Courtney Hutch's living, breathing magical face was right there smiling at me, her sexy, smoke-tainted voice curling through the air.

"You were such a gentleman, Dave."

"What??"

"You strapped me in."

I froze for a moment, stared at her seat belt and slowly grinned. For the first time in ever, everything made perfect sense.

"Yeah. I'm a gentleman…"

"What are you waiting for, baby?"

"Huh?"

"Doesn't it start at midnight?"

An inner thunderbolt struck me. Of course! The car seats beneath us were turning to black leather, and a faux wood sheen spread across the compacting dashboard. The radio had popped back on, and "Wind of Change" by Scorpions was playing with its signature haunting whistle, and I looked in the rear view mirror and saw curly-haired, drop-dead tan and handsome Dave Leonardo sitting behind the wheel, and it was spring of 1992 and hot damn, time to make that beach party in Hobo Canyon.

✄ TWENTY ✄

The custom Camaro RS could have driven there by itself. I was a regular at Hobo Canyon, but this was going to be special: the first midnight beach party of the year and the first time I was bringing Courtney. Tomorrow was Mother's Day, so I needed to get her home at a decent hour, but who knew how a beach party would unfold?

"Who's going to be there?" Courtney asked, as I gently weaved around the sparse late-night traffic along the coast. I glanced at her, ignored the short red hair and focused on the black string bikini top visible beneath her crisp white linen top.

"Benny for sure…P.K. and Sue…Brian and Tara…probably Finner…" The names spun out of my mouth with ease, and the taste of impending tequila shots replaced them. My loins tingled just knowing what was likely in store for us, as long as I was patient, and Courtney was as willing as she hinted…

I wasn't sure when they started calling our spot Hobo Canyon Beach. There was an actual Hobo Canyon in the Aliso Wilderness Park bordering the place, but it probably had something to do with the occasional bums caught napping on the sand down there. I thought those guys were vermin, and made it a point to not even look at them whenever they passed me on a Dana Point sidewalk, a response I had probably inherited from someone else.

I peeled into the beach parking lot, joined the small clump of Chargers and Mustangs I recognized at the south end. There was a fiery glow just over a rising dune.

"I don't see Joanna's car," said Courtney, "Isn't she coming?"

"I'm uh…not sure. Do you always do everything with her?"

Courtney sat up in the seat, her rhapsodic face inches from mine. "You know I do, Dave…We're like sisters…"

"Yeah, but isn't it good to do stuff on your—"

"How do you think I found you tonight, hmm?...How did I track you down?" Her small hand found and undid a button on my skin-tight shirt, slipped inside over my hard belly.

"I-I don't know, actually—"

"Over the days and months and years...you're all I ever wanted, Dave...all I ever wanted...Joanna knew it, too...knew it the second we saw each other again..."

"We should maybe go check who's here now—"

"Why did you run away, Dave? Huh?"

"Run away?"

"Didn't you love me?" Her mouth was on mine, and all worries melted. The night we sat in the back row at *Scent of a Woman* and her first kiss parted my lips in a way I never knew possible came flowing back along with her cinnamon scent, her long nails on my neck. No one would ever kiss better than Courtney Hutch; that was written in stone.

In seconds we were out of the car, hauling ourselves away from the fire pit and its acoustic guitar sound, its shadowy forms. Waves pounded the oncoming beach and she led me through whispering sea grass to a hidden gulley, ripping off her shirt and bikini top as we walked. The wind was fierce here, blowing sand, but she tripped me playfully, dropped on my chest.

"I have to have you, Dave...Can't sleep till I do..."

Her jeans seemed to dissolve off her white legs, and in seconds she'd tugged mine down to my knees. I'd been terrified of losing my erection the first time I did it, one of the reasons I kept putting her off, but now that we were here and she was lowering herself on top of me, and then she was squeezing me from the inside and the surf crashed my ears, her motion increased and it was happening, my god it was happening.

"I love you Courtney." She was smiling now, her white face and green eyes glowing beneath the starry black sky, smiling so hard it was forming tears.

"I knew you did, Dave...I knew it..."

The edge of an icy wave found my back and bare ass and excited me even more, and I thought I saw a shooting star paint a portion of sky.

"Faster, baby!"

I thrust myself heavenward, grabbed her glorious face and took in her scorching tongue as I came and came until there was nothing left inside me and I felt her insides shudder as she did the same in a series of whimpering moans, and then the waves seemed to retreat from the shore as if deciding to leave us alone.

When I opened my eyes again we were back in the Camaro, but for some reason not in the beach parking lot. There was a guardrail on the right, and Courtney was giving me the same coy look she'd mustered earlier.

"What are you waiting for, baby?"

I stared at her and she tugged my hand.

"Doesn't it start at midnight?"

"Wait…Didn't we just—"

And then I realized. This was like that funny movie I'd heard about, where the guy keeps repeating the same dreadful day in his life, except mine would be different, because I'd be able to have Courtney, my only true love I never was able to make love to, over and over and over…

I shoved the Camaro into drive and roared onto the road, heading south. We weaved around the same Land Rover I'd seen before, passed the same Airstream camper heading north.

A different song was on the radio, though: "It's So Hard to Say Goodbye" by Boys II Men, a soft ballad that curled Courtney up beside me.

"Why did you run?" she softly asked.

My face tightened. "Run from where? Didn't I just take you to the beach party?"

"You know what I mean…"

"No, I don't think I do."

She slid off me, pointed to her buckle and shoulder strap. "You strapped me in!" she cried.

"I know, you said that! I'm a goddamn gentleman already—"

"So it wasn't your fault, Dave!"

I frowned. "What wasn't my—"

"It was never your fault…"

"What are you talking about? What—"

The bobcat or coyote or whatever the hell it was darted in front of the Camaro. I jerked the wheel left to avoid it, saw nothing in the oncoming dark blue Escort except the horrified faces of Marc Driscoll and Laura Figg and then ducked below the dash as the cars collided head on, my windshield shattering, the young couple's bodies flying, the Camaro spinning and spinning across the slick highway and slamming into cheap struts holding a thin metal road sign that sailed over my hood, right through the open window and sliced off Courtney Hutch's head like the top of a bean.

The Camaro bounced off an embankment and lay still but when I tried to lift myself all I saw was Courtney's severed head, sitting in my lap and gurgling blood, her eyes wide open, gazing at me in shock and dismay before they finally clouded over. I screamed and screamed like I was completely unable to do before, and the thing rolled onto the floor with a sickening thud.

Then the wind and rain picked up, and the radio crackled off.

❧ TWENTY-ONE ❧

Ruby wasn't sure what woke her up first: the fighting seagulls or the garbage man knocking on the car window. The Honda's right front wheels were lodged in sand off the far end of the Aliso Beach parking lot, less than a foot away from a giant dumpster the maintenance man was determined to empty.

"Yeah, yeah…" she muttered through the glass, groggy beyond belief. What the hell happened to her last night? One second she was staring at this girl's photo in the yearbook, and then she was all feverish and queasy as though something was taking over her body and the next thing she knew she was in dreamland.

Yet they weren't the worst dreams. Leo was in them but he'd been reborn as Dave, tan and buffed with presentable hair and it really, really felt like they were doing it. Ruby had had plenty of fantasy dream moments with Kevin or Brad or Nicole Kidman or whoever over the years but they always ended quick and unfulfilled. This thing seemed to go on forever.

Then the garbage guy rapped on the window again and it shook the rest of her awake. She sat up, buttoned her shirt and looked around. I was not in the car, but in the foggy dawn light she could make out bare footprints leading away from the driver's side.

Her keys were still in the ignition, and with the help of a second and third maintenance guy lifting the front bumper she was able to back the car out of the sand and into one of the dozens of empty spaces. Then she got out and started following the footprints.

They led her toward the water, and pieces of my strewn clothing began to appear. She picked up speed as the waves grew louder. It was tough to see too far ahead through the fog, but as she grabbed my pants off the sand she could make out a hulking figure seated in the surf.

I was naked, knees drawn up to my chest, gazing out at the

blank sea. The tide was mercifully low, so I was able to keep my bottom planted in the wet sand, but it wouldn't be low for long. Ruby crept up behind me and crouched.

"Dave?"

I didn't answer. She put a gentle hand on my shoulder.

"Dave, you okay?"

I might have exhaled, but can't remember. Both of my eyes were wide open, and my mouth seemed to be moving as I mumbled to myself.

"You have to get up, okay? The tide's coming in."

She tried to tug on my arm but I wouldn't budge or even acknowledge her. Ruby stood back up, looked around with worry. Dug into her pocket for her cell phone.

The South Coast Medical Center in Laguna was a giant health palace overlooking the ocean, and as Ruby sat waiting to talk to a doctor she couldn't help thinking it had to be the greatest place in the world to be sick. Just looking out at the expensive beachfront property and crystal water beyond was enough to heal a brain tumor.

Yet because the place was so massive, it had been a fierce struggle getting them to look at me. I had no I.D., let alone health coverage, and if the ambulance hadn't brought me into the E.R. while I was babbling and having a small seizure, Ruby probably would have been tossed out the front door with me.

Dr. Pashi was a young, handsome guy with thick black horn rims and a slightly annoying way of sniffing while he talked, but at this point Ruby would have met with a dentist if he showed any compassion.

"We have him on fluids," he began, "He seems pretty stable for the time being."

"Good, good. He doesn't need a room or anything, but maybe you can just keep him in the E.R. overnight."

"That will also cost money."

"Yeah, I know. I'll take care of it. I just want him talking again."

"There's no guarantee he will…" The doctor turned a ballpoint pen around in his fingers. "What exactly was happening yesterday when you blacked out?"

Ruby shrugged. "Looking at his high school yearbook. And a picture of his old girlfriend." She stared into a tall water glass Dr. Pashi had poured for her. "Courtney Hutch…"

"Did you know this girl?"

Ruby heard him, but was suddenly listening to something else: a soft girl's voice spinning through her head. The doctor frowned.

"What was that?"

"You'll be happy together…"

"Ms. Mellon? Did you say something?"

"Take good care of him…"

"Well, that's what we do here. I'm a little concerned about you now, though."

She continued to stare into the water glass. He got up and touched her hand, snapping her out of her weird trance.

"What's that?"

"I think you just went somewhere."

"I did?? Jesus…"

"You said something before about your friend being psychic. Have you ever had psychic feelings yourself?"

She thought for a long moment, then looked at him with sudden, simple clarity.

"My mother has."

I had the best sleep I'd had in years, but wasn't sure if the drugs or my mind were responsible. I dreamt about a fish taco stand called Buzzy's that was down close to La Jolla, a place me and my buddies on the baseball team would sometimes go after games. They had a hot sauce that could singe the hair inside your nose, and Finner never failed to use too much.

It had been wonderful seeing Courtney again, and the love-making was as glorious as I thought it would be. Even though I knew it was her ghost, that it either happened in my mind or with Ruby's help, it was still a complete feeling that tied the bow on this supernatural package I'd been lugging around. Courtney was determined to lose her virginity the night of the accident—hell, so was I—and how could she rest until she could relieve both of our torments? She sensed my growing suicidal thoughts all month, but without her damn head was unable to speak to me, so why not use Marc and Laura and her best friend?

I half-remembered Joanna Kranson back in school, but she had transferred there during junior year and Courtney had a way of keeping her girlfriends separate. Courtney also preferred alone time with me, and had obviously communicated this to Joanna because I was only getting Jo visions and the other dead ones when I was alone or in a small group. Hempwood's TV fiasco was an unfortunate byproduct of this; the channeling incident in the Bel-Air suite didn't stop because the maid knocked, but because Hunter announced he was going out to get a cameraman.

The purpose of the spirit visits cleared up, I still had a few holes in my memory that needed patching. It's what I dwelled on in the surf that morning, hoping that each fresh wave would bring me a new thought. If I drowned in the process, well, at least I could make love to Courtney again.

They had me on a corner gurney with a nurse eyeing me every few minutes. It was hard to tell what time it was because there were no windows in the E.R., but at one point the automatic doors swung open and I caught a glimpse of dawn light.

I waited until the nurse wasn't looking and then carefully plucked out the IV tube. Peered under the gurney and saw a shopping bag full of my clothes. The phone at the nurse's station rang, and the second she answered it I swung my legs onto the floor, grabbed the entire bag and ducked into a nearby restroom.

When I emerged again fully dressed, I avoided the nurse's station altogether and found a side door that exited into the waiting area. Ruby was there, curled up on a couch, sitting far away from the only two other people in the room. I tiptoed across the rug, trying not to let the nurse see me, and carefully took a seat in a plastic chair beside her. Reached out with a hand to shake her awake but then spotted her car keys, very visible in her open purse on the floor.

I chewed on a thought, then lifted out the keys and went back in for a ten dollar bill peeking out of her wallet. She snored a little and I quietly stood back up, headed for the outside door.

It took me forever to find the Honda in the adjacent garage, and after I finally drove out I somehow found a quaint little downtown, but two flower shops I drove past weren't open yet, so I opted for a Ralph's. Lillies would be nice, I thought.

The coast road back from Laguna was like driving through gauze, but for once there were no accompanying whispers, no hitchhiking cadavers. I never went above thirty miles an hour.

When I reached Dana Point the route to the house I was looking for unfurled itself in my brain as though it had never left, and I took a left at the first traffic signal and wound my way into the hills, high above the school. Birch Lane became Oak Terrace and then the right turn on Mill Ridge Road made me brake the car.

It was amazing; they still had their giant red barn mailbox with HUTCH painted on the side. I backed the car up until it was one house away, killed the engine and reached for the bouquet beside me. A new thought surfaced and I opened Ruby's glove box. Found a pen and an old car repair receipt, then turned over the receipt and wrote the word SORRY as large as I could.

I climbed out, hurried up to the front walk of their house. The curtains were drawn. There were already Christmas lights strung under the eaves, though maybe they'd never taken them down. I debated whether I should ring the doorbell, finally choosing to set the flowers and note on the stoop, loudly knock once, and run away.

I was back in the car by the time a woman in a yellow night-gown opened the door. I recalled Mrs. Hutch as being pretty and in her 40s and even from a house away could tell this was a sad deterioration. I dropped down in the seat, peered over the dash and watched the woman pick up the bouquet, read the note and step out on the walk to quickly look around.

Mr. Hutch joined his wife momentarily in a purple robe but like her, wasn't venturing out too far. They turned, went back inside with the flowers in appreciative bafflement and shut the door.

It was then that I first noticed a small yellow sticky note that was either wedged under the brake pedal or stuck to it. I flashed on the thing being in Ruby's hand when we were leaving the Aliso golf club, and peeled it off the pedal, unfolded it:

12 Happy Village
Oceanside

I knew that Oceanside was south on Interstate 5, past Camp Pendleton and almost in Carlsbad, but I sure didn't remember ever living there. Certainly not being happy there. Still, Ruby had gotten this address from someone at the club so it must have been important.

❧ TWENTY-TWO ❧

It was still plenty early, and most of the Route 5 traffic was heading north to Orange County or Los Angeles. Camp Pendleton was a massive U.S. Marine base that stretched across a mountain-flanked plain leading to the sea. It was pleasantly green on this morning from the recent rain, and with fog wisps licking its corners it seemed like a dreamy tribute to Ireland or Middle Earth. I found a Ruby-esque classical station on the radio to accompany the landscape, and was calmly leaning back in the driver's seat in no time.

I took the first Oceanside exit and drove aimlessly around, before a guy with a military haircut loading his car with beer at a convenience store told me that Happy Village wasn't a street at all but a trailer park community a few miles south of there. I thanked him, went in the store for a go-cup of coffee and kept driving, over a set of railroad tracks.

Happy Village had tall palms, an ocean view and American flags everywhere. It was also a gated community but no one was guarding it. I parked on the road just outside, climbed out and used my Ordway house method of waiting for a friendly resident to exit the place.

The trailers were beautifully kept, adorned with striped awnings, flowers, flamingoes, pinwheels, and knick-knacks of every stripe. San Diego Padres and GO MARINES bumper stickers were the other hot items. Nearly everyone I saw gave me a friendly wave.

I got lost in a couple of cul-de-sacs, then located number 12 at the shady end of another one. The trailer was tucked under a dried-out Chinese elm, desperately needed a paint job, and had a side window screen with a raccoon-sized hole in it. There was no car in its carport.

The front door was partly open, and I could hear television voices inside. I knocked, faintly heard some movement. A birdbath that may not have been used since the Clinton administration leaned against the wall beside the door, and I took a moment to prop it back up while I was waiting. In doing so, I revealed a cheap metal nameplate screwed into the outside wall: D. LEONARDO.

I stared at it in sudden, frosty horror. Was I visiting myself?

"Put it on my tab and leave the food!"

No. I wasn't. The voice was hoarse, nicotine-scarred, slammed me with instant visions of biblically awful days I'd spent well over fifteen years trying to evaporate from my mind.

"Who's out there?"

I stared down at my shoes a moment, turned to leave but couldn't. The Tragic Day had been rainy and dark, and I was drunk and stoned by eight in the morning and there was no way I was going to the funeral with them, not to mention the cemetery I was sure still had angels over its gate. All roads pointed north, called to me, and my thumb would be the magic carpet to fly me out of the morose hell I'd been pitched into.

But this day was not rainy, and I was more sober than a priest, and the only tragedy within ten miles might have been just inside this door. I had to find out.

"Census bureau, Mr. Leonardo…We need some information."

A pause, then a shuffling sound.

"Oh. It's open."

I exhaled and stepped inside. All blinds in the room were closed, and the only light was from the studio of the ESPN news team, flickering from a TV in the corner. The floor and a coffee table were littered with stacked empty pizza boxes, piles of drained soda cups and take-out bags from In-n-Out Burger and KFC that were luring fly colonies. I could make out two slippered feet on the table and beyond that, pale hairy legs, striped boxers and a flabby torso squirting out of a sleeveless undershirt. I couldn't see the man's head but smelled his cigarettes and when his hand leaned forward to put a glass on the table containing a small puddle of orange juice and crushed ice, I knew who it was.

"Are you…Donald Leonardo?" I was banking on the room's shadows and my own figure, silhouetted against the grey daylight from the door.

"Seems that way. I can't see too good anymore." Donald belched. "But you don't look like any census taker."

"Umm, right…We're more casual now. Like mailmen in shorts."

A low rumble seemed to come out of the floorboards, and the entire trailer rattled. I spun around, saw an Amtrak passenger train roll by just outside the park.

"Coast Starlight!" said my host. He stood and turned to the small kitchen area, toting his glass. What I saw was a formerly handsome fit man with thick blonde hair who had totally gone to shit. "Screwdriver?" he asked, jiggling his glass in my direction.

"No thanks."

"I make them with Stolichnaya Elit." He poured from a tall, clear bottle until the glass was half full, then added O.J. as an afterthought. "No sense greeting a new day with anything but the best, right?" His eye caught a football highlight on the TV and he banged the glass on the counter, splashing some vodka on his hand.

"Goddamn Chargers lost again. Can't believe I stil root for those turds after they abandoned us. Who's *your* team?"

"I uh, don't have one. Is your…wife home?"

He licked his fingers clean like a mutt. "No sir. Dead for fifteen years."

I stood there in a slight coma, unsure how to react. Fighting back liquid in my eyes.

"I'm so sorry…"

"Hell, it wasn't your fault." There was another knock on the door. "Put it on my tab! Leave the food, por favor!" He shuffled across the room and I ducked into the shadows to let him pass.

A delivery kid had left a large brown bag outside the door. Donald grabbed it, carried it back to the kitchen, pulling out the Styrofoam box inside and letting the bag fall on the carpet. He popped it open and groaned.

"Never fails. Stupid beaner forgot the extra salsa."

"Do you have any children living here, Mr. Leo—"

"Him we don't talk about."

I looked at my father, retreated a bit deeper into the shadows. "Well…for the report I'm gonna need–"

"Just say he's dead, okay? May as well be…"

He lifted out a massive breakfast burrito and bit into it. Sour cream squirted over his chin.

"I don't understand, sir. You'll have to explain."

"He had everything, okay? A-minus average, God-given talent in two sports, big house on the hill with parents who loved the snot out of him. What more could we have done?" He plowed through more of the burrito, washed it down with his screwdriver.

"So…did something happen that—"

"He killed my boss's daughter, that's all! Took out two other kids in the process! Couldn't even show my face at work or the club anymore. Lois' tumor kicked in a year later and she was on her way, too."

I turned and raised my hands as if pretending to write something on a pad, even though I was just crying. I gazed out the half open door and fixated on a goofy weather vane across the lane to keep from giving myself away.

"So Dave...died in the accident?"

He looked up from his food and drink. Squinting.

"David, you mean. So you got his name."

"Umm…right. Guess it was in my file after all."

The old man nodded, having no weather vane of his own, and dove back in the screwdriver. "He survived somehow, but didn't talk for six months. We had him on every drug imaginable, saw half the shrinks on the south coast."

"Sounds like he might have been traumatized. By something he saw..."

"Hey mac, I was a marine in Nam Phong, so I don't wanna hear about it. We barbequed three villages in one day and you never saw me running away."

"So David...your son just left?"

"More like vanished. Sent us a P.O. box number up in L.A. but that was useless soon enough." He polished off the burrito, tossed the empty container on the floor pile. "See, when someone you raise disappoints you that much, he may as well be dead."

I was shaking, had to clasp my hands together to stop. "But he strapped her in..."

"What's that?"

I cleared my throat. "I said it doesn't sound like it was his fault, though."

"Oh you think so? Mr. Census Man? What the hell do you know about it?"

What I knew was practically everything, but should I share it with this wreck of a man once known as my father? I could only imagine the hell I'd put he and my mother through in the weeks and months after the accident. There was a speck of a memorial service at school, with many flowers and constant sobbing in the air, but that was soon lost in a swamp of rage and bafflement and horrible silence that filled every waking moment in our house, whatever street that was on. I had willfully pushed it out of my mind, along with everything else in the last eighteen or so years.

And now I could do the same with this. Just because you find your demons it doesn't mean you have to befriend them.

"Nothing at all," I said, and turned away from my father, "Forgive me." I took a big step toward the open door.

"Where are you going?"

"I guess...back to my office."

"So we're done here?"

"Definitely. I got everything I need...Thanks."

I walked outside. All of the stray morning fog wisps were gone, and I found my way back to the main gate and squeezed around the side of it. Then I heard that weird rumbling sound again and strolled across the road to the train tracks.

Another long Amtrak coach was coming from the opposite direction. I put a sleeve to my cheeks; they were still wet from crying. I put one foot over the rail, then the other, and stood there. The engineer blasted his horn but did not slow down. He blasted it again. I waited until the train was a city block away, then jumped back off the track and let the thing roar by.

Its violent breeze whipped my hair around, actually felt good on my face. When the thing finally passed, I let out an endless sigh, then returned to the Honda.

I started the engine, lowered the window, and let a fresh morning breeze overwhelm me. I had to get back to the hospital and pick up Ruby because I suddenly really missed her, especially that angelic face of hers, and we had a lot to talk about on the drive back to Los Angeles.

More than anything, I wanted to get home.

THE END

LOVED ONES

Screenplay by
Jeff Polman

Registered WGAW

EXT. PARKING LOT - DAY

Young, beefy CARLOS bites his lip. EXHALES.
He's looking at something very longingly.

                    JIMMY
                   (O.S.)
          Beautiful, isn't she?

                    CARLOS
          Oh yeah. Very beautiful.

Jimmy, late 20s, mildly dashing in a peach shirt
and skinny purple tie, leans into his ear.

                    JIMMY
          And you want her, don't you?

Behind them palm fronds CRACKLE in the hot,
dry wind. Carlos lifts the bill of his GOMEZ
FERTILIZER cap, mops his brow.

                    CARLOS
          I think so. Tough decision,
          y'know?

                    JIMMY
          Oh, I know. Made many of
          them myself. Let me ask you
          something, Carlos. What would
          it take me to get you and
          your family driving this
          Wagoneer off the lot today?

                    CARLOS
          What would it take?...
                   (shrugs)
          A lot less than what you're
          askin'.

Jimmy POPS a gum bubble. Peers around at the
mammoth lot for HONEST JOHN'S USED JEEP AND
VAN. At Carlos' THREE KIDS and exhausted WIFE,
waiting patiently a few yards away. He leans in
again.

                    JIMMY
          Do you know who I sold one of
          these babies to a year ago
          last Thursday? Take a guess.

                    CARLOS
          A guess?...I don't know—

                    JIMMY
          Gina...Coogan.

Carlos draws a blank.

                    JIMMY
          Ever watch <u>Windy City</u>?

                    CARLOS
          Naw, we don't got HBO.

                    JIMMY
          It's on the Cinebox Channel,
          dude. You can watch it on
          your pad.

                    CARLOS
          I don't got one of those
          either.

                    JIMMY
          Forget it. Anyway, I had to
          give <u>Gina</u> a deal because I'm
          deeply in love with her, but
          I'll tell you what I'm gonna
          do...
               (puts a friendly arm on
               his shoulder)
          I'm gonna give you the exact
          same deal I gave Gina Coogan.
          And you don't even have her
          red hair and green eyes.

                    CARLOS
                 (LAUGHS)
          Maybe I should just talk to
          Honest John, y'know?

                         JIMMY
          Actually, Honest John is tied
          up right now. But you can
          call me Honest Jimmy if you
          want. I mean, the two of us
          are cut from the same honest
          cloth. Damn. We go back so
          far I can't even remember how
          we met.

                                   CUT TO:

INT. DEALERSHIP OFFICE - DAY

Where JOHN GRIFFIN JR. leans over his computer.
Nudging 30, with hip round glasses, rolled-up
shirtsleeves and a checked blue tie. Jimmy's
clean-cut, suburban alter ego. He's also a
younger, softer version of the stern man in the
painting over his desk: "HONEST JOHN" GRIFFIN,
1927-1988.

                         CUMMINGS
                          (O.S.)
          John, are you listening?

                         JOHN
               Sure am...

John is logged into THE GINA COOGAN CHATROOM,
typing a response to someone he doesn't know.
Even from a small, scanned-in photo atop the
screen, the young actress' fresh, girl-next-
door face and haunting eyes have him slightly
mesmerized.

                         CUMMINGS
                          (O.S.)
               So what should I do?

                         JOHN
               Nothing yet.
               (eye-scrolls some of the responses)
               If his TransAm is parked out
               front it doesn't exactly mean
               they're doing it.

CUMMINGS rubs his baggy eyes and pours himself

a coffee from John's pot. In his 50s, he's the
lot's resident "old-timer".

                    CUMMINGS
          We were married 28 years,
          John. I know the woman. She
          wouldn't be playing Scrabble
          with this guy.

                    JOHN
          Weren't you the one who left?

                    CUMMINGS
          Hey, when you're close to
          someone for that long you get
          addicted to them no matter
          how it turns out. All that
          for better or worse shit?
          They didn't just make it up.
                    (sips the coffee)
          Someday you'll get it.

                    JOHN
          Well...I hope he's driving
          something better than a
          TransAm.

He smiles, exits the website. Neatly arranges
everything on his desk.

                    CUMMINGS
          Seriously, though. Ever feel
          this way about Polly?

                    JOHN
          Sure. Right after I met her.
           (pulls on his sport jacket,
              adjusts the sleeves)
          Before the marriage thing,
          the house thing, the kid
          thing...

He walks over to a mirror to check his hair. A
signed, framed photo of Gina Coogan is beside it.

          TO MY FAVORITE HONEST GUYS—
          THANKS FOR THE WHEELS!
                    XXX GINA

                    JOHN
          You've been pretty wound up
          lately, Cummy. Why don't you
          take a fishing day next week?

                    CUMMINGS
          Honest?

                    JOHN
          That's my name!

Jimmy blows in, loosening his tie.

                    JIMMY
          Had to play my Johnny Pachango
          CD, but I think I got a close.
          How much time we got?

                    JOHN
                (checks his watch)
          Six minutes.

                    JIMMY
          Not a problem. That Ms.
          Carlos, ooh la la...

He opens a drawer on his cluttered desk, shoves
three pieces of Hubba Bubba in his mouth. Grabs
a sales contract and salsas back out, blowing a
quick kiss, then a gum bubble at Gina's photo.

                    CUMMINGS
          Oh right. It's Thursday.

                    JOHN
          That's why you need to fish,
          Cummy.

                                        CUT TO:

INT. GRIFFIN FAMILY ROOM - NIGHT

Shoes are off. Chairs arranged. Jimmy tugs on a
WINDY CITY ballcap, and John's big flat screen
FIZZES to life on the CINEBOX CHANNEL logo.

                    JIMMY
          Waiting a week between new
          episodes is just brutal. Why
          can't they stream all the
          episodes at once?

                    JOHN
          Because they want geeks like
          us to still have a life?

                    JIMMY
          Fat chance.

John launches WINDY CITY, EP. 9 as Jimmy flips
open their giant take-out pizza box and grabs a
slice.

The jazz-fusion THEME MUSIC and scenic shots
of Chicago kick in. Jimmy HISSES shots of the
two MALE LEADS, then SWOONS with John as GINA
COOGAN'S lovely face appears.

John pours them Sierra Nevadas while the
credits run.

                    JOHN
          Almost everyone online thinks
          Delbert's road kill.

                    JIMMY
          That would be sweet. Highly
          unlikely, though.

                    JOHN
          Why? Gina was sick of him two
          weeks ago.

                    JIMMY
          You mean when they lip-locked
          at the Art Insitute? Hardly
          sick of him, amigo.

                    JOHN
          She was tired of him. I could
          see it in her eyes.

                    JIMMY
          Hey man. Gina's eyes never
          look tired.

                         JOHN
          Sorry, my infatuated one.

Jimmy CHUCKLES. Smothers his pizza with crushed
red peppers.

                         JIMMY
          Life's a bitch, amigo. And a
          little serious fantasy never
          hurt anyone.
                    (glances up at the TV)
          We have liftoff!

                                        CUT TO:

INT. FAMILY ROOM - 45 MINUTES LATER

John and Jimmy are still on the couch, leaning
forward like suicidal natives peering into a
volcano.

On screen, Gina is visited at her ad agency
computer by DELBERT, a cute but shallow cohort.

                         GINA
          This is not a good time.

                         DELBERT
          When the hell is it a good time?

Gina frowns, gently drums fingers on her mouse.

                         GINA
          To refresh, Delbert...I like
          who I am...What I do, what I
          believe in...I'm even happy
          with the way I look. But if
          there's one thing that makes
          me real unattractive, it's
          pressure. And since I've
          started seeing you, I've been
          feeling pretty damn homely.

She reaches up and tugs at the bottom of his
rayon shirt.

                    GINA
          Throw your map away, Delbert.

                    DELBERT
          My map?

                    GINA
          Yeah. As in...get lost.

                    JIMMY and JOHN
          YES!!!

They leap off the couch, high-five and do a
little victory jig.

POLLY GRIFFIN walks in the door at that moment,
toting a boy's sports equipment bag. She's a
bright Manhattan Beach girl with short blonde
hair and motherly fatigue in her eyes. Takes
in the TV screen and impromptu celebration and
EXHALES loudly.

                    POLLY
          So do they have a twelve-step
          program for this or what?

                    JIMMY
          C'mon, Poll. Of the 42
          obsessions your husband and
          I have shared since high
          school, only three are left:
          golf, Angels games, and Gina
          Coogan on Windy City.

                    JOHN
          He's speaking for himself, of
          course.

                    POLLY
          I doubt that. Anyway, I hear
          she might leave the show
          soon, which means you'll need
          a new obsession!

                    JIMMY
          If you're referring to media-
          driven, gossipy innuendo
          again, it's a charade. Every
          time her contract is up she
          threatens and threatens,
          then signs a new one a week
          later. Believe me, Gina knows
          exactly what she's doing.

Polly rolls her eyes and walks to the kitchen.
Eight-year-old ROY GRIFFIN mopes into the house
in his Little League uniform.

                    JOHN
          Hey sport, how'd you make out?

                    ROY
          We lost again...But I got a
          double.

                    JOHN
          Well, that's something.

                    JIMMY
          Your dad's right, Roy.
          Personal statstics are what
          count. Screw the team!

Roy YAWNS, grabs his sports bag and goes down
the hall. Polly pops back in.

                    POLLY
          His curve ball could use some
          work.

                    JOHN
          How do you know?

                    POLLY
          I guessed. They got 15 hits
          off him. Maybe you can see him
          pitch next time.

                    JOHN
          Honey, please. You knew it
          was a <u>Windy City</u> night.

She forces a smile, grabs a stack of mail by
the door and leaves the room. Jimmy shakes
his head and they turn back to the TV for the
show's closing credits.

INT. JOHN AND POLLY'S BEDROOM - HOURS LATER

Polly sits up in bed with a big T-Shirt on,
writing out bills. John washes up in the
adjoining bathroom.

                    POLLY
          I'm thinking of putting some
          red highlights in my hair.
                    (hears no response)
          What do you think?

John dries his face. Kills the bathroom light
and slips into bed next to her.

                    JOHN
          You're funny.

                    POLLY
          Hell, I'm serious. At least
          it'll get your attention...Or
          if not yours, maybe your male
          wife's.

                    JOHN
          No one's forcing you to like
          him, Polly.

                    POLLY
          I never said I didn't like
          him. He's just...intense.

                    JOHN
          Yeah, hey...Sometimes Jimmy
          gets on my nerves too. But
          he's also excited about life,
          and he makes me laugh. Would
          you rather I have boring
          friends?

                         POLLY
              Listen...
                 (slips an arm around his waist)
              I realize the two of you are
              close, that you were there
              for him when he lost his
              folks, etcetera etcetera. It
              doesn't mean you have to be
              joined at the hip so often.

                         JOHN
              I think I know what this is
              really about. You're jealous
              of Gina, right?

Polly CRACKS UP LAUGHING. Reaches behind her
and holds up a fat wad of unpaid bills.

                         POLLY
              My obsessions are a little
              more grounded in reality,
              John.

John doesn't know what to say. Shuts off his
bedside lamp instead.

INT. JOHN AND POLLY'S BEDROOM - AN HOUR LATER

Darkness. Silence. John's CELL PHONE RINGS,
startles him awake. He fumbles for it on the
night table.

                         JOHN
              Hello?

                         JIMMY
                 (V.O., hysterical)
              Put your TV on!!

                         JOHN
              Huh? Why—

                         JIMMY
                 (V.O.)
              NEVER MIND!! PUT IT ON!!

                         JOHN
              Okay, okay. Hang on—

Polly sits up as he hops out of bed.

                    POLLY
          What's wrong?

                    JOHN
          I don't know...

                                        CUT TO:

INT. FAMILY ROOM - NIGHT

John finds the remote in the dark. The TV boots
up.

                    JOHN
          What channel?

                    JIMMY
                    (V.O.)
          ANY CHANNEL!!

He drops his phone by accident and disconnects
the call. Locates CNN and we see a live
picture from SHERMAN OAKS, CA. An ambulance
and police cars parked in the drive of a gated,
tree-shrouded Craftsman-style house. John's
skin crawls. Something about the place looks
familiar. Polly appears behind him in her robe.

                    POLLY
          Sherman Oaks? Isn't that
          where—

                    JOHN
          Gina lives...

                    REPORTER VOICE
          Again, here's what we can
          confirm. Gina Coogan, popular
          star of the Cinebox dramatic
          series Windy City, found dead
          less than an hour ago outside
          the open front door of her
          Sherman Oaks home.

                    JOHN
          Oh no...Oh no, it's a
          mistake.

                    REPORTER VOICE
          According to police, cause of
          death appears to be cerebral
          hemorrhage, from a severe
          blow to the head. Hold on...
          They seem to be taking her
          out now...

PARADEMICS wheel a body bag on a gurney out the
front gate. John is too numb to respond.

                    REPORTER VOICE
          Again, there is no indication
          of robbery, and at present...
          no murder weapon has been
          found—

His CELL RINGS again. he knows who it is, picks
it off the floor.

                    JOHN
          Tell me this isn't happ—

                    JIMMY
                    (V.O.)
          He's dead, right? He's gotta be.

                    JOHN
          Who's dead?

                    JIMMY
                    (V.O.)
          Who d'ya think? The guy who
          did this. I mean, someone's
          gonna find him. Maybe not the
          cops but someone. 'Cause
          when you do something like
          this you can't fuckin' hide,
          right?

                    JOHN
          Jimmy, I'm sure the police
          are everywhere. They'll find
          whoever it was—

                    JIMMY
                   (V.O.)
          BullSHIT they will! Look
          at them now, man! Standing
          around, not doing squat! Why
          aren't they out there finding
          the motherfucker??

                    JOHN
          Jimmy, the thing just
          happened! They have to do
          fingerprints, an autopsy, find
          evidence...

                                        CUT TO:

INT. JIMMY'S PALISADES CONDO - NIGHT

Every light in Jimmy's place is on, as well as
his TV at top volume. He paces in his boxer
shorts, mind speeding.

                    JIMMY
          Uh-huh...Uh-huh...How about
          the loser she was engaged
          to...Mark Hansen. The one she
          broke off.

                    JOHN
                   (V.O.)
          What about him?

                    JIMMY
          No, wait! I know. The bass
          player from that shitty
          metal group! She met him in
          Telluride, remember? He was a
          complete and total dick. I'm
          sure it was him!

INT. JOHN'S HOUSE - NIGHT

Polly embraces John from behind, her eyes
clamped shut.

                    JOHN
          Listen. I have to hang up now
          and get some sleep, okay—

                    JIMMY
                   (V.O.)
         SLEEP?? How can you sleep?
         Gina's dead!!

                    JOHN
          (EXHALES, lowers his voice)
         I know she is, Jimmy. I
         know...But we can't change
         that. And I have to sleep.
         Let's talk in the morning...
         Sorry, man.

He hangs up. As Polly holds him tighter, he
stares at the flashing police lights on the
silent TV screen.

                                        DISSOLVE TO:

EXT. SUBURBAN STREET, 1999 - DAY

Ten-year-old John on his stopped bicycle,
staring at the flashing lights of a police
cruiser parked two driveways away. A handcuffed
MAN is being put into the cruiser. A WOMAN
holds a SOBBING, SCREAMING nine-year-old Jimmy
in her arms. Little John frowns, tugs on an
unseen woman's skirt beside him.

                    JOHN
         Mom? What's a manslaughter?

                                        DISSOLVE TO:

EXT. PALISADES BALCONY - NIGHT

Jimmy outside in a deck chair, smashed on Jack
Daniels. Wrapped in a Mexican blanket. Gazes up
the black coast at a convoy of airplane lights
drifting down from the Bay Area.

Picks up a smashed TV remote, lying in his lap.
Leans back and looks straight up at the stars.
A virtual planetarium.

                    JIMMY
         Don't you worry, baby...
         They'll find him.

Downs some more whiskey from a Gina Coogan
plastic cup.

INT. GRIFFIN KITCHEN - MORNING

Dead silence. Polly is at the counter,
buttering muffins. Sleepless John sits at the
table, reading his morning phone.

                    JOHN
          I hate this country...We have
          to move.

                    POLLY
          Famous people get attacked
          everywhere, John. Remember
          the tennis star Monica Seles?

                    JOHN
          I hate this planet.

Roy enters, finds himself some cereal in the
cupboard.

                    POLLY
          Morning, sweetie! Toast or
          muffin?

                    ROY
          Toast, please.

He floods his bowl with milk, joins his father
at the table.

                    ROY
          Angels win, Dad?

                    JOHN
          Umm...I don't know.

                    ROY
          You don't know?

                    POLLY
          Don't bother your father
          today, Roy.

Roy is puzzled a moment, then glances at a news
headline on John's phone: "WINDY CITY" ACTRESS
SLAIN.

      ROY
  Wow. I didn't know she was so
  important...How come she was
  so important?

      JOHN
  She wasn't, Roy. People
  just...liked her. Now finish
  your cereal please.

      ROY
    (eyeing John)
  She was your favorite, huh?

      JOHN
  Yeah...I liked her a lot.

      ROY
  Was it because she was a
  luscious babe—

      JOHN
  Hey! Just eat your cereal,
  okay??

Roy stares at him, hurt and confused. Picks up
his bowl and leaves the kitchen. Polly lets out
an exasperated SIGH.

      POLLY
  He's eight years old, for
  God's sake.

John looks at her a second, then nods. Puts his
phone face down on the table. Polly reaches out
for his hand.

      POLLY
  You know what? I think you
  and your intense buddy should
  get away this weekend. Play
  some golf.

                    JOHN
          Are you kidding? We'd end up
          talking about Gina for two
          days.

                    POLLY
          Sounds like you need to. It
          also wouldn't hurt to focus
          on something else, like a
          little white ball.

He sips his coffee, thinking.

                    JOHN
          Kind of hate to miss church.

                    POLLY
               (with a little smile)
          I think He'll give you a
          pass.

INT. HONEST JOHN'S EMPLOYEE LOUNGE - DAY

Jimmy sits on the food table, back against
the wall. Styrofoam cup of black coffee doing
nothing to improve his sleepless appearance.
John enters. They share a brief, silent glance,
before John walks over to him. Attempts to give
his friend a man-hug but Jimmy stiffens up and
just goes through the motion.

The air thickens. John sets his briefcase on a
chair. Goes to the counter and pours himself a
second cup of coffee.

                    JOHN
          Early start for you.

                    JIMMY
          Couldn't fuckin' sleep...

                    JOHN
          I hear ya.

Another long silence. John sips his coffee,
looks through a window at the showroom floor.

                    JOHN
          There's a Range Rover
          candidate out there if you
          want him.

                    JIMMY
          Not especially.

                    JOHN
          Work's always a good
          distraction, y'know.

Jimmy gives him a long, vacant face, then gets
off the table. Makes an attempt at straightening
his tie and goes out to the showroom.

INT. SHOWROOM - DAY

A muscular DUDE with a Marine haircut is in the
Range Rover's driver seat. Adjusting it back
and forth.

                    JIMMY
          Got any questions?

                    DUDE
          Yeah, like for the last ten
          minutes. What does she come
          with?

                    JIMMY
          She?

                    DUDE
          You might wanna drink that
          coffee, friend. I said the
          thing I'm sitting in. What
          does she come with?

Jimmy sets his coffee down and stares at him.

                    JIMMY
          It comes with whatever you
          see on the sticker.

                    DUDE
          Great. You mind telling me
          what it says?

                    JIMMY
          Sure. It says the vehicle
          comes with an engine,
          seats, four tires, glove
          compartment, headlights, and
          a steering wheel. Assuming
          the driver has the mental
          capacity to grip one.

The dude's face turns inside out.

INT. DEALERSHIP OFFICE - SECONDS LATER

John at his computer. Staring numbly at a
spread sheet. Hears LOUD VOICES and looks
through the showroom glass. Jimmy's customer is
SCREAMING something into Jimmy's face.

                    JOHN
          Oh God.

INT. SHOWROOM

                    DUDE
          'Cause I don't take lip from
          pricks like you, that's why!

John rushes in behind them.

                    JIMMY
          Oh look! Aren't you lucky!
          Here comes Honest John, my
          commanding officer!

                    JOHN
             (pulling the dude aside)
          John Griffin Jr., sorry about
          this...Let me show you
          something wonderful over
          here—

                    JIMMY
          SHOW HIM YOUR ASS, JOHN!

                    JOHN
          Jimmy, stop it!

The dude climbs out of the Range Rover, puts on

a pair of aviator sunglasses.

                    DUDE
          You fags have a nice day.

And walks out. Jimmy is ready to leap at the
guy but John contains his friend with a menacing
stare.

                    JOHN
          Satisfied?

                    JIMMY
          Its a start.

                    JOHN
          What the hell did you say to him?

                    JIMMY
          Obviously not enough.
          (drains and CRUNCHES his cup)
          Fuck it...Y'know maybe I
          should just take off. I can't
          deal with these clowns today.

                    JOHN
          No kidding.
                    (watches Jimmy pull on
                     his sport jacket)
          Hey wait. Listen. I've been
          thinking...Why don't you and
          I head out to Rancho Vista
          tomorrow?

                    JIMMY
          Rancho Vista. You're kidding,
          right?

                    JOHN
          Not at all. Little swimming,
          lots of golf. Couple of
          Cuervo Gold margs on the
          veranda...
          (Jimmy scratches his chin)
          C'mon. Pick you up at 9, we
          make the desert by 11...
          Cummings and Taylor can
          cover. It'll be good for us.

                         JIMMY
          Can we listen to Meteor
          really loud? 'Cause I don't
          even wanna <u>think</u> about Gina,
          man.

                         JOHN
          Promise. Full metal Meteor.
          With maybe a little break for
          some downtempo Spotify.

                         JIMMY
          Yeah, whatever. See ya in the
          morning.

He heads out. Cummings wanders over.

                         CUMMINGS
          Watched the news last night.
          You guys okay?

                         JOHN
          We're holding up.

                         CUMMINGS
          Don't know where you get the
          patience with him, John.

                         JOHN
          Yeah, well...I guess it's
          some of that for better or
          worse stuff.

INT. JIMMY'S EXPLORER - DAY

Jimmy stops at a light. Peers up at a huge
billboard for WINDY CITY. Gina is still on it,
posing and smiling with the other cast members.
She's radiant.

He looks away. Squeezes the wheel in pain.
Gets a thought and punches in an address on his
dashboard GPS. An address in the San Fernando
Valley.

EXT. 405 FREEWAY - DAY

Jimmy's Explorer zips under Mulholland, flies up
and over the pass into the vast, smoggier San
Fernando.

EXT. SHERMAN OAKS - DAY

Pulls onto a quiet residential street lined with
oaks and sycamores. Rounds a curve and parks
behind a line of cars and media vans. Slowly
climbs out.

Gina Coogan's Craftsman house is completely
surrounded by yellow police tape. Bunches and
bunches of flowers are heaped on both sides of the
entrance gate, where a pair of POLICE OFFICERS
keep back two dozen or so quiet SPECTATORS.

Jimmy moves into the crowd. All ages, all types.
A MIDDLE-AGED WOMAN does a slow pan of the house
with her phone camera while she WEEPS, pausing
to wipe her eyes every few seconds. A MILENNIAL
COUPLE snap selfies of themselves in front of the
gate.

Jimmy sides up to a young LATINO OFFICER.

                    JIMMY
          Buenos dias, man...Catch
          anybody yet?

                    OFFICER
                (sizing him up)
          Uh-uh.

                    JIMMY
          Any leads?

                    OFFICER
          No leads.

                    JIMMY
          Hmm...Do you know how he—
          how the person got on the
          property?

                    OFFICER
          (hesitates, then lowers his voice)
             Suspect scales that wall over
             there, lands in the flower
             bed...Knocks on her door and
             WHAM-O. Drops her like a
             watermelon.

Jimmy nods, somewhat repulsed. Turns and moves
back through the crowd. A YOUNG WOMAN is there
handing out yellow flyers.

                    WOMAN
             Prayer service for Gina
             tomorrow. 10 a.m., Hollywood
             Arts Church. Prayer service
             for Gina tomorrow...

Jimmy takes a flyer, looks it over.

EXT. JOHN'S DRIVEWAY - MORNING

John breaks open a fresh bag of Titleists,
loads the balls in his golf bag and zips the
pouch shut.

Polly stands there with a bulging overnight
bag.

                    POLLY
             I threw in more sunblock. No
             sense getting fried.

                    JOHN
             Thanks, hon.

                    POLLY
             Oh, and Ted and Sandy's
             barbeque is Sunday at 4.

John lifts the two bags into his trunk.

                    JOHN
             We'll be back. Where's Roy?

                    POLLY
             Still asleep.

He nods. Suddenly indecisive. A HORN BLOWS and
Jimmy's Explorer SCREECHES into the driveway.
Sunroof open, METEOR HEAVY METAL blasting from
the speakers. He hops out, noticeably cheerier
and POPPING a fresh gum bubble.

       JIMMY
  We have liftoff! Who's
  storming the desert today?

       JOHN
  I thought I was driving.

       JIMMY
  Keyword: was.
   (grabs the overnight bag,
    brings it to his car)
  Just this and your clubs,
  right?

       JOHN
  Y-yeah. Listen, we really can
  take mine—

       JIMMY
  Why bother? I'm here, I got
  the 4-wheel drive, the kick-
  ass tuneage—

       JOHN
  Yeah, but...You're okay to
  drive?

Jimmy grins. Walks over to Polly.

       JIMMY
  Polly? How do I look?

       POLLY
  Oh...Ready to golf and relax.

       JIMMY
  Ya see?
   (pecks her on the cheek)
  Thanks, Poll. I'll pay you
  later. And as for you—

Surprises John with a warm, five-second hug.

                    JIMMY
          Sorry about yesterday, man. I
          was a puddle.
                    (CLAPS his hands)
          Okay! Let's roll!

Jumps back into his Explorer. John shakes his
head, gives Polly a kiss.

                    JOHN
          Tell Roy I'll call him from
          the hotel.

                    POLLY
          You better.

John hesitates a second, then lifts his bags
back out and carries them to the Explorer.

INT. JIMMY'S EXPLORER - DAY

Jimmy weaves through light freeway traffic,
blasting his METEOR metal. John munches on a
donut, trying to focus on his phone's weather
app. Motions to Jimmy to drop the volume a
notch but Jimmy hesitates, so John does it for
him.

                    JOHN
          Looks like a furnace out
          there. 105 yesterday in Palm
          Desert.
           (sees them zip past an exit)
          Hey, wasn't that the 57?

                    JIMMY
          That it was. Don't worry,
          we'll hook up with the Pomona
          later.

                    JOHN
          Later? Where are we going?

Jimmy reaches under his seat, hands John the
yellow flyer.

                    JIMMY
          I called. It's legit.
          Actually, it was Gina's
          manager who set it up.

                    JOHN
          A prayer service? Are you
          nuts? I thought we were
          getting away from all this—

                    JIMMY
          I went to Shady Terrace
          yesterday.

John stares at him in disbelief.

                    JIMMY
          I had to, man. It was kinda
          creepy, okay, but I definitely
          felt better afterwards. Like
          I really got to say goodbye.
                    (points at the flyer)
          Now here's your chance.

                    JOHN
          Jimmy, I really don't think—

                    JIMMY
          We won't be staying long.
          Promise. It'll be good for
          us, man. And make the desert
          even sweeter.

John folds up the flyer and gazes out his window
at some sprawling industrial park. His thoughts
and feelings in a blender.

EXT. HOLLYWOOD ARTS CHURCH - DAY

A complete zoo. Cars, press vans parked
everywhere. HAWKERS selling GINA LIVES
T-shirts. An outdoor courtyard packed with well
over a hundred MOURNERS. Flowers and a giant
Gina Coogan poster adorn a makeshift stage.

Jimmy and John squeeze into the courtyard, find
a pocket of space at the rear. Listen to a
young, hip MINISTER addressing the crowd on a
microphone.

                    MINISTER
          ...Why even think of the
          darkness that embraced
          her? The evil shadow that
          extinguished Gina's warm,
          creative light? That much
          has passed, and so we cannot
          dwell. For dwelling will not
          let us heal...

SNIFFLES fill the air. John glances around,
uncomfortable. A HAGGARD YOUNG GUY with bone
white skin and three days of stubble stands
just beside him. Gently rocking with his eyes
closed, tears rolling down his cheeks.

                    MINISTER
          Gina was as giving a soul as
          there ever was, and she would
          have wanted us to continue
          that giving, so I ask you
          now...
             (raises his hands benevolently)
          ...to turn to the person
          beside you—whoever it is—and
          embrace that person, and all
          of the light inside them...

John turns to Jimmy. He's already occupied,
hugging the hell out of a SEXY GIRL he was
standing next to. John turns the other way.

The haggard guy is there, clenching his fists,
BLUBBERING like a baby. John hesitates, then
puts his arms around him. The guy tenses up,
but chokes off his crying. John pats his back.

                    JOHN
          It's okay...

                    GUY
          She was so...so...pretty...
          Why why why why why...

John slips free. Digs out an extra napkin from
the donut place and hands it to him. The guy
nods gratefully, wipes his eyes with it.

                    GUY
          I'm sorry...

                    JOHN
          Don't be. It's a terrible,
          painful thing.

The guy BLOWS his nose in the napkin, drops it
on the ground.

                    JOHN
          You um...just can't prepare
          for something like this.

                    GUY
          I know...Last time I cried
          was when Kinky got run over.

                    JOHN
          Kinky...Oh—you mean Gina's
          cat on the show!

                    GUY
          Yeah...second season. She
          loved that little Kinky...
          Remember when he jumped on
          the counter and ate her
          sushi?

                    JOHN
          Oh God yes. Right before the
          dinner party with, uhh...

                    GUY
          Patchevsky!

They share a comforting LAUGH. Jimmy turns away
from his extra long squeeze with the hottie,
his face still flushed.

                    JIMMY
          Great hugger, doesn't golf...
          How we doing over here?

                    JOHN
          Recuperating. This is...

                    GUY
          Tom.

                    JIMMY
          Hey, Tom. Pretty incredible,
          huh? All these Gina fans in
          one place.

Tom nods dully.

                    JOHN
          Shall we...hit the desert?

                    JIMMY
          Why the fallujah not?

                    TOM
          Which desert?

                    JOHN
          What's that?

                    TOM
          Which one? If you go north
          you're in the Mojave. If you
          go east you're—

                    JIMMY
          East for us. Assuming we can
          get out of here.

They start to exit the courtyard with the huge
throng. Tom picks up a weather-worn backpack
and trails behind them.

                    TOM
          Oh. Because I could sure use
          a ride to Indio if you're
          headed that way.

                    JIMMY
          Indio, huh?
             (shares a look with John)

                    TOM
          Yeah. 'Cause I missed the
          morning bus out there a half
          hour ago.

                    JIMMY
          You're saying you bussed to
          L.A.?

                    TOM
          Sure. There's Greyhounds so
          why not use 'em? Especially
          when your car's in the shop.

He lets out a little CHUCKLE. Jimmy eyeballs
his grungy jeans, long, uncombed hair. Sweating
in his buttoned-up flannel shirt.

                    TOM
          I can give you ten dollars
          for gas. And buy you both
          lunch.

Jimmy laughs to himself. Looks at John again.

                    JIMMY
          Think Tom needs a ride?

                    JOHN
                (shrugs)
          Well...Indio is right off the
          10. And it's been kind of a
          rough day for everyone.

                    JIMMY
          Sure damn has...
                (pats their new friend on the back)
          Hey, Tom. Ever hear Meteor?

                                        CUT TO:

INT. JIMMY'S EXPLORER - DAY

Jimmy abusing the fast lane on the Pomona
Freeway. Bobbing his head to another METEOR
dirge. Tom seems oblivious in the back seat,
but John is rubbing his forehead.

                    JOHN
          Either we stop and get some
          Advil or we play something
          else.

                    JIMMY
          Fine, fine. Hit us with your
          slow grooves, J.G.

                    JOHN
          Thank you.

He connects his phone to Jimmy's system with
a few button taps. Middle Eastern downtempo
rhythms from LOOP GURU begin playing.

                    JOHN
          Perfect desert relaxation
          music.

                    JIMMY
          If you say so.

                    TOM
          What I think happened is that
          she tried to be too nice to
          someone...She's always nice
          to people on the show and
          then she gets mean to them,
          so I think she wanted to make
          it up by being extra special
          nice. That's why she let the
          person in her gate.

                    JIMMY
          Got news for ya. The "person"
          climbed over the wall...A cop
          at the house told me.

Tom's eyes nearly pop out.

                    TOM
          You went to her house??

                    JIMMY
          Sure damn did.

                    TOM
          Wow. Did you see that little
          bird feeder on the side
          that's shaped like a big
          owl?...They showed it in the
          US Magazine feature last
          year, the November 17th issue
          with all that junk about her
          old boyfriends. I love that
          bird feeder!

                    JOHN
          Tom? I'd be willing to bet
          that no one knows more about
          Gina than you.

                    TOM
               (with a shy grin)
          That's just because I love
          her so much. When you love
          someone you want to know
          everything about them. That
          way they're always inside
          you. Even when they go
          away...Here, look—

He grabs the backpack. Begins to zip it open
but hesitates.

                    TOM
          Remember Season 3, Episode
          7 when she went to San
          Diego for that publishing
          convention and stayed at the
          Coronado? I took a bus there
          and watched them film the
          whole thing, and a wardrobe
          lady dropped something on the
          ground, so I grabbed...this.

He reaches into his backpack and pulls out a
girl's flimsy tangerine tank top. Hands it to
John, who stares at it.

                    JIMMY
          Jesus. And I thought we were
          hooked.

                    TOM
          It's nice, isn't it? She
          had a blue one in the Grant
          Park episode, but this one's
          better. If you want, you
          can...smell it.

John makes a face and hands it back.

                    JOHN
          No, that's okay.

                    JIMMY
               (trying not to laugh)
          Hell, pass it over, John!
          I'll friggin' eat it!

He sees Tom giving him a strange look in the
rear view mirror.

                    JIMMY
          Oops. Just kidding, man.

Tom lets out his shy smile. Neatly folds the
shirt and slips it back into his pack.

                    TOM
          Horace won't smell it,
          either. He doesn't even watch
          the show.

                    JOHN
          Horace?

                    TOM
          Yeah. He spends all day fixing
          cars.

                    JIMMY
          He working on yours?

                    TOM
          Uh-huh. A 1993 Buick LeSabre.
          I don't like it anymore.

                    JIMMY
          Can't imagine why. Actually,
          a guy like you who travels
          around a lot might wanna
          invest in a new road vehicle.

He snaps a business card out of his visor and
flips it backward to him.

                    JIMMY
          If you're ever in Manhattan
          Beach, stop in. We'll cut you
          a deal.

Tom pockets the card with a reluctant nod. John
throws Jimmy a glare.

                    JOHN
          You dog...

                    JIMMY
          Always lookin' out for us,
          podner.

EXT. MORENO VALLEY - DAY

The Explorer has finally left the L.A. basin
and entered clearer, hotter air. Flies past an
endless sea of tract housing toward the De Anza
hills and desert mountains beyond.

INT. EXPLORER - DAY

Tom leans back, gazes out at the approaching
hills.

                    TOM
          Gina never changes...When I
          get home to my DVDs she'll be
          waiting for me...and she'll
          still be pretty.

Jimmy tries to adjust his visor to keep the
morning sun out of his eyes but it's being
difficult. He smacks it into place.

                    JIMMY
          They just better fry the
          coward that did it, that's
          all I know. Eyeball for an
          eyeball, right?

                    JOHN
                  (to TOM)
          Our favorite argument. Jimmy
          actually thinks that killing
          a killer brings the original
          victim back.

                    JIMMY
          No...But you sure as shit
          feel better.

John shakes his head, and the Explorer soars
into the curving, dipping De Anza hills. In the
back seat, Tom's eyes get distant. His mouth
curls into a soft smile.

                    TOM
          When they kill him it should
          be on national TV. And
          they should walk him out
          on a ledge. A ledge that's
          in a big arena filled with
          thousands and thousands of
          Gina lovers...And they should
          let him say he's sorry, and
          then let him take a running
          start and dive into all the
          Gina lovers and get ripped to
          bits.

                    JIMMY
          That um...sounds like a plan,
          Tom.
                  (rolls his eyes at John)
          Written your congressman?

Tom doesn't seem to get the joke.

EXT. BANNING, CA STREET - DAY

A homely commercial strip wedged between the

desert and San Giorgino Mountains. Jimmy pulls
the jeep into a Taco Bell, but the drive-
through line is backed up.

                    JIMMY
          Shit. Let's just bag the
          lunch, okay?

                    TOM
          Oh no. I promised I'd treat!

He gets out of the car. John throws up his
hands and goes with him.

                    JIMMY
          Extra salsa on mine or you're
          dead!

                    JOHN
          Yeah, yeah...

Jimmy pulls the Explorer into a space, kills
the engine. Notices a half dozen or so
splattered bugs on the windshield and GROANS.
Reaches behind his seat for a bottle of Windex
on the floor.

Notices Tom's backpack, laying there with its
zipper half open. A yellowed, weather-worn
map of some kind sticking out. Jimmy frowns,
curiously moves the pack a bit closer. Slides
out the map.

It's a GUIDE TO THE STARS' HOMES. Looking like
it's been carried around for ten years. A red
magic marker leads somewhere on the map.

Jimmy carefully unfolds the thing. Follows the
fat red line. It starts from downtown L.A.,
heads west. Curls over the 405 freeway and into
the San Fernando Valley. Off the 405 at Sherman
Oaks and straight to a large X on Gina Coogan's
street.

                    JIMMY
          Sweet Jesus...

The inside of the car suddenly feels hot.

Jimmy starts the engine a sec and rolls his
window down. Sees Tom and John through the
restaurant's glass, waiting at the counter.

He stares at the red X again, then quickly
folds the map up. Leans over, grabs the pack
and zips it open a little more. Peers inside.

A change of rolled-up clothes. A toothbrush.
Something heavy, wrapped in newspaper. Jimmy
pauses, then slowly unwraps it.

Inside is a long, metal pipe, some kind of tool
with a round, bulbous socket on its end.

Jimmy's skin crawls. He digs deeper. Pulls out
a pair of soiled tennis shoes. Thick brown dirt
caked on one of the soles.

                    JIMMY
          Holy shit..

Looks up, sees Tom and John approaching the
car. Frantically puts everything back in the
pack, zips it half-shut the way it was. Drops
it back on the floor seconds before they climb
in.

                    JOHN
              (tosses him a burrito)
          With extra salsa for the
          presidente.

Jimmy nods, his head spinning. Starts the jeep
and backs out.

                    JOHN
          Don't you want to eat first?

                    JIMMY
          That's okay. I'll wait.

And ZOOMS out of the lot.

INT. EXPLORER - DAY

Back on the freeway. Passing the jagged

mountains on the right, windmills on the left.
Into the desert oven.

John and Tom MUNCH their Taco Bells. Jimmy is
sweating.

                    JOHN
          How come the air is off?

                    JIMMY
          Oh. Sorry.

He cranks it back up. It doesn't seem to help
him. A sign goes by for INDIO 8 MILES and he
picks up speed. John looks at him.

                    JOHN
          You okay?

                    JIMMY
          Oh yeah. Just...wanna get
          there.

EXT. INDIO STREET - DAY

Jimmy comes down the exit ramp, makes a hard
right. An endless, sun-baked, two-lane road
stretches to the horizon.

INT. EXPLORER - DAY

                    TOM
             (peering ahead)
          There's a local bus stop at
          the next light. You can drop
          me there—

                    JIMMY
          Yeah, in a second...

He pulls the Explorer into a seedy, near-
abandoned gas station.

                    JOHN
          Didn't we just fill up?

                    JIMMY
          We did, I um, just have to
          ask how to get somewhere.
          Come with me a second,
          okay? You're better with
          directions.

John is puzzled. Jimmy gives him a serious
nudge, then kills the engine, gets out with the
keys. John slowly follows. Tom stays in the
back seat, curious.

EXT. GAS STATION - DAY

Jimmy leads John toward the dark, open garage,
then detours them around the side. Stops and
grabs John by the shoulders.

                    JIMMY
          He's in our car.

                    JOHN
          Who's in our car—

                    JIMMY
          The motherfucker.

                    JOHN
          What are you talking about?
          Tom is in the car—

                    JIMMY
          Exactly. Tom Q. Motherfucker.
          The Gina-killer.

John gazes at him, speechless.

                    JIMMY
          It's him, man! I looked in
          his pack. Exhibit A: Map with
          a red line to Gina's house,
          where he said he's never
          been. Exhibit B: Muddy tennis
          shoes, and need I remind you
          of the footprint found in
          Gina's garden yesterday.

                    JOHN
Tennis shoe footprints?

                    JIMMY
Exhibit C: Nasty-looking
metal pipe wrapped in a
newspaper.

                    JOHN
So you—...These were all
in his backpack? You don't
think—

                    JIMMY
What? That he stopped at a
hardware store? Did a few
errands after taking a bus
there? You can't <u>do</u> an errand
in L.A. without a car.

                    JOHN
Well...Maybe this pipe thing
was <u>for</u> his car. Did you see
blood on it?

                    JIMMY
I didn't have time to look
close. But he could've washed
it off, and believe me, the
thing was nasty.

                    JOHN
I don't know, Jimmy...He
seems to me like a goofy Gina
nerd who just wants to get
home to his—

                    JIMMY
They always seem that way.
Quiet. Nice. Keeps to
himself. When was the last
time you heard a psycho's
next door neighbor say, "Hey,
I'm not surprised Bobby Gene
shot up that pot luck church
dinner at all. He was a
fucking loon." Uh-uh, man.
This guy toasted Gina, and
his ass is ours.

John is quiet for a long moment.

                    JOHN
          What's that supposed to mean?

                    JIMMY
          Meaning I wish I brought my
          hunting rifle. But that's
          okay. That's okay. For now...
          maybe I'll just go ask him
          why he did it—
               (abruptly walks away)

                    JOHN
          Jimmy, wait!

Hurries around the corner after him and SLAMS
into his back.

The two of them are staring at an empty
Explorer.

                    JIMMY
          Mother...fucker...

They back away from each other, looking in all
directions. Jimmy squints into the sun. Spots a
figure wearing a backpack, running down the road
to a waiting local bus at the next corner.

                    JIMMY
          There!

He hops in the Explorer. John hesitates, then
gets in and they SCREECH after him.

INT. EXPLORER - DAY

Jimmy hunches over the wheel, weirdly enjoying
himself.

                    JIMMY
          Look at the guilty prick run.

                    JOHN
          I think he's just trying to
          catch the bus, Jimmy.

                    JIMMY
          No shit. wouldn't you?

Tom reaches the idling bus, hurries aboard.
Jimmy SLAMS on his brakes right behind the
bumper. Reaches for the door handle and John
grabs his arm.

                    JOHN
          What are you doing?

                    JIMMY
          What do ya think I'm doing?
          Kicking his ass.

                    JOHN
          No you're not.

                    JIMMY
          I'm not?

John reaches over and switches off the ignition.

                    JOHN
          No. Because right now you are
          very out of control.

                    JIMMY
          Oh, I see. Mr. Tank Top
          Smeller just bashed Gina's
          head in, and I'm out of
          control?

                    JOHN
          Jimmy, you can't go through a
          guy's stuff once and assume he
          killed a person—

                    JIMMY
          Who's assuming? I know it—

                    JOHN
          You don't know squat!
          You're mad because Gina was
          murdered! So am I! But we
          have to be sensible here,
          okay?

                    JIMMY
          (SLAMMING his door shut)
     Fine. Let's be sensible. Tell
     me what to do.

                    JOHN
     First...we calm down. Then...
               (pulls out his cell)
     We call the police. Describe
     Tom, tell them what bus he's
     on and let them handle it—

                    JIMMY
     No. Way. In hell.

                    JOHN
     Why not—

                    JIMMY
     BECAUSE THEY'LL FUCK IT UP,
     THAT'S WHY!!

John is startled. Jimmy nudges his phone away.

                    JIMMY
     And if they don't, the
     lawyers will. And if <u>they</u>
     don't, some bored, overworked
     son-of-a-bitch in the D.A.'s
     office puts the wrong address
     on a form and the prick is
     back on the street in three
     months.

                    JOHN
     Jimmy, there are laws and
     there are systems—

                    JIMMY
     And they don't work! You
     know that, I know that, the
     monkeys at the zoo know that—

                    JOHN
     If this has to do with your
     dad, it's a dumb reason.

Jimmy looks at him a long beat. Slides a stick
of gum in his mouth and pulverizes it.

                    JIMMY
          Cold, man...That's really
          cold.

                    JOHN
          Look. All I'm saying is
          that Tom should not be held
          responsible because of a
          mistake some jury made twenty
          years ago—

                    JIMMY
          One hell of a mistake, wasn't
          it? Bad enough to give my mom
          a fatal stroke.

John hangs his head, somewhat guilty.

                    JOHN
          Hey. I didn't mean anything
          by that. I just don't think
          it's healthy to be so
          paranoid.

                    JIMMY
          Yeah, well if twelve
          incompetent dicks fucked up
          your upbringing, you'd be a
          little paranoid, too.

Suddenly the bus pulls away, leaving them in a
cloud of exhaust.

                    JIMMY
          Shit.

John REVVS the Explorer, puts it into drive.
Looks at John.

                    JIMMY
          Now or never, amigo. Gina's
          killer is getting away and we
          have a chance to stop him.

John stares at the bus as it moves down the

endless road. He can't decide.

                    JOHN
          Okay, but—

                    JIMMY
          Okay! Good idea!

He peels out after it. John frantically buckles
himself in.

                    JOHN
          But we need evidence first!

                    JIMMY
          Evidence?

                    JOHN
          Right. If we catch up to him,
          I mean. We need concrete
          evidence he did it.

                    JIMMY
          You mean like a confession?
          Be a pleasure!

                    JOHN
          Or something else! Like
          another item he has in his
          possession. Maybe we can
          follow him home and watch him
          for a little.

                    JIMMY
               (chews that over)
          Hmm. Not as thrilling. But
          I like the way you think,
          Honest John.

The streets and houses of Indio fall away from
the road, and broiling, unforgiving desert
envelops them.

EXT. TWO-LANE ROAD - DAY

The Explorer stays a good distance behind the
bus. The flat terrain morphs into a line of dry,

jagged hills.

INT. EXPLORER - DAY

John has a map open.

                    JOHN
          This road dumps out near El
          Centro. The guy could live in
          Mexico, for all we know.

                    JIMMY
          Doubtful. That's a local bus
          he's on.
               (peers off to the left)
          What's all that water?

John glances up at a distant strip of blue-
brown water. Checks the map again.

                    JOHN
          The Salton Sea...God, it's
          huge.

He's not kidding. Thirty-five miles long and
fifteen across, the northern end of this bizarre
inland lake appears on the left, its murky
water rippling in the hot desert breeze.

                    JOHN
          Actually, I've read about
          this place. I think it was a
          mistake...They were making
          irrigation cuts from the
          Colorado River like over a
          hundred years ago and the
          thing overflowed, set water up
          here...

The SUNBURST TRAILER PARK appears on the left.
A dozen or so shabby, immobile units and a few
Airstreams, perched along the Salton Sea shore.

                    JIMMY
          "You too can live next to a
          mistake."

Suddenly the bus slows down, pops on its brake

lights. Jimmy hangs back, watching.

The bus door opens. Tom gets out with his pack,
crosses the road to the trailer park.

                    JIMMY
          Lift-off...

They wait in silence for Tom to vanish between
two of the trailers, before Jimmy pulls into
the gravel lot and kills the Explorer's engine.

The only sounds are a PINGING flagpole rope
and gently CREAKING sign below it: RENT NOW
BY MONTH OR YEAR. Beside a stack of abandoned
truck tires and a mini-trailer is an ancient
phone booth, all four of its sides tinted brown
from months of blowing dust.

                    JIMMY
          Whaddya think?

                    JOHN
          I think you should do this
          yourself.

                    JIMMY
          Aw c'mon, for chrissakes. All
          we're gonna do is scope the
          place out, see what he's up
          to.

                    JOHN
          Somehow I don't believe you.

                    JIMMY
          Okay. How's this? If we
          somehow find out he's
          definitely the killer, I hold
          him down while you call the
          cops.

                    JOHN
          We could make this a lot
          easier and just call them
          now—

                    JIMMY
          Forget that. This is <u>our</u>
          show, amigo. Gina's done so
          much for us and we owe her
          one back.

                    JOHN
          What do you mean "owe" her?
          We gave her three grand off on
          a Wagoneer!

                    JIMMY
          I'm talking about <u>Windy City</u>,
          man. The good times we've had
          watching her. Nutball Tom is
          right. We've known and cared
          about her more than most
          people we see every day...At
          least <u>I</u> have.

He glances around at the desolate landscape.
Nudges John's arm.

                    JIMMY
          You're gonna wuss out on me,
          aren't ya?

John stares at the trailer park. EXHALES.

EXT. TRAILER PARK - DAY

Late afternoon light basks the trailers in
a dusty gold. Towels and sheets hang on
clotheslines between a few of the units, but
otherwise the place seems deserted.

Jimmy and John make their way on foot through a
shadowy trailer alley. Jimmy sniffs the air.

                    JIMMY
          Something is very reeking
          here.

                    JOHN
          Don't tell me. The bodies in
          Tom's freezer.

                    JIMMY
          <u>Now</u> you're making sense.

They hear some VOICES and hold up. Listening.
One of them is definitely Tom's but the words
aren't clear. They keep moving. Come to the end
of a rack of kayaks. Peer around the corner.

Before them is a decrepit "lakefront" trailer.
RENTAL OFFICE badly painted on its window. The
entire trailer tilts slightly toward the water
on cracked cinder blocks. There's no sign of
Tom, but they can hear some FOOTSTEPS gravel-
CRUNCHING into the distance.

They inch out closer to the trailer, checking
all directions. A whirlwind of dust blows
through, stings their eyes. For a moment they're
disoriented, have to pause to rub them dry.

When they look up again, a shirtless BRUTISH
MAN stands in the open trailer doorway. Deep
into his 60s, perspiring heavily in a stained
pair of black overalls. Holds a PET GOPHER
in his somewhat greasy hands. His skin is
leathery, sun-cracked, his hard expression the
product of liquor and apparent bitterness.

He gives them a long, blank stare.

                    MAN
          Office is closed.

                    JOHN
          Oh—that's okay. We were just
          looking around.

                    MAN
          Lookin' at what?

There's a long, awkward silence. The man pets
the gopher's neck, then pockets the critter in
his overalls and walks a little closer.

                    MAN
          Saw your fancy-ass jeep out
          there. You here to collect
          money from me?

                    JIMMY
          No, man. We're checking out
          local trailer parks and
          that's all we're doing.
          C'mon, John—

He blocks their way. Looks them over again,
haircuts to shoes. Nods to himself, then works
a mouthful of yellow, crooked teeth into a
startling smile.

                    MAN
          Good Christ. I owe both of
          you bastards a cherry-lime
          Rickey on my sundeck.

                    JIMMY
          A what—

He throws his arms around them, gets them in a
bear hug.

                    MAN
          Horace never takes no for an
          answer, y'know.

John and Jimmy share a stunned glance, then nod
uneasily.

                                        CUT TO:

INT. HORACE'S TRAILER - DAY

Part office, part garage. Barely a living space.
Shelves and shelves of auto parts, tools, and
rusting household appliances line the shelves
and walls. A cobwebbed adding machine, ledger
and manual typewriter sit on a desk in the
corner. Like everything else in the place, the
desk leans at a slight angle toward the Salton
Sea.

Horace leads them through the trailer. Drops
his gopher in a shoebox, then zips open a
massive green canvas on the far wall. A twenty-
foot square redwood deck has been built onto
the trailer, complete with sun chairs, stand-up

bar, gas grill and motorboat dock.

                    HORACE
          Life ain't worth a crap
          without a sun deck, y'know.

                    JIMMY
          Huh. Pretty soon it could be
          a water deck.

Horace eyes him a second. John quickly motions
around at the auto parts collection.

                    JOHN
          Horace? I bet you fix cars.

                    HORACE
          You bet right. Hope you
          like ice in your Rickeys
          'cause that's how I make the
          bastards.

He opens a SQUEAKY little fridge, pulls out
a glass pitcher of bright red, slightly
crystallized liquid. Jimmy nudges John, points
to the back of Horace's overalls.

The long black pipe from Tom's backpack—minus
its newspaper—is protruding from his back
pocket. He turns suddenly and catches them
staring.

                    JOHN
          Oh! W-we were just noticing
          that weird thing in your
          pocket...What is that?

He carefully slides it out. Looks it over and
lays it on a table.

                    HORACE
          Tie rod. Got an old Buick
          that's been needin' a new
          one.
                    (looks at them again)
          What's the matter? Don't like
          my sun deck?

                    JOHN
          Oh right. Sorry.

Ushers Jimmy outside.

EXT. SUN DECK - DAY

Leads him across to the far rail. The repugnant
stench is back, and it nearly knocks them over.
They peer over the side.

DEAD, ROTTING FISH are washing up everywhere.

                    JIMMY
          Charming...

                    JOHN
          Let's have this stupid drink
          and get out of here, okay?
          We saw the thing. It's a tie
          rod for Tom's car that he
          probably picked up for him in
          L.A. End of mystery.

                    JIMMY
          Sure. Unless he planned it
          that way.

                    JOHN
          Planned what?

                    JIMMY
          Remember that old Alfred
          Hitchcock Presents about the
          wife who beats her husband to
          death with a frozen leg of
          lamb? The cops come over to
          question her and she serves
          it to them for dinner. It
          was brilliant. And I bet Tom
          watched that.

John just shakes his head. Horace steps onto
the deck with two cherry-lime Rickeys served in
beer mugs. Hands them over, then stands there
until they take their first sips.

                    JOHN
          It's um...refreshing.

                    JIMMY
          Yeah. Kind of neutralizes the
          dead fish smell.

                    HORACE
          Yep...Salt kills 'em. If not
          that the low water levels. If
          not that the red tide—y'know,
          Mexican pollution. Been goin'
          on so long it seems like
          it's supposed to. Actually,
          caught a few live ones out in
          the cove this mornin' I'll
          be grillin' up soon. First I
          gotta get _my_ Rickey.
                    (winks at them)
          With the added kick.

He ducks back inside. John and Jimmy take
second sips of their drinks, gaze off at the
line of adjacent trailers.

And see Tom step out of one in a bathrobe,
carrying a towel and shampoo bottle. Walks
around the side and curtains himself into an
outdoor shower.

                    JIMMY
          Did you see that? What's the
          first thing people do after
          they do something bad? Take a
          shower.

                    JOHN
          And also if they're hot and
          dirty. You see too many
          movies, Jimmy.

                    JIMMY
          Señor. Life _is_ a movie. Gimme
          your glass—

He grabs it, pours most of his Rickey into
John's, tosses the rest over the rail.

                         JOHN
                What are you doing?

                         JIMMY
                Getting in that trailer. Keep
                an eye out.

                         JIMMY
                Are you craz—

Too late. He walks inside and collides with
Horace, who's on his way out carrying his
Rickey in one hand and an ice bucket filled with
fresh trout in the other.

                         HORACE
                Christ O'Leary! Where you
                goin'?

                         JIMMY
                Can you believe it? Promised
                to call my wife and left my
                phone in the car. Back in a
                few minutes...
                   (hands him the empty mug)
                Delicious Richie!

He hurries back through the trailer and out the
door. Horace SNORTS.

                         HORACE
                Peckerhead...

Comes out on the deck, sets down the ice bucket
and squeezes himself into a plastic deck chair.
Draws a large shearing knife from his overalls.

                         HORACE
                Would've spiked your drinks
                too, but I was a little low
                on the old Popov.

He picks a trout out of the bucket, lops its
head off and begins gutting the thing right on
the deck. John turns away.

EXT. TRAILER PARK - DAY

Jimmy darts around a few trailers, doubles back. Reappears on the far, shadowy end of Tom's trailer, a glorified U-Haul with a door, window, and its own mini-satellite dish on top.

He hears the outdoor SHOWER going, sees water from it running on the ground from around the side.

EXT. HORACE'S SUN DECK - DAY

John glances down the trailer line in search of Jimmy. No sign. Horace lops off another fish head.

                    JOHN
          Those are...non-polluted
          ones, I take it.

                    HORACE
          Hope so.

John glances around him again. Spots Tom sliding open a side window on Tom's trailer and lifting himself inside.

John is a nervous mess. Horace gazes out at the putrid water and SNIFFS the air. John prays he doesn't look behind him.

                    HORACE
          Yep...Red tide night.

John forces a smile.

INT. TOM'S TRAILER - DAY

Jimmy looks around the dim, sweltering room he's dropped into. Waits for his eyes to adjust.

A dirty shag rug and piles of unwashed dishes add to the aroma outside. Jimmy sees a lamp next to an unmade futon on the floor, picks his way over some soiled underwear and SWITCHES it on. Looks up.

                    JIMMY
          Jesus...

The ceiling over the bed is plastered with
the same half dozen Gina Coogan glossies.
Meticulously arranged so that they fan out
directly over his stained pillow. Walls haven't
been spared, either, covered top to bottom with
Gina Coogan magazine articles. Across from the
bed, a 47-inch flat screen TV takes up half the
trailer.

The SHOWER WATER outside loses its pressure
for a moment. Jimmy's heart stops. The water
RECOVERS, and he continues his search.

EXT. SUN DECK - DUSK

Dusty, tangerine light now paints the water and
deck. John is too frazzled to enjoy it, and
Horace is staring at him again.

                    HORACE
          You guys got money to buy a
          trailer?

                    JOHN
               (shrugs)
          Guess that depends on the
          trailer, doesn't it?

                    HORACE
          You sassin' me?

                    JOHN
          What's that?

                    HORACE
          You sassin' me back? I don't
          like people sassin' me back.

                    JOHN
          I wasn't, Horace. Believe me.

Sips some more Rickey. Glances down at Tom's
trailer and can faintly hear the SHOWER still
going.

                    HORACE
          You boys fairies?

John looks at him in disbelief.

                    HORACE
          'Cause one thing I don't
          tolerate is sick love. Hard
          enough to find real love in
          this world. Don't need the
          screwy kind.

John toys with saying something unkind. Then
hears Tom's shower suddenly TURN OFF.

INT. TOM'S TRAILER - DUSK

So does Jimmy. He lurches back to kill the
lamp and knocks over a carton. Notepaper and
envelopes spill across the floor.

                    JIMMY
          Shit—

Gets on his knees, frantically gets everything
back in the box.

Pauses when he sees what he's looking at.

Batch after rubber-banded batch of returned,
unopened letters, addressed to:

          GINA COOGAN
          C/O WINDY CITY,
          CINEBOX ENTERTAINMENT
          STUDIO CITY, CA

Jimmy's eyes widen. He stuffs a batch of the
envelopes in his back pocket. Hears FOOTSTEPS
walking around the side of the trailer and
ducks behind a counter in a tiny kitchen area.

EXT. SUN DECK - DUSK

John squirms as he spots Tom entering the
trailer, towel wrapped around his waist. He
sets his mug down. Rises and moves across the
deck, backpedaling away from Horace.

                    JOHN
          Uhhh...Listen, this probably
          isn't the best time to see
          that trailer. Y'know, getting
          late. We'll call you back in
          a few days, okay?

Horace glowers at him as he leaves. Already
buzzed from his drink.

                    HORACE
          Fairy peckerheads...

INT. TOM's TRAILER - DUSK

Jimmy holds his breath while Tom peels the
towel off his pale, scrawny body and rubs his
hair dry. Turns and brushes right past him.
Swings open the door to a narrow closet. While
he rummages around for clothes, Jimmy quietly
slips out the trailer door.

EXT. TRAILER PARK - DUSK

A frantic John sees Jimmy heading for the
Explorer and hurries after him.

                    JOHN
          Did you talk to him—

                    JIMMY
          Get in.

INT. EXPLORER - DUSK

Jimmy REVVS the engine, backs around.

                    JIMMY
          Where's the nearest town? I
          need a fuckin' drink. A real
          one.

                    JOHN
          (quickly checks his phone)
          Uhh—left in a few miles. Did
          you talk to him or not?

                         JIMMY
               Wasn't the best time.

He reaches into his back pocket, tosses the wad
of envelopes in John's lap.

                         JOHN
               What's this?

                         JIMMY
               Possible evidence. Signed,
               sealed, and not delivered.

                         JOHN
               You took these?

                         JIMMY
               Well, I couldn't exactly sit
               and read them there, right?

                         JOHN
               Then how do you know they're
               evidence?

Jimmy smiles impishly.

                         JIMMY
               I don't...That's why we need
               a bar.

INT. ROAD RUNNER SALOON - NIGHT

A dark, practically empty watering hole.
Soft WILLIE NELSON playing on a jukebox. The
BARTENDER sleepily reads a Weekly World News on
the nearly empty bar.

Jimmy and John hunker down with their beers at
a back table. Two or three of the letters are
already opened. Jimmy reads from another.

                         JIMMY
               "I can't remember if I ever
               asked what your favorite
               color is. Mine is maroon,
               because it has lots of red in
               it."

He scratches his chin stubble. Looks at John.

                    JIMMY
          Interesting. He likes the
          color red.

                    JOHN
          This is pathetic...

                    JIMMY
          You wouldn't say that if you
          saw his trailer.

                    JOHN
          I wouldn't? The last time I
          checked, it wasn't against
          the law to be a groupie.

                    JIMMY
          Okay...Then why did he lie to
          us about being at Gina's?

                    JOHN
          Jimmy, a map with an arrow
          doesn't prove he was
          anywhere.

He pauses to rub some lingering dust out of his
bleary eyes.

                    JOHN
          And I'm not buying this muddy
          shoe business. If he really
          killed her he would've tossed
          them by now. Same with the
          tie rod.

Jimmy downs the rest of his beer. Glances back
at the open letter in his hand.

His eyes narrow. He sits up a little
straighter.

                    JIMMY
          Hey.

                    JOHN
          Hey what?

                    JIMMY
          Hey this:
                    (reading again)
          "Please don't do this to me,
          Gina. You are all I care
          about. Anyone they replace
          you with will be an absolute
          fraud."

He raises an eyebrow at John. Skims the rest of
the letter. Stops at the end.

                    JIMMY
          "How dare you leave me!
          Neglecting your loved ones is
          a serious, horrible crime,
          Gina...I hope you don't
          regret it."

Jimmy's face flushes red.

                    JOHN
          What's the date on that one?

                    JIMMY
          Postmarked...April 4th. Two
          weeks ago. Which means he
          must've gotten this returned
          undelivered last week!

                    JOHN
          (staring at the other letters)
          Open the one before that one.
          If it's there...

Jimmy finds it, practically tears the envelope
in half.

                    JIMMY
          Let's see, let's see..."Do
          we have to wait a whole week
          between new episodes? Can't
          you make them stop doing
          that? When I wait seven days
          to see your angelic face,
          wondering what you'll say
          and do next, then get stuck
          watching an old episode and
          lines I know by heart, it's
          actually criminal."

                    JOHN
          He knows them by heart...

                    JIMMY
          "You were in my dream again
          last night. This time we were
          sitting in my back seat at
          a drive-in movie that had
          nothing on the screen, and
          we started kissing and your
          mouth tasted like spearmint,
          and before you knew it—"
                    (he tenses up)
          "Before you knew it I had
          my hand inside your shirt,
          feeling one of your...
          titties. And you just kept
          kissing me, and the cars
          around us grew lizard heads
          and crawled on top of each
          other and it looked like the
          famous junkyard"—whatever
          that is—"but if felt safe to
          stay clamped on your lips,
          moving my tongue—"
                    (tosses it aside)
          Aw, shit. I can't read this.

John picks up the letter, skips to the last
graph.

                    JOHN
          "If you ever left me, nothing
          would exist anymore. I would
          lay my head on a railroad
          track and squash it. Maybe
          you can...squash yours with
          me. Or maybe I'll just squash
          yours first."

He looks at Jimmy, mortified.

                    JIMMY
          Guess he didn't wait around
          for a train.

                    JOHN
          Guess not...
               (neatly folds up the
               letter, slides it back
               in its envelope)
          I gotta...use the bathroom.

INT. SALOON HALLWAY - NIGHT

John hesitates at the bathroom door, keeps
walking to a shadowy corner and takes out his
cell phone. Glances back to make sure Jimmy
can't see him.

                    OPERATOR
                    (V.O.)
          9-1-1 emergency.

                    JOHN
          Hi, I need...the local
          police. For like...the Anza-
          Barrego Desert area.

                    OPERATOR
                    (V.O.)
          State your emergency, please.

He pauses. hears a CREAK in the wood floor and
turns to see Jimmy standing right behind him.
Not happy.

                    JOHN
          I um, want to report someone—

Jimmy snatches the phone out of his hand and
hangs up the call.

                    JIMMY
          Who would that be? Tom? Or
          me?

                    JOHN
          We need a third opinion. This
          has gotten too weird.

                    JIMMY
          What's weird? You just don't
          wanna believe it.

                         JOHN
              It's not a matter of wanting
              to. Unless we have absolute,
              concrete proof that he—

                         JIMMY
              SCREW the proof!!

He draws a dirty look from the bartender. Jimmy
motions them out the saloon's rear door.

EXT. SALOON BACK PARKING LOT - NIGHT

                         JIMMY
              You know what our proof is?
              It's Lover Boy Tom on his
              hands and fucking knees,
              begging forgiveness. Now I
              don't know about you, but
              that's something I would pay
              to see.

                         JOHN
              Good. You pay. I'll watch
              the film at 11. Can I have my
              phone back?

                         JIMMY
                (keeping it away from him)
              What are you gonna tell them?
              That we followed the guy,
              broke into his trailer, and
              opened his mail? That's one
              federal offense already.

                         JOHN
              Jimmy, we are way over our
              heads on this.

                         JIMMY
              You might be. I'm not.

He sees how distressed John is and lays a calm
hand on his shoulder.

                    JIMMY
          Listen, man. The guy they
          should've jailed instead of
          my dad? I'll never find him.
          Nobody will. But this is a
          once-in-a-lifetime chance
          here. Tom murd—excuse me—
          might have murdered a woman
          close to us.

                    JOHN
          I don't care if she was our
          sister. It doesn't give us
          the right to—

                    JIMMY
          Talk to him? I think so.
          For five very calm fucking
          minutes? I think so. And
          I promise: The second he
          confesses, we call the cops.

                    JOHN
          Great. And what if he won't?

Jimmy smiles, pats John's back and gingerly
hands him his cell phone back.

                    JOHN
          Have a little faith, amigo.

EXT. TRAILER PARK - NIGHT

Jimmy backs the Explorer up to a fenced-off
transformer across the road from the park.
Kills the engine and lights. A hot night wind
has kicked in, blows dust, litter, and a few
tumbleweeds around in mini-cyclones.

INT. EXPLORER - NIGHT

John scrolling around on his cell phone. Jimmy
is very antsy.

                    JIMMY
          You got it or not?

                    JOHN
          Yeah, yeah. I put it in my
          notes. Hang on...
               (clicks on his notes app)
          Okay, here. 442-399-1214

Jimmy dials the number on <u>his</u> cell. They stare
at the old phone booth across the road, by the
park's entrance. It starts to RING, faintly.

                    JIMMY
          Come on, someone.

It RINGS. And RINGS.

                    JOHN
          Forget this. Let's go.

Jimmy ignores him. The phone keeps RINGING.
Finally a dim light switches on outside the
mini-trailer behind the booth. An OLD WOMAN
emerges with a walker and clunks her way to the
ringing phone.

                    WOMAN
                    (V.O.)
          Sunburst Park. Help you?

                    JIMMY
          Hi! I'm uh...looking for a
          resident there named Tom? I
          don't know his last name or
          have his number, but he lives
          alone in that real small
          trail—

                    WOMAN
                    (V.O.)
          Wait a minute.

She leaves the open booth, slowly clunks her
way into the shadows. Jimmy taps out a rhythm
on the steering wheel. John can't sit still.

                    JOHN
          He's never going to buy this.

                    JIMMY
          Don't know unless you try.

They see the woman re-enter her trailer,
shut the door. Seconds later, a barefoot and
bathrobed Tom appears. Shuts himself in the
phone booth.

                    TOM
                   (V.O.)
          Hel-lo?

                    JIMMY
          Tom? Hi, it's Jimmy! We
          gave you a ride to Indio,
          remember?

                    TOM
                   (V.O.)
          Oh. Yeah.

                    JIMMY
          You disappeared on us, man.
          What happened?

                    TOM
                   (V.O.)
          I had to catch the bus...How
          did you know where I live?

                    JIMMY
          How? Umm...somebody at the
          gas station recognized you.
          Listen—

                    TOM
                   (V.O.)
          Who was that?

                    JIMMY
          Aw, didn't get his name.
          Anyway, listen. Before you
          split I was gonna tell you
          that I have a whole carton
          of Gina paraphernalia in the
          back of my vehicle here.

                    TOM
              (V.O., after a pause)
          What do you have?

Jimmy nudges John with delight.

                    JIMMY
          Oh, clippings, posters, press
          kits. Some real good <u>Windy
          City</u> swag. I got a buddy at
          Cinebox who gets it for me.
          Anyway, we're kind of in
          your neighborhood. How about
          we swing by your trailer in
          about fifteen minutes and you
          can take a look at the stuff?

There's a very long pause. Tom peers through
dirty phone booth glass at the windy darkness,
though not in their direction.

                    TOM
                  (V.O.)

          Okay...

                    JIMMY
          Cool! We'll see you in
          fifteen!

He hangs up. Watches with John as Tom leaves
the booth and hurries back to his trailer.

                    JOHN
          Think he bought it?

                    JIMMY
          Sure seems so.
                  (points to the letters
                  in John's lap)
          Stick those somewhere for now.

He starts the Explorer's ENGINE, drives a good
hundred yards down the road before putting his
lights back on and making a U-turn.

INT. TOM'S TRAILER - NIGHT

Tom sits on his bed, excitedly tugging on some shoes and socks. Stares at a gorgeous close-up of Gina Coogan on his massive TV.

                    TOM
          I don't have to tell you
          anything, Scott.

                    GINA
               (seconds later)
          I don't have to tell you
          anything, Scott.

She does a quick shake-toss with her scarlet hair. Tom grabs a remote, backs up and plays the shake-toss again in super slow motion. A relieved, mildly ecstatic smile crosses his face.

INT. EXPLORER - NIGHT

They wait on the side of the road, watching the entrance to the trailer park. John is behind the wheel now, while Jimmy plays around with the GPS on the dash.

                    JIMMY
          The entire area is the Anza-
          Borrego Park. Pick any road
          you want, man.
               (glances up ahead)
          And there's our boy...

EXT. TRAILER PARK DRIVEWAY - NIGHT

Tom approaches the jeep as it pulls into the lot. Jimmy hops out, pats him on the back with a grin.

                    JIMMY
          Can you believe it? We left
          the stupid carton at this bar
          we were at.
               (opens the back door for him)
          C'mon, we'll get you there and
          home in like twenty minutes.

Tom doesn't move.

                    TOM
          Are you sure?

                    JIMMY
          Of course. C'mon, I'll even
          buy ya a beer. Or a ginger
          ale. Anything you want.

Tom hesitates, then lets out a nervous smile
and climbs in back.

INT. EXPLORER - NIGHT

Heading up a pitch black two-lane road.
Nobody's talking yet. Jimmy fiddles with his FM
radio tuner.

                    JIMMY
          Can't get shit out here.
          Bet you got one of those
          satellite dishes, huh?

Tom doesn't answer. Jimmy finds some CHRISTIAN
CHORAL MUSIC on the radio and leans back.

                    JIMMY
          So Tom! What's it like living
          by the old Salty Sea?
                    (nudges John)

                    JOHN
          Right. Yeah. seems pretty
          remote!

                    TOM
          It's quiet...Except when it's
          windy.
          (worriedly peers out the window)
          Where's this bar?

                    JIMMY
          Up ahead. A few more miles.

Tom seems unconvinced. Squirms in his seat.
John tightens his grip on the steering wheel,

feels around with his toe for the brights
switch.

And a JACKRABBIT darts in front of the car.
John tries to jerk the wheel but SPLATTERS the
thing across the road.

                    TOM
          What the heck was that??

                    JOHN
          A rabbit! God, I hate doing
          that.

Tom is stricken. Softly begins to CRY. Jimmy
turns, looks at him.

                    JIMMY
          Hey man, it's okay...Isn't
          that what they do out here?
          Y'know, play Car Keepaway?

Tom looks at the floor. Wipes his eyes on a
sleeve. John gives Jimmy a disapproving stare.
Jimmy's face hardens.

                    JIMMY
          Pull over a sec, okay? I
          gotta take a whiz.

                    JOHN
          Are you sure?

                    JIMMY
          Dude. My bladder is sure.

EXT. TWO-LANE ROAD - NIGHT

John brakes the Explorer in the narrow
emergency lane. Jimmy waits for a pickup to
ZOOM past them doing about 65, then gets out,
walks a yard or two and has to fight to stay on
his feet in the hot, whipping wind. Fumbles
with his zipper.

                    JIMMY
          Christ. Gonna need a goddamn
          wet suit out here.

INT. EXPLORER - NIGHT

John gnaws on a fingernail. Can hear Tom's rapid
BREATHING in the back seat.

                    TOM
          He said we're going to a
          bar...but there's no bar this
          way.

                    JOHN
          No, no. There really is.
          It's...a brand new one, I
          think.

                    TOM
              (his voice cracking)
          I don't believe you.

John locks eyes with Tom in the rear view
mirror. The guy is actually shaking. John
begins to say something—

And Jimmy throws the back door open, jumps in
beside Tom.

                    JIMMY
          Hey, Tom...Got a minute?
          (smacks a hand on the front seat)
          Lock up and drive, John.

John pauses, then hits a CHILD-PROOF LOCK on
the door panel and drives away. Tom starts to
freak out. Jimmy puts a comforting arm around
him.

                    TOM
          What's happening??

                    JIMMY
          Nothing man, nothing. It's
          just...Before I show you the
          stuff we have, I thought we
          should have a little talk
          about Gina. Y'know, find out
          how really committed you
          are to carrying her torch
          and stuff. 'Cause we don't
          wanna lay this stuff on just
          anybody.

                    TOM
          But...I thought we talked
          about her already. I told you
          her horoscope, and-and I let
          John hold her shirt—

                    JIMMY
          I know, Tom. I was there. But
          what we want now are more
          specific details. Things about
          Gina that only you know...

John is distracted, nearly swerves into an
oncoming, HONKING car.

                    JIMMY
          Jesus! Excuse me—
                    (to John)
          I don't like this road. Pull
          off behind that building up on
          the right.
                    (back to TOM)
          Oh—I just remembered. We
          stashed the box in this
          buiding up ahead. We've been
          all over the map tonight and
          I've had a couple too many.
          That's why <u>he's</u> driving.

EXT. THE QUIET MAN LODGE - NIGHT

John turns off on a dusty service road. Cuts
around the back of a ghostly, abandoned motor
lodge that was probably built in the early
'60s. Weeds grow out of its pool. Eighty
percent of the windows broken or shot out.

INT. EXPLORER - NIGHT

John pulls up in front of a row of first floor
"rooms". Kills the engine. They can almost hear
Tom's heart pounding.

                    TOM
          This place is scary. C-can
          you bring out the stuff for
          me?

                    JIMMY
          What are you scared of? It's
          empty! John, don't forget the
          flashlight under the seat,
          okay?

John nods, but doesn't move right away.

                    JIMMY
          And could you please let us
          out?

John SMACKS the UNLOCK button with his hand.
They all get out.

EXT. BACK OF LODGE - NIGHT

Jimmy trains the flashlight on the row of
rusted, half-open doors.

                    JOHN
          Which one was it?

                    JIMMY
          Umm...The first one!

He reluctantly leaves Tom next to John and
edges up to the first room. Peers inside with
the flashlight. Turns. Tom and John have barely
moved.

                    JIMMY
          C'mon, guys! The box is
          friggin' heavy. I need both
          of ya!

John motions for Tom to lead the way.

INT. ABANDONED MOTEL ROOM - NIGHT

The flashlight beam reveals what's left.
Stripped TV wires protruding from a wall.
Shredded Bible under a bent, overturned patio
chair. Desert dust caked on everything. Tom
walks in between them, CHOKES once from the
dust, then looks around. Confused.

                    TOM
          There's no box in here...

Turns to John and Jimmy's hand CLAMPS onto his
shoulder.

                    JIMMY
          Why'd you do it, Tom?

Tom stares at him. Dumbstruck. Jimmy grabs the
patio chair with his free hand and flips it over
for him.

                    JIMMY
          Have a seat.

Tom doesn't want to sit. Jimmy firmly shoves him
into the chair with his hand, then crouches in
front and aims the flashlight in his face.

                    JOHN
          God, Jimmy. Enough with the
          damn cop shows—

                    JIMMY
          Hey. We're doing this.
                    (to TOM)
          I'll ask you again. Why did
          you kill Gina?

                    TOM
          W-what??

                    JIMMY
          C'mon, c'mon. You think we're
          that dumb? We saw the tie rod
          and the muddy shoes in your
          pack. For all we know there's
          a tank top missing from her
          laundry hamper right now.

                    TOM
          Oh no...You don't understand.
          I <u>loved</u> her!

                    JIMMY
          Breaking news, buddy: We
          all did. But only one of us
          killed her, and me and John
          were tucked in our beds when
          it happened.
                    (leans in)
          Where were <u>you</u>?

Tom begins to CRY again. Huge, racking SOBS
this time.

                    JOHN
          Jimmy, he didn't do it—

                    JIMMY
          COOL IT, MAN! WE'RE CLOSE!!

He drops the flashlight, grabs the front of
Tom's shirt.

                    JIMMY
          Where were you? Huh? On Shady
          Terrace in Sherman Oaks,
          right? We saw the giant red
          arrow on your stars map, so
          don't tell us you've never
          been there.

                    TOM
               (through his sobs)
          I would never...hurt...her...

                    JIMMY
          Oh really? Then what was
          the crazy-ass shit we read
          in your letter? "I hope you
          don't regret it." What the
          hell was that??

Tom suddenly stops crying. Gets real quiet and
just stares at Jimmy with chilling, venomous
eyes.

                    JIMMY
          Motherfucker doesn't believe
          us. Keep him in here.

                    JOHN
          What?

                    JIMMY
          Keep him the fuck in here!

He stalks back outside. John isn't sure what to
do. Picks up the flashlight and holds it over
Tom in a half-assed threatening manner. Hears a
weird LEAKING SOUND and looks down at a little
piss puddle forming beside Tom's shoe.

EXT. MOTEL LOT - NIGHT

Jimmy throws open the back of the Explorer,
CURSING under his breath.

INT. MOTEL ROOM - NIGHT

Tom stares up at John, shaking. John keeps
finding excuses to look away.

                    TOM
          You were reading my
          letters?...

                    JOHN
          Yeah. I guess we got nosy...
               (EXHALES)
          You havbe to admit
          there's some pretty weird
          coincidences—

                    JIMMY
               (O.S., from outside)
          Where the fuck are they??

                    JOHN
          In my bag!
               (to TOM)
          I have to apologize for my
          friend, okay? He's had it
          kind of rough. See...when he
          was a kid his father was put
          in prison for something he
          didn't do. And he died in a
          knife fight there.

He finally meets Tom's eyes.

> JOHN
> I guess he picked you to take
> it out on this time.

Tom hunches forward in the chair, focused on
one thing only.

> TOM
> How did you get my letters?

> JOHN
> Actually, Jimmy did. He
> didn't mean—

> TOM
> They're private.

> JOHN
> I know they're private, Tom.
> Believe me, you'll get every
> one of them back. For now,
> though, just deny everything
> he asks you, okay? And wait
> for him to calm down. Because
> I know him. He will.

Tom doesn't respond. John leans closer.

> JOHN
> Okay?

Tom's hand FLASHES from below, and a SHARD OF
BROKEN GLASS is at John's throat.

> TOM
> I have to go home now. Gina's
> waiting for me.

> JOHN
> Tom, wait—

> TOM
> If I don't get back and watch
> her, she'll be very, very
> mad...

                    JOHN
          Tom?...Calm down, okay?

                    TOM
          Oh, I'm calm...I'm calm.
          Because Gina is with me all
          the time now. She really
          didn't want to come, but I
          convinced her...

                    JIMMY
                    (O.S.)
          I can't find 'em, man! Which
          bag are ya talkin' about?

                    JOHN
          Jimmy—
               (Tom jerks the shard, nearly
               slicing John's neck open)
          H-hold on!!

                    TOM
          She was a lot shorter than I
          thought she'd be...And she
          had this beautiful nightgown
          on. In the moonlight you
          could see her titty circles
          sticking through...They were
          so pretty.
               (squints at John)
          Don't you ever think about
          her in a nightgown?

                    JOHN
          S-sometimes, yeah...Let's
          go outside now, Tom. Okay?
          G-give you your letters back.

INT. MOTEL LOT

Jimmy finally digs out the letters.

                    JIMMY
          Never mind, found 'em!

Hears FOOTSTEPS. Walks around the Explorer and
freezes in his tracks.

Tom has John's arms pinned behind him, the
glass shard still at his throat.

                    JIMMY
          You crazy asshole...

                    JOHN
          Don't move, Jimmy.

Jimmy takes a step toward them anyway and Tom
jerks John's head back.

                    JOHN
          Jimmy, no! He isn't kidding!

                    JIMMY
          I can see that.
          (puts up his hands, backs away)
          Fine! We're good. Just let
          him go, Tom.

Tom glances around at the dark, forbidding
terrain. Unsure what to do.

                    JIMMY
          I said let him go.

                    TOM
          How will I...get home?

                    JIMMY
          Not a problem. Drop that
          thing and we'll give you a
          ride.

                    TOM
          (desperate twinkle
             in his eye)
          You will?

                    JIMMY
          Sure we will...The ride of
          your pathetic life—

Lunges through the air and tackles him. John,
his glasses, and the shard go flying.

Tom flails around, ELBOWS Jimmy in the face.

Jimmy falls back, SLAMS his head against the
Explorer's front bumper. Drops on the ground,
GROANING.

John panics. Gropes around for his glasses.
Can make out the shard, lying in nearby dirt.
Scrambles over to it but Tom gets there first
with two limber strides. Grabs the shard and
puts John in a quick, brutal headlock. Tickles
his cheek with the sharp edge of the glass.
Blood trickles down his arm from where he's
unknowingly cut himself.

> TOM
> Know something?...I've been
> thinking all day about those
> Gina fans...the ones at
> the church...hugging and
> crying...What phonies...I
> mean, none of them love her
> like I do...Your friend Jimmy
> sure doesn't...He can't love
> anyone. He's too mean. He's a
> real phony...
>   (squints at John)
> Are you a phony, too?

> JOHN
> No, Tom...I'm not.

> TOM
> Huh. I guess I don't believe
> you...Oh well.

He raises the shard like a knife. John squirms
in terror and—

WHACK!!

A sand wedge takes a divot out of Tom's skull.
Jimmy WHACKS him again. Blood sprays the side
of Tom's face. Tom's eyes go white and he drops
the glass shard, topples into the dirt like a
dishrag.

John sits up, in complete shock. Jimmy
collapses against the Explorer, clutching the
golf club. Blood drips from the small gash on

his head.

They stare at Tom's lifeless body, afraid to
speak. The only sound is the desert wind,
whistling through the lodge's broken windows.

                    JOHN
          My God...

Jimmy crawls over to Tom and turns him over.
Feels for a pulse and heartbeat.

                    JOHN
          We're dead...We're positively
          dead.

                    JIMMY
          Correction...He's dead. And
          you would've been.

Jimmy achingly stands, walks away from the
vehicle to look around at the dark landscape.
John slowly gets to his feet, staring at the
body.

                    JOHN
          Okay. Okay. First thing we
          do...is find a town with a
          police station, right? And
          you need stitches—

                    JIMMY
          Uh-uh. Things have changed,
          amigo. We just killed
          someone.

John can't believe what he's hearing.

                    JOHN
          What? You mean you killed
          someone—

                    JIMMY
          No, John. We did. But that's
          okay. It doesn't matter.
          Because no one is ever gonna
          know about it.

                         JOHN
          Oh really? How are they not
          going to know?

                         JIMMY
          Look around, man. See any
          witnesses? No one saw...or
          even heard...shit. Meaning
          all we gotta do is hide his
          dead ass up in those hills,
          grab us a box of Band-aids at
          the 7-Eleven, go home to our
          little lives, pop a couple of
          Advils and treat this thing
          like it never happened.

He walks around to the open back of the
Explorer. Reaches under their golf bags and
hauls out a giant camping tarp.

                         JOHN
          I can't believe this.

John walks away a few yards, shielding his eyes
from the constantly blowing dust. Turns back.

                         JOHN
          Do you know what my name is?
          Honest John Griffin. They run
          a damn commercial about me
          ten times a week!

                         JIMMY
          And what a commercial.

                         JOHN
          Yeah. The same one my dad
          did fifteen years ago. Now he
          might've had the personality
          of a paperweight, but he did
          teach me what honesty is. And
          I'm not about to kiss off the
          entire family reputation with
          one idiotic lie.

Jimmy doesn't respond. Lays the open tarp on
the ground beside Tom's body.

                    JOHN
          This isn't right.

                    JIMMY
          What the fuck is "right"?
          Was what he did right? I
          don't know about you, but the
          thought of this turd getting
          off on an insanity plea or
          signing a million dollar book
          deal was making me puke—

A WHITE LIGHT flashes over the desert behind
them. They turn, see a POLICE CRUISER coming up
the service road on the other side of the motor
lodge. Scanning the area with a searchlight.

                    JIMMY
          Shit! Get down!

They crouch and wait. Hearts racing. Each of
them praying for a different result. The cruiser
slows as it passes the front of the lodge.
Light beam poring through every motel room and
broken window. Jimmy stares down John, afraid
his friend is going to stand and wave his arms.

After a second or two the cruiser moves on by.

                    JIMMY
          It's a sign, man. We're doing
          the right thing.
               (lifts TOM's legs onto the trap)
          You with me or not?

John hesitates a long moment, then dizzily
sinks to his knees. Gently lifts a corner of
the tarp and tucks it under Tom's legs.

INT. EXPLORER - NIGHT

Jimmy's headlights barely illuminate the steep,
twisting road they climb into the desert
foothills.

Suddenly he slows, makes a left into a wide,

sandy wash. Shoves the Explorer into four-wheel
drive. John peers out the windshield with him.

Two large boulders block their way on the first
bend. It's the end of the road. Jimmy knocks
out his last stick of gum. Looks at John.

EXT. WASH - NIGHT

The wind out here is vicious. Jimmy and John
can barely look up as they lift the tarp with
Tom's body out of the back, carry it along a
sandy ridge.

The body is heavy, and they stop repeatedly to
pry their sinking shoes out of the sand. After
a hundred yards or so they stop at the edge of
a cliff, set the tarp down. BREATHING HARD. Wait
for the wind to subside a notch, then look up.

The Anza-Borrego badlands stretch out below
them. Miles of rippling, sandy ridges, dotted
with scattered brush and rocks. The drop
directly below them is a good 600 feet.

Jimmy looks at John. John can't take his eyes
off the drop. Jimmy nudges him. John gives him
a very slow nod and together they unwrap the
tarp. Roll the body off of it, to the lip of the
cliff.

                    JIMMY
          Ready?

John puts up a hand. MUTTERS a prayer to
himself. Looks down at Tom's bone-white face,
then grabs hold of his shoes—

And Tom GURGLES.

                    JOHN
               (jumping back)
          Crap!

A blood bubble forms in his half-open mouth.
John looks at Jimmy, panicking. Jimmy
hesitates, then SHOVES Tom off the cliff.

                    JOHN
          NO—

He falls...falls...falls...

Lands on a flat rock with a THUD, rolls
lifelessly into the dirt. The WIND stirs up
again, blowing sand over his ruined head.

                    JIMMY
          In a half hour you won't be
          able to see him.

He shields his eyes from the dust, starts
back to the Explorer. John slowly rises, then
follows. In a disturbed trance.

INT. EXPLORER - NIGHT

Jimmy bounces them down the main road at a good
clip. John doesn't look too good.

                    JOHN
          Stop the car.

                    JIMMY
          Why?

John is shaken. Ashen. Throws a foot out and
SLAMS the brake pedal.

EXT. SIDE OF ROAD - NIGHT

The Explorer SCREECHES to a stop. John leaps
out, walks three feet and VOMITS his guts out.
Jimmy looks away. Waits. John regains his
stamina. Takes a few DEEP BREATHS of desert
air. Climnbs back in the vehicle and lays a
hand on Jimmy's sleeve.

                    JOHN
          I just want you to know...
          that you can do whatever you
          want...but if the cops drag
          me in...I'm telling them the
          truth.

Jimmy just sits there, simmering with rage. But
speechless for once. SLAMS the Explorer into
drive and keeps going.

EXT. INDIO NEIGHBORHOOD - NIGHT

Jimmy drags the end of a garden hose away from
a dark, shuttered house. Signals to John. John
gently turns the outside faucet on. Water spits
out and Jimmy wets the gash on his head.

John hurries over, takes the hose. Douses his
hands and face like he's been laying in toxic
waste.

INT. EXPLORER - NIGHT

Approaching the lights of Palm Springs now.
Their windows are open, and a warm, calmer
night breeze fills the car.

John is dozing. Wakes to a view of a starry
sky, fanned by tall, spotlit palms. Like
another planet. Realizes where they are and
suddenly sits up.

The snaking driveway of RANCHO VISTA, a plush,
heavily irrigated golf resort wedged into
a small local canyon. Jimmy guzzles from a
Snapple behind the wheel. Angels cap over his
dried gash.

                    JOHN
          What the hell are you
          doing?...We can't stay here!

                    JIMMY
          Why not? We got a killer
          roo—I mean, a dynamite room
          waiting for us.

                    JOHN
          And you feel good about
          taking it?

Jimmy avoids the vested VALET GUY, turns into a
self-parking lot.

                    JIMMY
          Sure. It's good for our
          alibi.
                  (pulls into a space)
          John, the smartest thing we
          can do right now is get on
          with our lives. That doesn't
          mean I'm up for 18 holes
          tomorrow, but I'm not about
          to let the sorry fate of
          one psychotic keep me from
          a Cuervo Gold marg and hot
          jacuzzi.

                    JOHN
          You're incredible. Does it
          occur to you that Tom was a
          living human being like an
          hour and a half ago?

Jimmy kills the engine, stares at him.

                    JIMMY
          I know he was. He was also
          evil garbage. And y'know
          what? It was a joy to empty
          that trash.

Pops the rear hatch, climbs out and walks
around for his overnight bag.

                    JIMMY
                    (O.S.)
          Coming in?

                    JOHN
          I don't know...

                    JIMMY
          You sure? Might be a message
          from Polly.

                    JOHN
          She would call my cell.
          Actually, I think I'll stay
          out here and call her.

                    JIMMY
          Think talking to her right
          now is the best idea?

                    JOHN
          She's my wife, Jimmy.
          Don't worry, I won't "say
          anything".
           (looks at his phone, GROANS)
          Damn it. Out of juice.

                    JIMMY
          Bummer. So let's go in,
          charge that sucker and hit
          the jacuzzi bubbles.

EXT. RESORT LOBBY - MINUTES LATER

Jimmy finishes up registering for them at the
hotel desk. Glances back at John, pacing around
the lobby nervously.

                    DESK WOMAN
          Two keys apiece?

                    JIMMY
          Yeah. That would be great.

                    CHUCK
           (O.S., from a yard away)
          Well kiss my big butt! It's
          the Two Musketeers!

Jimmy and John spin around. See mammoth CHUCK
and scrawny FRED, a pair of occasional golf
cronies, still in their checked slacks and
teetering from alcohol.

                    JIMMY
          Hey um...Chuck. What a
          surprise!

                    CHUCK
          You remember Fred Wellberger,
          right? Think you talked him
          into a Wrangler too once.

John stays a few feet away, trying not to be
sociable.

                    JIMMY
          Right, right...How's she
          running?

                    FRED
          Got us here in this bake-off,
          didn't it?
                    (to John)
          And hey! I remember you.
          Honest John Junior!

John manages a nod, nervously eyes the exit
door.

                    CHUCK
          So Jimmy! Play any holes
          today?
                    (squints at their
                     soiled clothes)
          Looks like you spent the
          afternoon in the 14th sand
          trap!

                    JIMMY
          Actually, we were taking a
          hike up in Joshua Tree and
          um...got a little too rugged
          for our own good.

                    CHUCK
          You adventurous types...Hey,
          feel like making last call
          with us at Pink Pepe's?

Jimmy glances over at John.

                    JOHN
          Sorry, we can't. Got an early
          tee tomorrow.
                    (walks over, grabs a
                     room key from Jimmy)
          All set?

He turns before his friend can answer and heads
for the elevator. Jimmy grins sheepishly at

Chuck and Fred.

                    JIMMY
          Tough day for him. Marital
          stuff.

Chuck and Fred nod silently. Jimmy picks up his
bag and follows John.

INT. HOTEL SHOWER - NIGHT

John stands under the hot spray. Exhausted.
Soaking his head to death. Draws back the
curtain and opens the bathroom door a crack.

                    JOHN
          Should I leave it on for you?

Jimmy is in a chair, cold beer pressed to his
swollen head gash. Staring at a COWBOY MOVIE IN
SPANISH on the hotel TV.

                    JIMMY
          Hell no. I'm hittin' the
          jacuzzi.

John shuts the door again, closes the shower
curtain. Puts his head back under the water, as
if afraid to come out.

INT. HOTEL ROOM BALCONY - NIGHT

John sits in a patio chair, gazing out at
the swaying palm fronds lining the dark golf
course. Turns and waits for Jimmy to salute him
and leave the hotel room with a bathing suit on
and towel around his neck. Then takes out his
charged phone. Braces himself and auto-dials
his home.

                    ROY
                   (V.O.)
          Hello?

                    JOHN
          Hey Roy...

                    ROY
                   (V.O.)
          Hi Dad! You kick Jimmy's butt
          today?

                    JOHN
          Kind of...Mom around?

There's a long pause.

                    POLLY
                   (V.O.)
          I tried you before.

                    JOHN
          I know. Just heard the
          message. Had the phone off to
          y'know...decompress.

                    POLLY
                   (V.O.)
          And how'd that go?

                    JOHN
          It went...Jimmy actually
          needed to more than me.

                    POLLY
                   (V.O.)
          Big surprise there. Trying to
          stay away from the news, but
          it's hard for me too...They
          still have no leads on this
          killer.

John nervously scratches the arm of the chair.

                    JOHN
          That so?

                    POLLY
                   (V.O.)
          Yeah. So you'll be able to
          make it back for Jerry and
          Linda's barbeque on Sunday,
          right?

                    JOHN
          Uhh...sure. To be honest,
          we're both still kind of
          stressed and there's a chance
          we might come back tomorrow
          and just lay low. The golf
          isn't really helping.

                    POLLY
                    (V.O.)
          Aw, sweetie. I'm sorry.

                    JOHN
          Yup...Me too.

EXT ROADSIDE DINER - MORNING

Jimmy wolfs down a lumberjack breakfast of
pancakes, three eggs, hash browns. John sits
in the booth across from him with coffee and
a partially-eaten muffin. Peers over at the
counter, where an OLD PATRON has a morning
paper open.

                    JIMMY
          How's Polly?

                    JOHN
                    (with a SIGH)
          Thankfully oblivious.

Jimmy nods, sees John looking at the guy with
the paper.

                    JIMMY
          Look at the news on your
          phone already. You're driving
          me nuts.
                    (drops his voice)
          And who knows? Maybe they
          arrested some other guy.

He CHUCKLES. John doesn't even smile.

INT. EXPLORER - DAY

Heading home. Jimmy has an ANGELS game on the
radio but neither of them seem to be paying
attention. John has his seat tilted way back.

                    JOHN
          I did get caught shoplifting
          once...Ever shoplift?

                    JIMMY
          Uh-uh.

                    JOHN
          Stuck a comic book down my
          pants and they nabbed me five
          steps out the door. Took me
          up to this little room, tried
          to impress me with their one-
          way mirrors and spy cameras
          and stuff...Mom came and got
          me, and I begged her not to
          tell Dad, so she didn't...

He gazes out at a sprawling tract neighborhood.

                    JOHN
          Until the day he died, I was
          convinced he'd found out
          somehow. My dad had a way of
          judging you without saying a
          word.

EXT. JOHN'S DRIVEWAY - DAY

Jimmy pulls in. John sees both cars in his open
garage and gets nervous again.

                    JIMMY
          Just be your cool self, man.

                    JOHN
          Right. But not my honest one.

Jimmy has no comeback for that, so just pats
his arm. John hesitates, then pats his back
before climbing out.

INT. JOHN'S HALLWAY - HOURS LATER

John peers out of their bedroom. Hears Polly in
the kitchen, making something with a CUISINART.
He quickly darts across to the laundry room
with a bundle of dirty clothes under his arm.

INT. LAUNDRY ROOM

Stuffs the soiled garments in the washer and
adds some extra bleach before turning the thing
on.

Polly appears in the doorway, startling him.

                    POLLY
          I could've done those.

                    JOHN
          No...It's fine. What are we
          having?

                    POLLY
          One of your faves. Butternut
          squash soup.

He turns and gives her a warm hug. Kisses her
neck and just holds on like he's afraid to let
go.

                    JOHN
          Missed the hell out of you.

                    POLLY
          I can tell.
            (he finally lets go of her)
          Too bad Jimmy doesn't have
          anyone right now.

                    JOHN
          Oh...He'll make up for that
          somehow.

                    POLLY
                (shakes her head)
          I just can't believe they
          don't have any leads yet.

                    JOHN
          It's only been a day or two.
          Who knows, maybe they'll
          never find the person.

                    POLLY
          Are you serious? People
          are foaming at the mouth
          right now. They have to find
          <u>someone</u>.

John is silent for a moment, then puts on the
WASHER, drowing out further conversation.

INT. CAR WASH - DAY

Jimmy sits in the Explorer. Exhausted. A car
wash ATTENDANT approaches his open window.

                    ATTENDANT
          Want us to vacuum the back,
          señor?

                    JIMMY
          No—I mean...I did it already.
                (hands him a five)
          For your friends.

                    ATTENDANT
          Gracias! Close the window and
          put in neutral, por favor!

Jimmy closes the window. Inches the vehicle
forward until it catches on the drive-thru
chain. Puts the gear in neutral and stares into
the approaching dark abyss of brushes and soap.

EXT. NEIGHBOR'S BACKYARD - DAY

John stands over an open grill, prodding a rack
of pork ribs. Smoke is everywhere. He turns,

puts a rib on a GUEST's plate. Then another.
Then another.

                    TOM
                   (O.S.)
             Well done, please.

John turns. Tom stands there with an empty
plate. Bloodied, covered in sand from head to
toe. His face half rotted away—

                                        CUT TO:

INT. NEIGHBOR'S BACKYARD -DAY

And John jumping awake in a lounge chair.
Rattled. Looks around at the festive barbeque.
At Polly, their neighbors JERRY and LINDA, and
six other GUESTS seated around a table, mopping
up their plates. John takes a sip of his iced
tea, tries to relax.

                    JERRY
             No. What I'm saying is you
             choose that career, you
             choose that lifestyle.
             Autograph hounds and internet
             trolls and occasional nutjobs
             come with the territory.

                    LINDA
             Nobody knows exactly who it
             was yet, Jerry.

                    POLLY
             I still say it was someone
             she knew.

                    GUEST
             Did you catch that interview
             with her folks last night?

Mournful SIGHS all around. John scratches his
head, trying not to listen.

       GUEST
Poor things...Y'know, they're
trying to pass bills in the
few states with the death
penalty to allow victim
family members to witness
executions. It's kind of
sick, but I like it.

       POLLY
I still think the death
penalty is sick. Except for
the guy who shot John Lennon,
of course.

       JERRY
Hypocrite.

       POLLY
And proud of it.

       GUEST
John, did you see that
interview?

John stands wth his iced tea glass.

       JOHN
I don't...watch the news
anymore. Excuse me.

And walks away. The group shares a concerned
look.

       POLLY
He was _crazy_ about her.

John wanders past a pool filled with KIDS to a
shady section of grass. Spots Roy, baseball and
glove in hand, talking to another BOY.

       JOHN
Hey! How about showing me
that curveball?

       ROY
Yeah!

Flips his dad the glove and jogs to the corner
of the yard. John crouches down, happy to be
doing anything to distract himself. Roy goes
into a little windup, floats a high curve into
the glove, chest-high.

                    JOHN
          Good drop! You'd fool Ohtani
          with that. How's the blister?

                    ROY
          Almost all gone...
               (gets the ball back,
                goes into a stretch)
          Hey Dad?

                    JOHN
          Yeah?

                    ROY
          How come they haven't caught
          that actress-killer yet?

He throws the ball and it bounces off John's
glove. He picks it off the grass and inspects
the seams. Visibly disturbed.

                    JOHN
          I don't know, Roy...Maybe the
          police aren't smart enough.
               (tosses the ball back)
          Let's see your heater, okay?

INT. THE DRAYCOTT, PACIFIC PALISADES - NIGHT

Jimmy tips a few at the bar in this British-
themed bistro pub. Eyes a pair of COLLEGE
GIRLS sharing a laugh a few stools away. The
BARTENDER appears, points to his empty beer
glass.

                    BARTENDER
          Another?

                    JIMMY
          Sure, why not?

Above the bar, the DODGERS are playing
Cincinnati and leading 12-2.

                    JIMMY
          Hey. Mind putting the Angels
          on? This game's over.

The bartender grabs a remote, runs through some
channels and gets a teaser for the local 11:00
news.

                    JIMMY
          Hold on a sec!

                    REPORTER
          ...admits being stymied in
          their search for clues or
          even a motivation for the
          murder.

They show the outside of Gina's house, still
taped off.

                    REPORTER
                     (O.S.)
          According to Chief Dodd,
          "We're back at square one."

                    JIMMY
               (with a snicker)
          Dipshits.

He signals for the bartender to keep changing
the channel.

INT. JOHN'S FAMILY ROOM - NIGHT

John dozes in his Barcalounger, all lights off
except for the blue-white glow from an ARCTIC
DOCUMENTARY on the Nature Channel.

Something RATTLES and SQUEAKS outside and his
eyes snap open. He reaches for the remote and
kills the TV.

Another SQUEAK. Like someone trying to open

something. A gate?

John's heart pounds. He gets out of the lounge chair, inches up to a curtained glass door to the backyard. Peers outside.

Just sees the yard. Flowers, lawn, hose. Volleyball net.

But the backyard gate CREAKS. RATTLES. And there's virtually no wind.

INT. KITCHEN - NIGHT

John hurries in. Takes a flashlight from a drawer, then a good-sized butcher knife from the counter.

INT. BACKYARD - NIGHT

Steps out the sliding door. The gate is still RATTLING. He moves around the perimeter of the yard. Knife and flashlight poised. Eyes glued on the gate...

And TRIPS headlong over a sprinkler! John CURSES, gropes for his dropped flashlight. Hears RUNNING FOOTSTEPS, then a CAR ENGINE chugging to life. He gets back on his feet, runs to the latched gate and throws it open.

Just as a beat-up car with one tail light RUMBLES out the end of the alley and vanishes. John stares into the darkness a moment, then trains the flashlight at the asphalt just outside the gate.

Whoever was standing there had a lot of dirt on their shoes.

INT. JOHN AND POLLY'S BEDROOM - MINUTES LATER

John slips into bed behind Polly. Shaken. Burrows up to her backside like a newborn pup.

INT. JOHN AND POLLY'S BEDROOM - MORNING

Dawn light tickles John's eyes.

                    ROY
              (O.S., from hall)
          Hey Ma! Where'd you put the
          Pop Tarts?

John sits up and stretches, glad to see
daylight and hear his son's voice.

INT. JOHN'S CAR - DAY

He sits behind the wheel, dressed for work, but
still in the driveway. Scrolling through a news
site or two on his phone. Satisfied, he starts
the ENGINE.

INT. JOHN'S CAR - DAY

Cruises up a commercial strip. A JAZZ COMBO on
the radio lightens his mood a little more.

Honest John's Used Jeep and Van comes into view
on the left and he brakes the car. Stunned.

Two POLICE CRUISERS are parked at tne entrance.
John idles in the middle of the road for a
moment. Unsure what to do. A car HONKS behind
him and he pulls left into the lot.

INT. SHOWROOM - MINUTES LATER

A HANDYMAN sweeps up broken door glass. One of
three POLICE OFFICERS dusts for fingerprints.

John and Cummings stand there in mild shock.
Jimmy is a few feet away, adjusting his shirt
cuffs.

                    JOHN
          Why didn't the alarm go off?

                    JIMMY
          Ask Mr. Reliable here.

                    CUMMINGS
          Sorry, John. There were so
          many things on my mind when I
          left last night—

                    JOHN
              (heads for the offices)
           Did they get the computers?

INT. JOHN'S OFFICE - DAY

An absolute mess. Drawers open, papers
everywhere, but the computers are still intact.

                  CUMMINGS
           They trashed my desk, too.
           Dirtbags even got my cigars.

                  OFFICER
           Most likely a local gang
           looking for cash. Did you
           keep any around?

                    JOHN
           Not in the office, no...

He crouches beside a tipped-over file cabinet.
Leafs through some manila folders scattered on
the floor.

                  CUMMINGS
           You'd think they'd help
           themselves to a nice SUV if
           they got in here.

                    JOHN
           Right...

His face suddenly turns white. He walks from
the room.

EXT. LOT - DAY

Jimmy leans against a van, enjoying his morning
stick of gum. John walks up, trying not to look
nervous to the police.

                    JOHN
           What do you think?

                   JIMMY
           About what?

                    JOHN
The break-in!

                    JIMMY
                (shrugs)
Cops got it pegged. Druggies
or gang members or gang
druggies—

                    JOHN
The directory is missing.

                    JIMMY

Directory?

                    JOHN

The personnel file? With all
our names and addresses?

                    JIMMY

Yeah?

                    JOHN

Why would a druggie take
<u>that</u>?

Jimmy gives him an annoyed look.

                    JIMMY
To send us all Christmas
cards. I don't know, John,
the office is a disaster area.
Did you really look for it?

                    JOHN
I don't think he's dead,
Jimmy...

                    JIMMY

What's that?

                    JOHN

Tom. I don't know how it
happened, but I think he's in
town, and I think he's after
us.

A long pause. Jimmy holds in his laughter as
long as he can, then loses control and nearly
swallows his gum.

                    JIMMY
          Know what you need, man?
               (pats him on the back)
          A weekend in the desert!

He doubles over. Sees John isn't laughing and
a police officer is watching them and quickly
calms down.

                    JOHN
          Listen. The cop told me that
          the guy at the taco stand
          next door heard noises in
          the office around midnight,
          right? An hour later someone
          was trying to get in my back
          gate.

Jimmy stares at him.

                    JOHN
          Someone wearing dirty shoes
          and driving an old beat-up
          car like the one you-know-who
          was having fixed.

                    JIMMY
          Sure you didn't dream this?

                    JOHN
          Jimmy, it was him! You gave
          him our damn business card
          before we dropped him in
          Indio, remember? He could've
          tracked us down easy—

                    JOHN
          Science fucking fiction, man.
          We both saw the guy. He
          dropped off a steep cliff and
          he was barely alive <u>before</u> he
          fell!

He leans in, drops his voice.

                    JIMMY
          This break-in is just what
          it was, okay? Don't go loony
          tunes on me. Now if you don't
          mind...there's a customer in
          the lot I need to bamboozle.

He POPS a gum bubble and walks toward this
customer.

EXT. JOHN'S HOME OFFICE - EVENING

John slouches in his desk chair with an empty
wine glass. Playing a slow game of chess
with his computer. He's losing badly. Polly
strolls in, points to the glass and bottle of
Chardonnay on the desk.

                    POLLY
          That your third?

                    JOHN
          Roughly.

She sits on the edge of the desk, facing him.

                    POLLY
          So what did the insurance guy
          say?

                    JOHN
          Nothing much. The place is
          covered...He also suggested
          we put the alarm on next
          time.

He reaches for the bottle and Polly grabs his
wrist.

                    POLLY
          What else is wrong?

                    JOHN
          W-what do you mean? Shouldn't
          I be upset when someone
          breaks into our—

                    POLLY
          No, not that. Something else.

John makes a quick chess move and loses a pawn.

                    JOHN
          There's nothing else.

                    POLLY
          Come on...You drive to Rancho
          Vista to relax and come back
          like a stressed-out zombie.
          Is this Gina Coogan thing
          still bothering you? Because
          if it is I know a couple
          of good therapists you can
          contact—

                    JOHN
          I'm over that, Poll. Really.
          It's just...it's kind of
          everything at once. The
          murder, the break-in, the
          heat...I'm just wiped out.

Polly folds her arms skeptically.

                    POLLY
          You guys didn't...meet some
          cute little Gina look-alikes
          out there?

                    JOHN
          God! Can't you stop? What
          kind of question is that?

                    POLLY
          I'm sorry. Strike it from the
          record, your honor...
               (softly strokes his arm)
          I guess I've just been...
          missing you lately. And it
          makes me a little paranoid.

He reaches up, caresses her cheek. EXHALES.

                    JOHN
          You and me both...

INT. SUPERMARKET - NIGHT

Jimmy cruises by the check-out lines with a
small basket of items. Each line is longer than
the next, but he manages to find a short one. He
sets his basket down, eyeballs the trash mags
and tabloids. A screaming headline catches his
eye.

    FOUR MEN AN HOUR CLAIM TO HAVE KILLED GINA

He freezes. Virtually every publication on
display has a loud, scandalous headline about
Gina.

He turns away from the rack. Sees a tall,
smartly-dressed REDHEAD in the next aisle,
parking her basket on a self-checkout stand.
Jimmy is instantly entranced, grabs his basket
and walks around to stand behind her.

She has similar features and is definitely
taller than Gina. But her clothes, statuesque
posture, and sensual aura are definitely Coogan-
esque.

She starts scanning her items. Jimmy eyes every
curve of her pale, exposed shoulders. Sees
she's unloading about sixteen cans of cat food.

                    JIMMY
          What's your cat's name?

She turns. Takes him in with one glance and
smiles.

                    REDHEAD
          Cats. Vincenzo and Ed.

                    JIMMY
          Nice...How'd you come up with
          those names?

                    REDHEAD
          Ex-husbands. My landlord
          wouldn't allow dogs, you see.

                    JIMMY
          Aha.

                    REDHEAD
               (uses her debit card)
          Actually dogs bark too much.
          And they slobber. And they
          don't know when to leave you
          alone. Excuse me.

Grabs her bag and walks out. Jimmy makes a
glum, defeated face and starts scanning his
groceries.

INT. JIMMY'S CONDO COMPLEX - NIGHT

He exits his elevator, armed with two grocery
bags. Sees CLARA, his frumpy downstairs
neighbor, heading into the laundry room.

                    JIMMY
          Whassup, Clarabelle?

                    CLARA
          Hey! Comin' to my party next
          weekend?

                    JIMMY
          Wouldn't miss it!

                    CLARA
          Awesome. Hey. where'd you
          meet the lumberjack, anyway?

                    JIMMY
          The what?

                    CLARA
          The guy in your apartment
          with the heavy shoes. Figured
          it was some delivery guy.

                    JIMMY
          When was this?

                    CLARA
          Like an hour ago. I don't
          know, maybe it was from
          Benjy's place. Anyway, gotta
          big wash to do here—

                    JIMMY
          Yeah, okay. Later...

She disappears into the laundry room. Jimmy
looks down the hall at his shut condo door with
trepidation. Slowly walks toward it.

He inspects the lock and the doorknob. No one
seems to have messed with them.

Takes out his keys, unlocks the dead bolt and
gently pushes the door open.

INT. CONDO - NIGHT

The bathroom light is on down the hall, but
otherwise the place is dark. And quiet.

He flicks on a wall switch. Nothing disturbed.
He frowns, shuts the door, then takes the
grocery bags to the kitchen area. Turns to a
round bluetooth device on the counter.

                    JIMMY
          Alexa, play some grunge rock.

                    ALEXA
                    (V.O.)
          Now playing...Todd Rundgren.

                    JIMMY
          Whatever.

"HELLO IT'S ME" starts up. Jimmy unloads the
first bag, carries some milk and butter to the
fridge.

Stops and looks down.

Dirty shoe prints are all over the floor.

His face turns white. He steps around them,

sets the milk and butter on the counter. Looks
around and spots an empty shot glass at the far
end, beside an empty bottle of Old Bushmill's.

                    JIMMY
          What the F?...

Backs out of the kitchen, scanning the rug and
other floors. Dirty shoe prints are everywhere.
He follows them down the hall.

Stops at every room and puts on the light.
Nothing. Hurries the last few feet to his
bedroom.

INT. BEDROOM - NIGHT

Giant, bachelor-friendly bed with a mirror on
the ceiling. Jimmy enters and throws open his
closet.

A long, comforting rack of shirts and suits. He
reaches onto the top shelf.

Brings down a Browning autoloader hunting
rifle. Checks the chamber. Loaded. Hears a soft
FLAPPING sound and looks right.

One of his blinds FLAPS against the windowsill
in the night breeze. Okay. But why is that
window even open? He takes one step toward it
and

     HORACE EXPLODES FROM THE CLOTHES RACK!!

Eyes wild—

Fingers reaching—

Jimmy raises the gun. Horace KNOCKS it away and
grabs Jimmy by the throat. Jimmy GASPS for air,
reaches up. SCRATCHES Horace's face. He HOWLS,
SMACKS Jimmy over a chair.

Drops on him like a pro wrestler. Pins him to
the floor, gagging Jimmy with his foul, boozy
breath.

                    HORACE
            Where...is he??...

In the other room, "HELLO IT'S ME" continues to
play.

INT. JOHN AND POLLY'S BEDROOM - NIGHT

John lies on the bed in his clothes, arm over
his eyes. Bottle of Advil on the night table.
Roy enters, shakes his ankle.

                     ROY
            Hey Dad. Mom said you'd help
            me with my Spanish history.

                    JOHN
            A little later, okay?...Your
            dad needs a nap right now.

Roy mopes out of the room. John rolls onto his
side, tries to fall asleep again.

His CELL PHONE RINGS.

                    JOHN
            God almighty.

He digs it out of his back pocket. JIMMY M. is
calling.

                    JOHN
            Hey.

He hears silence. Then a sudden burst of
LABORED BREATHING.

                    JOHN
            Hello? Jimmy??

The CALL DROPS. Jimmy sits up, quickly calls
him back. The connection RINGS.

                    JIMMY
                   (V.O.)
            Hi, Jimmy here. Who are you?

BEEP.

                    JOHN
          Jimmy? You there? I think you
          just called me.
          (waits a beat, then hangs up)
          Damn...

INT. FAMILY ROOM - NIGHT

Polly lays on the couch, trying to stay awake
with a novel. John blows through, pulling on
his windbreaker.

                    JOHN
          Need to go meet Jimmy about
          something, okay? Back in a
          few. Maybe you could...help
          Roy with the Inquisition.

                    POLLY
          My specialty. Something
          wrong?

                    JOHN
          No. Just um...business stuff.

And he's out the front door.

INT. JOHN'S CAR - NIGHT

John races north on the 405.

EXT. JIMMY'S CONDO BUILDING - NIGHT

John swings open the unlocked gate, enters the
complex. Moonlight glimmers on the pool. A CAT
IN HEAT lets out a chilling WAIL, freezes him
for a moment. He disappears into the elevator.

INT. CONDO HALLWAY - NIGHT

He exits the elevator, jogs down to Jimmy's
door. KNOCKS and it opens slightly. There's
blood on the knob. John's heart pounds.

INT. CONDO - NIGHT

He enters and looks around.

                         JOHN
          Jimmy?

Sees the same dirty shoe prints on the floor and
moves down the hall to the bedroom.

INT. BEDROOM

It's in shambles. Like the aftermath of a
western saloon brawl. Jimmy lies across the
floor in a pool of blood, wedged between the
bed and a shelf of <u>Windy City</u> T-shirts,
sweatshirts, and mugs.

                         JOHN
          Damn!

He rushes over. Jimmy's eyes are swollen shut,
fingermarks around his neck. His body looks
crooked. Someone has kicked and choked him into
a stupor. A spit bubble leaks from his mouth
and he WHEEZES. John carefully raises his head
and shakes him.

                         JOHN
          Can you hear me, Jimmy? Who
          did this? Who was it??

Jimmy WHEEZES again but doesn't respond. John
whips out his cell phone, jabs 9-1-1.

                         JOHN
          Yeah, I need a paramedic up
          here! 19344 West Coastline
          Drive. #12. Hurry!...My name?
                (pauses a moment)
          John Griffin.

Jimmy MUMBLES something. John drops the phone,
props his head up a bit more.

                         JIMMY
          Directory...

                         JOHN
          What was that?

Jimmy grips the sleeve of John's jacket. A

sliver of eye opens.

                    JIMMY
          The trailer guy...took the
          directory...knows where you
          live.

                    JOHN
          Trailer guy? You don't mean
          Tom, right?
               (gets a sudden thought)
          Oh shit. That old geezer
          Horace? Why the hell would
          Horace—

                    JIMMY
          Because we killed his kid!

John is blown away. A weird, painful grimace
appears on Jimmy's face.

                    JIMMY
          Eye...for an eye...for an
          eye...
               (GASPING)
          Can't stop those fuckin'
          eyes...

He loosens his grip. Blood GURGLES in his mouth
and he lies still.

                    JOHN
          Jimmy?

He feels for a heartbeat. Gets one and breathes
easier.

                    JOHN
          They're comin' for you,
          buddy...They'll fix you up.

Then he remembers something and grabs his
phone. Is about to dial Polly but stops
himself. We hear a DISTANT AMBULANCE SIREN.

John is suddenly panicked. Gets to his feet
and hurries out of the condo, leaving its door
open.

EXT. JOHN'S CAR - NIGHT

John drives back down the 405 to the South Bay
like a madman, weaving around cars.

EXT. JOHN'S HOUSE - NIGHT

He SCREECHES into his driveway. Hops out and
looks down the street in both directions,
scopes out their yard.

INT. GRIFFIN FAMILY ROOM - NIGHT

Polly is passed out on the couch. Wakes with a
start as John bursts in, breathless. Pacing.

                    JOHN
          We have to get out of here.

                    POLLY
          What??

He helps her up. Walks over to a sliding glass
door to their backyard, shuts and locks it.

                    JOHN
          I can't explain now. Pack a
          bag for yourself, and one for
          Roy—

                    POLLY
          What happened?? Did you find
          Jimmy?

                    JOHN
          Jimmy's hurt pretty bad,
          honey. And the guy who hurt
          him might be on his way here.
          Now please. Let's just leave.

INT. HALLWAY - NIGHT

John KNOCKS on Roy's door, opens it.

                    JOHN
          Wake up, sport. We're takin'
          a drive—

Peers into the dark, quiet room a second.
Switches on the light.

Roy's bed is empty. And his window is wide
open.

                    POLLY
          (hushed, coming down the hall)
          Don't tell him about Jimmy
          yet—

John SLAMS the door shut. Stricken. Stares at
his wife.

                    POLLY
          What's wrong?

He gives her a desperate hug, starts walking
her back to the family room.

                    JOHN
          It's okay. We have to sit
          down now.

                    POLLY
          Why?? Where's Roy?

He won't answer and she breaks free, runs back
to his door and throws it open. Sees that he's
gone.

                    POLLY
          Oh my God.

Throws off his bedcovers. Looks in the closet.
Under the bed. Out the open window. John tries
to grab her and she pushes him away. Crazed.

                    JOHN
          I know who has him, okay? I
          know—

She SCREAMS and swings at him. He grabs her
arms, drops her on the bed and holds her there.

                    JOHN
          We got in some bad trouble,
          Poll...Jimmy and me...We did
          something very stupid...But
          it's okay—

                    POLLY
          WHO TOOK HIM??

                    JOHN
          Okay...His name is Horace,
          and he runs a trailer park at
          the Salton Sea—

                    POLLY
          What the hell are you waiting
          for?? Call the police!!

John pauses a moment. Keeps hold of her arms.

                    JOHN
          We can't...Not yet.

                    POLLY
          What do you mean you
          can't?...
               (shoves him off her and sits up)
          WHY CAN'T YOU??

John stands, paces the floor again.

                    JOHN
          We met this other guy,
          Poll...At a mass for Gina
          we met the guy who killed
          her. And we gave him a ride
          without knowing that, and
          then we found out and Jimmy
          went too far...and Jimmy hit
          him. And now...his father's
          come after us and OH CHRIST—

He PUNCHES a wall. Polly is speechless.

And then John's CELL PHONE RINGS. He looks at
Polly a second, then takes it out of his back
pocket.

                    JOHN
                 (anxiously)
          Hello?

                   HORACE
          (V.O., weird industrial
           sounds in the background)
          Howdy...Missin' anyone?

                    JOHN
          Where is he?

                   HORACE
                   (V.O.)
          Close by. Still breathin'.

                    JOHN
          I want him back, Horace.

                   HORACE
                   (V.O.)
          Heh. Thought you might...How
          'bout you folks take me to my
          boy and then you get yours?

                    JOHN
          Uhh...Okay. But I'm not
          exactly sure where he is. He
          fell, you see—

                   HORACE
                   (V.O.)
          Fell?

                    JOHN
          Right. He was showing us this
          ridge in the Anza-Borrego
          park—

                   HORACE
                   (V.O.)
          Bullcrap. You picked him up
          to show him something. And he
          wasn't sure about you two.
          Told me so before he left and
          gave me your business card.

                    JOHN
Listen, Horace. I'm sorry about
Tom, but he was dangerous—

                    HORACE
                   (V.O.)
I'm sorry too. DAMN sorry.

                    JOHN
And I don't think you know
what Tom did.
          (Polly jabs him)
For now, though, let's just
work this out, so I can get
Roy back, and then I'll fill
you in—

                    HORACE
                   (V.O.)
Oh, that's his name. I've just
been callin' him Pissant.
Heh...Little Roy can fall,
too. Know a whole bunch of
places he can take a nasty
tumble—

                    JOHN
Stop it, okay?? Let's just do
this. Your way.

                    HORACE
 (V.O., after a labored pause)
Well, my way's gonna be Follow
the Leader. I'm parked down
the road from the Arco station
on Harbor. Across from that
smelly factory with the fire
pipes.

                    JOHN
You mean the refinery...Okay,
give me fifteen minutes.

                    HORACE
                   (V.O.)
And if I see one badge and
holster I'll be doing away
with your boy.

                    JOHN
          You won't, okay? Promise.

He hangs up. Embraces a horrified Polly.

                                        CUT TO:

INT. ARCO STATION OFFICE - NIGHT

Horace hangs up the phone on the desk, one
side of his face still bleeding from Jimmy's
scratch. The lone STATION ATTENDANT lies
motionless on the floor, his head bashed in.

Horace walks outside, slowly rounds the back of
the Buick. Freezes until a car goes by, then
climbs in.

INT. BUICK - NIGHT

Horace drops behind the wheel, fatigue and a
profound sadness in his eyes.

Takes out an old snapshot of Tom, age 14.
Pitching horseshoes with Horace in a dusty
parking lot.

                    HORACE
          No one takes you away from
          me...

EXT. JOHN'S DRIVEWAY - NIGHT

John marches out to his car, Polly fast on his
heels.

                    JOHN
          Polly, you're going to get
          hurt—

                    POLLY
          No, you will! Meanwhile I'll
          be sitting here tearing my
          hair out!

He stops, tries to take her by the shoulders

but she knocks him away and gets in the
passenger seat.

                    POLLY
          Let's go.

EXT. ARCO REFINERY - NIGHT

Marshland surrounds an industrial city of
tanks, catwalks, and flame-jeting pipes. John's
car turns down a dark road past the Arco
station. Slows to cruising speed.

The Buick is parked just off the road, a hundred
yards ahead. Its lights and engine off. John
slows a little more, passes the car. Can't see
inside. He makes a wide U-turn, parks directly
across the road from it. Kills his engine.

INT. JOHN'S CAR - NIGHT

They eye the shadowy Buick.

                    POLLY
          He's gotta be in there,
          right?

                    JOHN
          Actually, he doesn't.

A sea breeze whips the marsh grass around them.

                    POLLY
          Why isn't he calling you?

                    JOHN
          I don't know. But I'm not
          waiting.
               (reaches for the door handle)
          Damn! Wish I had grabbed
          Jimmy's rifle.

                    POLLY
          You don't need it. We just
          have to take him to his son,
          and then we get Roy. Go!

She gives him a nervous hug, and he climbs out.

EXT. ROAD - NIGHT

Hands at his side, John crosses the road. No
movement or sounds from the Buick. He reaches
the car, glances back at Polly and shrugs.
Peers through the dark windows.

INT. JOHN'S CAR - NIGHT

Polly's heart races. The marsh grass RUSTLES
around her. She turns to look at it—

And HORACE stands at the window! SMASHES his
fist through the glass!

EXT. ROAD - NIGHT

John spins. Sees Horace dragging Polly out of
the car.

                    JOHN
          HEY!!

Too late. In seconds his arm is around her
neck, Jimmy's rifle against her cheek.

                    HORACE
          What'd I say about inviting
          guests. Huh??
                    (to John)
          Get in the car, fella.

                    JOHN
          Let go of her first.

He turns and SHOOTS OUT two of John's tires.

                    HORACE
          Whoops. Looks like you're
          drivin' the Buick now.

                    JOHN
          I said let go of her.

He nods calmly. Loosens his grip, then SMACKS
her to the pavement with the gun butt.

John's eyes go wild. He charges, grabs the gun.
They struggle, but Horace is stronger, SHOVES
him against the Buick and sticks the rifle
barrel in John's nose.

                    HORACE
          How 'bout gettin' your
          pathetic ass behind that
          wheel now.

Polly opens her eyes. She's dazed, bleeding.
The Buick RUMBLES to life and goes past her.
She achingly gets to her feet and starts
limping toward the Arco station.

INT. BUICK - NIGHT

Horace slouches against the passenger door,
rifle trained on John's head. John gives him a
quick, incensed look.

                    JOHN
          Where's my boy?

                    HORACE
          Guess that's the slogan for
          <u>this</u> night, ain't it?

                    JOHN
          I said where—

                    HORACE
             (cocks the rifle)
          Got myself a medal in Korea,
          fella. Don't make me too
          nostalgic now.

John slowly, carefully looks back at the road.

EXT. INTERSTATE 15 - NIGHT

The Buick flies south on a fairly sparse freeway
past Lake Elsinore.

INT. BUICK - NIGHT

Horace fiddles with the AM radio's tuning knob,
finds a STATIC-filled ROGER WHITAKER tune. Leans
back again, gun still poised.

                    HORACE
          Now that's music...You a
          Roger Whitaker fan?

He HUMS to the melody. John is trying his best
to relax.

                    JOHN
          Can I ask you something?
            (Horace raises an eyebrow)
          Why do people act so crazy
          sometimes?

                    HORACE
          Heh...You're the crazy one
          here...Couldn't leave a sweet
          young soul alone.

                    JOHN
          Well, to be honest...He
          wasn't <u>that</u> sweet.

Horace squints at him. Sits up a little
straighter.

                    HORACE
          You tellin' me I don't know
          my own boy? Maybe it's you
          don't know yours.

                    JOHN
          That's not what I'm—

                    HORACE
          You ever love anybody? Love
          'em so much your guts spill
          out every time they cry?

                    JOHN
          I have a kid, remember? Why
          do you think I'm here?

                    HORACE
          Yeah, you got a kid...A nice
          one with a good momma, no
          doubt.

He stares John down. A DIONNE WARWICK song
comes on and Horaces punches the radio off.

                    HORACE
          Take this exit.

                    JOHN
          W-why?

                    HORACE
               (COCKS the gun)
          Never mind why.

John swerves across two lanes, drops down the
next exit ramp.

EXT. HILLY TWO-LANE ROAD - NIGHT

John puts the Buick into low gear, CHUGS it
up a twisting bend. Rounds the corner and a
fenced-off auto junkyard comes into view. RAY'S
WRECKS.

INT. BUICK - NIGHT

                    HORACE
          Pull in there.

John turns into its dirt driveway, stops in
front of the locked gate. They peer in at a
spooky, hundred-foot mountain of dead cars.

                    HORACE
          Used to be Horace Goodwine
          Auto Scrap.

                    JOHN
          Right. The "famous junkyard"
          in Tom's letter...Why are we
          stop—

                    HORACE
          Shut up.

He slouches against his door, gazes at the pile
of cars. Fetching a memory.

                    HORACE
          A squirrel-engine Toyota with
          ten thousand good miles left.
          Can you imagine?...Bitch
          could've gotten to Bangor,
          Maine in that thing. Yup...
          She could've gotten to lots
          of places.

                    JOHN
          You mean the car? Or...

                    HORACE
          Only saw Tommy's momma for
          twenty seconds, but she was
          one pretty young bitch...
          White skin. Red hair. Wearin'
          one of those see-through
          hippie dresses.

WIND GUSTS through the junkyard, RATTLES a
couple of fenders. Horace looks out, FLASH-
IMAGINES a SLENDER YOUNG WOMAN—a Gina clone—
rushing by in the headlights.

                    HORACE
          Caught her leavin' the yard
          one night. Said she was using
          my Port-O-San...Didn't think
          much about it...

He COUGHS up something ugly, drops his window
and spits it out.

                    HORACE
          Anyway...Got back two days
          late from my sister's. Around
          midnight...Rainin' like a
          bastard. Park my truck, get
          out...then I hear this sick,
          everlovin' wail. Like a cat
          under somebody's foot. Except
          it ain't. Walk up between
          the wrecks and there's this
          Toyota I never seen.

His eyes get distant. Voice lowers to a
whisper.

                    HORACE
          With a cold, starvin' baby
          boy in the back seat.

His jaw tightens. Tears form in his eyes. John
tries to look away and Horace grabs his arm.

                    HORACE
          Didn't bother callin' the
          county. Why should I? Found
          him on my own property,
          right?

John nods. Peeks at Horace's dark back seat.
FLASHES on a shivering INFANT, swaddled in a
ripped blanket. The baby has Tom's face, and
it's staring at him...

                    HORACE
          Kept askin' about his evil
          bitch of a mother, so I told
          him at one point. Yup. Raised
          him hard but raised him
          honest...He was always around
          weekends, always around when
          he said he'd be.
               (fixes John with a stare)
          Then couple days ago he
          wasn't. That's how I knew you
          two were lyin' sacks of shit.

                    JOHN
          Listen, Horace..That's a real
          moving story about him, but
          Tom...has some mental issues
          I don't think you're aware
          of. This TV actress he's been
          addicted to—

BLAM!!!

Horace takes out the driver's side window with
one rifle shot. John covers his head, waits for
the glass shards to stop TINKLING. And for his
hearing to return.

                    HORACE
          Shut up and back us out of
          here.

EXT. BUICK - NIGHT

They're back on the quiet, dark freeway, but
heading down another exit ramp.

INT. BUICK - NIGHT

On a straight two-lane road now into desert
blackness.

Something SPLATS on the windshield. John jerks
the wheel a second and Horace sits up, inspects
a cloudburst of dripping bug guts on the
windshield.

                    HORACE
          Dumb bastards...

He looks over the next hill and catches a pink
strip of dawn sky, and the reflection of the
approaching Salton Sea.

                    HORACE
          We better get us some coffee.
          You like coffee?

                    JOHN
          Sometimes...

                    HORACE
          Well, Ginger makes the best
          in the world. She's gonna
          wanna meet you, too. Hell—she
          might go with us.

                    JOHN
          Who's Ginger?

EXT. SUNBURST TRAILER PARK - DAWN

John parks the Buick next to the mini-trailer
at the entrance. Horace reaches over and HONKS
THE HORN.

                    HORACE
          Brought company, Ginger!

After a few seconds there's a steady CLUNKING
sound, and GINGER, the old lady with the walker
we saw earlier, swings open the door and waves
them inside.

INT. LOCAL PATROL CAR - MINUTES LATER

Two YOUNG COPS cruise past the trailer park.
Spot the Buick parked at the entrance and slow
to a crawl. The one on the passenger side
punches up some info on a monitor.

                 PASSENGER COP
          Wife didn't get the plate
          number but the description
          sure's a match.

The driving cop unhooks his dashboard phone.

INT. GINGER'S MINI-TRAILER - DAWN

Smaller than Tom's rig, if that's possible.
Horace, John, and Ginger sit cramped around her
tiny table with full coffee cups. Horace still
has Jimmy's rifle trained on John.

                    HORACE
          Mighty wicked brew today,
          Ginger.

Ginger can't take her rheumy eyes off John.

                    GINGER
          Who's this again?

                    HORACE
          I just told ya. Him and
          his pal are the ones took
          Tom away the other night,
          remember? They talked to ya
          on the phone!

Her mouth stiffens. Horace points to her tiny
counter.

                    HORACE
          Got any more of that sweet
          roll?

She creaks to her feet, gets behind her walker
and CLUNKS slowly to the counter.

EXT. TRAILER PARK - DAWN

The two cops have parked their car fifty yards
or so from the entrance and have split up. Move
toward Ginger's trailer.

INT. GINGER'S TRAILER - DAWN

Ginger is back at the table, still glaring at
John. Horace picks away at the homemade sweet
roll with his dirty fingers.

                    GINGER
               (barely audible)
          You find Tommy...

                    JOHN
          Excuse me?

She achingly reaches under the table, slides
out a metal cane and WHACKS John's shoulder
with it.

                    GINGER
          YOU FIND TOMMY!!

                    JOHN
          Hey—

                    GINGER
               (SMACKS him again)
          YOU BRING HIM HOME! YOU FIND
          TOMMY!

John jumps out of his chair, tries to defend
himself. Ginger keeps whipping the cane around
at him, SMASHES three or four dishes on the
counter. Horace is LAUGHING but finally gets up,
grabs John around the waist and hauls him to
the trailer door.

                         HORACE
              Thanks for the coffee, Ginger!
              We'll see ya later!

EXT. TRAILER PARK - MORNING

Horace shoves John outside and kicks him back
to the Buick.

                         HORACE
              Shame on you! Upsettin'
              Ginger like that—

                      PASSENGER COP
                        (O.S.)
              Drop the weapon, sir!

Horace whirls. The cop is ten yards away. legs
apart, .38 Berretta aimed at Horace's chest.
The driving cop COCKS his gun on the other side
of the Buick.

Horace shrugs. Raises the rifle barrel and BLOWS
the passenger cop off his feet with one shot.
The driving cop FIRES three or four times,
hitting the side of the Buick and Horace's left
arm. Horace turns and drops. SHOOTS the cop in
the leg.

John tries to tackle Horace but gets RIFLE
BUTTED in the head and loses his glasses again.
Horace hauls him up and stuffs him in the
Buick's passenger seat. Walks around, his arm
dripping blood, sees the wounded cop crawling
to his gun. Calmly puts the rifle to his head
and FIRES.

                         HORACE
              So much for that. Now how
              about we go get my boy?

EXT. ANZA-BORREGO BADLANDS - DAY

It's 92 degrees at 7:30 in the morning. Horace
churns the Buick up a winding dirt road. Off to
the left are the badlands, a series of gullies

and washes turned pink, red, yellow, and green
from iron deposits in the soil.

INT. BUICK - DAY

Blood now streams from the hole in Horace's
arm. He winces, glances at the wound.

                    HORACE
          Good thing it's clean...
               (sees John is fading and JABS
                  him with the rifle)
          We there yet?

John sits up, squints over the dash.

                    JOHN
          Don't have my glasses so it's
          hard to see...but maybe.

                    HORACE
          Maybe ain't gonna save your
          little pissant son, y'know.

John squints harder. The badlands don't look
familiar, but the road in front of them sure
does.

                    JOHN
          Is that a ridge over there? I
          think that's where he fell—

Horace SLAMS on the brakes.

                    HORACE
          Good enough for me.
               (JABS John with
                  the rifle again)
          Get out.

Horace follows John out, holding the rifle with
his good arm.

EXT. BADLANDS - DAY

A hot, dry wind has kicked in. A bank of rare
clouds loom over the Santa Rosa Mountains.

Horace nudges John to the ridge. John peers over its edge, but again, it's hard for him to see.

> JOHN
> Not sure this is the right
> spot.

> HORACE
> (glancing around)
> Yeah...But everything here
> leads to the below.

He motions John to a nearby path, leading down into a steep, rocky gorge. The heat is suddenly brutal, the terrain unforgiving. Every time John pauses, Horace jabs him with the gun.

EXT. FURTHER DOWN GORGE - DAY

The sky has darkened. HEAT LIGHTNING crackles nearby. Horace and John plod along, dragging their feet through the thick, pink sand.

They round a bend and stop. The gorge ends at a small cave entrance. John collapses against a rock.

> JOHN
> This isn't it...We have to go
> back.

> HORACE
> Thought you couldn't see. My
> boy's down here somewhere and
> you're gonna find him!

He steps away, scans the immediate area. Spots something lying in the sand and hurries over.

Picks up a torn piece of flannel shirt. The same one Tom had been wearing before his "fall". He feels the material. It has some kind of wet goo on it.

Horace's eyes narrow. He looks around. Sees a depression in the ground, as if something has been dragged or pulled out of windblown sand.

Follows a straight line of tracks in some dirt,
studded with paw prints.

He pauses at the cave entrance. Notices
something a few feet away.

Tom's body, lying in the shadows. Ripped apart
by wild animals like a barbequed chicken.

He glances back at John in fury, gun still
pointed at him. Hears a loud YIP and spins.

TWO COYOTES emerge from the cave. Horace
quickly FIRES the rifle at them. Hits one in the
leg and they both scamper away.

He drops to his knees beside his mangled son.
Horace's entire body shakes like a runaway
freight car. Tears pour from his eyes.

                    HORACE
          What have they done to you—

John painfully stands, makes his way over.
eyeing the rifle. And can hardly look at the
body.

                    JOHN
          All he did was fall, Horace.
          I swear.

Horace says nothing. Tightens his grip on the
weapon.

                    JOHN
          I'll help you get...what's
          left of him back up there.
          But then...you need to tell
          me where Roy is—

                    HORACE
          Yer pissant's dead.

                    JOHN
          What's that?

Horace stands, a malevolent grin on his face.

                    HORACE
          You didn't deserve no loved
          one. Not after what you did
          to mine.

                    JOHN
          What happened to him?...
                    (anger swelling)
          WHERE IS HE??

He lunges for the rifle, rips it away. Knocks
Horace down with the butt end. The old man
lands in the dirt on his hands and knees.
Stunned. John flips the gun around, steps toward
him—

Horace ROARS. Grabs the tail of John's shirt
and wrenches him to the ground.

They struggle, churning up dust. Heat lightning
CRACKLES nearly on top of them. John loses his
grip on the gun. Horace gets his meathook hands
around John's neck. Presses. Tears fused to his
vengeful eyes.

                    HORACE
          No one takes my Tommy away
          from me...

He presses harder. John GASPS for air. It could
be over...

WHUP-WHUP-WHUP!! A POLICE CHOPPER shoots over
their heads. Circles. Horace is distracted
for a split second and John KNEES him in the
crotch. Horace WHEEZES, doubles over. John
grabs the rifle again and drops on his chest
with it.

Lodges the gun barrel under his chin. Horace
CHOKES, lets out a snide, throaty LAUGH.

                    HORACE
          Care about yer pissant
          offspring now, don't ya? Now
          that he's gone—

                    JOHN
          I don't believe you. Where is
          he?

                    HORACE
          I told ya. Being dead
          somewhere—

John jabs the rifle barrel in his adam's apple.

                    HORACE
          Shoot me, why don't ya? Go
          ahead...You killed my boy and
          I got yours, so now you gotta
          kill _me_. Ain't that the eye
          for an eye law of life?

HEAT LIGHTNING singes a yucca tree just yards
away. Sweat pours down John's face. He COCKS
the gun. Horace gives him a final, rotting death
grin.

                    HORACE
          C'mon, son...Do me proud.

John's finger tickles the trigger. Starts to
squeeze it—

                    JOHN
          NO!!

Stands back up. Turns and whips the gun over a
nearby ledge.

                    JOHN
          The eyes close here, Horace.
          All those eyes...Right here.

He turns, begins trudging back up the gorge.
Horace, still angry but also a traumatized
mess, crawls backward into the cave shadows.
Gathers what's left of Tom's corpse in his arms
and squeezes it. SOBBING.

EXT. BADLANDS ROAD - DAY

John stumbles back up the path to the Buick.
His hair is dirty and weirdly frizzed out from

the static in the air. Reaches the Buick and
slumps against the back wheel. Buries his face
in his hands.

Something THUDS LOUDLY behind him. We hear a
MUFFLED CRY. He stands, looks around.

It's coming from the Buick's trunk. A trunk
thankfully peppered with bullet-made oxygen
holes. John scrambles around to the driver's
side.

The keys aren't there. He panics. Grabs a
nearby rock and HAMMERS the trunk lock with
it. HAMMERS and HAMMERS again until the lock
breaks. Tries to wedge his fingers under the
lid. Another MUFFLED CRY.

                    JOHN
          I'm here, Roy!

Scrambles over to a sharper, flatter rock.
Shoves it under the lid and pounds it with the
first rock. The trunk pops open.

Roy is bound with rope, gagged with his own
sock. Dangerously deydrated. John rips him
loose. Lifts him out and hugs him. CRYING.

The POLICE CHOPPER buzzes over the ridge, and
a convoy of POLICE VEHICLES churn up from the
main road.

Polly leaps out of one of the cruisers. Runs
over and joins John and Roy's embrace. LAWMEN
slowly move around them, waiting for John. But
this family is hugging too hard to notice.

SUPER: SEVEN MONTHS LATER

INT. STATE CORRECTIONAL CENTER - NIGHT

A thinner, unshaven John sits on his neatly-
made cot, reading a letter.

                        POLLY
                       (V.O.)
          "I can't get over the amount
          of letters and emails we're
          getting. Guess there's more
          Gina fans out there than I
          was willing to admit.
                   (John smiles)
          Roy misses you a lot. You
          should see him. I bet when
          you get out he'll be up to
          your shoulders—

                        GUARD
                       (O.S.)
          Visitation time, Griffin!

The GUARD slides the cell door open. John puts
his slippers on, pats him on the back as he
exits.

                        JOHN
          Thanks, Luke.

INT. PRISON CORRIDOR - NIGHT

John is escorted down a shiny, waxed hall.
Through an electronic door. Down two flights
of metal steps. Through a second electronic
door marked MEDICAL WARD. The guard unlocks a
private room and John enters.

INT. PRIVATE ROOM - NIGHT

Harsh fluorescent lighting. A stained mattress.
Table with old car magazines. And a haggard,
emaciated Jimmy, his twisted body doomed to a
wheelchair.

                        JOHN
          Hey, Jimmy.

Jimmy raises his bleary eyes. Smiles weakly.
John moves around the room, collecting some of
his things: pill tray, plastic water bottle,
cloth napkin.

                    JOHN
          Cummings called Polly
          the other day. Said the
          dealership sold nine vans
          and seven SUVs last weekend
          alone. Can you imagine?
                    (laughs to himself)
          Maybe we should've thought of
          this a long time ago.

Jimmy makes a GURGLING sound. John takes the
cloth napkin, wipes Jimmy's mouth.

                    JOHN
          Anyway, the chaplain heard
          a rumor about our parole
          hearing. That it might get
          moved up before Memorial
          Day...God...It would sure be
          nice to hit a warm, sunny
          beach again.

Jimmy looks at a spot on the floor. John
realizes what he just said, grabs Jimmy's hand
and squeezes it.

                    JOHN
          Sorry, buddy...I'll find a way
          for you to hit it with me
          anyway. For better or worse,
          right?

Jimmy doesn't respond. John moves his half-
eaten soft dinner aside. Reaches into a pocket
on his prison-issued garment, takes out a fresh
pack of Hubba Bubba gum. Slides out a couple of
sticks and puts them in Jimmy's mouth. Jimmy
manages a small grin, begins chewing.

The guard at the door points to his watch. John
nods, follows the guard as he pushes Jimmy's
wheelchair out of the room.

INT. MEDICAL WARD LOUNGE - MINUTES LATER

A half dozen other sick or crippled PRISONERS
fill the room, doing jigsaw puzzles, playing
cards. Watched by a PAIR OF GUARDS.

Suddenly the lilting THEME MUSIC from <u>Windy City</u> spices the lifeless air.

Jimmy's wheelchair has been parked in front of a raised TV over a DVD player. John sits in a plastic chair beside him.

                    JOHN
          See okay?

Jimmy nods weakly, continues to chew his gum as he gazes up at the screen.

                    JOHN
          I just loved her in this one.

Onscreen, GINA COOGAN walks out on her Chicago balcony with a cup of coffee, wearing a gorgeous peach nightgown. She looks past the camera at the summer sunrise over Lake Michigan and breathes in the fresh, dewy air.

John and Jimmy BREATHE with her.

                              FADE TO BLACK

JEFF POLMAN is the author of *Mystery Ball '58* and three other historical baseball fictions, a young adult comic novel, and two produced thriller screenplays. Originally from New England, he lives in Culver City, CA, the self-dubbed "Heart of Screenland".

Website: jeffpolman.com
Twitter: @ReddJeff8

www.ingramcontent.com/pod-product-compliance
Lightning Source LLC
Chambersburg PA
CBHW031046110726
47900CB00003B/821